MW00655502

Critical Praise for Lee and Miller's Liaden Universe®

"No one does space opera better than Lee and Miller."

– **SF Site**

"The writing is as rich with detail as anything by C. J. Cherryh, while the general approach... reminds of Andre Norton."

– **Tom Easton, Analog**

"...tight, well-wrought prose, economical characterization, and basically charitable vision of humanity – characteristics I found in all of these stories."

– **Thomas Marcinko, Tangent**

"...the authors' craftsmanship is top-notch, recalling the work of Elizabeth Moon and Lois McMaster Bujold..."

– **Publishers Weekly**

"The combination of wit, relationship, and space opera may appeal to readers of Lois McMaster Bujold."

– **Booklist**

"The craftsmanship and love that clearly went into them makes them easy to read, the way a well-made chair feels good to sit on. There's an element of wish-fulfillment in these stories, but the wish is to reach some kind of meaningful understanding with a strange or estranged Other. It's one of the great themes of science fiction, and it's a wish well worth having."

– **Thomas Marcinko, Tangent**

"...good, solid space opera. ...a very fine piece of entertainment."

– **Don D'Ammassa, Chronicle**

"As a writer, I admire (the authors') deft turn of phrase, subtle humor, and elegance of prose. As a reader, I especially enjoy stories in which a member of one culture must find a way to adapt to another."

– **Susan Krinard, author of *To Tame a Wolf***

"Sharon Lee and Steve Miller are so good it's scary."

— **S. L. Viehl, author of the Stardoc novels**

"These authors consistently deliver stories with a rich, textured setting, intricate plotting, and vivid, interesting characters from fully-realized cultures, both human and alien."

— **Elizabeth Moon, author of *Speed of Dark***

"Imagine Georgette Heyer crossed on James Bond in a universe of starships and psychic wizardry, and you'll have something like the Liaden novels of Sharon Lee and Steve Miller—nobody else in the field combines space opera and comedy of manners with the same deftness and brio as these two."

— **Debra Doyle, co-author of the *Mageworlds* novels**

"...I loved the action, the conflict of cultures, the characters, the romance. But best of all, and what makes each story enduringly special to me, is the strong sense of honor that impels the actions of the main characters and is often the basis of the conflicts among them. The Liaden world is an admirable world. Bravo!"

– **Mary Balogh, author of *The Secret Pearl***

Liaden Universe®
Companion
Volume 2

Sharon Lee
and
Steve Miller

SRM Publisher, Ltd
PO Box 179
Unity, ME 04988

This is a work of fiction. All the characters and events portrayed in this book are fictitious. Any resemblance to real people or events is purely coincidental and really amazing.

Liaden Universe® Companion, Volume 2

All stories have previously appeared in SRM Publisher chapbooks
Sweet Waters, ©2002 Sharon Lee and Steve Miller, first appeared in 3SF #1 Naratha's Shadow © 2000 Sharon Lee and Steve Miller, first appeared in Such a Pretty Face A Matter of Dreams © 1999 Sharon Lee and Steve Miller, first appeared in A Distant Soil #27 Phoenix © 2001 Sharon Lee and Steve Miller; first appeared in Loose Cannon, SRM Publisher
Veil of the Dancer © 2001 Sharon Lee and Steve Miller, first appeared in Absolute Magnitude #19 Quiet Knives © 2003 Sharon Lee and Steve Miller, first appeared in Quiet Knives, SRM Publisher Heirloom © 2002 Sharon Lee and Steve Miller, first appeared in Shadows and Shades, SRM Publisher Changeling © 1999 Sharon Lee and Steve Miller, first appeared in Absolute Magnitude #14 This House © 2002 Sharon Lee and Steve Miller, first appeared in Stars Lord of the Dance © 2004 Sharon Lee and Steve Miller, From With Stars Underfoot, SRM Publisher This House © 2002 Sharon Lee and Steve Miller, first appeared in Stars Lord of the Dance © 2004 Sharon Lee and Steve Miller, From With Stars Underfoot, SRM Publisher

Published by SRM Publisher, Ltd.
PO Box 179
Unity, ME 04988-0179
www.srmpublisher.com
First Printing
October 2007

ISBN 978-0-9776639-5-8 Hardcover
ISBN 978-0-9776639-6-5 Softcover

Printed in the United States of America
0 9 8 7 6 5 4 3 2 1

Liaden Universe® Companion
Volume 2

Sharon Lee
and
Steve Miller

Dedicated
to

Mary Shelley
Andre Norton
Anne McCaffrey
Georgette Heyer
C J Cherryh

With love...
And dragons

Contents

Sweet Waters

THE TRAP HAD TAKEN a kwevit–a fat one, too.

Slade smiled, well-pleased. Beside him, Verad, his hunting-partner and his oldest friend among the Sanilithe, saving Gineah, grunted in mingled admiration and annoyance.

"The Skylady Herself looks after you, small brother. Three times this day, your spear failed to find its target, yet you return to your tent with a fair hunting of meat."

"The hunters before us this morning were noisy and hurried–making the game scarce and distant even for your arm," said Slade. "My spear flies not quite so far."

Verad waved a broad hand at the sky in a gesture meant to take in the whole of the world, and perhaps the whole of the universe.

"It is the trail we find today, hunter."

Slade nearly smiled–Verad's stern-voiced lesson could have as easily come from one of his merchant uncles, for all that those uncles would scarcely acknowledge Verad human and capable of thought, much less sly humor. The humor was lacking at the moment, so Slade kept his smile behind his teeth, and moved quietly toward the trap and its skewered victim.

"If I am a poor hunter," he asked, "is it wrong to find another way to take meat?"

"The tent must eat," Verad allowed. "Still, small brother, a hunter should keep several blades in his belt, and be equally skilled with all."

Slade knelt on the wiry moss, put his spear down, and carefully removed his kill from the trap.

"One skill at a time," he murmured. "The tent must eat speaks with a larger voice than Slade must hunt with *erifu*."

From the side of his eye, he saw his friend make the sign to ward ill luck. Slade sighed. *Erifu*–"art," or, as he sometimes thought, "magic"–was the province of women, who held knowledge, history and medicine. Men hunted, herded, and worked metal into the designs betold them by the women.

"If you are a bad hunter and discourteous, too," Verad

commented, settling onto a nearby rock, "you will be left to stand by the fire until the coals are cold." He blinked deliberately, one eye after another.

Slade frowned, rubbing the trap with nesom, the herb hunters massaged into their skin so the game would not scent them.

"What if I am left unChosen?" he asked, for Gineah had been vague on this point. He situated the trap and set the release, then came to his feet in one fluid motion.

"Those left unChosen must leave the Sanilithe and find another tribe to take them."

Slade turned and stared–but, no, Verad's face was serious. This was no joke.

"So, I must be Chosen." He chewed his lip. "What if I do not come to the fire?"

Now, Verad stared. "Not come to the fire? You must! It is law: All blooded hunters who are without a wife must stand at the fire on the third night after the third purification of the Dark Camp's borders."

Tomorrow night, to be precise, thought Slade. He would be there, around the fire –a son of the grandmother's tent could do no less than obey the law. But . . .

"Sun's going," Verad said.

Slade picked up his kwevit by the long back legs and lashed the dead animal to his belt. He recovered his spear, flipped his braid behind a shoulder with a practiced jerk of his head, and nodded at his friend. "I am ready."

*

The scattered tents of the Sanilithe came together for Dark Camp in a valley guarded by three toothy mountain peaks. It was toward the third mountain, which Gineah had taught him was called "Nariachen" or "Raincatcher" that Slade journeyed, slipping out of the grandmother's tent after the camp was asleep. He went lightly, with a hunter's caution, and spear to hand, the cord looped 'round his wrist; the broad ribbon of stars blazing overhead more than bright enough to light his way.

He should not, strictly speaking, be away from night camp at all. Man was prey to some few creatures on this world, several of which preferred to hunt the night. But come away he must, as he had during the last two Dark Camps–and which he might never do again, regardless of tomorrow night's outcome.

To the left, a twisty stand of vegetation formed out of the shadow–what passed for trees. He slipped between the spindly trunks and into the shocking darkness of the glade, where he paused. When he had his night eyes, he went on, angling toward the mountain face–and shortly came to that which was not natural.

It might seem at first glance a shattered boulder, overgrown with such vegetations as were able to take root along its pitted surface.

At next glance, assuming one hailed from a civilized world, it was seen to be a ship, spine-broke and half-buried in the ungiving gray soil.

Slade moved forward. Upon reaching the remains of his ship, he fitted the fingers of both hands into an indentation of the tertiary hatch, braced himself and hauled it back on its track, until there was a gap wide enough to admit him.

Inside was deep darkness, and he went slowly, feeling his way along the broken corridor, his soft-soled boots whispering against the dusty plates. His questing fingers found an indention in the wall, he pressed and a door clicked open.

Carefully, for there was torn and broken metal even inside the one-time supply cabinet, he groped within.

His search gained him several small vials, a single cake-bar of the survival food he'd wrinkled his nose at in pilot training class, and an ironic appreciation of his situation. He had fought the ship to the plains, knowing it unable to survive a planet-fall in any of the world's salty seas.

By the seas, he might have found a mix of food and vitamins better suited to his off-worlder needs–but the scant beaches below the cliff-lined continents were all of shale and broken rock, and he had thought an inland grounding might preserve his ship.

Choices made. Or as Verad might put it, *this* was the trail he found today.

He unzipped the cake wrap, the burp of preservative gas letting him know it was still edible, and–though the sweetness of it was surprising–ate it as if it were a delicacy as he continued to rummage through the former larder.

One more tiny container came into his hand –the last of the wide-spectrum antibiotics. He tucked it into his pouch with the others, pushed the door shut, and crept onward in the dark.

As he moved, his back brain did the calculations: if he rationed himself to a single dose every three days, he could stretch the vitamins he needed to survive through one more migration cycle.

At last, he gained the piloting chamber, where a single go-light glowed, faint. He inched forward and sat in the chair which, with its webbing and shock absorbers, had doubtless saved his life, and reached out to touch a switch.

The stats computer came up sluggishly, the screen watery and uncertain. Despite this, he felt his heart rise. His ship was alive.

Alive, yet mortally wounded. The distress beacon, its power source undamaged, gave tongue every six Standard hours, hurling ship ID and coords into the heedless chill of space. For two full turns of the Sanilithe seasons–almost three Standard Years– the distress beacon had called.

With no result.

A less stubborn man might by now have given up hope of rescue. He supposed, sitting there at the dim board in the shattered belly of a dead ship, on the eve of being either mated or cast out, that he *ought* to give up. Surely, the choices before him were daunting.

Were he cast out of the Sanilithe and left to his own methods, he might hunt well enough to feed himself. Perhaps. Certainly, he could not expect any other nomadic, hardscrabble tribe to adopt him. It bewildered him yet, that Gineah had taken him in– undergrown, wounded, and without language as he had been.

As to the probability of being Chosen at the fire–he considered that approached negative numbers. Worse, if he were, by some passing madness of the local gods, Chosen, he would forthwith have broken every non-fraternization reg in a very substantial book.

The consequences of which were merely academic, unless he were rescued.

And surely, he thought, flipping his braid behind a shoulder and leaning toward the board, if he were Chosen, his underfed and nutrient-lacking seed would quicken no child among the Sanilithe.

If he were, against dwindling odds, *rescued*, and left thereby the tent of his wife, she would not suffer. Her sisters would care for her, and share with her the profits of their tents, until all converged upon the wintering Dark Camp again, and she might Chose another hunter to serve her.

And if he were Chosen and remained unrescued–well.

The day's trail did not always yield good things.

He touched a key.

The screen blanked, then swam back into being, displaying the last entry he had made in the log, on the night before the Sanilithe broke apart into its several Light Season bands and roamed far, gathering what foodstuffs could be wrested from the sullen land.

Carefully, he placed his fingers on the pad and began, slow and hesitant over his letters, to type, giving as the date Dark Camp, Third.

Last night, the final purification was done by the eldest and most holy of the grandmothers. Tomorrow night, I am to stand around the fire as a candidate husband, for the choice of any woman with need. If this chance comes to me, I shall seize it, in order to remain in proximity to the ship and to the beacon.

If I am not chosen, I will be forced away from this kin-group. Should that transpire, I will shelter in the ship for the remainder of the Dark Season. Then, if rescue has not found me, I will attempt to reach the sea. If I make that attempt, I will record my plan here.

I have this evening withdrawn the last of the nutrient drops and antibiotics from the emergency locker.

He hesitated, his right hand rising to finger the length of

metal in his right ear, which named him a son of Gineah's tent, just as the heavy braid of hair identified him as unmarried. Married hunters, such as Verad, had their hair cut short, and wore the earring of their wife's tent with pride in their left earlobe. Slade sighed, thinking that one might wish for a mating, if only to be rid of the braid.

He put his fingers back on the keys. When he had begun this log, he had filled it with observations of custom and language. There had been less of that, as odd custom became that code by which he lived, and the curiously nuanced language the tongue in which he dreamed. Likewise, he had previously recorded the weakness which came to him when he denied himself the supplements and ate only local food. There was no need to repeat that information for those who . . . might . . . read what he had been writting.

He moved his fingers on the keypad, laboriously spelling out his name:

Tol Ven yo'Endoth Clan Aziel

Scout survey pilot

Then, as an afterthought–though he'd done the transliteration earlier in the report–he added one more typed line:

Slade, second named son of Gineah's tent.

*

Slade stood, Arb on his right hand, Panilet on his left, before them the man-high blaze of the Choosing Fire. It was difficult to concentrate in the flame-swept darkness, for which he blamed the various brews he had been compelled to swallow during the purifications, as well as the chants and songs of those of the tribe gathered to witness the Choosings.

Briefly he closed his eyes, seeing the flames still dancing on the inside of his eyelids. The day had begun at sunrise, with Verad rousing him from Gineah's tent and hustling him, with neither meat nor berries to break his fast, to the far side of the encampment, where the hunters of the Sanilithe gathered, each bachelor under the patronage of a married man. Verad stood as Slade's sponsor, for which he was grateful.

There were prayers to recite, smokes to inhale, and strange beverages to drink. There was no water, nor tea, nor aught to eat. Still, he was not hungry and as the day with its duties progressed he found himself remarkably calm, if slightly lightheaded.

At last the waning sun disappeared behind toothy Nariachen. Slade, bathed and oiled by Verad, shivered in the sudden coolness, his naked skin pebbling.

"Drink," his friend said, offering yet another horn cup. Obedient, Slade drank, feeling the liquid take fire in his blood. He handed the cup back, blinking to clear the tears from his eyes.

Verad grinned. "That will put the heat of the hunt into you!"

An aphrodisiac? Slade wondered, as Verad carried the cup away. It seemed likely–and too late to wonder to what lusty adventures the dose in the cup, meant for a broad shouldered and heavily muscled specimen such as Verad, might incite his shorter and more slender self.

"*Now. . .* " Verad returned, bearing a strip of soft, pale leather. He showed the length between his hands. "Up with your arms, brother! I will dress you finer than any who will stand beside you." He slipped the skin 'round Slade's hips, wrapping it in an arcane pattern. "I took this one after last year's Choosing, when Gineah had held you back from the fire, saying that next year was soon enough." He worked swiftly, making the leather kilt tight.

"One throw of the spear brought it down, and I asked my wife for the skin, for I had a brother-gift to make." A final flourish and he stepped back, pride plain on his wide face, his grin displaying several broken teeth.

"There, now," he said. "What woman wouldn't Choose you? That's the question!"

It was certainly, thought Slade, slowly lowering his arms, a question. He looked down at himself. The kilt was . . . brief, and he suspected, from what seemed a very great distance, that he looked ridiculous.

"Don't be so long-faced," Verad said, leaning forward and

slapping him on the belly. "All muscle and lithe as a finoret, too! There will be Choosers brawling to have you!" Another broad grin, then a wave of the hand. "Turn around, small brother. I have one more gift to give you."

Careful on feet gone slightly silly, Slade turned, and felt his braid tugged, loosened. Heavy, his hair unwound across his shoulders–two long seasons of growth.

"Like honey," Verad crooned, and Slade felt a comb slip down the length of his mane. "You will glow in the firelight, like a star. The eyes of the women will be dazzled. Doubt not that you will be Chosen. And when you are . . ." The combing and Verad's crooning whisper resonated weirdly in his head–or perhaps it was that last drink. Slade closed his eyes.

"When you are Chosen," Verad continued. "Your wife will lead you to her tent. There, she will reveal a great mystery. A very great mystery." The comb stroked downward, soft and hypnotic. "In the morning, she will cut away all of this honey-colored hair and you will return to us as a man and a husband.

"Your wife will take you to the metal worker, and she will put the hot wire through your ear and twist it into the sign of her tent. Then . . ." The comb whispered down once more . . . stopped. "And then, we will hunt together as full brothers." He snorted, for a moment the workaday Verad. "And you will practice with your spear until it is said truly that you never miss a cast."

Yes, very likely. Slade tried to say that, but it was too much trouble. Behind him, he heard Verad laugh, and felt a calloused hand on his shoulder.

"To the Fire, brother."

Slade opened his eyes, and glanced quickly to each side. Arb yet stood at his right hand. Panilet was gone. Chosen. Despite the heat from the fire, Slade shivered, and closed his eyes once more.

*

Arb had long been Chosen, and the man who had stood beyond him.

The Fire was a black bed upon which a few red embers kept vigil. Slade frowned at them, wondering laboriously if one of the witnesses beyond the circle would come and tell him to leave; if he would be brought his spear, and his tough hunter's leathers, or if he would be cast forth weaponless and all-but-naked.

His mouth was dry, his head heavy; his blood still warm from that last draught. Altogether, he thought painfully, hc was in a dangerous and most discouraged state and ought by rights to simply curl up on the moss by the dying fire and sleep off the sorrows of the day.

In the heart of the fire, an ember exploded in a rush of scarlet ash. Slade jerked– and froze.

Walking swiftly across the trampled and vacant moss came a tall reed of a woman, her dark hair braided with feathers and flowers, her short robe of soft suede, her legs and feet naked.

Forward she came, until he could see her face in what remained of the firelight. Wide, pupil-drowned eyes stared down at him from a bony, long-jawed face. Abruptly, she checked and looked wildly about, but there were no other hunters shivering and lachrymose around the dying fire. He was the last.

As if the realization galvanized her, she jumped forward and grabbed his wrist. Her fingers were cold; her grip strong. Without a word, she turned and marched into the darkness beyond the fire. Slade, perforce, went with her; all but oblivious to exalting songs and catcalls from the standers-by.

The sounds and warmth fell away behind them, and there was dust underfoot, her shape distant in the night, and her hand, unrelenting, to guide him.

She came at last to a small tent in the next-but-last circle. Brusquely, she pushed the flap aside and ducked within, dragging him after, her fingers bruising his wrist.

Inside, he was at last released, as his captor–his wife–turned to lace the flap. Slade looked about, finding the interior of the tent as cluttered as Gineah's had been neat and shipshape. In the center, beneath the air hole, was the fire, banked for the night, bed unrolled beside it.

He felt a hand on his arm and turned to look up into the face of his wife.

In the relative brightness, he saw that she was younger

than he had at first supposed–scarcely more than a girl, even by the standards of Sanilithe–her forehead high, and her jaw square. Her lean cheeks had been painted with stripes of white and yellow and red; those on her left cheek were smeared. Her eyes were the color of summer moss–gray-green– and very wide.

Still, she said nothing to him, merely reached with hands that trembled to begin working the knot in his kilt. His manhood leapt, eager, and she gasped, the first sound he had heard from her, snatching her fingers away.

Gods, Slade thought, his mind sharpening slightly within the shrouds of drugs and exhaustion. *She's terrified.*

"Wait," he said softly, catching her hands. She flinched, and looked at his face– at least she did that–and did not pull away. "Wait," he said again. "Let us trade names. I am Slade."

She swallowed, and glanced to one side. "Arika."

"Arika," he repeated, struggling toward gentleness. "It is not necessary–"

She pulled her hands free. "This tent requires a hunter."

"Yes," he said, trying to soothe her with his voice, trying to ignore the increasing demands of his body. "Yes, I will hunt for the tent. But it is not necessary to continue this, now, with both of us tired and frightened."

She stiffened at that, and awkwardly reached for his hands, looking sideways into his face.

"I–there is nothing to fear, inside my tent," she said, haltingly. "Slade. There is no harm here. I am–Tonight, I will teach you a mystery which will, will bond us and make us stronger for the tent."

A set piece, poorly learned, he realized, holding her cold fingers. And all honor to her, that her first thought was to soothe his fears. He smiled, carefully.

An unmarried hunter of the Sanilithe was a naive creature. He learned of the mystery of sex on the night of his Choosing, from the woman who had Chosen to become his wife. It was that same wife who would later decide how many children the tent might rejoice in–and a married hunter was not at all certain quite how those children came to be. Verad spoke of seeds, but in the context of a fruit eaten, perhaps from a tree known only to the *erifu* of women.

Though obviously herself terrified of the upcoming mystery, Arika would be scandalized to find that her new and unshorn husband came to her fully tutored. Still, Slade thought muzzily, he was the elder here, and it was his duty to ease her way, as much as it was hers to ease his fear.

"First," Arika said, breathlessly, slipping her hands away. "We must remove these skins . . ." Her fingers were at the knot again, somewhat steadier. Slade left her to it and reached to the laces of her robe. She froze.

"What do you?"

He smiled again, as guileless as he might, in which endeavor he was no doubt assisted by the drugs.

"If we must remove the skins, it will go quicker, if you remove mine and I remove yours." He affected a sudden shyness, dropping his eyes. "Unless there is some reason in *erifu* that I should not . . . ?"

She frowned, as if trying to recall a long-ago and not very well attended lesson. Finally, she jerked a shoulder–the Sanilithe negative. "It does not offend *erifu*. You may continue."

Continue he did, taking care with the laces while she fumbled with his kilt. He did not wish to reveal her too soon. Best, if they became naked and equal in the same moment.

He felt the knot at his hip loosen all at once, slipped the last of the lacing free and slid his palms over her shoulders, easing the garment up, just as the kilt fell unceremoniously to the floor. Softly, he smoothed his hands down her back, slipping the robe down and off, to pool about her feet.

She visibly swallowed, her pale eyes moving down his body in quick glances. Obviously, she hadn't the least idea what to do now.

Slade stepped forward, lifting a hand to her hair, stroking it back to reveal an exotic and enticing little ear. He heard her gasp, but she had heart, did Arika. She slid her fingers into his hair, silking it back to reveal his ear. Greatly daring, she ran her finger 'round the edge and he felt his blood flare as he copied the motion, then stroked the line of her jaw. She followed his lead, her fingers moving in a long stroke down the side of his neck.

He cupped her breast, she ran a light hand down his chest; he bent and put his lips around one pert nipple. She gasped, back arching, and it came to him that *erifu* would have required that she also drink the Choosing drugs, to be ready to welcome the new husband in fullness . . .

"Slade," she said huskily, and her hands were in his hair, drawing his face up, her gray-green eyes looking deep into his. "We–should lie down."

A good idea, he thought, *before one or the other of us falls into the fire.*

He stretched out beside her, and she touched him, tentative fingers warm now, and indescribably exciting. He moaned, and pulled her to him, exhaustion burning away into the brilliance of passion.

*

Slade opened his eyes to a tent wholly unfamiliar, a heavy weight pinning his arm to the sleeping mat. Carefully, he turned his head, and discovered his wife, Arika, deeply asleep, her head on his shoulder, hair tangled with last night's passion, lashes sooty smudges on her thin cheeks. In the spill of morning light from the fire hole, her face was achingly young.

Surely, he thought wildly, *surely a child of this age ought to be with her tutor and not roistering about in the darkness, soliciting strange men into the service of her tent?*

He drew a hard breath. The Sanilithe came quickly to adulthood, and quickly to old age. Gineah, revered grandmother that she was, with two daughters and a hunter-son, all grown and mated–Gineah had between fifty and fifty-five Standard Years. On the planet of his birth, she would have just reached the height of her powers, with another thirty to fifty years before her . . .

The planet of his birth, he thought, suddenly bitter; which he had wished with all his heart to escape–and found his wish well-granted.

Carefully, not wanting to awaken the girl-child asleep on

his shoulder, he drew a breath, and looked about him.

It was not the largest tent he had seen among the Sanilithe, nor the tidiest, though it might, considering the numerous patches in the skin walls, make some claim to the shabbiest.

Scattered around, in no order he could discern, were baskets, pots, robes, and rugs. Poles lined the walls, and from them hung familiar clusters of dried herbs and medicinal plants.

Gineah had divided her tent into sections–a place which was *erifu* and off-limits to ham-fisted sons of the tent, a place to store foodstuffs and water, a place for that same ham-fisted son to keep his weapons, his skins, and his bedroll. The center was common area, where meals were made and where grandmother and son might dawdle over their warmed beer, talking far into the night.

Well, and Gineah's tent was as distant from him as his mother's house, now that he was married.

He sighed and brought his gaze back to the child's sleeping face. The stripes of paint adorning her cheeks were smeared and faded. The Sanilithe did decorate their faces–certain signs were erifu, others were, as far as he understood, nothing more than exuberance. It seemed to him that he had seen stripes like these before–white, yellow, red, in alternation–and suddenly, he remembered.

Mourning stripes. Someone of this tent had died–recently. The stripes were worn only for three days after the deceased had been commended to the fire.

Outside, a woman's voice rose in the welcome-morning song. The girl asleep on his arm stirred, and opened her eyes, face tensing. He smiled, deliberately.

"Good morning, Arika," he said softly.

Her face relaxed, though she did not go so far as to smile. "Good morning, Slade," she returned, seriously, and looked upward to the patch of sullen sky visible through the smoke hole.

"We must rise," she said abruptly, snaking out of their tumbled bed and rolling to her feet. "There is much to do."

Naked, she hesitated, staring about the disordered tent, then darted to one side, where she found a tunic. She pulled it over her head, emerging, she frowned at Slade, still slugabed.

"Rise!" she snapped, and reached for the pair of leather leggings hanging over a cracked storage pot.

Sighing, he rose, found his kilt on the dirt floor by the edge of the fire, picked it up, shook it out, and wrapped it around his loins, feeling even more foolish, now that there was no kindly drug diluting his perceptions. Quickly, he knotted the leather, wishing for shirt and leggings.

"Slade."

He turned. Arika held her hands up, showing him the blade in her right, and the comb, in her left. "I will cut your hair, now, and we will go to the smith. Then we will go to the tent of Grandmother Gineah and bring away those things she allows to be yours." She smiled, very slightly. "The sooner we do these things, the sooner we may eat."

Eat. His stomach, reminded of its fast, set up a complaint, and he moved sprightly indeed and sat on the floor at her feet.

"Be still now," she said, and plied the comb, surprisingly gentle; and then the knife, in long, practiced sweeps.

Slade closed his eyes as the weight of his hair fell away, leaving the back of his neck chill.

"Done."

He lifted his hands to his head, feeling strands barely two fingers long. Gods alone knew what he looked like, but at least he was rid of the braid, which had a penchant for becoming entangled in twigs, and flirting with fires . . .

"Come." Arika was already unlacing the flap. "The smith."

Indeed, the smith. He rolled to his feet and followed his wife out into the new day.

*

Some while later, earlobe stinging and stomach rumbling, he stood two paces behind his wife, before Gineah's tent.

A shadow moved and the grandmother stepped out, plump and grizzled, her arms encircled with the many bracelets of her station.

Before him, Arika spread her arms wide in the traditional

greeting to one of the Wise.

"Grandmother," she murmured, respectfully.

"Daughter," Gineah replied, and moved her eyes, pinning Slade with a bright blue glance. "Hunter."

He bowed, which the Sanilithe did not do. "Grandmother."

She stepped forward, her eyes on Arika. "You could have come to me."

Arika bit her lip, and shook her hair back in what Slade was beginning to understand as a nervous gesture. "I swore to Keneple that the tent would endure," she said, her voice not quite steady.

"And a tent must have a hunter." Gineah sighed.

"Child . . ." She stopped.

"Please," she said, after a moment, "allow your hunter to enter my tent and collect those things which have been made ready for him."

"Yes . . ." Arika whispered. She straightened shoulders that had begun to sag and looked to him, chin up.

"Slade, you may find what Grandmother Gineah has left for you and bring it forth."

"Yes," he said in his turn and slipped into the tent that had been his home for two full turns of season.

Inside, all was neat and familiar; it smelled of herbs, and leather; smoke and the scent of Gineah herself. Tears rose to his eyes. Blinking them away, he turned toward the corner which had been his.

There were several bundles there, as well as his spear, his knives, and the unfinished length of braided hide he had been working on as he sat at the fire with Gineah in the evenings.

He knelt and examined the bindings of each pack, in no hurry, wanting to give Gineah as much time as possible to share what wisdom she might with his girl-wife. It came to him that it was Keneple who had died, and who Arika mourned. The name meant nothing to him, but that was not unusual. Well as he knew the names of those with whom his tent traveled in the seasons of gathering, little did he know the names, or the faces, of those who traveled other routes.

Kneeling on the mat among his bundles, his Choosing became real to him: he was now tied to a tent that would follow a different route, come the Light Season, and which held allegiances and debts that he did not understand. The ones he would hunt beside would not be the same men he had come to know–who had come to know and accept him, with all his incomprehensible difficulties– as a brother.

He gasped. This time, the tears escaped to moisten his cheeks. To be taken from everything and everyone he knew–and, yet, what did it matter? He was the alien here, shipwrecked and dead to all he had been. To lose one tent, one old woman, half-a-dozen savage brothers–what was that, against the magnitude of his other losses?

Crouched beside the small pile of his belongings, he wept, then wiped his face with his forearm and forced himself to his feet.

He draped the bundles about himself as Verad had taught him to do, slipped his knives, carefully, into the waist of his kilt and hefted the spear.

Outside, Gineah embraced Arika, and stepped aside. "Take care of my son, who is now your hunter, daughter."

"Grandmother, I will." Arika swallowed, and Slade saw that her cheeks were also damp. "You are welcome in my tent, always."

Gineah smiled upon them, and raised her hands in blessing above their heads. Then, wordless, she re-entered her tent.

Arika licked her lips, nodded to Slade. He followed her across the camp, to their shabby and disordered home.

*

Kneeling on the dirt floor next to the fire pit, Slade unrolled his bundles. The first held his hunting leathers and boots, as well as a vest sewn of kwevit hides with the fur attached. He dressed quickly, rolling the kilt and putting it with the vest, then turned his attention to the rest, chewing on a strip of dried meat Arika had given him.

She was at the back of the tent; he could hear her moving

things, possibly attempting to impose order upon the clutter, a project of which he heartily approved.

Opening the next bundle, he found the furs and skins of his own bed, and several sealed medicine pots. He smiled, profoundly warmed, for Gineah took care with her potions, which were genuinely soothing of bruises, cuts and strained muscles.

Another bundle gave up his second pair of leggings, three sitting mats, and pots containing dried legumes, jerked meat, and raisins. Too, there was the bag ritually made from the skin of the very first kwevit he'd taken and meant to carry what Verad called "the hunter's touch," which was the only property besides his weapons and his clothes that a hunter could be said to own. The knot was undisturbed, and inside, among the scent-masking potions, feathers, and special stones that he had been given by his brother of the hunt, was his paltry supply of Liaden nutrients. Slade smiled again, and thanked Gineah in his heart.

"Where do those things come from?" Arika's voice was shrill. He spun on his knees and looked up, seeing her face twisted with anger, her eyes blazing green fire.

"Gineah gave them," he said, keeping his voice gentle.

She was not soothed. "Return them! I am the mother of this tent–and this tent is not in need!"

Very slowly, hands loose at his sides, Slade rose. Deliberately, he looked about him, at the clutter, at the tatters, at the soot. He looked back to her angry face.

"The tent must eat," he said.

"The tent *will* eat," she snapped. "The hunter will see to it."

"Yes." He moved a hand, showing her the bounty Gineah had sent. "These were given by the grandmother, to the hunter. I have seen that the tent will eat."

She glared, lips parting, then turned and stomped away.

Sighing, Slade looked about him for an uncluttered corner to call his own.

*

They worked in silence, he on his side, she on hers. It was

not so large a tent that they were unaware of each other, and had they been in charity, Slade thought ruefully, they might have made a merry time of it. And, really, it was wrong that they continued thus in anger. Unless he did something very stupid on a hunt, they would be partners for–some time. They needed each other's goodwill and willing cooperation– the tent could not function, else.

Sighing, he straightened from tidying away his sleeping roll, and turned.

Across the tent, Arika stood with a pot cradled in her arms, her head bent, hair obscuring her face.

Biting back a curse, Slade crossed to her side, and put a careful hand on her arm.

She gasped, and started, eyes flying to his face, her lashes damp, the remains of the mourning paint running in long, smeary lines down her cheeks.

"Peace," he said, as gently as he knew how. "Gineah meant well. We should not be at odds because of her kindness."

She swallowed, and shook her hair back from her wet cheeks. "I–Tales of Grandmother Gineah's good works are told around story fires wherever the Sanilithe gather. I will be proud to tell my own story, that the grandmother so valued her son she gave his wife-tent a Dark Season's worth of provisions, as a measure of her regard."

"A good story," he said, softly. "And nothing to weep for."

Arika snuffled, and raised a hand to scrub at her cheeks.

"I weep because–" Another gulp, and a wave around at the general chaos. "It was not like this. It was orderly and, and *erifu* and–and the babe was born dead, and Keneple caught the milk fever, and the grandmothers did what there was to do . . ." The tears were flowing again, and she hugged the pot tight to her chest.

"So, she died," she whispered. "It was past time to leave for Dark Camp . . . They helped me with the pyre before they left. I packed the tent in haste and, and–" She bent her head, hair falling forward to shroud her face. "*Erifu* has been broken, and I don't know how . . ."

He slipped an arm around her waist, as she cuddled her pot and wept, offering the comfort of his warmth.

Gently, he asked, "Keneple was your mother?"

Arika sniffled. "My elder sister. Elae–her hunter–fell from a rock ledge at Far Gathering and broke his neck. We–" Her grief overtook her, then, and there were no more words for a time.

Slade stroked her hair, murmuring nonsense phrases, as he had heard Gineah murmur to soothe a sick child.

Gods, he thought, the tragedy unrolling before his mind's eye. *Every one of the tent dead, save herself, within the space of one summer walkabout?* Mother, hunter, and hopeful babe–gone, leaving one grieving girl-child, who had promised her dying sister that she would not allow the tent to lapse . . .

"Arika," he murmured. "Gineah taught me. We can together put things right. Our tent will be erifu and the envy of every hunter!"

She looked at him sidewise through her hair. "The grandmother taught you how to order a tent? But that is–"

"Who says no to a grandmother when she requires a thing?" he asked, smoothly.

That argument had weight. Arika straightened. "We do as the grandmother says."

"We do," he said, and smiled at her. "Let us begin in the Windward corner."

*

Slade shivered in the light wind and held his end of the braided leather rope loosely by the knot. The other end was tied to the most robust of the shrub-like trees in the thicket with a knot Verad would have frowned upon had he seen it, for it looked to be more erifu than the knots men might use. All around, the rocks, bushes and moss glittered silver in the starlight–ice, and treacherous footing for even a skilled hunter.

As had become his habit since his mating, Slade hunted alone. He regretted the loss of Verad's companionship, but the elder hunter had grown even more disapproving of Slade's methods. Hunting alone, he had perfected those methods. It was seldom, now, that their tent was without fresh meat.

Today, Slade thought, might be one of those rare days when he returned empty-handed. If the binkayli failed to swarm, if his throw went awry, if the leather parted, if the branch gave way–if, if, if . . .

One-handed, Slade reached to his belt and worked the knot on the hunter's touch. Though he hunted solitary, he was often enough among other hunters at the end of the day, when casual groups might form to discuss the weather, the hunting, the lie of the land for tomorrow's hunt. Thus, he had added several odd quartz bits, the tail fur of an ontradube, and the sharply broken stub of the same creature's small antler to his collection of magical items, as further camouflage.

Finding the vial of vitamins by touch among the lot was a chore, but he succeeded, and squeezed the drops into his mouth. He grimaced at the taste, and at the state of the container, and dropped it back into the bag.

Checking his hold on the leather, his nose hair bristled. Cold, cold, cold.

From his left came a rolling rumble, as of dozens of hooves hitting the frozen ground. Slade tensed, then forced himself to relax, pushing all thought of failure–all thought–from his mind, just as the binkayli burst out of the silvered thicket, barely six paces from his crouching place, running hard across the open land.

He threw, the lasso arced into the spangled air, spun and fell about the neck of a well-grown binkayli stallion.

Oblivious, the stallion raced on. The rope stretched, the noose tightened. The branch held, held–and broke in a clatter of scattered ice.

Slade swore and leapt. His boots skidded on the icy surface, he twisted, clawing for balance, and fell badly, left leg bent beneath him, head cracking against the ground.

Half-dazed, he saw the rope and the branch speed across the icy ground in the wake of the stallion. The pounding of hooves vibrated through his head, and finally faded away.

*

It was late when he limped back into camp, leaning heavily on his spear. He staggered to his own tent, standing silver and serene 'neath the changeless winter sky, pushed the flap back, ducked inside–and froze.

The air was pungent with some unfamiliar odor, and thick with smoke. Arika sat, cross-legged and naked, before the fire, eyes closed, holding a hunter's gutting knife between her palms. Two women he did not know knelt, fully clothed, facing her.

Slade moved as quietly as he was able, meaning to retire to the corner where he kept his hunter's gear, to warm himself, and rest his injured leg.

One of the strangers looked over her shoulder and leapt up, her eyes wide and angry. She grabbed his arm, none-too-gently, and shoved him toward the flap.

"You are not allowed here!" she hissed. "Go! Do not return until you are summoned!" Another shove, and a third, which sent him stumbling out into the cold, ice-rimed camp.

Slade stood for a moment, gathering his wits; shivering, aching and angry. Then, leaning hard on his spear, he limped away, toward Gineah's tent.

*

"Rest, tomorrow and tomorrow," Gineah said, rising from her inspection of the injured leg. "The muscles are angry, and you–you are a very fortunate hunter, young Slade. You might have broken that leg, and then you would have been a dead hunter, alone in the freezing darkness, without a brother of the hunt nearby to aid you."

He smiled up at her. "I was fortunate, I know. I will be more careful, Gineah."

She snorted and motioned him to sit up, as she crossed to the cookfire and the pot hanging there. "At least your head is hard," she said–and then, "You should not hunt alone."

"I must," he said. "My methods frighten Verad, and the others are more timid still."

Gineah ladled soup into bowls and brought them back to the hearth fire, handing one to Slade.

"Eat." She ordered. "And while you eat, tell me what your wife was about, to allow a stranger to send you from her tent."

So he ate, and told her of his strange homecoming, with Arika entranced or uncaring, the smoke, the knife, and the woman who had banished him.

"So." Gineah looked at him straightly across the fire. "Your wife, young Slade, is a Finder."

He blinked, trying to read her face, and, as usual, failing.

"What is a Finder, grandmother?"

"A woman of great *erifu,* who may cast her thought out to find that which is lost. The best Finders improve their tents many times over. Your wife is young, she has some years before she reaches the fullness of her gift. But she is already known as a Finder of great talent. The tent will improve quickly, I think, and you will no longer live on the edges of the Dark Camp."

Surely, Slade thought, *this was good news?* In the house of his mother, the birth of a Healer was cause for rejoicing. Yet, Gineah looked more doleful than joyous.

"This troubles you . . ." he said, tentatively.

Gineah sighed. "Finders . . . do not thrive. The heat of their gift consumes them. Not all at once, but over a time. Sometimes, a very long time."

He stared at her, thinking of Arika, young and frail and fierce, and his eyes filled. "Is there no–"

"Cure?" she finished for him. "Child, there is no cure for destiny."

"Then," he asked, blinking the tears away, though the empty feeling in his chest remained. "What should I do?"

"Be the best hunter you are able. Be her friend, as I know you can be, O, wisest and most *erifu* of hunters. If children come to the tent, care for them. And pray that they were not born to be Finders."

Something moved near the flap of the tent, loud to Slade's hunter-trained ears. He came around, began to rise–and fell back as fire shot through his leg.

"Rest!" Gineah hissed at him, and went to unlace the flap.

"Grandmother," he heard Arika's voice, thin and vulnerable. "Is Slade with you?"

"He is. A woman pushed him from your tent while you were Finding, child. What greeting is that for a hunter returned to his tent wounded?"

"Wounded?" He heard her gasp and called out–

"A fall, nothing more. Gineah . . ."

She stepped back, motioning, and Arika entered.

She was wan, and unsteady on her feet, her eyes great and bruised looking.

"A fall?" she repeated, and knelt beside him, touching the leg Gineah had wrapped. "Is it broken?"

"No," he soothed her. "Not broken."

"He must rest," Gineah said. "Tomorrow and tomorrow. Eat from stores. If there is a call upon your gift, you will come to me, rather than turn this hunter out. Am I understood?"

Arika hung her head. "You are understood, grandmother." She looked up, and Slade saw tears shining in her eyes. "Slade. You should not have been cast out. Next time, I will be certain that those who watch know that your presence will not disturb me."

"Thank you," he said, sincerely, and touched her thin cheek. *The heat of their gift consumes them* . . . he thought, and wanted nothing more than to fold her in his arms and protect her from that fate.

"So," said Gineah, and his wife stood, to attend the grandmother with due respect, and to receive two medicine pots.

"Rub the leg with this, morning, mid-day, night. If there is swelling, three drops of this, in noginfeil tea. If there is fever, send and I will come."

"Yes, grandmother," Arika murmured, and tucked the pots into her pouch. She looked down at him doubtfully.

"Can you walk?"

The leg was considerably stiffer, despite the warmth, but he thought he could walk. "If I can rise," he said.

Gineah held out a plump arm, and Arika offered a thin one. It took the support of both, but gain his feet he did, and stood wobbling, arm around Arika's waist for balance, while Gineah fetched his vest and his spear.

*

They made love, their last night in Dark Camp. After, in the soft silence, Arika snuggled against his chest, and he put his arms around her. She had gained weight since they had married, and the tent had improved as well–in some part due to his efforts; in greater part, so he had it, to hers. As the Dark wore on, more came to ask the Finder to locate this or that misplaced item, animal, or–rarely–person. They paid well, those seekers–in fur, in food, in good metal knives and spear tips. He watched her closely, having taken Gineah's words much to heart, but, truly, she seemed more well, not less.

"Slade," Arika murmured. "Tell me about your home."

He stirred, breathing in the perfume of her hair. "My home?" he repeated, lazily.

"Gineah told me that you were not of the Sanilithe," she said, nestling her head onto his shoulder. "She said you were not of the Trinari, or of the Chinpha. She said that you had fallen out of the starweb, and were no ordinary hunter at all."

Shrewd Gineah, he thought, stroking Arika's hair; *and really–what does it matter now?*

"She said," Arika continued, "that she expected your tribe to come for you, and held you away from the Choosing. But when they did not come after two full rounds of seasons, she sent you forth, for a hunter of the Sanilithe must live by the law of the Sanilithe."

Slade sighed.

"Did you fall out of the starweb?" Arika asked him.

What does it matter? He thought again. For surely Gineah was correct–no one would come for him now.

"My . . . starship . . . was caught in a storm," he murmured, which was true, if not factual. "Yes, I fell out of the starweb."

"And before it fell? Did you live on your starship?"

As much as I was able, he thought, and sighed again.

"Much of the time. I was . . . the hunter . . . who went ahead, to find how the land lay, if danger crouched, or if sweet waters sang . . ."

This she understood, the order of march during the gathering season being: scouts, hunters, gatherers, tents. She also knew that scouts often took harm from their duty. She shifted, pressing her body against him in a long hug, and nestled her cheek more closely against his shoulder.

"Tell me about your mother's tent."

His mother's tent–almost he laughed. Instead, he stroked her hair and stared up into the darkness.

"My mother's tent was . . . full," he said slowly. "We lived in–a permanent camp. It was not necessary to wander in the Warm Days, to spread ourselves thin so that we did not strain the land. It was," he said, even more slowly, feeling his way, "a land of plenty. The camp—it was called—Solcintra'."

"There must have been many people in your camp, Solcintra," Arika said after he had been silent for a time.

"Yes," he said, "many, many hands of people."

"What else?" she asked, and this time he did laugh.

What else, the child asks.

"Is my question funny?" Arika demanded, between hurt and angry.

"Not at all," he assured her, smoothing her shoulder with his hand. "Not at all. Listen, now, and I will tell you . . ."

And so he told her, of spaceports, and shops, and healers, and traffic, and sometime before the gray uncertain dawn wavered into being, she fell asleep. He held her then, silent, his thoughts still on the city, his kin, the sky he would never see again . . .

*

Arika gained weight as they traveled into the light, until he was forced to believe what he had not thought possible. And one night, as they sat companionably at the fire; he mending a frayed rope, she mending a broken basket, he asked a question.

"I wonder," he said, watching her face out of the sides of his eyes. "Will the tent soon welcome a child?"

Her hands froze, and she raised her head to stare at him across the fire.

"Perhaps," she said haughtily. Arika was always haughty in fear.

He preserved his pretense of oblivious industry. "A child in the tent would be–a joy," he said. "But the hunter should be informed, if he will soon need to hunt for more."

She looked away, throat working. "As to that–it is not certain. The women of my tent . . . do not always . . . birth well."

Her sister, he remembered, whose baby had been born dead–and who had herself died of the birth. He plaited his rope in silence for a few heartbeats, then asked, quietly, "Is it the Finder blood that puts the babes at risk?"

She swallowed. "The grandmothers believe so. They call it a 'gift', but it eats us up, even those it allows to be born."

"It does not have to be," he said, carefully. "My mother, my brother, my sister– all are gifted as you are, with an extra pair of eyes, that see what others cannot." He raised his head and met her stare across the fire.

"You have the blood," she said, with certainty.

"I do. My mother bore three healthy children; my sister and my brother, who have extra eyes; myself, who has but two. So . . ." Here was the dangerous ground, for hunters knew nothing of such matters. "So, Arika, my wife, if the child in your belly is one that we made together, it may be that my . . . blood . . . will lend her strength enough to be born–and to thrive."

"It may be," she said quietly, and sighed, putting her basket aside. "Slade. How do you know these things?"

He opened his eyes wide and made a show of innocence. "Things?"

"That without a hunter, there is no child. How does a hunter put a child in a belly, Slade?"

Well, he had botched it. He sighed, then smiled at her. "Why, when we enjoy each other, and you take me into yourself . . ."

"Enough." She sighed in her turn. "These things are *erifu.*"

"Among the Sanilithe, they are *erifu*," he allowed. "In my

mother's tent, these things are common knowledge, shared among sisters and brothers."

She closed her eyes. "You make me tremble," she murmured, and looked at him once more. "But I see the fire has not leapt up to consume you, so it must be that the spirits of your grandmothers allow you this knowledge." She bent her head. "The child who–will–come to us is a child of my blood–and yours." She smiled, very slightly. "May your blood make her strong."

*

Arika waned as the child waxed. Slade held her at night and tried to will his strength into her, for she, his precious, for whom he hunted, did not have his blood to make her strong. Lying awake in the dark, he made plans to dose her from his dwindling supply of supplements; plans which he abandoned as morning overtook him. His Arika was a child of this world, and even as her world was slowly poisoning him, so his needed vitamins might very well poison her.

He did insist that she refrain from gathering, and when she protested, told her that he would gather. Gineah had taught him something of plant lore. This was true enough, though not as she heard it. Gineah had shown him the fruits of her labors in the evenings when they both had returned to the tent, laying out and naming those things she had gathered.

"I will bring everything to you, and you will decide if it is good," he told Arika. "But you will not go out alone, soft on your feet as you are! You put our daughter and yourself in danger, and I do not allow it!"

A grave breach of *erifu*, that, and yet, strangely, she laughed.

"Slade. How will you hunt and gather? Or will you give your spear to me?"

"No, never that," he said, lightly. "A tent mother must not kill."

"A hunter's work fills the day–and a mother's work, too. How will you fit two days into one?"

"Let me try," he said, urgently, and took her hands. "Two

days. If I fail to gather, or to hunt, we will–think of something else."

It was perhaps a measure of how weak she was that she allowed him his two days of proof.

*

His scheme worked well: In the morning, he set his traps; his afternoon went to gathering plant stuffs. When his sack was full; he turned toward the camp of the day, collecting game from his traps as he went.

On the morning of the sixth day, he encountered Tania, the grandmother of their group, at the edge of the camp, gather-bag in hand.

"Good morning, hunter," she said politely.

Slade touched the tip of his spear to the ground in respect. "Good morning, grandmother."

"I see that the mother of your tent sends you to gather in her name."

This, Slade thought, *could be bad.* He allowed no trace of the thought cross his face. Instead, he replied calmly, "Grandmother, it is so. Her talent gnaws the mother of my tent to bone."

Her eyes softened. "It is a harsh gift," she said slowly. "Do you prepare the gather?"

"No, grandmother; she prepares what I bring, and shows which I should choose more of, and what is not as needful to the tent."

"So." She stood up, shaking out her bag. "*Erifu* is preserved. Good hunting."

After that, no one questioned him.

And Arika grew ever more fragile.

In the evening, she sorted and prepared what he had gathered, while he performed other needful tasks. After, they would lie in each other's arms and he would stroke her until she fell into uneasy sleep.

So, the short summer proceeded. Slowly, the sky darkened, and the wind carried an edge of ice, warning that the time to turn to Dark Camp approached.

Slade returned to their tent somewhat later than usual, burdened by numerous kwevits and an especially heavy sack of gatherings.

At first, he thought the tent unoccupied, then, he saw the shape huddled, far in the back, where the medicines were kept.

Heart in mouth, he dropped his burdens and rushed forward. Arika was barely conscious, her body soaked with sweat. Carefully, he straightened her, turned her . . .

Her eyes opened, and she knew him. "Slade. The child comes." Her body arched, and she gasped, eyes screwing shut.

*

The baby had come quickly, which had been a blessing. He cleaned her and put her to Arika's breast, turned–and looked up into Tania's hard, old eyes.

"Hunters do not deliver children," she said, coldly.

"This hunter does," he snapped, perhaps unwisely.

"So I see." She stepped forward. "I will examine the mother of your tent, hunter. She is frail and I am many years your elder in the healing arts."

He took a hard breath. "Grandmother, I know it."

"Good," she said, kneeling at Arika's side. "Walk around the camp, twice. Slowly, as if you search for hunt-sign on hard rock. Then you may return."

Almost, he protested. Almost. He had just reached the entrance when he heard his name and turned back.

"Grandmother?"

"You did well," she said softly. "Now go."

*

The child–Kisam, their daughter–clung to her small life by will alone, and in her stubbornness Slade saw generations of Clan Aziel. She nursed, but it seemed her mother's milk nourished her only enough to keep her soul trapped in her body–and in that, too, he saw the effect of his blood.

His blood.

She sucked the supplement from the tip of his finger while

he cuddled her and prayed, chaotically, expecting the tiny body at any moment to convulse, and release his child's willful spirit–

"She is stronger," Arika said next day, Kisam tucked in the carry-cloth against her breast. "Slade, does she not seem stronger to you?"

"Yes," he murmured, leaning over to stroke the small head covered already with plentiful dark curls–her mother's blood, there. "Yes, she does."

*

They traveled slowly toward Dark Camp, for Arika's strength was low, and Kisam yet frail, though much improved. And truthfully, the slower pace was not only to accommodate the child and her mother. Slade walked sometimes unsteady, his legs weak, and betimes a high, busy humming in his ears, and flashes of color across his vision. The spells passed shortly, and he did not speak to Arika of the matter. And every other night, as his wife lay in the sleep of exhaustion, he would nurse Kisam from his dwindling supply of vitamins and tried not to think what would happen, when, finally, they were gone.

So they arrived at Dark Camp among the last, and pitched their tent in the fourth tier, considerably higher than last year. There was firewood waiting, and a fire-circle, built properly by women's hands, by those who owed still on Findings past.

Slade saw Arika settled by the fire, and Kisam on the nurse before he turned to stow his weapons–and heard the buzzing begin, growing until it was a black well of sound into which he toppled, head first, and swooning.

*

He opened his eyes to Gineah's somber face.

"He wakes," she said, and Arika was there as well, her eyes wide and frightened.

Carefully, he smiled. "Forgive me, grandmother. A stupid faint . . ."

"Not stupid, perhaps," another voice said, speaking the Sanilithe tongue slowly and with an odd nuance.

Slade froze, looked to Arika, who touched his face with fingers that trembled. "A woman of your mother's tent has come, Slade."

A woman of his–

He pushed himself into a sitting position, despite Arika's protesting hand on his shoulder, and Gineah's frown. For a heartbeat, his vision was distorted by spangles of light; when they melted, he saw her, seated like any ordinary guest by the fire, the baby's basket at her side, a horn cup cradled between her two hands.

She wore leather, and a wide Scout-issue belt, hung about with a profusion of objects. Her hair was brown and curly, her face high-boned and subtle.

"Do I find Slade, second named son of Gineah's tent?" she asked, in the native tongue.

"Hunter," he corrected, "for the tent of Arika Finder."

Her eyes flickered. "Of course. No insult was intended to the mother of the tent." She raised her cup, sipped, then looked to him, face bland. "I have come to take you back to the tent of your mother, hunter. You have been sore missed."

Arika was gripping his shoulder hard enough to bruise. He reached up and put his hand over hers.

"My mother's tent has many hunters, this tent has but one."

The Scout inclined her head. "Yet this tent's hunter is ill, and soon will die."

Which was certainly true, thought Slade. Death or departure equally deprived the tent of its hunter. And the hunter would rather die than depart.

"His mother, his sisters–they may heal him?" Arika's voice was thin, her hand beneath his, chill.

The Scout inclined her head respectfully. "Tent mother, they will."

"And after he is healed," Gineah–shrewd Gineah–murmured, "he will be returned to the tent of his wife."

The Scout considered her. "The grandmother knows better than that, I think," she murmured. "Between the *erifu* of the Sanilithe and the *erifu* of we who are not the Sanilithe, there is a . . . disharmony. We are each correct, in our way, but not in the way of the other."

In her basket, Kisam awoke and began to cry, and Arika rose to go to her. Slade watched them for a moment, then looked back to the Scout.

"It is possible," he said to her bland and subtle eyes, "that the addition of a third *erifu* will balance the disharmony and allow health to bloom."

She raised an eyebrow, but said nothing.

Slade leaned forward. "Take this tent to the sea. I will give you a message for my mother and my sisters." *And for Scout Headquarters,* he thought.

"The sea will not aid you. It–" The Scout frowned, looked to Gineah. "Grandmother, I apologize for the breach of courtesy, but I must speak to Slade in the tongue of his mother's tent."

Gineah moved a hand. "Speak, then."

Yet, having gained her permission, the Scout did not at once speak, and when she did, she spoke the language of home as slowly as if it, too, were uneasy on her tongue.

"I had seen your log, and your determination to gain the sea, were you turned out. Not a bad plan, in truth, pilot, excepting only that this world lacks those things which your body must have in sufficient quantity to sustain you. I have done the scans and can show you the results. Those who are born to this world, they have adjusted to the lowered levels and function–as you see. You, who were bred upon a world rich in nutrient–you can only sicken here, and die."

So, then. Slade took a breath. "Our daughter will die soon. A few days, now."

Comprehension lit the Scout's bland eyes. "You have been giving the child your supplements."

"What would you?" he said irritably, the words feeling all odd angles in his mouth. He sighed. "If I must go, then, allow them to come. My wife, she is–a Healer of a sort, and frail. Perhaps home will heal her, too."

The Scout paused, head to one side . . .

"Slade." Arika was back at his side, Kisam in her arms. "What does this woman say?"

"She says that the sea will not aid us."

Arika frowned. "The sea? What do the Sanilithe have to do with the sea?"

"I thought that the *erifu* of the sea might bring the child of our tent to health, and myself."

She bent her head, her hair falling forward to shroud their child. "The little bottle," she whispered, "it is almost empty?"

He reached out and stroked the hair back from her face. "You knew?"

"I woke in the night and saw you give–it is a medicine from your mother's tent, isn't it? She shares the *erifu* of your blood."

"Yes," he whispered, stroking her hair. "Arika–come with me to my mother's tent." From the corner of his eye, he saw the Scout start, but she held her tongue. He *knew* the regs forbade just what he proposed. *Damn the regs.*

Arika raised her head, showing him a face wet with tears. "And then I will die, sooner than my gift would eat me."

He glanced to the Scout, saw her incline her head, very slightly, and lost her face in the wash of tears. He bent forward and gathered his heart into his arms.

"Arika . . ."

"No. Slade." Her arms tightened, then loosened, as she pulled away. "You must take our child, make her strong, so that she may do the work of our tent–and yours." She reached to his face, smoothing away the tears with cold fingers.

"It is the trail, hunter. The only trail that is given."

He stared at her, unable to speak. She rose, and he did–Gineah and the Scout, as well.

Arika held their daughter out; he took the small burden, numbly.

"Commend me to your mother," Arika whispered, then spun and was gone, out of their tent and into the night.

He moved, meaning to go after her–and found Gineah before him. "I will look after her, Slade. Go, now."

In his arms, his daughter whimpered. He looked down

at her, and then to the Scout, standing patient and silent by the fire.

"It is time, then. My daughter and I are ready."

Naratha's Shadow

For every terror, a joy. For every sorrow, a pleasure. For every death, a life. This is Naratha's Law.

-- From Creation Myths and Unmakings: A Study of Beginning and End

"TAKE IT AWAY!" The Healer's voice was shrill.

The Scout leapt forward, slamming the lid of the stasis box down and triggering the seal in one smooth motion.

"Away, it is," she said soothingly, as if she spoke to a child, instead of a woman old in her art.

"Away it is *not,*" Master Healer Inomi snapped. Her face was pale. The Scout could hardly blame her. Even with the lid closed and the seal engaged, she could feel the emanation from her prize puzzle–a grating, sticky malevolence centered over and just above the eyes, like the beginnings of ferocious headache. If the affect was that strong for her, who tested only moderately empathic as the Scouts rated such things, what must it feel like to the Healer, whose gift allowed her to experience another's emotions as her own?

The Scout bowed. "Master Healer, forgive me. Necessity exists. This . . . object, whatever it may be, has engaged my closest study for–"

"Take. It. Away." The Healer's voice shook, and her hand, when she raised it to point at the door. "Drop it into a black hole. Throw it into a sun. Introduce it into a nova. But, for the gods' sweet love, *take it away!*"

The solution to her puzzle would not be found by driving a Master Healer mad. The Scout bent, grabbed the strap and swung the box onto her back. The grating nastiness over her eyes intensified, and for a moment the room blurred out of focus. She blinked, her sight cleared, and she was moving, quick and silent, back bent under the weight of the thing, across the room and out the door. She passed down a hallway peculiarly empty of Healers, apprentices and patrons, and stepped out into the midday glare of Solcintra.

Even then, she did not moderate her pace, but strode on until she came to the groundcar she had requisitioned from Headquarters. Biting her lip, feeling her own face wet with sweat, she worked the cargo compartment's latch one-handed, dumped her burden unceremoniously inside and slammed the hatch home.

She walked away some little distance, wobbling, and came to rest on a street-side bench. Even at this distance, she could feel it–the thing in the box, whatever it was–though the headache was bearable, now. She'd had the self-same headache for the six relumma since she'd made her find, and was no closer to solving its riddle.

The Scout leaned back on the bench. "Montet sig'Norba," she told herself loudly, "you're a fool."

Well, and who but a fool walked away from the luxury and soft-life of Liad to explore the dangerous galaxy as a Scout? Scouts very rarely lived out the full term of nature's allotted span–even those fortunate enough to never encounter a strange, impulse powered, triple-heavy *something* in the back end of nowhere and tempted the fates doubly by taking it aboard.

Montet rested her head against the bench's high back. She'd achieved precious little glory as a Scout, glory arising as it did from the discovery of odd or lost or hidden knowledge.

Which surely the *something* must carry, whatever its original makers had intended it to incept or avert.

Yet, six relumma after what should have been the greatest find of her career, Montet sig'Norba was still unable to ascertain exactly what the something was.

"It may have been crafted to drive Healers to distraction," she murmured, closing her eyes briefly against the ever-present infelicity in her head.

There was a certain charm to Master Healer Inomi's instruction to drop the box into a black hole and have done, but gods curse it, the thing was an artifact! It had to do something!

Didn't it?

Montet sighed. She had performed the routine tests; and then tests not quite so routine, branching out, with the help of an interested, if slightly demented, lab tech, into the bizarre. The tests stopped short of destruction, the tests, let it be known, had not so much as scratched the smooth black surface of the thing. Neither had they been any use in identifying the substance from which it was constructed. As to what it did, or did not do . . .

Montet had combed, scoured and sieved the Scouts' not-inconsiderable technical archives. She'd plumbed the depths of archeology, scaled the heights of astronomy, and read more history than she would have thought possible, looking for a description, an allusion, a *hint*. All in vain.

Meanwhile, the thing ate through stasis boxes like a mouse through cheese. The headache and disorienting effects were noticeably less when the thing was moved to a new box. Gradually, the effects worsened, until even the demented lab tech–no empath, he– complained of his head aching and his sight jittering. At which time it was only prudent to remove the thing to another box and start the cycle again.

It was this observation of the working of the thing's . . . aura that had led her to investigate its possibilities as a carrier of disease. Her studies were–of course– inconclusive. If it carried disease, it was of a kind unknown to the Scouts' medical laboratory and to its library of case histories.

There are, however, other illnesses to which sentient beings may succumb. Which line of reasoning had immediately preceded her trip to Solcintra Healer Hall, stasis box in tow, to request an interview with Master Healer Inomi.

"And much profit you reaped from that adventure," Montet muttered, opening her eyes and straightening on the bench. Throw it into a sun, indeed!

For an instant, the headache flared, fragmenting her vision into a dazzle of too-bright color. Montet gasped, and that quickly the pain subsided, retreating to its familiar, wearisome ache.

She stood, fishing the car key out of her pocket. Now what? she asked herself. She'd exhausted all possible lines of research. No, check that. She'd exhausted all orderly and reasonable lines of research. There did remain one more place to look.

*

The Library of Legend was the largest of the several

libraries maintained by the Liaden Scouts. The largest and the most ambiguous. Montet had never liked the place, even as a student Scout. Her antipathy had not escaped the notice of her teachers, who had found it wise to assign her long and tedious tracings of kernel-tales and seed-stories, so that she might become adequately acquainted with the Library's content.

Much as she had disliked those assignments, they achieved the desired goal. By the time she was pronounced ready to attempt her Solo, Montet was an agile and discerning researcher of legend, with an uncanny eye for the single true line buried in a page of obfuscation.

After she passed her Solo, she opted for field duty, to the clear disappointment of at least one of her instructors, and forgot the Library of Legends in the freedom of the stars.

However, skills once learned are difficult to unlearn, especially for those who have survived Scout training. It took Montet all of three days to find the first hint of what her dubious treasure might be. A twelve-day after, she had the kernel-tale.

Then, it was cross-checking–triangulating as it were, trying to match allegory to orbit; myth to historical fact. Detail work of the most demanding kind, requiring every nit of a Scout's attention for long hours at a time. Montet did not stint the task–that had never been her way–and the details absorbed her day after day, early to late.

Which would account for her forgetting to move the thing, whatever it was, from its old stasis-box into a new one.

*

"This is an alert! Situation Class One. Guards and emergency personnel to the main laboratory, caution extreme. Montet sig'Norba to the main laboratory. Repeat. This is an alert . . ."

Montet was already moving down the long aisle of the Legend Library, buckling her utility belt as she ran. The intercom repeated its message and began the third pass. Montet slapped the override button for the lift and jumped inside before the door was fully open.

Gods, the main lab. She'd left *it,* whatever it was, in the lab lock-box, which had become her custom when she and the tech had been doing their earnest best to crack the thing open and learn its inner workings. It should have been . . . safe . . . in the lab.

The lift doors opened and she was running, down a hall full of security and catastrophe uniforms. She wove through the moving bodies of her comrades, not slackening speed, took a sharp right into the lab's hallway, twisted and dodged through an unexpectedly dense knot of people just *standing* there, got clear–and stumbled, hands over her eyes.

"Aiee!"

The headache was a knife, buried to the hilt in her forehead. Her knees hit the floor, the jar snapping her teeth shut on her tongue, but that pain was lost inside the greater agony in her head. She sobbed, fumbling for the simple mind-relaxing exercise that was the first thing taught anyone who aspired to be a Scout.

She crouched there for a lifetime, finding the pattern and losing it; and beginning again, with forced, frantic patience. Finally, she found the concentration necessary, ran the sequence from beginning to end, felt the agony recede–sufficiently.

Shaking, she pushed herself to her feet and faced the open door of the lab.

It was then she remembered the stasis box and the madcap young tech's inclination toward explosives.

"Gods, gods, gods . . ." She staggered, straightened and walked, knees rubbery, vision white at the edges—walked down the hall, through the open door.

The main room was trim as always, beakers and culture-plates washed and racked by size; tweezers, blades, droppers and other hand tools of a lab tech's trade hung neatly above each workbench. Montet went down the silent, orderly aisles, past the last workbench, where someone had started a flame on the burner and decanted some liquid into a beaker before discovering that everything was not quite as it should be and slipping out to call Security.

Montet paused to turn the flame down. Her head ached horribly, and her stomach was turning queasy. All praise to the gods of study, who had conspired to make her miss the mid-day meal.

The door to the secondary workroom was closed, and refused to open to her palmprint.

Montet reached into her utility belt, pulled out a flat thin square. The edges were firm enough to grip; the center viscous. Carefully, she pressed the jellified center over the lockplate's sensor, and waited.

For a moment–two–nothing happened, then there was a soft *click* and a space showed between the edge of the door and the frame.

Montet stepped aside, lay the spent jelly on the workbench behind her, got her fingers in the slender space and pushed. The door eased back, silent on well-maintained tracks. When the gap was wide enough, she slipped inside.

The room was dim, the air cool to the point of discomfort. Montet squinted, fighting her own chancy vision and the murkiness around her.

There: a dark blot near the center of the room, which could only be a stasis box. Montet moved forward, through air that seemed to thicken with each step. Automatically, her hand quested along her utility belt, locating the pin-light by touch. She slipped it out of its loop, touched the trigger–and swore.

The stasis box lay on its side in the beam, lid hanging open. Empty.

Montet swallowed another curse. In the silence, someone moaned.

Beam before her, she went toward the sound, and found the charmingly demented lab tech huddled on the floor next to the further wall, his arms folded over his head.

She started toward him, checked and swung the beam wide.

The thing, whatever it was, was barely a dozen steps away, banked by many small boxes of the kind used to contain the explosive trimplix. The detonation of a single container of trimplix could hole a spaceship, and here were twelves of twelves of them, stacked every-which-way against the thing . . .

"*Kill it,*" the tech moaned behind her. "Trigger the trimplix.

Make it stop."

Carefully, Montet put her light on the floor. Carefully, she went out to the main room, drew a fresh stasis box from stores and carried it back into the dimness. The tech had not moved, except perhaps to draw closer 'round himself.

It was nerve-wracking work to set the boxes of trimplix gently aside, until she could get in close enough to grab the thing and heave it into the box. It hit bottom with a thump, and she slammed the lid down as if it were a live thing and likely to come bounding back out at her.

That done, she leaned over, gagging, then forced herself up and went over to the intercom to sound the all-clear.

* *

Panopele settled her feet in the cool, dewy grass; filled her lungs with sweet midnight air; felt the power coalesce and burn in her belly, waking the twins, Joy and Terror. Again, she drank the sweet, dark air, lungs expanding painfully; then raised her face to the firmament, opened her mouth–and sang.

Amplified by Naratha's Will, the song rose to the star-lanes, questing, questioning, challenging. Transported by the song, the essence of Panopele, Voice of Naratha, rose likewise to the star-lanes, broadening, blossoming, listening.

Attended by four of the elder novices, feet comforted by the cool, dewy grass, strong toes holding tight to the soil of Aelysia, the body of Panopele sang the Cycle down. Two of the attendant novices wept to hear her; two of the novices danced. The body of Panopele breathed and sang; sang and breathed. And sang.

Out among the star-lanes, enormous and a-quiver with every note of the song, Panopele listened, and heard no discord. Expanding even further, she opened what might be called her eyes, looked out along the scintillant fields of life and saw–a blot.

Faint it was, vastly distant from the planet where her body stood and sang, toes comfortably gripping the soil– and unmistakable in its menace. Panopele strained to see– to hear–more clearly, hearing–or imagining she heard–the faintest note of discord; the barest whisper of malice.

Far below and laboring, her body sang on, voice sweeping out in pure waves of passion. The two novices who danced spun like mad things, sweat soaking their robes. The two who wept fell to their knees and struck their heads against the earth.

Panopele strained, stretching toward the edge of the song, the limit of Naratha's Will. The blot shimmered, growing; the malice of its answering song all at once plain.

Far below, the body of Panopele gasped, interrupting the song. The scintillation of the star-lanes paled into a blur; there was a rush of sound, un-song-like, and Panopele was joltingly aware of cold feet, laboring lungs, the drumbeat of her heart. Her throat hurt, and she was thirsty.

A warm cloak was draped across her shoulders, clasped across her throat. Warm hands pressed her down into the wide seat of the ancient wooden Singer's Chair. In her left ear the novice Fanor murmured, "I have water, Voice. Will you drink?"

Drink she would and drink she did, the cool water a joy.

"Blessings on you," she rasped and lay her left hand over his heart in Naratha's full benediction. Fanor was one of the two who wept in the song.

"Voice." He looked away, as he always did, embarrassed by her notice.

"Will you rest here, Voice? Or return to temple?" That was Lietta, who danced, and was doubtless herself in need of rest.

Truth told, rest was what Panopele wanted. She was weary; drained, as the song sometimes drained one; and dismayed in her heart. She wanted to sleep, here and now among the dewy evening. To sleep and awake believing that the blot she had detected was no more than a woman's fallible imagining.

The Voice of Naratha is not allowed the luxury of self-deceit. And the blot had been growing larger.

Weary, Panopele placed her hands on the carven arms of the chair that dwarfed all present but herself and gathered her strength. Her eyes sought the blue star Alyedon: The blot approached from that direction. That knowledge fed her strength and resolve. Slowly she leaned forward and, as the chair creaked with her efforts, pushed herself onto her feet.

"Let us return," she said to those who served her.

Lietta bowed, and picked up the chair. Fanor bent to gather the remaining water jugs; Panopele stopped him with a gesture.

"One approaches," she told him. "You are swiftest. Run ahead, and be ready to offer welcome."

One glance he dared, full into her eyes, then passed the jug he held to Darl and ran away across the starlit grass.

"So." Panopele motioned and Zan stepped forward to offer an arm, her face still wet with tears.

"My willing support, Voice," she said, as ritual demanded, though her own voice was soft and troubled.

"Blessings on you," Panopele replied, and proceeded across the grass in Fanor's wake, leaning heavily upon the arm of her escort.

*

There was of course nothing resembling a spaceport on-world, and the only reason the place had escaped Interdiction, in Montet's opinion, was that no Scout had yet penetrated this far into the benighted outback of the galaxy.

That the gentle agrarian planet below her could not possibly contain the technology necessary to unravel the puzzle of the thing sealed and seething in its stasis box, failed to delight her. Even the knowledge that she had deciphered legend with such skill that she had actually raised a planet at the coordinates she had half-intuited did not warm her.

Frowning, omnipresent ache centered over her eyes, Montet brought the Scout ship down. Her orbital scans had identified two large clusters of life and industry–cities, perhaps –and a third, smaller, cluster, which nonetheless put forth more energy than either of its larger cousins.

Likely, it was a manufactory of some kind, Montet thought, and home of such technology as the planet might muster. She made it her first target, by no means inclined to believe it her last.

She came to ground in a gold and green field a short distance from her target. She tended her utility belt while the hull cooled, then rolled out into a crisp, clear morning.

The target was just ahead, on the far side of a slight rise. Montet swung into a walk, the grass parting silently before her. She drew a deep lungful of fragrant air, verifying her scan's description of an atmosphere slightly lower in oxygen than Liad's. Checking her stride, she bounced, verifying the scan's assertion of a gravity field somewhat lighter than that generated by the homeworld.

Topping the rise, she looked down at the target, which was not a manufactory at all, but only a large building, and various outbuildings, clustered companionably together. To her right hand, fields were laid out. To her left, the grassland continued until it met a line of silvery trees, brilliant in the brilliant day.

And of the source of the energy reported by her scans, there was no sign whatsoever.

Montet sighed, gustily. Legend.

She went down the hill. Eventually, she came upon a path; which she followed until it abandoned her on the threshold of the larger building.

Here she hesitated, every Scout nerve a-tingle, for this *should* be a Forbidden World, socially and technologically unprepared for the knowledge-stress that came riding in on the leather-clad shoulders of a Scout. She had no *business* walking up to the front door of the local hospital, library, temple or who-knew-what, no matter how desperate her difficulty. There was no one here who was the equal–who was the master– of the thing in her ship's hold. How could there be? She hovered on the edge of doing damage past counting. Better to return to her ship, quickly; rise to orbit and get about setting the warning beacons.

. . . and yet, the legends, she thought–and then all indecision was swept away, for the plain white wall she faced showed a crack, then a doorway, framing a man. His pale robe was rumpled, wet and stained with grass. His hair was dark and braided below his shoulders; the skin of his face and his hands were brown. His feet, beneath the stained, wet hem, were bare.

He was taller than she, and strongly built. She could not guess his age, beyond placing him in that nebulous region called "adult."

He spoke; his voice was soft, his tone respectful. The

language was tantalizingly close to a tongue she knew.

"God's day to you," she said, speaking slowly and plainly in that language. She showed her empty hands at waist level, palm up. "Has the house any comfort for a stranger?"

Surprise showed at the edges of the man's face. His hands rose, tracing a stylized pattern in the air at the height of his heart.

"May Naratha's song fill your heart," he said, spacing his words as she had hers. It was not quite, Montet heard, the tongue she knew, but 'twould suffice.

"Naratha foretold your coming," the man continued. "The Voice will speak with you." He paused, hands moving through another pattern. "Of comfort, I cannot promise, stranger. I hear a dark chanting upon the air."

Well he might hear just that, Montet thought grimly; especially if he were a Healer-analog. Carefully, she inclined her head to the doorkeeper.

"Gladly will I speak with the Voice of Naratha," she said.

The man turned and perforce she followed him, inside and across a wide, stone-floored hall to another plain white wall. He lay his hand against the wall and once again a door appeared. He stood aside, hands shaping the air.

"The Voice awaits you."

Montet squared her shoulders and walked forward.

The room, like the hall, was brightly lit, the shine of light along the white walls and floor adding to the misery of her headache. Deliberately, she used the Scout's mental relaxation drill and felt the headache inch, grudgingly, back. Montet sighed and blinked the room into focus.

"Be welcome into the House of Naratha." The voice was deep, resonant, and achingly melodic, the words spaced so that they were instantly intelligible.

Montet turned, finding the speaker standing near a niche in the left-most wall.

The lady was tall and on a scale to dwarf the sturdy doorkeeper; a woman of abundance, shoulders proud and face serene. Her robe was divided vertically in half–one side white, one side black—each side as wide as Montet entire. Her hair was black, showing gray like stars in the vasty deepness of space. Her face was like a moon, glowing; her eyes were dark and insightful. She raised a hand and sketched a sign before her, the motion given meaning by the weight of hcr palm against the air.

"I am the Voice of Naratha. Say your name, Seeker."

Instinctively, Montet bowed. One *would* bow, to such a lady as this–and one would not dare lie.

"I am Montet sig'Norba," she said, hearing her own voice thin and reedy in comparison with the other's rich tones.

"Come forward, Montet sig'Norba."

Forward she went, until she stood her own short arm's reach from the Voice. She looked up and met the gaze of far-seeing black eyes.

"Yes," the Voice said after a long pause. "You bear the wounds we have been taught to look for."

Montet blinked. "Wounds?"

"Here," said the Voice and lay her massive palm against Montet's forehead, directly on the spot centered just above her eyes, where the pain had lived for six long relumma.

The Voice's palm was warm and soft. Montet closed her eyes as heat spread up and over her scalp, soothing and—she opened her eyes in consternation.

The headache was gone.

The Voice was a Healer, then. Though the Healers on Liad had not been able to ease her pain.

"You have that which belongs to Naratha," the Voice said, removing her hand. "You may take me to it."

Montet bowed once more. "Lady, that which I carry is — ." she grappled briefly with the idiom of the language she spoke, hoping it approximated the Voice's nearly enough for sense, and not too nearly for insult.

"What I carry is . . . accursed of God. It vibrates evil, and seeks destruction–even unto its own destruction. It is–I brought it before a . . . priestess of my own kind and its vibrations all but overcame her skill."

The Voice snorted. "A minor priestess, I judge. Still, she

did well, if you come to me at her word."

"Lady, her word was to make all haste to fling the monster into a sun."

"No!" The single syllable resonated deep in Montet's chest, informing, for a moment, the very rhythm of her heartbeat.

"No," repeated the Voice, quieter. "To follow such a course would be to grant its every desire. To the despair of all things living."

"What *is* it?" Montet heard herself blurt.

The Voice bowed her head. "It is the Shadow of Naratha. For every great good throws a shadow, which is, in its nature, great evil."

Raising her head, she took a breath and began, softly, to chant. "Of all who fought, it was Naratha who prevailed against the Enemy. Prevailed, and drove the Enemy into the back beyond of space, from whence it has never again ventured. The shadows of Naratha's triumph, as terrible as the Enemy's defeat was glorious, roam the firmament still, destroying, for that is what they do." The Voice paused. The chant vibrated against the pure white walls for a moment, then stopped.

This, Montet thought, was the language of legend–hyperbole. Yet the woman before her did not seem a fanatic, living in a smoky dream of reality. This woman was alive, intelligent–and infinitely sorrowful.

"Voices were trained," the Voice was now calmly factual, "to counteract the vibration of evil. We were chosen to sing, to hold against and equalize– what slighter folk cannot encompass. We were many, once. Now I am one. Naratha grant that the equation is exact."

Montet stared. She was a Liaden and accustomed to the demands of Balance. But this–

"You will die? But by your own saying it wants just that!"

The Voice smiled. "I will not die, nor will it want destruction when the song is through." She tipped her massive head, hair rippling, black-and-gray, across her proud shoulders.

"Those who travel between the stars see many wonders. I

am the last Voice of Naratha. I exact a price, star-stranger."

Balance, clear enough. Montet bowed her head. "Say on."

"You will stand with me while I sing this monster down. You will watch and you will remember. Perhaps you have devices that record sight and sound. If you do, use them. When it is done, bring the news to Lietta, First Novice, she who would have been Voice. Say to her that you are under geas to study in our library. When you have studied, I require you to return to the stars, to discover what has happened to the rest of us." She paused.

"You will bring what you find to this outpost. You will also initiate your fellow star-travelers into the mysteries of Naratha's Discord." The wonderful voice faltered and Montet bent her head.

"In the event," she said, softly, "that the equation is not–entirely–precise." She straightened. "I accept your Balance."

"So," said the Voice. "Take me now to that which is mine."

*

The Voice stood, humming, while Montet dragged the stasis box out, unsealed it and flipped open the lid. At a sign from the other woman, she tipped the box sideways, and the thing, whatever it was, rolled out onto the grass, buzzing angrily.

"I hear you, Discord," the Voice murmured, and raised her hand to sign.

Montet dropped back, triggering the three recorders with a touch to her utility belt.

The Voice began to sing.

A phrase only, though the beauty of it pierced Montet heart and soul.

The phrase ended and the space where it had hung was filled with the familiar malice of the black thing's song.

Serene, the Voice heard the answer out, then sang again, passion flowing forth like flame.

Again, the thing answered, snarling in the space between Montet's ears. She gasped and looked to the Voice, but her face was as smooth and untroubled as glass.

Once more, the woman raised her voice, and it seemed to Montet that the air was richer, the grassland breeze fresher, than it had been a moment before.

This time, the thing did not allow her to finish, but vibrated in earnest. Montet shrieked at the agony in her joints and fell to her knees, staring up at the Voice, who sang on, weaving around and through the malice; stretching, reshaping, *reprogramming*, Montet thought, just before her vision grayed and she could see no longer.

She could hear, though, even after the pain had flattened her face down in the grass. The song went on, never faltering, never heeding the heat that Montet felt rising from the brittling grass, never straining, despite the taint in the once clean air.

The Voice hit a note, high, true and sweet. Montet's vision cleared. The Voice stood, legs braced, face turned toward the sky, her mighty throat corded with effort. The note continued, impossibly pure, soaring, passionate, irrefutable. There was only that note, that truth, nothing more, in all the galaxy.

Montet took a breath and discovered that her lungs no longer burned. She moved an arm and discovered that she could rise.

The Voice sang on, and the day was brilliant, perfect, beyond perfect, into godlike, and the Voice herself was beauty incarnate, singing, singing, fading, becoming one with the sunlight, the grassland and the breeze.

Abruptly, there was silence, and Montet stood alone in the grass near her ship, hard by an empty stasis box.

Of the Voice of Naratha–of Naratha's Shadow–there was no sign at all.

A Matter of Dreams

ON SINTIA, it's the dreaming that first marks a witch.

A child will dream the minutiae of life, relate the sending in the morning, all innocent and dewy-eyed; astonished when the dream events turn true next day—or next one.

She's watched then, for grandma will have contacted Temple, never doubt it; and after a time the child will dream the name of the one she had been Before. Then she'll be brought to Circle and trained to be one with the Dream.

I know the way because Jake used to talk about his Mam, my gran'mam, who'd Dreamed a Dream and had the training and then left the Temple and who she'd been—for love, Jake said, and for stars.

I've never dreamed the naming-Dream, being outworlder, even though witch-blood. I figure only the damned come to me—those who died unquiet or outside the love of the Holy; those who somehow lost their Name. I figure that, but I don't say it. I dream the dreams and I let them go. Sometimes they come back. Sometimes they come true.

The first time I saw Her was dreamsight.

She was in a port side bar—too coarse a place for Her to be—standing straight in her starry blue robe, with her breasts free and her face shining with power, black hair crackling lightning and spread around her like an aurora. Her eyes—her eyes were black, and in the dream she saw me. At her feet was broken glass; the shine of a knife.

She was young—not above fifteen—with the silver bangles hiding half of one slim arm. But for all that, I wanted to go down on my knees in front of her and lay my cheek against her mound from which had sprung the worlds and the stars and the deep places between. That's how it was, in the dream.

But then the dream ended, as they do, and there was Lil, yelling about orbit and was I conning or not, so it was out of the cot and let the dream go and get about the business of making a living.

I never talked to Lil about the dreams. They scared her, and there's nothing worth that. Still, she's witch-blood too and knows as sure I do when I've dreamt, though she never dreams at all.

"Well?" she spat at me, spiteful the way sisters are, within the protection of Us against Them. "Was it wet this time?"

"Keep it down and keep it clean," I answered, no more gentle, because there was the flutter in the nine-dial I didn't like, which meant relying on number eight, a thing that had been a bad idea since I was co-pilot and Mam on prime.

"Where's the passenger?" I asked, because there was a certain amount of care taken, when you'd been paid hard coin to deliver someone intact to a place.

"Webbed in gentle as a roolyet," Lil said and I gave a grin for the old adventure, though putting *Mona Luki* through the orbiting sequence was proving more of a problem than usual.

"Shit," muttered Lil, hands over her part of the business. "We gotta get that reset before we lift, Fiona."

"On Sintia?"

"Federated port," she answered, which was true. And, "Credit's good," which was not.

"Yeah," I said, not wanting to argue the point and have her start to worry. "We'll let our passenger off and see if we can't patch it. Bound to be junkyards."

"Flying a junkyard," she answered, which I should have known she would. "Mam'd have a fit, Fiona..."

And that was another line of thought better left alone.

"Mind your board," I growled, and she sighed, and looked rebellious, and turned her head away.

Tower came on in another few seconds, with an offer of escort, if we had equipment trouble. I turned down the escort, which was expensive, but requisitioned a repair pad, which came gratis, they having noted trouble, and we got her down without any bad glitches.

Our passenger, that was something else.

Cly Nelbern got her first sight of Sintia Port there in screen number one, looked sour and flung herself into prime pilot's chair like she had a right to it. Lil had her mouth half opened before she caught my headshake, but I doubt Nelbern would have heard a shout just then.

I finished making my coffee-toot and ambled over, leaned a hip against the chair-back and spoke over her head. "We can give you a hand with your baggage," I said; "or you can leave it stored. We'll be here a day or two. Repairs."

Nelbern gave one of those snorts we'd decided between us passed for her laughing and shook her head, real gentle, eyes still and always on that screen.

"So eager to lose me, Captain?"

"Not to say," I answered, calm, like Mam'd taught us to talk to dirtsiders. "It's just that you paid cash money for Jumps in a hurry. I figured you had an appointment."

"An appointment," she repeated and snorted. "An appointment." She licked her lips like the phrase tasted sweet and glanced up at me out of wide blue eyes.

"As it happens, Captain, I do have an—appointment. Yes." She smiled, which I had never liked in her, and nodded. "I wonder if I might impose upon the good natures of yourself and your sister just a bit further."

I gritted my teeth and brought the cup up to keep it from showing; feeling Lil tense up behind me. I was mortally sick of dirtside manners and a stranger on our ship, whether she carried an ambassador's ransom in Terran bits or no. It was on the tip of my tongue to say so, though not as blunt as that, when she turned full around to face me.

"I noticed a bit of a boggle on the way in, I thought," she said, in that conversational way officials use when it's bound to cost you plenty. I stared down at her and shrugged.

"Told you we'd be here a day or so."

"Indeed. Repairs, I think you said." She stared, sizing me up, maybe, though I was sure she'd done that long ago. "Repairs to the central mag coil don't come cheap, Captain; and it's hardly anything you'd like to trust to the junkyard and a gerryrig." She smiled. "If you had a choice."

I felt Lil behind me like a wound spring, and in my heart I cursed all dirtsiders—especially this one. I gritted my teeth and then bared them, not caring a whit for manners.

"So now I've got a choice, have I?"

"Certainly you have a choice." She brought her hand up, and I focused on the thing that gleamed there; did a double-stare and nearly dumped my drink in her lap.

She was holding a Liaden cantra piece.

I stared, not at the coin—enough money for several choices and maybe a luxury, too—but at her face—and read no more there than I ever had, save it was the first time I thought her eyes looked mad.

"What in starlight do you *want*?" That was Lil, coming up like she was stalking tiger, bent at the waist, her eyes on the shine of the money.

Cly Nelbern looked up at me and she smiled before turning to face my sister and hold the coin up high.

"An escort," she said softly. "Just an escort, Ms. Betany, as I walk around the town. In case the natives are restless."

"An escort," I scoffed, around the cold dread in my belly. "On Sintia a woman needs no escort—unless you'll be breaking into the Temple?"

The mad eyes gleamed my way, though she forbore to smile again. "Not the Temple, Captain. Of course not." She did smile then, her eyes going back to Lil. "That would be foolish."

"Then us not being fools—" I began, short-tempered with something near terror.

But Lil shot a glance that silenced me long enough for her to gabble: "A *cantra*, Fiona! *New* parts, backups, a new 'doc, coffee..." Her eyes were back on Cly Nelbern and I knew right then I'd lost her.

"Lillian!" I snapped, as much like Mam as I could.

Too late. "I'll do it," she told the dirtsider.

And held out her hand for the money.

I sat down slow on the arm of the co-pilot's chair and brought the tepid coffee-toot up to sip. There was nothing else to do, the word having been given. Nothing except:

"I'll be coming along as well, then. If that coin's so wide a treasure, I reckon it'll pay berth-cost while we escort this lady 'round town."

Nelbern laughed, a half-wild sound no more pleasant than her smile. "Think I won't pay, Captain?" She sent a brilliant glance into my face, and flicked the coin to Lil.

"Order your repairs," she said, standing up. "And you'll—both—be ready to come with me in one hour."

She sauntered off toward her cabin and I looked at my sister, standing there with her hand clenched 'round that money, and her cheeks flushed with lust of it and I sighed and hovered a second between sad and mad; figured neither would mend it and stood up myself.

"I'll take first shower," I said, tossing the cup into the unit as I went past.

At the door I looked back, but she was showing back to me, head half-tipped, like she hadn't even noticed that I'd gone.

*

WE WANDERED, that endless afternoon, visiting trade-bars, dives, and talking-booths on both sides of the river. Some places folk eyed us; some places they eyed our employer. Other places they ignored us entirely, and those I liked least of all.

The last was near the city-line, close enough to the Temple that the evening chant echoed off the dirty windows and the tawdry buildings, making even Cly Nelbern look up for a moment before turning down the short, ill-kept walk.

This place at least made some pretense of cleanliness: the window was clear enough to let the evening light come through; the bar was chipped but polished; the tender's tattered apron had recently been washed.

I was three steps into the room before I realized why it felt so comfortable. It reminded me of *Mona Luki*: desperately ship-shape and tidy; and showing the worn spots despite it.

It hadn't always been so. When Mam and Jake had run her, back when I was little enough to be strapped in a net slung between their seats, watching baby-eyed while they worked the Jumps between them—then *Mona Luki*'d gleamed, oiled and cared-for and prosperous as you like. Then there'd been coffee—yes, and chocolate—and repairs when they were needed and spare parts in third hold. Lil was too young to remember those days—too young, just, to remember Jake, killed in the same mishap that had taken Mam's leg.

I'd dreamed that accident; I'd even told Mam. They'd gone out to make the repair anyway, of course, as who, save on Sintia, would not? I'd climbed into the netting with the baby and held her til Mam started to scream.

Six years old, I was then, but it got me thinking hard about dreams.

"So!" That was Cly Nelbern and here was the present. I came alert to both, sending my gaze along hers to the man in Sintian town clothes—shabby, bright blue overshirt, bold with raveling embroidery, darker blue pants, worn wide and loose in respect of the heat, with matching fancy-work around the hems.

He had a tired face, used honestly, I thought, with eyes showing desperation far back. Likely I looked the same: respectability balanced on the knife-edge of despair, needing only one more disaster to send us all over into thieves.

He gulped, brown eyes darting from her face to mine, barely glancing from me to Lil before his face softened a touch and he bowed, gesturing toward the rear of the little room.

"I have a table, La—ma'am." His voice was agreeable, though it quavered. Nelbern shrugged and pushed forward.

"Delightful," she said, and the edge in her voice put the shine of fear in his eyes. "Lead on."

It was a small enough table in a snug, ill-lit corner, tight seating for four, but he'd clearly been expecting only her.

"My—companions," Cly Nelbern said to his startled glare. "Captain Fiona and Ms. Lillian Betany, of the *Mona Luki*."

It gave me a chill, being named there, and by the sudden dart of Lil's eyes, it chilled her, too. But she stayed tight where she was, perched on a chair crammed next to the man—and Cly Nelbern smiled.

"Well?" she said, and the icy edge was back in her voice. "Where is it?"

He gulped, sent a hunted glance around the room at my back and firmed his face to look at her.

"In the office at the Port House, Lady. And that's where it's going to stay."

Nelbern didn't frown, which was what I expected. She picked up her drink and had a sip, eyeing him over the chipped rim.

"Indeed." She set the glass aside. "That wasn't our agreement."

Mild as it sounded, it was evidently bad enough. The man stared at her dumbly, pale to the lips.

"Our agreement," she pursued, still in that mild-as-milk voice, "was that you provide me with a certain item, in return for which I provide you with a particular sum of money." She stared at him. "That *was* the agreement?"

He gulped. "Yes, Lady."

"'Yes, Lady'," she repeated softly, then leaned suddenly across Lil, to put her face right up to his and hiss: "Then what in the name of the Last Hell do you mean by telling me you don't have that file?"

"I-" he tried to pull back, but there was nowhere to go. He licked his lips. "There is a—a Maiden out of Circle House, come to study and catalog the files. She—Lady, I dare not! If Circle House finds me—"

"What I'll leave for the Temple to find if I don't have that file within the day will be far beyond worrying about witches," Cly Nelbern snarled. "Do you mark me, Pirro Velesz?"

If he hated the speaking of his name, in that place and in such company, he gave no sign other than the roll of an eye.

"The Maiden," he said, "is named Moonhawk." Nelbern leaned back and reached for her glass. "What do I care for her name? If you can't match wits with a half-grown chit out of Circle House—"

"Moonhawk," the man interrupted, with an intensity that raised the hairs along the back of my neck, "is the oldest Name in Circle. Moonhawk is the most powerful servant of the Goddess—every life she lives is exceptional—historic..."

"Don't prate at me like an abo! So the girl had the wit to pick an elite name—she's still in school. Come to Port House to study the records, you said. Where's the danger—"

"The girl," Velesz interrupted again, "is Moonhawk's incarnation in this life, Lady. Fact. She is young, but the power abides within her. The danger is that she has not yet relearned control. The training her elders-in-world provide is to ensure that she will not—accidentally—use more force than might be necessary."

"Loose cannon." That was Lil, unexpected and great-eyed, but still well away from fright.

The man turned his head, eyes easier for looking at her again. "Loose cannon," he repeated and nodded, a smile coming and going in the second before he looked back to Cly Nelbern. "Power without guidance."

"Well, then we'll see to it that she has no need to expend her powers." Nelbern finished her drink and put the glass away. "I have a client, can you understand that? An—organization—that has paid me to—collect—a certain fact. The only place this fact has come to light is Sintia. My client has paid for proof. I *will provide* proof, whether you earn your fee or not." She looked closely at Velesz.

"My client is not easily thwarted, you see? Satisfaction earns reward. The wages of inefficiency are destruction and disgrace." She leaned forward, and I saw fear bloom at last in my sister's eyes and saw the sweat bead on the man's face.

"Disappoint me and be sure that your name will pass higher."

"Lady—" he began, but Cly Nelbern had pushed back her chair and turned away, carelessly flinging a handful of coin to the table.

"Tomorrow midday," she said softly. "At Diablo's, in the port. Have it." And she was gone.

I half-rose, but Lil stayed put, the fear like lunacy in her eyes. If she wasn't ship and blood I'd have left her but—

"Let's move," I said, gruff-like, so not to spook her, but she stared at me like she had when Mam died, and never moved a hair.

"Lil—"

"Lady Lillian," that was Pirro Velesz, leaning over to take her hand, oh so gently. His voice was soft, and I seemed to hear it, like a cat's burr, somewhere in the middle of my brain. "You cannot stay here, Lady Lillian. Go with your captain."

Incredibly, the fear subsided and she turned her eyes to him. "What're you gonna do?" she asked, matter-of-fact as if they were old shipmates and she had every right of an answer.

He smiled and pressed her hand, speaking as if to a child, "Why, I will go to the Port House and do what I may, and trust that the Goddess is good."

It seemed to satisfy her, who never had patience with my dream-tellings. She nodded and rose, Velesz with her, and he gave her hand into mine with a little bow, as if all were right and tight with him.

But the eyes he lifted to mine in the moment he gave Lil over were blighted with dread. His lips held the ghost of the smile he'd shown her, but his eyes were the eyes of a man looking at his death, or worse. I hesitated, thinking to offer—what? I had no aid to give, trapped likewise by Cly Nelbern's coin. I nodded my thanks and went away, my sister's hand warm in mine.

*

IT'S A MARVEL how many repairs can be done to a ship, in the course of six short hours. A marvel, too, how much it all cost: enough to put a sizable dent in Cly Nelbern's cantra-piece. Though, truth told, the leavings of money would be enough to give *Luki* some semblance of credit again—enough, even, to claim a small amount of interest, if Lil would agree to forego real coffee for a time.

I had just thought that comfortable thought, musing among the itemizations on the screen, when I caught a sound behind me and spun the chair, fast.

Cly Nelbern smiled her ugly smile and came forward another step, to lean companionably against the co-pilot's chair and nod at the bill on the screen.

"Everything put to right now, Captain?"

"Everything'd take a deal more than a cantra," I said, reluctantly honest; "but we're set to fly."

"Good," she said, somewhat absent, and I asked the next question even more reluctantly.

"You'll be wanting our escort tomorrow?"

She looked up at that, alert as a dock-rat. "But of course—and a lift out, too. If we're up against the Temple—if that fool out there trips up..." The words faded and she focused on me again. "Have us moved to a hot-pad, Captain."

I looked at her hard. "We're ready to fly, I said. I didn't say we were champing on it. Plan to look around, take on cargo."

"You have a passenger." The voice was milk-mild and I felt my heart shudder, remembering her at the tavern.

I shook my head. "We're through with passengers. Trade's what we were born to; trade's what we'll stay with."

"Indeed." She pointed at the screen, at the invoice still visible, waiting for my thumbprint so the funds could leave *Luki's* account. "I demand return of my loan, Captain Betany."

I stared at her. "That was no loan, and you well know it. Payment for escort, was what you said."

"Really?" she purred and then I knew how far Lil had lost us. "Do you have a contract stating so, Captain?"

I held onto my glare with an effort. "No."

"No." She smiled. "But I have a contract stipulating that I offered a cantra in loan for needful repairs, payable upon demand, else the ship resolves to me."

My mouth dried and my heart took up thumping so hard I thought the scans might read it. "You have no such thing."

"Oh, I do," she assured me; "and so do you. Right there in the daily log." She leaned away from the chair and started back toward the companionway. "Do move us to a hot-pad, Captain; there's a good girl."

It took me a long time to move, after she was gone. The first thing I did was open the log and read the thing she'd put there, sealed with my own codes.

Ship and blood. Mam'd told me to save things in that order, always. Ship first, then blood. I'd never in life have signed such a thing, nor agreed for the sake of a cantra...

Ship and blood. I thumbprinted the invoice and put the call through for the ready-pad. I okay'd those charges, too, forgetful of the meaning of the numbers; and then I went to my bunk to lie down, sealing the door and detaching the bell.

After a time of lying there in cold terror, eyes screwed shut against the awful sight of the ceiling, I fell asleep and I dreamed.

The dream was a confusion of pointing fingers and harsh voices making accusations that echoed into meaninglessness. At the center of it all stood my goddess of the barroom, her hair quiescent, though her eyes were not; and the one word that echoed clearly from the finger-pointers was "Recant!"

The word that I woke with among pounding head was hers, shaping my mouth with Her will: "No."

*

THE SHIP WAS QUIET. World-clock showed midnight, straight up. Ship clock showed 0200.

I made myself a cup of 'toot and slid into the pilot's chair, worry gnawing at my gut. Cly Nelbern was surely mad, with more than grounder lunacy. No simple dockside bully, she; but a dangerous woman, and on more levels than gave me comfort.

The man? The man was desperate, and that carried its own brand of danger. But he seemed sane enough, and perhaps might be turned a card—made a pawn. Sacrificed for ship and blood.

It was snatching at starlight, of course, and madness in its own way, but I had to try something, there in the dark quiet; had to make some stab at saving my ship, my sister.

Curiously, it was Nelbern's money that bought me a way to make that stab, sorry as it might be. I set aside my cold drink and cycled the chair forward. I'd never had the credit to tap into a current planetary data bank before. We'd always bought old records—last week's cargo movements, yesterday's closing prices, and left it at that—but not this time.

I typed in Pirro Velesz' name. I tapped the dot for full database inspection. I offered up a prayer to whatever gods might be awake and listening, there in the deep heart of the night.

Then I went to sleep.

*

CLY NELBERN WOKE me by laughing, waving a hand at the

screen where Velesz' information glittered like an unexplored star system.

"That's close to the way I found him, Captain, except that I didn't have a name—I just looked for a desperate person."

She laughed again, harder.

"That's how I found *Mona Luki* , too. Hard as you try to hide it, the information's there. I *know* how to read that spiral. Dreamers like you and that greengrocer—always thinking you'll find a way to beat the universe.

"I've seen it over and over again. You think you're something special. Think luck'll be with you. Well, you got lucky, Captain. I found you, thought you'd be useful and pulled you out of your downspin. *I'm* your luck, and if you're a smart girl, you'll ride easy with me, no arguments."

She waved at the screen again.

"But you want to know all about Senor Velesz —go ahead—read it. It's not a secret, is it?" Her words bit, deep and bitter, but I couldn't think of anything useful to say to a dirtsider who held mortgage to my ship and my kin, so I spun the chair back around and I read.

*

THE SHORT OF IT was that Pirro Velesz got himself suckered on a contract to supply some upcountry Temple with vittles for a year. When he couldn't make delivery the Temple took his business and put him to work at the rate of a standard year for each month the Temple had to buy its food from someplace else. He had the option of buying himself out, of course—but he'd rolled everything on that losing deal—and no one on Sintia would lend money to a Temple debtor.

I sagged back into the pilot's chair, yanked two ways: pity and despair. So much for the stab to save us. Pirro Velesz was in worse case than *Mona Luki* or either of her sorry crew.

*

MIDDAY AT DIABLO'S. Too far from the city to hear the Temple chanting. Too close to the port to see anything but outworlders, half of them drunk and the other half out of luck, hunched over the bar like their last hope of salvation, eyes blurred like the middle of Jump.

Not one of them took note of us at all.

Lil was jumping terrified—the move to the hot-pad in the middle of our night and the guilt that came with knowing she'd sold our ship, however unknowing, had her in a state already. The bar filled with chancy spacers wired her even higher.

Pirro Velesz was nowhere to be seen.

Cly Nelbern found us a ringside table, ordered up a round of drinks and leaned back. She sipped from her glass now and then, and her hands were steady when she did, but for all of that I thought she looked tense and I tried not to think what she'd do, if she were forced into hunting him out.

The crowd thinned soon enough, as my drink sat untouched on the table. Lil's was long swallowed and Nelbern had all but finished her own.

She had just waved her hand for the waiter when there was a flicker at the doorway and a ripple of city-clothes in the corner of my eye. Nelbern came to her feet in one smooth flow, moving through the knot of patrons.

Lil charged to her feet the next second, wailing something inarticulate under her breath.

"Lillian!" I cried as she went by, but her eyes were full of anguish and she never heard me at all.

A circle had opened around them—Cly Nelbern and Pirro Velesz—a circle of the dead-eyed incurious, who turned back to drinking after a glance determined the business was none of theirs.

"Well?" I heard her say, as Lil pushed a way to his side.

"Well." He looked tired, his shabby blue tunic draggled and dirty. He swayed where he stood and Lil put a hand under his elbow to steady him.

I saw a smile come and go on his face, like a whisper of might-have-been; then he reached in his sleeve and pulled out a thin white envelope of the kind used for dirtsider's mail and handed it to Cly Nelbern.

She shook her head toward a table and we moved that way, Lil bright in the reflection of the man's wan smile.

"So." A purr of satisfaction as Nelbern opened the folder and pulled out a strip of film. "The original?"

He nodded. "As agreed."

"Delightful. And I have payment for you." She patted her own sleeve. Something in the gesture chilled me, and I saw Lil clutch after the man's arm, her eyes showing white at the edges.

It was then that I saw Her, in life as in dreaming, walking into that place in Her cleanness and her power, as if nothing evil could ever touch Her.

"Witch!" screamed one of the drunks at the bar, and threw a glass, which fell, stone-heavy, and broke on the floor at Her feet. She turned Her head and there was silence at the bar; raised a hand and drew a sign in the fetid air. The silence shimmered, then broke apart, as the one who had thrown the glass lay his head upon the bar top and wailed.

She turned back then, fixed us with those eyes, which saw us and saw through us.

"Pirro Velesz." Her voice was deep, not ungentle; I heard it in my heart.

He licked his lips. "Mercy, Lady."

"Return what you have stolen."

"Lady, I cannot."

The smooth brow creased; then those eyes moved again, pinning Cly Nelbern.

"Return what you have stolen."

The older woman smiled, and bowed a trifle, one hand over her heart. "Why certainly, child," she said agreeably, and reached into her sleeve.

Lil cried out—a single wild shriek of protest. The man flung out a hand, too late, to stop the throw. I jumped half-forward, not sure if my mark were Lil or Nelbern, and saw the knife arc silver-bright, straight for Moonhawk's breast.

It fell, as had the glass; there was a clatter of shards where it struck. Cly Nelbern was already moving, the shine of another blade in her hand, swinging for an undercut that would take the girl out as Nelbern charged on—

"STOP!"

The world rocked and the stars shook in their places. I froze where I was, unable to do otherwise, my muscles commanded by Her will, not mine. I saw Cly Nelbern fall, and Lil. I saw Pirro frozen upright like myself, and heard the silence; wondered if everyone in the bar were like froze...

Moonhawk lifted a hand, bangles tinkling like carnival, and pointed a slender finger at Pirro.

"Return what you have stolen."

He moved, wooden-like, and went to his knees at Nelbern's side. He pulled the envelope from her belt, but tarried, his fingers straying to her wrist. Slowly, he stood and bowed to the girl.

"Lady, this woman is dead."

The power shimmered, and I saw the girl through the goddess; frightened by what she had done, and saddened. She bent her head and when she raised it again, the girl was gone.

Pirro bowed, offered the envelope with its strip of film.

She took it and slipped it away, her eyes, black and brilliant, boring into his. In a moment, she had moved, turning like attention to me, so that I felt Her hovering over my soul; felt Her touch on my heart; felt, at last the loosening of Her will and blurted out: "My sister is dead!"

The black eyes seared into me. "Your sister is alive, Fiona Betany. Give thanks to the Goddess and honor your gifts. All of them."

She went to Lil then, and spoke two words which my ears somehow refused to hear. Then she reached down Her own hand to help my sister rise, and stepped back to survey the three of us.

"You will return to your ship and you will leave this world. You are forbidden to return, on pain of punishment from the Circle."

She motioned, drawing burning signs within the air. "Go now! Be prosperous and true." A tip of a hand toward what had been Cly Nelbern. "Leave that one here."

She paused, looking at us with those eyes, that saw us and saw through us and forgave everything they saw.

"Goddess bless," she said. "Now run!"

It might have been that easy, had the others not come just then:

Temple robes of starry blue, cowls half-hiding faces that woke the echo of "Recant!" within me. There were three, or five, or eight of them: Their magics so shimmered air and truth that I could not count the number.

"HOLD!" demanded on of the group, and, perforce, we did.

One witch pointed at me; I heard the word "Talent!" and nothing else until a second witch pointed at Lil, and me, and Pirro and waved us all into a circle with the word "Conspiracy" binding us together like rope.

A third snatched open the envelope that Moonhawk had meekly given her and let out a smoking curse. "They would have stolen the secret of the catalyst molecule!"

There was charged silence, as if a great secret had been revealed; and the oldest among them laughed, all brittle.

"So, someone seeks to manufacture witches. Little enough success would have attended them! The Temple way is best. As all know—and believe."

She glanced about and took a brisker tone. "The wrong is that they dared to steal from us—the Temple! Retribution is demanded."

She gestured at us, and there was certainty in my heart: Ship and blood—and a good man, too...doomed.

The shortest witch raised a hand, began to trace a sign—and stopped because Moonhawk was abruptly there, meek no longer, slashing across the other's sorcery with a jangle of bracelets.

"Let be!" she snapped. "Moonhawk has looked and Moonhawk has forgiven. This was a dream-matter! Their way is clear, guaranteed by the Goddess!"

The shorter witch gaped, hand suspended in mid-sign. "*Moonhawk* has forgiven! Heresy, Maiden. By what right—"

The argument raged, words unsayable were said and then sign against sign was raised and the witches contended there—

But I found my limbs were my own again and I grabbed Lil's arm with one hand and Pirro's with the other and we took Moonhawk's last advice—we ran, and none chased after.

*

JUST AS WELL THAT Moonhawk banned us from her world, for *Mona Luki's* liftoff and out-travel that day is now legend among traders and Port Masters (who all too often add an extra watch-minder to our bill), and most likely we'd be shot down on approach for traffic violations alone. But Moonhawk had told us to *run!*

And we did what she told us—all of what she told us; and we're as prosperous as a three-crew ship can be.

Pirro calms Lil as none since Mam did; she has found the best truth possible. I have found Pirro practical, a man of his word, always.

We share shifts or switch about to cover the boards. It works well, two sisters and their husband—not an odd arrangement, among small traders. Two babies on the way, which will fill the ship nicely and give us all too much to do.

I take the dreaming seriously now, which accounts for some of our luck in trade—and in other things.

Now and again over the months I dreamt of her—Moonhawk. Not happy dreams. A burning. A hacking away of her long black hair. A mort of hard times among strangers, too much work, not enough food—things I remember all too well myself, so could be those dreams weren't true. Sometimes I'd wake and find myself with my arms pushed tight against the cabin's wall as if I'd tried to push those hard times away...

Just lately, though, I dreamed her again, after a long time of no dreams at all. It woke me and I lay there, listening to Pirro breathe and considering what I'd seen: Moonhawk, short hair all curly, dressed in prosperous trader clothes, bending to embrace a fair-haired boy while a tall man looked on, smiling.

The dream had felt true, I thought, and turned over, to nudge Pirro awake and tell him.

He smiled sleepily and hugged me, the motion of his hands a comfort.

"Will our daughter be a dream-witch too?" he asked and I had no quick answer, for of our daughter the dreams are just beginning.

-Standard Year 1375

Phoenix

CYRA HURRIED THROUGH the bustle of the pre-dawn, head down, and face hidden.

She traveled early, when the friendly shadows helped hide her deformity, allowing her to negotiate the eight chancy blocks from the anonymous apartments she kept in a nondescript building where the floor numbering was in fresher paint in Terran numerals than in the older Liaden to the streets she depended upon for her living.

Once on those streets no one remarked her, and few noticed her passing or her business, except those who had need to buy or sell this or that bauble of stone or made-stone or metal. The half-light suited her purpose, and even so she sometimes found herself automatically facing away from the odd passerby of Liaden gait and stature who would consider her worthless, or less.

On some worlds, Cyra would have been valued for her intelligence and her skills. On others, her demeanor and comeliness would surely have been remarked.

On others but none of that mattered, for here on Liad she was marked for life by the knife of her Delm, and guaranteed a painful existence without the support of clan or kin for at least the remaining ten years of the dozen she'd been banned from clanhouse and the comforts of full-named society.

At one time, of course, she'd been Cyra chel'Vona, Clan Nosko. Now, on the streets where she was seen most, she was "*that Cyra*," if she was anything at all.

The marks high on her cheeks were distinctive, but hardly so disfiguring or repulsive in themselves to have people of good standing turn their heads or their backs on her until she passed. Yet, those of breeding did . . . .

This was scarcely a problem any longer, for she had long ago moved the shambles of her business from the streets of North Solcintra, where she had served the Fifty, to the netherworlds of Low Port, where her clientele were most frequently off-worlders, the clanless, outlaws, and the desperate.

Her own fortunes had fallen so far that she opened and closed her small shop by herself, working daily from east-glow to midday, and then again from the third hour until whatever time whimsy-driven traffic in the night faltered. Occasionally even these hours were insufficient to feed her, and she would work in the back-house at Ortega's cleaning dishes, turning sheets, cooking, pushing unruly drunks out the back door where her face would not be remarked and thereby eating and sometimes earning an extra bit or two.

That was the final indignity. Very often her purse was so shrunken that she measured her worth not in cantra or twelfths but in bits Terran bits! and was pleased to have them. For that matter, being employed by a pure blood Terran was, by itself, enough to turn any of the polite society from her face, no matter that the Terran was a legal land-holder.

Things had been somewhat better of late; the new run of building on the east side of the port gave many of her regulars a chance at day labor and those of sentimental bent often returned in hope for the items they'd sold last week, or even last year.

This morning she was tired, having spent much of the evening at Ortega's, filling in for a cook gone missing. Shrugging her way into the store after touching the antiquated keypads she caught a glimpse of someone standing huddled against the corner of the used clothing store.

Closing the door behind her, leaving behind the sound of the morning shuttles lifting under the clouds, and the jitneys in the streets, she settled into the quiet of the thick-walled old building, checking the time to see that she was early enough to set tea to boil, and to warm and wolf the leftover rolls she carried from last night's work. She started those tasks, glancing through the scratched flex-glass of the door as she moved the few semi-valuable pieces from their hiding places to the case, and uncovered the special twirling display that held her choice Festival masks behind a clear plastic shield.

Cyra admired the green feathered mask as it twirled by, recalled the evening her aunt had brought her the ancient box and said, "This green does not become me, and I doubt I'll go again to

Festival. This was *my* aunt's, after all, and is much out of style but if you wish it, it is yours."

And so she'd worn it to her first Festival, finding delight in the games of walking and eyeing, the while looking for people she might know and seeking one who might not know her . . .

Later, she'd been doubly glad of that Festival, for the marriage her uncle found for her was without joy *or* success, which had scandalized him despite the medic's assurance that she was healthy and quashing her chance at full time study at the Art Institute.

Now, of course, she was denied the Festival at all.

She took her hand from beneath the plastic shield, where it had strayed, unbidden, and returned to routine, eyes drawn to the sudden flash of color outside the window, as the light began to rise with real daybreak.

He - at the distance the wildly abundant Terran beard was about all she could be sure of, aside from the bright blue skullcap he wore to hide his hair - *he* was dressed in what may have once been fine clothes, but which looked somewhat worse than they ought. She doubted he could see her, but his face and eyes seemed to spend about half their time watching her shop door and the other half watching chel'Venga's Pawnshop.

She sighed gently. The ones who had not the good sense to wait until the store was respectably open were the ones who were selling something. She wasn't sure which sort was worse, the ones who needed something they wouldn't be able to afford or the ones who couldn't afford to sell what they had to offer for a price she was able to give. At least he'd be out soon, no doubt, and she'd be able to keep the fantasy she held to heart from being overly tarnished yet again, the fantasy that ***Port Gem Exchange*** was yet a jewelry store and not yet a pawnshop in truth.

The clock stared back at her. Once upon a time she had slept until midday when she wished. Now she used each hour as if there was not a moment to waste. And for what this early morning? So that she might eat without being observed, and without companions. No need to rush chel'Venga's Pawnshop rarely opened on time.

*

THE TERRAN STOOD at his corner across the way, left hand in pocket, watching across the way as the increasing jitney traffic blocked his view from time to time, his beard waving in the wind. He'd seen her work the door and had straightened; and was there when she went back inside to get the rope-web doormat that welcomed her visitors. The pawnshop had no such amenities as rugs or mats. Perhaps it made no difference to her customers, but such were among the few luxuries she had these days.

He was not on the corner when she straightened from placing the mat in the doorway and a quick glance showed him nowhere on the street. The lights had gone on in the pawnshop. They'd likely stolen the man away. Now Cyra regretted not giving in to the impulse to beckon to him as she unlocked the door, no matter the poor manners of it. It was hard to keep good melant'i in this part of the city, after all.

And then he was back, this time carrying a large, flat blue package of some kind, and he was hurrying, fighting the wind and the traffic, threatening at one point to run into a jitney rather than risk his burden.

Then he was there, larger than she'd realized, his relative slenderness accentuating his height, the dense beard distorting and lengthening his already long face, and his plentiful dark brown hair, brushed straight back from the high forehead, making him seem that much taller now that he'd taken the hat respectfully off to enter her store.

He came in quietly, with the noise of a large transport lifting from the port masking not only his sounds but those of the door until it closed, leaving his breathing - and hers - loud in the room.

He glanced down at her, nodded Terran-style, and looked over the shop carefully. Somehow she felt he might be looking at the tops of the cases: it had been many days since she'd thought to dust them, for who ever climbs a stool to inspect them?

He smiled at her, his light brown eyes inspecting her face so quickly that she hadn't time to flinch at the unexpected attention;

nodded again, and said in surprisingly mannered Liaden, "I regret it has taken me so long to find your operation. I suspect we are both the poorer for it. "

At that he pulled from his pocket a large handful of glittery objects, some jeweled, some enameled or overlaid; pins, rings, earrings, necklaces . . . .

And, she suspected quickly, all of them real.

"These are for sale," he said, "for a reasonable return. Since I am very close to crashing I will not haggle nor argue. I will simply accept or reject your offers on each. I would hope to get more than scrap value. You are a jeweler, however, and will know what you need."

His hands were the competent hands of an artisan, she decided as he turned the items out on her sales cloth. Despite the items he sold, he was ringless and despite the worn look of his clothes the marks on his hands were those of someone who worked with them regularly, not one who was careless or unemployed. Indeed, there were spatters, or patterns of colors on his skin, masked somewhat by the unusual amount of hair on his wrists, on the back of his hands, even down to his knuckles. Cyra was distracted, yes, even shocked: she had never seen a man with hair so thick it looked like fur!

"Indeed, we shall look," she managed, fretting at herself for the incivility of staring at someone's hands.

Quickly she sorted, finding far too many items of real interest. A dozen earrings, some of them paired and some not, all of quality. A strangely designed clasp pin, set with diamonds, starstones, and enamel work. A necklace, of platinum she thought, set with amethyst. Then the glass was in her hand, and the densitometer turned on, and the UV light, as well.

In a twelve day she would rarely expect to see so many fine pieces, much less at once.

"The pin," she said finally, "is obviously custom work, of a scale we rarely see. I suspect it of more value to the owner or designer than to me . . . ."

"My great-uncle designed that himself," said the man, "and he is always one for the gaudy. Set it aside and we can talk about it later. Else?"

Cyra looked up, way up,into those brown eyes. He looked at her without sign of distress, and so she continued, oddly comforted.

"I would offer to buy the lot if we were closer to Festival," she admitted, "even the pin. But these are all quality items, as you do know, and they are somewhat more, extravagant, let us say, than I might usually invest in at this season."

"That's not an offer," the Terran returned, his face suddenly strained. "And I will need something for later, too."

"Perhaps," she suggested, "you should choose those least dear to you and point them out to me. I will offer on them."

His hands carefully moved the earrings to a small pile, and the necklace, leaving the pin by itself, and retrieving deftly other pins and the two rings. He leaned his hands on the counter then, as if tired.

"An offer," he said, "with and without the pin. You know that it is platinum; know that it is platinum from the very Amity object,and the provenance can be proved . . . ."

Cyra grabbed up the pin, admiring its weight and the clasp design. Impulsively she touched his hand, the one that held the other retrieved objects, and turning it over, pressed the pin into it.

"In that case, this is better placed with someone among the High Houses. They fail to arrive here in sufficient number to make my purchase worthwhile . . . ."

And then she named a price which was far more of her available capital than she normally risked, but far less than the value she perceived before her, and was oddly annoyed by the man's rather curt, "That will do."

She was even more annoyed by the rapt attention he paid as she counted the cash out, as if each coin was in doubt. The she realized he was looking at her face. Involuntarily, she colored, which made her angry. Too long among the Terrans if she could blush so easily . . . .

"No," he said suddenly, his Liaden gone stiffly formal. "I did not mean to disturb you. I sought, I was trying to see if I might read or recognize the etchings or tattoos on your face."

Cyra felt her face heat even more. She covered the scars with close-held fingers, looking up.

"Our transaction is finished. You may go."

He reached his hand toward her face and she flinched.

"Ah," he said, wisely. "The rule is that you may reach and touch my hand, but I, I may not reach and touch yours. When the crash is coming I see things so clearly . . . ."

Startled, she stepped back.

"Forgive me," she managed, and paused, seeking the proper words. Indeed, *she* had overstepped before he had; it was folly to assume that one who was Terran had no measure of manners.

Then: "But why this crash? Crash? You do not seem to be on drugs or drink, and . . ."

Now she was truly flustered; more so when he laughed gently.

"In truth, I am very much on drugs right now. I have been drinking coffee constantly for the last three days. Starting last night, I have been drinking strong tea, as well. It has almost been enough, you see, but I could tell it would not continue to work, so I need to buy food. I should eat very soon and I need to write the notes, though, and look once more before the crash."

Cyra held her hands even closer to her face.

"You need not look at all. These are none..."

But he was shaking his head, Terran-wise.

"No, you misunderstand. I need to look at the art so I remember what comes next . . . sometimes it is not so obvious to me when I start moving again."

Cyra was sure she *must* be misunderstanding, but before she could reply he pocketed the coins from the counter top and hefted the fabric-covered blue case or portfolio he'd brought in, laying it across the counter and reaching quickly for the seals.

"You, you love beautiful things, you must see this!" he said, nearly running over his words in his haste. "This one is my best so far! This is the reason I have come to Liad . . . this is where the Scouts are!"

Now he wasn't staring at Cyra at all, and she found the

willpower to bring her hands down and come forward to see what might be revealed.

Some kind of tissue was swirled back from inside the case and before her was a photograph of a double star, with one redder and the other bluer, taken from the surface of an obviously windswept desert world with tendrils of high gray clouds just entering the photograph.

But sections were missing or else the photo-download had been incomplete or....

Now the odor came to her, eerily taking her back to the brief time she studied painting before turning to jewelry.

"You painted this? You are painting it now?" She looked up into his face and rapidly down to the work again. The detail was amazing, the composition near perfect, the....

"Yes," he was saying, "yes, it is my work. But I must not paint *now*, because now I am tired and spent and will only ruin what I have done. For now, the work is not safe near me!"

Cyra recalled working long and hard on her first real commission, so long and hard in fact that she'd finally fallen asleep in the midst, and woke to find the beaten metal scratched and chewed in the polishing machine, destroyed by the very process which should have perfected it.

She heard her voice before she realized she was speaking.

"If you need a place, I can keep it here. It will be safe! Then, when you are awake and ready, you can claim it."

He laughed, sudden and short, and with an odd twist of amusement pulling his grin into his beard.

"When I *wake*. Yes, that is a good way to put it. When I *wake*."

With a flourish he waved his hand over the tissue, swept it back over the painting, and sealed the portfolio.

"My name," he said quite formally, "is Harold Geneset Hsu Belansium. Among my family I am known as Little Gene. To the census people I am BelansiumHGH, 4113." He paused, smoothed his beard, and smiled wryly before continuing.

"When I'm lucky, the pretty ladies of the universe call me Bell. Please, lady, if I may have your name, I would appreciate it if you would call me Bell."

With that he handed the portfolio into her care.

She bowed. "Bell you wish? Then Bell it is. I am Cyra the Jeweler to the neighbors here, or simply Cyra. I will see you when you wake."

*

SOUND RUMBLED THROUGH the walls and rattled the room around Cyra, who involuntarily looked toward the ceiling. This one was an explosion then, more blasting, for the expansion, and not a re-routed transport flying low overhead. Rumor had it that several of the older houses two streets over were settling dangerously, but that was just rumor as far as she was concerned. Her store would be fine. It *would*.

She tried to tell herself it was just the noise that was making her skittish, but she knew it wasn't so. She had moved the stool behind the counter to gain a better vantage of the street, and had developed a nervous motion: nearly a shake of the head it was, when surveying the street.

The knowledge that she had a masterwork of art in her back room awaiting the return of the absent Bell frightened her deeply.

Suppose he didn't return? Suppose he had "crashed" in some fey Terran way and was now locked in a quiet back room at Healers Hall, or worse?

A smartly dressed businessman carrying a bag from the pastry shop strode by and Cyra found herself looking anxiously past him toward the corner where she'd first spotted Bell. It didn't help, the businessman had slowed, eyes caught by one of her displays, perhaps, and now was peering in and reaching for the door, carefully wiping feet, and bringing the brusque roar of a transport in with him as he entered. He closed the door and the sound faded..

Cyra slid to her feet.

"Gentle sir." She bowed a shopkeeper's bow. "How may I assist you today?"

He bowed, and now that she did not have the advantage of the stool, she saw that he was very tall, with sideburns somewhat longer than fashionable and, no, it was a very thin Terran-style beard, neatly trimmed and barely covering chin.

"Cyra, I am here to bring you a snack and to collect my painting."

She gawked, matching the height, and the color of the beard, and the voice.

"Bell!"

He laughed, and said mysteriously "You, too?"

"Forgive me," she said after a moment. "You gave me great pause. I have been watching for you, but I did not . . ."

He put the bag on the counter and began rooting through it, glancing at her as if calculating her incomplete sentence to the centimeter.

"I clean up well, eh? But here, if you'll make some tea the lady at the pastry shop assures me you're partial to these . . ."

"Pastry shop? What does that have to do with anything?" She sputtered a moment, and, "Eleven days!" She got out finally, which was both more and less than she wished to say.

He lived very much in his face, the way Terrans do; his eyes were bright and his smile reached from the corners all the way to his bearded chin. He laughed gently, patting the counter, where there were now half-a-dozen pastries for her to choose from.

"Yes," he acknowledged. "Eleven. Not too bad. The worst was twenty-four, but that was before I knew enough to keep food by, and I'd been partying instead of painting."

"But what did you do for eleven days?"

He shook his head and the grin dissolved. He glanced down, then looked back to her, eyes and face serious.

"I crashed. I slept and I tried to sleep. I spent hours counting my failures, numbering my stupidities. I counted transports and the explosions and watched the crack in the wall get larger with each. Every so often I knew I'd never see my painting again, and I would know that I'd been taken and that you'd fled the city and I would never see you again, either."

He raised his hand before she could protest. "And then I would pull myself together and say 'Fool! Bewitched by beauty again!' And that way I'd recall your face and the painting, and try to sleep, knowing you'd be here, if only I could recall the shop name when I walked by. I nearly didn't, you know. I had to focus on that set of ear cuffs that match yours before I was sure."

She nearly reached for her ear, and then she laughed, somehow.

"Forgive me. I am without experience in this *crashing* you do. I was concerned for you, for your health, for your art!"

He smiled slowly. "We're both concerned for my health then, which I'm sure will be greatly improved if I can eat. My stomach has been growling louder than the shuttles! Please, join me! Afterward I will need to visit the port. It would be good if you could do me the favor of retaining my art until I return." The smile broadened. "I promise I will not be gone eleven days, this time."

The noise of the street invaded their moment then, as two young and giggling girls entered. They stopped short, staring at the towering, bearded figure before them.

"Please," said Cyra to Bell. "If you will come back here we can let my patrons look about!"

He nodded, and moved without hesitation.

She opened the counter tray to let him pass, indicated a low stool for him (his knees seemed almost to touch his ears!) and moved the pastries to the work table, where they would both be able to reach them.

He smiled at her as she lifted a pastry to her lips. She felt almost giddy, as if she'd discovered some new gemstone or precious metal.

*

DEBBIE, THE HALF-TERRAN pastry maker from the shop four doors down was in, again, when Cyra returned from apartment hunting. It didn't improve her mood much; the girl hardly seemed as interested in the goods as in Bell, and her language was sprinkled with Terran phrases Cyra could just about decipher on the fly. Likewise the assistant office manager from the Port Transient Shelter. *Didn't they realize that...*she shushed her inner voice, nodding, Terran fashion, to Bell in his official spot behind the trade counter. He winked at her and she sighed. Were Terrans always so blatant?

The conversation continued unabated: and there on the counter were actual goods; an item she didn't recognize, so it was for sale to the shop.

"Now," Bell was saying carefully, "I've seen places that these might have been in the absolute top echelon."

The women gazed at him.

Drawn to the story and the voice despite the crowd, Cyra leaned in to hear.

"Of course, that would only be if the local priestess had purified the stone before it was cut, blessed the ore the silver had come from, sanctified the day the day the ring was assembled, and then prayed over the ring-giver and scried the proper hour for giving."

"In other corners of the universe," he went on, "as, say, on Liad or Terra, the flaws in the stone might mark it ordinary. If I were you, I would ask Cyra if she'll set a price, knowing it for a nubiath'a hastily given . . ."

Cyra moved behind the counter to take up the office of buyer, but the women had both apparently heard tall tales from Terrans in the past.

"Bell, now really, were you on that planet," asked the assistant office manager, "Or have you merely heard of it?"

He rolled his eyes and surprised Cyra with a discreet pat as she squeezed by him.

"What, am I a spaceman, or a Scout, to have all my stories disbelieved?"

They laughed, but he continued, assuming a serious air.

"Actually, it was almost all a disaster. The planet you should never go to is Djymbolay. I arrived just after I finished a painting on board the liner, and was pretty well spent. I had my luggage searched twice for contraband, and then they confiscated the painting as an unauthorized and unsanctified depiction of the world."

He shook his head, then tapped it with his finger. "They wanted to have me put away for blasphemy or something, I think. It took a Scout who happened by, all thanks to little John!, to let me keep my papers and my paint and my freedom. Off with my head or worse, I expect was the plan! But the Scout was there on another matter and interceded. The locals walked me across the port under armed guard, and the Scout came, too, to be sure that it was gently done, and they kept me confined to the spaceport exit-lounge for the twelve days the ship was there. If several kind ladies hadn't taken pity, and brought me meals and blankets, I might well have starved and froze."

Cyra bit back a comment halfway to her lips; after all she knew not where he'd slept before she met him, nor, for that matter, that he always returned to his own rooms on the afternoons and evenings he went to the lectures at Scout Academy. She only knew he returned to the store with sketches and ideas and full of hope that he might eventually be permitted to visit a new world, to be the first painter, the first interpreter . . . .

In a few moments more, the transaction was made; she paid a fairly low price for the emerald ring—the one suggested by the seller—and agreed to look at earrings that might be a match.

The two women gone, Bell looked at her carefully.

"You're tired—and you've been angry."

Exasperated by his grasp of the obvious, Cyra waved her hands in the air in a wild gesture, and snapped, "How else?"

"You might be pleased, after all. The emeralds were got at a decent price."

"Yes, a decent price. But if I'm going to afford you, my friend, we'll need to do better."

He looked at her with the same air of frankness he'd used when talking about the disaster that had cost him a painting, and shook his head.

"Yes, I know; I am hardly convenient for myself, much less for anyone else."

"That's not what I meant!" she protested. "I mean that—I mean that it is difficult to find a larger place to live hereabouts, and nearer to my apartment there are those who will not rent to someone who—"

"Someone who might bring a Terran home of a night," Bell finished, as she faltered. "*Inconvenient* I said, and I meant!"

he insisted with heat. "I don't mind sleeping here in the store, after all, though the light is not always good. Perhaps you can offer to rent the corner place the next street over."

They had been over that before, too. Bell's situation was so changeable that neither knew how long they might find each other's company pleasant, useful, or convenient. He could hardly sign a lease, with his "*transient alien*" status in the port computers assuring that any who looked would laugh at his request. Even getting a room beyond the spaceport was difficult for him, except here in the Low Port area. Mid-port was too dear for his budget in any case.

He could hardly cosign with her, either. The conditions her Delm had set were strict and might well bear on that—if she wished to ever return to the House, she would, during her time of exile, refrain from forming formal alliances; she must not buy real estate; she was forbidden to marry, or to have children . . . .

There could be no cosigning; she could speak for none other than herself. But to add a place where some of his paintings could be shown—this close to the port, they might gain a better clientele with such a gallery.

Truth told, though, Bell's sometime presence permitted Cyra to cut her dependence on Ortega's chancy employ; in fact, twice recently they'd been there as patrons.

He looked at her, snatched the ring to his hand and began tossing it furiously into the air. This, after three previous ragged forty-day cycles, she recognized. Any day, perhaps any moment, he would drag out the rough sketches and ideas, choose one, and then hardly see her, even should she stand naked before him, while he took plasboard and tegg-paint and the secret odds and ends from his duit box and transformed them by touch of skilled hand and concentration and willpower unmatched to art as fine as ever she'd seen. Days, he would be one with the art.

And then he would crash; folding into a hollow and dispirited being barely willing to feed himself, with a near-fear of sunlight and a monotone voice and no plans to speak of . . . until the cycle came full and from the gray, desperate being emerged Bell, fresh and whole and new. Again.

He shook the ring, tossed it, glanced anxiously to his art kit where it was stashed near the door to the back room.

"I know," he said. "I know! It's almost time. I think we should close early, perhaps, and go someplace fine to eat—I'll pay!—and plan on a bottle of good wine and snacks—I've chosen them already—and a night, a glorious night, my beauty. And then, we can talk at breakfast, if the art's not here yet, and if it is, we'll talk in a few days."

In front of her then, the choice—and she knew already she'd take it, or most of it. Had she a clan to call on she would pledge her quartershare— to make this work, she'd—but what she would do *if* was no matter, now. Her quartershare would go—till the twelfth year, at least—nto the account of a dead child, just as her invitations—large and small—would go to her Delm, and be returned with the information that she was in mourning and not permitted.

She recalled the discreet caress a few moments earlier, her blood warming . . .

Tonight she would forget the she was poor and outcast. Bell would take them somewhere with his stash of cash and they would spend as if he were a visiting ambassador instead of an itinerant artist, and then he would—

"Bell," she said gently, "perhaps we should stay until nearer closing. My friend. I followed your instructions last time, you know—there are three prepared boards waiting—and I have already an extra cannister of spacer's tea and you gave me enough for two tins of Genwin Kaffe last time, so we have that. That is, if you are certain that you won't talk to the Healers this time."

He looked at her then and his eyes were hungry; she doubted that hers were not.

"I'll check the boards, Cyra, and make sure that you have room to work this time, too."

*

CYRA TASTED THE SALT on her lips, and nearly wept as she relaxed against him. He was so inexhaustible and inventive a lover, she thought, that perhaps she should have invited the office manager to help out—and she laughed at the silliness, and he heard her, Bell with his hands still willing and eager, and his quirky Terran words dragged out of him in the midsts.

"Now I'm funny. Oh, woe, oh woe . . ."

She could see him in the half-light he preferred for lovemaking; just bright enough that the mirrors on the wall might tell an interesting tale to a glancing eye. She remembered that he'd brought beeswax candles, along with wine and flowers, that first evening after his very first return, when he'd somehow parlayed her concern—

She laughed again, this time finding his hair and beard wooly near her face, and she gently moved to brush them orderly. He had something more on his mind though, as her hands came in contact with his cheek; but she held him a moment and he was willing to be calmed.

Of course, she should not stroke his beard and his cheek; she should not kiss his nose, nor lay her palm on his face, this Terran who never knew the taboo of it . . . .

"Let's trade," he said, very gently. "A story for a story, a touch for a touch."

Then he laid his hand on her cheek, spreading his wide hand so that his thumb and his forefinger spanned her face.

It was late in the night, very nearly morning; the sounds from the road were not yet impinging on their lair. His breathing, and hers, and his touch.

"I," he said after a moment. " I cannot go to the Healers, because when someone in my family is cured, we lose the art. My father, my grandfather, my uncle—myself. I tried, there once—"

He paused, brushed her hair away from her eyes, kissed her on her nose, covered the marks on her face as if he would wipe them away. "After that painting was stolen from me I could have been locked up forever there, but for the good luck of a Scout's intercession. So, I thought I should get over the crash. I spoke to a doctor and he seemed to make sense, and they gave me a therapy and drugs and an implant . . . ."

"Here!"

He guided her hand and held it against that long scraggly

scar on his leg. She'd found that scar before, but never dared question—there were things lovers were not to ask, after all; the Code was clear on that.

"Three months," he said very quietly. "Let me say about two of my usual cycles, though they change sometimes—be warned!—and I had not even the slightest twinge of being able to paint, and what I drew was stick figures and bad circles and patterns, and I spoke politely to people and one night I went home and picked up a cooking knife and thought that I would cut my throat."

He took her hand and placed it under his beard, where it was just above his throat, and let her feel the pulse of him, and the smaller, more ragged scar.

"I'd made a start, actually, when I realized that what I wanted was not my throat cut, but my art back. And so I took the knife and opened my leg and took the thirty-four months worth of implant that was left out of me, and I washed it down the drain."

She stared at him, at once fascinated and horrified, not knowing what to say.

"My cousin," he went on, after a moment. "My cousin Darby. He took the cure and has stayed on it. He's married, he goes to work, comes home, goes to work, comes home—and I have the last piece of sculpture he did before the implant. He was brilliant. He made me look like a bumbling student. But it is gone. Five years and he can't draw a face much less model one; he can't see the images in the clouds!"

He brushed his lips over the mark under her left eye, then kissed the one under her right eye.

"You know," he said quietly, "you are beautiful. I have known beautiful ladies, my friend, and you are very beautiful."

The realization hit her—what he would ask, in exchange for this tale from his soul. Very nearly, she panicked, but he caught her mouth with his, and in a few moments she relaxed against him.

"My friend," she said, "you can be as cruel as you are wonderful. To cut yourself so—the pain! But I am not so brave as you. I took the cuts from my Delm, in punishment—cut with the blade my family keeps from the early days. Then I wept and cried, and was cast from the house..."

"Does this person yet live?" Not in his deepest despair had she heard his voice so cold.

Cyra looked into his face and saw he meant it—that he contemplated Balance or revenge or—

"No, Bell, you cannot. My Delm was doing duty. I was cut to remind me and to warn others."

He said nothing, but kissed her face again, gently, waiting.

"We are not as rich a house as some others, Clan Nosko; and my Delm, my uncle, is not so easy a spender as you or I. As I was youngest of the daughters of the house—and lived at the clan seat, it being close to my shop—it fell my duty sometimes to spend an afternoon and a night, or sometimes two, doing things needful. And so . . ."

Here she paused a moment, gently massaging Bell's neck under the beard, imagining all too well . . . .

"So it was," she went on very quietly, with the blood pounding in her ears, "that I was briefly in charge of the nursery, the nurse having been given a discharge for cost or cause, I know not. I had put the child Brendar to bed; a likely boy come to the clan through my sister's second marriage. I changed him once, but he was otherwise biddable. I was trying for my Master Jeweler's license, so I was at study with several books. I read, and read more, hearing no fuss. Then my sister came home, and the child was not asleep, but had died sometime in the night."

There was quiet then.

Finally, he kissed her again, each scar, very carefully.

"I'd thought there must be more, but I see the story now, and I am near speechless. The child died of an accident—"

"My incompetence and negligence . . ."

He pressed a finger to her lips so hard it nearly hurt.

"I am a fool, Cyra, my beautiful friend. I thought it was your own anger, or your own desire, that placed those marks on your face; that you had rebelled against the rules of this world and even now wore them as badges. That they were inflicted by your family to humiliate and destroy you never came to mind . . ."

He brushed the hair out of her face again.

"I will paint your picture one day, I promise. Your face will be known as among the most beautiful of this world. And they will see that they have lost you, for I'll not let them have you back!"

She had no quick answer for this, and then he said, "Here!" and placed her hand again on the long leg scar.

She felt the welt there—he laughed, nibbled on her earlobe, and moved her hand a bit, murmuring, "Now, lady, here if you wish to be pleased!"

She did, and she was.

*

THREE DAYS LATER Cyra was not so very pleased.

To begin, Bell had become inspired sometime in the night of their pillow talk and when she awoke alone in the dawn she found him sketching like a madman on her couch, barely willing to drag himself away from his work long enough to share a breakfast with her.

He packed his sketches and walked with her to the shop, his eyes as elsewhere as his mind. Twice she had to repeat herself while she spoke with him, and then he disappeared into the back room to work as soon as they reached the store.

In the afternoon he had rushed out of the back room, complaining that she'd not told him the time, and stormed out, on his way to a lecture he particularly wanted to see. Worse, he stormed back, having left his sketchbook and wallet, and dashed off with nary a backward glance. When he didn't return by closing—he sometimes went to discussion groups after the lectures—she'd not expected him to come by her apartment, and he didn't, which grated mightily.

In the morning he wandered in very late, hung over and exhausted, explaining that he'd met a pack of Scouts at the lecture and talked with them until the barkeep announced shift-change at dawn. He was animated, nearly wildly so, explaining that he might "have a line on" the Scout who had helped him at Djymbolay; that his conversations of the evening had revealed that he owed Balance to that Scout; that he might have an idea for yet another painting;

and that when he had more money there was a world he'd have to travel to and—

"I have an appointment, Bell," Cyra said abruptly. "Tell me later!"

She rushed out the door, barely confident—and barely caring—that he'd heed the advent of a customer.

Her appointment was with her tongue—had she stayed and heard more she surely would have said hurtful words.

So she walked, nearly oblivious to the sounds of transports—more this day than others since a portion of the port would be closed late in the afternoon for some final tricksy bit of work for the expansion—and found herself several blocks from her usual streets, in a very old section, where the buildings and the people were barely above tumbledown.

Surprisingly, she saw Debbie-the-pastry-girl hurrying from one of the least kept brick-fronts; Number 83 it was, a regrettable four-story affair sporting ungainly large windows and peeling paint. The peaked, slate roof suggested that the building was several hundred Standards old, and it looked like it had no repair since the day it was built.

Heart falling, she reached into her card case, and removed the slip of paper she had from Bell the day he'd agreed to share his direction with her: Number 83 Corner Four Ave, Room 15.

A shuttle's long rumble began then; she could feel the sidewalk atremble as she watched the pastry girl's blue-and-green hair disappear in the distance. Also on the paper was the pad combination, and with the whine of the shuttle rising behind her, and then over, she stood, and for a moment was tempted to enter Number 83 and find Room 15, open the door, and see if—if . . .

She turned and walked all the way home for lunch, grasping the paper tightly in her fist.

When she got back to the store, calmer, but heartsore, there was Bell's back vaguely visible in the back room. He heard her enter and yelled out over his shoulder "Any luck?"

"No," she said, quietly. "No luck, Bell."

She slept badly alone, and the rumble of the transports, joined with the not entirely foreign sounds of proctor-jitneys blaring horns as they answered a nighttime summons hadn't helped.

And now, on her store step across the road in the dawn light?

Debbie, cuddling Bell's good jacket in her arms.

*

"BELL'S OK," THE GIRL said quickly, shaking her absurd hair back from a remarkably grimy face. "He wasn't bleeding all that much and the medic said he'll do. The proctor, now, he'll be OK, too, other'n his pride's pretty well hurt by getting really whomped—I mean decked in front of all his buddies. But there's gonna be some fines to pay, I guess, and he's gotta have a place to live and—"

Cyra stood staring, hard put to sort this tumbled message, clinging at last to the simple, "Bell's OK . . ."

Debbie was looking at her with desperate eyes. "Cyra, you're a lucky girl, you know? But you're gonna have to get someone down to the jail to get him out. He's not the kind of guy that'll get along there, and hey—what it'll take is 'a citizen of known melant'i, moral character, and resources.' I sure don't qualify for the resources part, the melant'i I ain't got and I'm not sure if I qualify for the character part . . . ."

Cyra wasn't too sure about the character part either, though the fact that the girl was here with so many of Bell's belongings argued for her. Arrayed on the step was a ship bag with "Belansium" printed on a tag, four or five studies—paintings and sketches of a woman, who Cyra realized must be herself by the detail of the face—nude in different positions, some small odds and ends in boxes, a small paint kit, a picnic box . . . .

"Tell me again," Cyra demanded. "After we got these inside. From the beginning. I'll make tea."

*

DEBBIE RUSHED OFF while the tea was heating and returned with pastries, and a damp towel, which she was using on the dust and grime on her bare arms.

"I was having company over and wasn't much paying

attention to other stuff when I heard one of the transports go over. Things started trembling and—well, wasn't at the stage I thought, then the next thing I know there was a big *cherunk* kind of noise and the front wall just fell out into the street. The whole place got shaky and we all got out. Bell come dashing out from his room carrying something big and square and rushing down the steps with it whiles bricks and roof-stuff falling all around.

"We was outside standing and staring—most everyone out by then, when the whole building kind of slanted over backwards and leaned into the alley. My guy, he's pretty smart, he'd grabbed a bottle of wine on the way out, and we all had a sip, and when it looked like there wasn't any more *up* to fall *down* we went in to see what we could save and to make sure no one was inside—and a bunch of snortheads showed up. One grabbed one of them sketches of you and yelled for some of the others—

"That Bell picked up part of a drainpipe and started hitting and bashing at them guys, and then my guy hit one of 'em with the empty bottle, and then the proctors showed up and Bell wasn't letting no one near his stuff. Proctor kind of waved something in his direction and Bell did this neat little dance step and brought his hand out and lifted the proctor right off his feet. Right quick they was all on him . . . and I had to explain—see it was my Ma's building, and all—but they still got Bell for drunk-and-disorderly, striking a proctor, and I don't know what else. And I can't speak for him!"

"Neither can I," Cyra admitted, staring down into her tea and trying not to think of Bell at the hottest part of his cycle, locked away from his paints and pens. "Neither can I."

*

"YOU HAVE ARRIVED," the receptionist told Cyra, "at a bad time. I have no one to spare to listen to your story, as interesting as it must be. The Scouts are not in the habit of interfering with the proctors on matters of Low Port drunk-and-disorderly . . ."

Cyra glared. "He was not drunk—not at this time in the cycle. Disorderly—he did strike a proctor, but—" she stopped, suddenly struck by a thought, and came near to the counter again.

"Have you a Scout named Jon?" she asked.

"Only several," a female voice said from close behind her. Cyra spun, face heating. The Scout tipped her head, eyes bright and manic, as the eyes of Scout's so often were. "Would you wish us to know that it is a Scout named Jon whom the proctors discovered to be drunk and disorderly? I don't find that impossible. Why, I myself have been drunk and disorderly in Low Port. It is excellent practice for the dining situations found on several of the outworlds."

"Captain sig'Radia . . ." the receptionist began, but the Scout waved a hand.

"Peace. Someone has arrived with time to spare for a story about a drunk and disorderly in Low Port." She cocked a whimsical eyebrow in Cyra's direction, looking her full in the face, as if the disfiguring scars were invisible, or non-existent. "The acoustics of this hallway are quite amazing, but allow me to be certain—I did hear you say 'struck a proctor'?"

Cyra admitted it dejectedly. "But it is not the Scout Jon who did this," she continued, feeling an utter fool. "I had merely thought, since my friend—Bell—was known to the Scout . . ."

"Ah. And something more of your friend—Bell—if you please? For I do not believe, despite our abundance of Jons, that we have any Scouts named Bell."

Cyra bit her lip. "He is a Terran—an artist. Last night, the apartment house he lived in fell down, and—"

"Now I have the fellow!" Captain sig'Radia cried, and grinned with every appearance of delight. "What we heard on the Port is that he knocked down a prepared, on-duty proctor, barehanded. Quite an accomplishment, though I don't expect the proctors think so. No sense of humor, proctors."

"It must be unpleasant," Cyra murmured, "after all, to be knocked down."

"Oh, wonderfully unpleasant," the Scout agreed happily. "Especially with the rest of your team looking on."

"Yes," Cyra bit her lip, wondering how possibly to explain the cycles, and the tragedy of Bell being without his paints now. "If you please, Bell—it is very bad . . ." she stammered to a halt.

"Complicated, eh?" the Scout said sympathetically. "Come, let us be private."

She took Cyra's arm as if they were long friends, and escorted her out of the main room and down a hall.

"Ah, here we are," the Scout said, and put her palm against a door, which opened willingly, utterly silent.

The lights came up as they walked down the room to the table and chairs. Cyra looked about, marveling at the size of the chamber, her eye caught and held by a projection on the front wall—a planetscape, it was, showing a sun and a great-ringed planet in the distance and a close up portion of bluish-green atmosphere—

Cyra gasped, recognition going through her like a bolt, though she had never seen this painting, but the composition, the eloquence the work—it could only be—

"That is Djymbolay, is it not?" She asked the Scout captain, her voice shaking.

The woman looked at her in open wonder. "It is, indeed. How did you know?"

"My friend Bell painted the original of that." She used her chin to point.

The captain looked, face very serious now. "I see. You will then be comforted to know that the original is safe in the World Room." She looked back to Cyra, her smile crooked.

"And your friend Bell is by extrapolations no more nor no less than Jon dea'Cort's glorious madman. Allow me to see if the Scout is within our reach."

*

SUMMONED, JON DEA'CORT arrived quickly and heard the tale out with a grin almost as wide as Bell's could be, when he stood at the height of his powers. When all was said, he looked to Cyra, and inclined his head.

"Your Bell, he is at what stage in his continuing journey?"

She blinked against the rise of unexpected tears, made herself meet his eyes squarely. "He is painting. Please—"

He held up a hand. "Yes. You were right to come to us." He looked to Captain sig'Radia, who lifted an eyebrow.

"A change of custody, I think," he said to her. "Certainly, they will insist that he be heard, and fined, but he must be got out of the holding tank at once and allowed to paint before drunk-and-disorderly becomes cold murder."

Cyra sat up, horrified. "Bell would not—" A bright glance stopped her.

"Would he not? Perhaps you are correct. But let us not put him to the test, eh?" He grinned suddenly, Scout-manic. "Besides, I want to see what magic flows from his brush this time."

*

THEY GAVE HER A room, and a meal, and promised to fetch her, when Bell was arrived. She ate and laid down on the bed, meaning to close her eyes for a moment only . . .

"Cyra?" The voice was quiet, but unfamiliar. "It is I, Jon dea'Cort. Your Bell is safe."

She sat up, blinking, and found the Scout seated on the edge of her bed, face serious.

"Is he well?" she demanded. "Is he—"

He held up a hand. "Would you see him? He is painting."

"Yes!"

"Come then," he said, and he led her out and down the hall to a lift, then down, down, down, perhaps to the very core of the planet, before the doors opened, and there was another hall, which they walked until it intersected another. They turned right. Jon dea'Cort put his hand against a door, which slid, silently, open, and they stepped into a large and well-lit studio.

Bell at the farther end of the room, his easel in the best light; he was working with that focused, feverish look on his face that she had come to know well—and to treasure.

The Scout touched her hand, and tipped his head toward the door. Cyra followed him out.

"Thank you," she said, feeling conflicting desires to sing and weep. "He will crash—sometime. Often, he knows when, but in a strange place, with this interruption—I do not know. Someone—someone should pay attention to him."

"Surely," the Scout said amiably. "And that someone ought to be yourself, if you are able?"

She hesitated for a moment, thinking of the shop in Low Port, and then inclined her head. "I am able."

*

"CYRA?" SHE LOOKED UP from her work, smiling, and found Bell gazing seriously down at her.

Having gained her attention, he went to a knee, and raised his hand to her face. She nestled her cheek into the caress.

"Are you sorry, Cyra? To leave your home, to be rootless, companioned to the very inconvenient Bell, and in the sphere of Scouts . . ."

She laughed and turned her face, brushing her lips against his palm, and straightening.

"What is this? You will be painting tomorrow, my friend; do not try to tease me into believing that you are on the down-cycle!"

He smiled at that, and touched a fingertip to her nose before dropping his hand to his knee. "You know me too well. But, truly, Cyra . . ."

She put the pliers down and reached out, placing her hands on his shoulders and gazing seriously into his eyes.

"I am not sorry, Bell. Did you not say that you would take me away? You have done so, and I am not sorry at all."

He had kept the other part of that pillow-sworn vow, as well, and the portrait of herself that he had completed in Scout Headquarters remained there, on display in the reception area, with other works of art from many worlds.

"I have the original," he had said to Jon dea'Cort. "Take you the copy, and let us be in Balance."

And so it had been done, and now they were—attached to Scouts, spending time on this research station, or that surveillance ship, while Bell painted, and sketched, and fed his art. Cyra fed her own art, and her jewelry was sought after, when they came to a world where they might sell, or trade.

"We do well," she said, leaning forward to kiss his cheek. "I am pleased, Bell."

He laughed gently and leaned forward, sliding his arms around her and bringing her on to his knee.

"You're pleased, are you?" he murmured against her hair. "But could you not be—just a little—*more* pleased?"

She laughed and wrapped her arms closely around his neck, rubbing her cheek against the softness of his beard.

"Why, yes," she said, teasing him. "I might be—just a *little*—more pleased."

He laughed, and rose, bearing her with him, across their cabin to the bed.

—Standard Year 1293

Veil of the Dancer

IN THE CITY OF Iravati on the world of Skardu, there lived a scholar who had three daughters, and they were the light and comfort of his elder years.

Greatly did the scholar rejoice in his two elder daughters–golden-haired Humaria; Shereen with her tresses of flame–both of these born of the wives his father had picked out for him when he was still a young man. Surely, they were beautiful and possessed of every womanly grace, the elder daughters of Scholar Reyman Bhar. Surely, he valued them, as a pious father should.

The third–ah, the third daughter. Small and dark and wise as a mouse was the daughter of his third, and last, wife. The girl was clever, and it had amused him to teach her to read, and to do sums, and to speak the various tongues of the unpious. Surely, these were not the natural studies of a daughter, even the daughter of so renowned a scholar as Reyman Bhar.

It began as duty; for a father must demonstrate to his daughters that, however much they are beloved, they are deficient in that acuity of thought by which the gods mark out males as the natural leaders of household, and world. But little Inas, bold mouse, did not fail to learn her letters, as her sisters had. Problems mathematic she relished as much as flame-haired Shereen did candied sventi leaves. Walks along the river way brought forth the proper names of birds and their kin; in the long neglected glade of Istat, with its ancient sundial and moon-marks she proved herself astute in the motions of the planets.

Higher languages rose as readily to her lips as the dialect of women; she read not only for knowledge, but for joy, treasuring especially the myths of her mother's now empty homeland.

Seeing the joy of learning in her, the teaching became experiment more than duty, as the scholar sought to discover the limits of his little one's mind.

On the eve of her fourteenth birthday, he had not yet found them.

*

Well though the scholar loved his daughters, yet it is a father's duty to see them profitably married. The man he had decided upon for his golden Humaria was one Safarez, eldest son of Merchant Gabir Majidi. It was a balanced match, as both the scholar and the merchant agreed. The Majidi son was a pious man of sober, studious nature, who bore his thirty years with dignity. Over the course of several interviews with the father and the son, Scholar Bhar had become certain that Safarez would value nineteen year old Humaria, gay and heedless as a *flitterbee*; more, that he would protect her and discipline her and be not behind in those duties which are a husband's joy and especial burden.

So, the price was set, and met; the priests consulted regarding the proper day and hour; the marriage garden rented; and, finally, Humaria informed of the upcoming blessed alteration in her circumstances.

Naturally enough, she wept, for she was a good girl and valued her father as she ought. Naturally enough, Shereen ran to cuddle her and murmur sweet, soothing nonsense into her pretty ears. The scholar left them to it, and sought his study, where he found his youngest, dark Inas, bent over a book in the lamplight.

She turned when he entered, and knelt, as befit both a daughter and a student, and bowed 'til her forehead touched the carpet. Scholar Bhar paused, admiring the graceful arc of her slim body within the silken pool of her robes. His mouse was growing, he thought. Soon, he would be about choosing a husband for her.

But not yet. Now, it was Humaria, and, at the change of season he would situate Shereen, who would surely pine for her sister's companionship. He had a likely match in mind, there, and the husband's property not so far distant from the Majidi. Then, next year, perhaps–or, more comfortably, the year after that–he would look about for a suitable husband for his precious, precocious mouse.

"Arise, daughter," he said now, and marked how she did so, swaying to her feet in a single, boneless move, the robes rustling, then falling silent, sheathing her poised and silent slenderness.

"So," he said, and met her dark eyes through the veil. "A

momentous change approaches your life, my child. Your sister Humaria is to wed."

Inas bowed, dainty hands folded demurely before her.

"What?" he chided gently. "Do you not share your sister's joy?"

There was a small pause, not unusual; his mouse weighed her words like a miser weighed his gold.

"Certainly, if my sister is joyous, then it would be unworthy of me to weep," she said in her soft, soothing voice. "If it is permitted that I know–who has come forward as her husband?"

Reyman Bhar nodded, well-pleased to find proper womanly feeling, as well as a scholar's thirst for knowledge.

"You are allowed to know that Safarez, eldest son of Majidi the Merchant, has claimed the right to husband Humaria."

Inas the subtle stood silent, then bowed once more, as if an afterthought, which was not, the scholar thought, like her. He moved to his desk, giving her time to consider, for, surely, even his clever mouse was female, if not yet full woman, and might perhaps know a moment's envy for a sister's good fortune.

"They are very grand, the Majidi," she said softly. "Humaria will be pleased."

"Eventually, she will be so," he allowed, seating himself and pulling a notetaker forward. "Today, she weeps for the home she will lose. Tomorrow, she will sing for the home she is to gain."

"Yes," said Inas, and the scholar smiled into his beard.

"Your sisters will require your assistance with the wedding preparations," he said, opening the notetaker and beginning a list. "I will be going to Lahore-Gadani tomorrow, to purchase what is needful. Tell me what I shall bring you."

Mouse silence.

"I? I am not to be wed, Father."

"True. However, it has not escaped one's attention that tomorrow is the anniversary of your natal day. It amuses me to bring you a gift from the city, in celebration. What shall you have?"

"Why, only yourself, returned to us timely and in good health," Inas said, which was proper, and womanly, and dutiful.

The scholar smiled more widely into his beard, and said

nothing else.

*

Humaria wept well into the night, rocking inside the circle of Shereen's arms. At last, her sobs quieted somewhat, and Shereen looked to Inas, who sat on a pillow across the room, as she had all evening, playing Humaria's favorite songs, softly, upon the lap-harp.

Obedient to the message in her sister's eyes, Inas put the harp aside, arose and moved silently to the cooking alcove. Deftly, she put the kettle on the heat-ring, rinsed the pot with warm water and measured peace tea into an infuser.

The kettle boiled. While the tea steeped, she placed Humaria's own blue cup on a tray, with a few sweet biscuits and some leaves of candied *sventi.* At the last, she added a pink candle, sacred to Amineh, the little god of women, and breathed a prayer for heart's ease. Then, she lifted the tray and carried it to her sister's couch.

Humaria lay against Shereen's breast, veils and hair disordered. Inas knelt by the end table, placed the tray, and poured tea.

"Here, sweet love," Shereen cooed, easing Humaria away from her shoulder. "Our dear sister Inas offers tea in your own pretty cup. Drink, and be at peace."

Shivering, Humaria accepted the cup. She bent her face and breathed of the sweet, narcotic steam, then sipped, eyes closed.

Shereen sat up, and put her head scarf to rights, though she left the *ubaie*–the facial veils–unhooked and dangling along her right jaw.

"Our young Inas is fortunate, is she not, sister?" Humaria murmured, her soft voice blurry with the combined effects of weeping and the tea.

"How so?" asked Shereen, watching her closely, in case she should suddenly droop into sleep.

"Why," said Humaria, sipping tea. "Because she will remain here in our home with our father, and need never marry. Indeed, I would wonder if a husband could be found for a woman who reads as well as a man."

Shereen blinked, and bent her head, fussing with the fall of the *hijab* across her breast. Inas watched her, abruptly chilly, though the night was warm and no breeze came though the windows that stood open onto the garden.

"Certainly," Shereen said, after too long a pause. "Certainly, our father might wish to keep his youngest with him as long as may be, since he shows no disposition to take another wife, and she knows the ways of his books and his studies."

"And certainly," Humaria said, her eyes open now, and staring at Inas, where she knelt, feeling much like a mouse, and not so bold, so bold at all.

"Certainly, on that blessed day when the gods call our father to sit with them as a saint in Heaven, my husband will inherit all his worldly stuffs, including this, our clever sister Inas, to dispose of as he will."

At her father's direction, Inas had read many things, including the Holy Books and domestic law. She knew, with a scholar's detachment, that women were the lesser vessel and men the god-chosen administrators of the universe the gods had created, toyed with and tired of.

She knew that, in point of law, women were disbarred from holding property. Indeed, in point of law, women were themselves property, much the same as an ox or other working cattle, subject to a man's masterful oversight. A man might dispose of subject women, as he might dispose of an extra brood cow, or of an old and toothless dog.

She knew these things.

And yet, until this moment, she had not considered the impact of these facts upon her own life and self.

What, indeed, she thought, would Safarez the merchant's son do with one Inas, youngest daughter of his wife's father? Inas, who read as well as a man–a sinful blot so dire that she could not but be grateful that the Holy Books also stated that the souls of women were small, withered things, of no interest to the gods.

Humaria finished the last of her tea, and sat cradling the blue cup in her plump, pretty hands, her eyes misty.

"There now, sweet, rest," Shereen murmured, capturing the cup and passing it to Inas. She put arm around Humaria's shoulders, urging her to lie down on the couch.

Inas arose and carried the tray back to the cooking alcove. She washed and dried the teapot and cup, and put the crackers back in their tin. The *sventi* she left out.

She was wise in this, for not many minutes later, Shereen slipped into the alcove, veils dangling and flame-colored hair rippling free. She sighed, and reached for the leaves, eating two, one after the other, before giving Inas a swift glance out of the sides of her eyes, as if Shereen were the youngest, and caught by her elder in some unwomanly bit of mischief.

"Our sister was distraught," she said softly. "She never meant to wound you."

"She did not wound me," Inas murmured. "She opened my eyes to the truth."

Shereen stared, sventi leaf halfway to her lips.

"You do not find the truth a fearsome thing, then, sister?" she asked, and it was Inas who looked away this time.

"The truth is merely a statement of what is," she said, repeating the most basic of her father's lessons, and wishing that her voice did not tremble so. "Once the truth is known, it can be accepted. Truth defines the order of the universe. By accepting truth, we accept the will of the gods."

Shereen ate her leaf in silence. "It must be a wonderful thing to be a scholar," she said then, "and have no reason to fear." She smiled, wearily.

"Give you sweet slumber, sister. The morrow will be upon us too soon."

She went away, robes rustling, leaving Inas alone with the truth.

*

The truth, being bright, held Inas from sleep, until at last she sat up within her *chatrue*, lit her fragrant lamp, and had the books of her own studies down from the shelf.

In the doubled brightness, she read until the astronomer on

his distant column announced the sighting of the Trio of morning with his baleful song.

She read as a scholar would, from books to which her father, the elder scholar, had directed her, desiring her to put aside those he might wish to study.

The book she read in the lamplight was surely one which her father would find of interest. A volume of Kenazari mythology, it listed the gods and saints by their various praise names and detailed their honors.

Nawar caught her eye, "the one who guards." A warrior's name, surely. Yet, her mother had been named Nawar. A second aspect of the same god, *Natesa*–"blade dancer" –in the Kenazari heresy that held each person was a spirit reincarnated until perfected, alternatively took the form of male and female. The duty of the god in either aspect was to confound the gods of order and introduce random action into the universe, which was heresy, as well, for the priests taught that the purpose of the gods, enacted through mortal men, was to order and regulate the universe.

Inas leaned back against her pillows and considered what she knew of her father's third wife. Nawar had been one of the married women chosen as guardians of the three dozen maiden wives sent south from Kenazari as the peace tithe. Each maiden was to be wed to a wise man or scholar, and it had been the hope of the scholars who had negotiated it that these marriages would heal the rifts which had opened between those who had together tamed the wildlands.

Alas, it had been a peace worked out and implemented locally, as the Holy Books taught, and it had left the mountain generals unsatisfied.

Despite the agreement and the high hopes of wise men, the generals and their soldiers swept through Kenazari shortly after the rich caravan of dowries and oath-bound girls passed beyond the walls of the redoubt. Fueled by greed, bearing off-world weapons, they murdered and laid waste–and then dispersed, melting back into the mountains, leaving nothing of ancient, wealthy Kenazari, save stone and carrion.

The priests of the south found the married escorts to be

widows and awarded them to worthy husbands. Reyman Bhar had lately performed a great service for the priests of Iravati, and stood in need of a wife. Nawar was thus bestowed upon him, and it had pleased the gods to allow them to find joy, each in the other, for she was a daughter of an old house of scholars, and could read, and write, and reason as well as any man. Her city was dead, but she made shift to preserve what could be found of its works, assisted gladly by her new husband.

So it was that numerous scrolls, books, and tomes written in the soon-to-be-forgotten language found their way into the house of Scholar Bhar, where eventually they came under the study of a girl child, in the tradition of her mother's house...

The astronomer on his tall, cold column called the Trio. Inas looked to her store of oil, seeing it sadly depleted, and turned the lamp back til the light fled and the smoky wick gave its ghost to the distant dawn.

She slept then, her head full of the myths of ancient Kenazari, marriage far removed from her dreams.

*

Their father sent word that he would be some days in the city of Lahore-Gadani, one day to the west across the windswept ridges of the Marakwenti range that separated Iravati from the river Gadan. He had happened upon his most excellent friend and colleague, Scholar Baquar Hafeez, who begged him to shed the light of his intellect upon a problem of rare complexity.

This news was conveyed to them by Nasir, their father's servant, speaking through the screen in the guest door.

Humaria at once commenced to weep, her face buried in her hands as she rocked back and forth, moaning, "He has forgotten my wedding! I will go to my husband ragged and ashamed!"

Shereen rushed to embrace her, while Inas sighed, irritable with lack of sleep.

"I do not think our father has forgotten your wedding, sister," she said, softly, but Humaria only cried harder.

As it happened, their father had not forgotten his daughters, nor his mission in the city. The first parcels arrived shortly after

Uncu's prayer was called, and were passed through the gate, one by one.

Bolts of saffron silk, from which Humaria's bridal robes would be sewn; yards of pearls; rings of gold and topaz; bracelets of gold; *ubaie* fragile as spider silk and as white as salt; hairpins, headcloths, and combs; sandals; needles; thread. More bolts, in brown and black, from which Humaria's new dayrobes would be made, and a hooded black cloak, lined in fleece.

Additional parcels arrived as the day wore on: A bolt each of good black silk for Shereen and Inas; headcloths, *ubaie*; silver bracelets, and silver rings set with onyx.

Humaria and Shereen fell upon each new arrival with cries of gladness. Shereen ran for her patterns; Humaria gave the saffron silk one last caress and scampered off for scissors and chalk.

Inas put her silk and rings and bracelets aside, and began to clear the worktable.

Across the room, the guest screen slid back and a small package wrapped in brown paper and tied with red string was placed on the ledge.

Inas went forward, wondering what else was here to adorn Humaria's wedding day, even as she recognized her father's hand and the lines that formed her own name.

Smiling, she caught the package up and hurried, light-footed, to her room. Once there, she broke the red string and unwrapped the brown paper, exposing not a book, as she had expected, from the weight and the size, but a box.

She put it aside, and searched the wrapping for any note from her father. There was none, and she turned her attention back to his gift.

It was an old box of leather-wrapped wood. Doubtless, it had been handsome in its day, but it seemed lately to have fallen on hard times. The leather was scuffed in places, cracked in others, the ornamental gilt work all but worn away. She turned it over in her hands, and rubbed her thumb along a tear in the leather where the wood showed through–gray, which would be ironwood, she thought, from her study of native product.

She turned the box again, set it on her knee, released the

three ivory hooks and lifted the lid.

Inside were seven small volumes, each bound in leather much better preserved than that which sheathed the box.

Carefully, she removed the first volume on the right; carefully, she opened it–and all but laughed aloud, for here was treasure, indeed, and all honor to her father, for believing her worthy of so scholarly a gift. She had read of such things, but this was the first she had seen. A *curiat* – a diary kept of a journey, or a course of study, or a penance.

These . . . Quickly, she had the remaining six out and opened, sliding the ubaie away from her eyes, the better to see the handwritten words. Yes. These detailed a scholar's journey–one volume dealt with geography, another with plants, another with minerals, still another with animals. Volume five detailed temples and universities, while volume six seemed a list of expenditures. The seventh volume indexed the preceding six. All were written in a fine, clear hand, using the common, or trade, alphabet, rather than that of the scholars, which was odd, but not entirely outside of the scope of possibility. Perhaps the scholar in question had liked the resonances which had been evoked by writing in the common script. Scholars often indulged in thought experiments, and this seven volume *curiat* had a complexity, *a layering*, that suggested it had been conceived and executed by a scholar of the highest learning.

Carefully, she put volumes two through seven back in the box and opened the first, being careful not to crack the spine.

"Inas?" Shereen's voice startled her out of her reading. Quickly, she thrust the book into the box and silently shut the lid.

"Yes, sister?" she called.

"Wherever have you been?" her elder scolded from the other side of the curtain. "We need your needle out here, lazy girl. Will you send your sister to her husband in old dayrobes?"

"Of course not," Inas said. Silently, she stood, picked up the box, and slipped it beneath the mattress. Later, she would move it to the secure hidey hole, but for now, the mattress would suffice.

"Well?" Shereen asked, acidic. "Are you going to sleep all

day?"

"No, sister," Inas said meekly and pushed the curtain aside.

*

The days of their father's absence was a frenzy of needlework. At night, after her sisters had fallen, exhausted, into their beds, Inas read the *curiat*, and learned amazing things.

First, she learned that the geographical volume mislocated several key markers, such as the Ilam Mountains, and the Sea of Lukistan. Distrustful of her own knowledge in the face of a work of scholarship, she stole off to her father's study in the deep of night, and pulled down the atlas. She compared the latitudes and longitudes given in the *curiat* volume against those established by the Geographical College, verifying that the *curiat* was off in some areas by a league, and in others by a day's hard travel.

Next, she discovered that the habits of certain animals were misrepresented–these, too, she double-checked in the compendium of creatures issued by the Zoological College.

Within the volume of universities and temples were bits of myth, comparing those found in Lahore-Gadani to others, from Selikot. Several fragments dealt with the exploits of the disorderly Natesa; one such named the aspect Shiva, another Nawar; all set against yet a third mythic creature, the *Coyote of the Nile*.

Then, she discovered that the whole of volume five had been machine printed, in perfect reproduction of the fine hand of the scholar. So the *curiat* was not as ancient as it appeared, which gave her cause to marvel upon the scholar who had created it.

Minerals–well, but by the time she had found the discrepancies in the weights of certain ores, she had made the discovery which explained every error.

She had, as was her habit, waited until her sisters retired, then lit her lamp, pulled up the board under the carpet, and brought the box onto her *chatrue.* She released the three ivory hooks, opened the lid–the box overbalanced and spilled to the floor, books scattering every which way.

Inas slipped out of bed and tenderly gathered the little

volumes up, biting her lip when she found several pages in the third book crumpled. Carefully, she smoothed the damaged sheets, and replaced the book with its brothers inside the box.

It was then that she noticed pieces of the box itself had come loose, leaving two neat, deep, holes in the wood, at opposite corners of the lid. Frowning, she scanned the carpet, spying one long spindle, tightly wrapped in cloth. The second had rolled beneath the *chatrue*, and by the time she reached and squirmed and had it out with the very tips of her fingers, the cloth covering had begun to unravel.

Daintily, she fingered it, wondering if perhaps the cloth held some herb for protection against demons, or perhaps salts, to insure the books kept dry, or–

There was writing on the inside of the cloth. Tiny and meticulous, it was immediately recognizable as the same hand which had penned the *curiat*.

Exquisitely careful, breath caught, she unrolled the little scroll across the carpet, scanning the columns of text; heart hammering into overdrive as she realized that she had discovered her nameless scholar's key.

Teeth indenting her bottom lip, she unrolled the second scroll next to the first, and saw that she had the complete cipher.

Breathless, she groped behind her for the box, and extracted a book at random.

Slowly at first–then more quickly as her agile mind grew acquainted with the key– she began to read.

Illuminated by the cipher, it was found that the volume geographical did not concern itself with mountain ranges and rivers at all, but was instead a detailed report of a clandestine entry into the city of Selikot, and a blasphemous subterfuge.

I regret to inform you, oh, brother in arms, that our information regarding this hopeful world was much misleading. Women are not restricted; they are quarantined, cut off from society and commerce. They may only travel in the company of a male of their kin unit, and even then, heavily shielded in many layers of full body robes, their faces, eyes and hair hidden by veils. So it is that the first adjustment in our well-laid plans has been implemented. You will find that your partner

Thelma Delance has ceded her route and her studies to a certain Scholar Umar Khan. And a damnable time I had finding a false beard in this blasted city, too. However, as you know to your sorrow, I'm a resourceful wench, and all is now made seemly. Scholar Khan is suitably odd, and elicits smiles and blessings wherever he walks. The project continues only slightly impeded by the beard, which itches. I will hold a copy of this letter in my field notes, in the interests of completeness.

Farewell for now, brother Jamie. You owe me a drink and dinner when we are reunited.

*

Inas was slow with her needle next morning, her head full of wonders and blasphemies.

That there were other worlds, other peoples, variously named "Terran" and "Liaden"– that was known. Indeed, Selikot was the site of a "space-port" and bazaar, where such outworlders traded what goods they brought for those offered by the likes of Merchant Majidi. The outworlders were not permitted beyond the bazaar, for they were unpious; and the likes of Merchant Majidi must needs undergo purifications after their business in the bazaar was concluded.

Yet now it seemed that one–nay, *a pair*–of outworlders had moved beyond the bazaar to rove and study the wider world–and one of them a woman. A woman who had disguised herself as a man.

This was blasphemy, and yet the temples had not fallen; the crust of the world had not split open and swallowed cities; nor had fires rained from the heavens.

Perhaps Thelma Delance had repented her sin? Perhaps Amineh, the little god of women, had interceded with his brothers and bought mercy?

Perhaps the gods were not as all-seeing and as all-powerful as she had been taught?

Within the layers of her at-home robes, Inas shivered, but her scholar-trained mind continued its questions, and the answers which arose to retire those new and disturbing questions altered the measure of the world.

"Truth defines the order of the universe," she whispered, bending to her needlework. "When we accept the truth, we accept the will of the gods."

Yet, how if accepting the truth proved the absence of the gods? Why had her father given her such a gift? Had he read the *curiat* before sending it to her? Did he know of the hidden–

Across the room, from the other side of the guest screen, Nasir's voice intruded.

"The Esteemed and Blessed Scholar Reyman Bhar is returned home and bids his daughter Inas attend him in the study."

*

Her father was at his desk, several volumes open before him, his fingers nimble on the keypad of the notetaker. Inas waited, silent, her hands folded into her sleeves. The light of the study lamps was diffused into a golden glow by the *ubaie*, so that her father seemed surrounded by the light of heaven. He was a handsome man, dark, with a masterful beak of a nose and the high forehead of a scholar. His beard was as black and as glossy as that of a man half his age. He wore the house turban, by which she knew he had been home some hours before sending for her, and the loosened braid of his hair showed thick and gray.

He made a few more notes, turned a page of the topmost book, set the notetaker aside, and looked up.

Inas melted to her knees and bowed, forehead to the carpet.

"Arise, daughter," he said, kindly as always.

She did so and stood quiet once more, hands folded before her.

"Tell me, did my packet arrive timely?"

"Father," she said softly, "it did. I am grateful to you for so precious a gift."

He smiled, well-pleased with her. "It is a curiosity, is it not? Did you mark the pattern of the errors? Almost, it seems a farce–a plaything. What think you?"

"Perhaps," Inas said, her breath painfully short, "it is a

test?"

He considered it, black brows knit, then nodded, judiciously. "It could be so. Yes, I believe you have the right of it, daughter. A test devised by a scholar of the higher orders, perhaps to teach discipline." He paused, thinking more deeply. Inas, waiting, felt ill, wondering if he knew of the hidden scholar's key and the blasphemies contained in the revealed text.

"Yes," he said again. "A test. How well the scholar must have loved the student for which it was devised!"

"Yes, Father," Inas whispered, and gathered together her courage, lips parting to ask it, for she *must* know . . .

"As you progress in scholarship, you will learn that the most precious gifts are those which are more than they appear," her father said, "and that hidden knowledge has power." He bowed, seated as he was, scholar to scholar, which was a small blasphemy of its own, face as austere as a saint's.

And so, Inas thought, she was instructed. She bowed. "Yes, Father."

"Hah." He leaned back in his chair, suddenly at ease, and waved her to the stool at his feet.

"Sit, child, and tell me how the arrangements for your sister's wedding progress."

*

The *curiat* buoyed her, frightened her, intrigued her. She spent her nights with it, and every other moment she could steal. She stored it now in the long-forgot sand-wood drawer– the hidden pass-through where it stood long out of use– where she could, if she wished, reach it as easily from the garden or her room.

Thelma Delance–she heard the woman's voice in the few hours of sleep she allowed herself–a loud, good-natured, and unwomanly voice, honest as women could never be, and courageous.

Inas read, and learned. Thelma Delance had been a scholar of wide learning. There were recipes for medicines among her notes; recipes for poisons, for explosives, and other disasters, which Inas understood only mistily; and lessons of *self-defense*, which held echoes of her mother's name. There was other knowledge, too–plans for establishing a base.

And there was the appalling fact that the notes simply ended, and did not pick up again:

They're on me. I've got one more trick up my sleeve. You know me, Jamie Moore, always one more trick up Thelma's wide sleeve, eh? We'll see soon enough if it's worked. If it has, you owe me–that's my cue. They're shooting . . .

There was nothing more after that, only the box, and the wound it bore, which might, Inas thought, have been made by a pellet.

She wondered who had wished to kill Thelma Delance–and almost laughed. Surely, that list was long. The priests–of a certainty. The scholars–indeed. The port police, the merchant guild, the freelance vigilantes . . .

And Inas realized all at once that she was crying, the silent, secret tears that women were allowed, to mourn a sister, a mother, a friend.

*

The day before Humaria was to wed, Inas once again attended her father in the study, where she was given the task of reshelving the volumes he had utilized in his last commissioned research. By chance their proper places were in the back corner of the room, where the convergence of walls and shelves made an alcove not easily seen from the greater room.

She had been at her task some time, her father deep in some new bit of study at his desk, when she heard the door open and Nasir announce, "The Esteemed and Honorable Scholar Baquar Hafeez begs the favor of an audience with the Glorious and Blessed Scholar Reyman Bhar."

"Old friend, enter and be welcome!" Her father's voice was cordial and kindly–and, to his daughter's ear, slightly startled. His chair scritched a little against the carpet as he pushed away from the desk, doubtless rising to embrace his friend.

"To what blessed event do I owe this visit?"

"Why, to none other than Janwai Himself!" Scholar Hafeez

returned, his voice deeper and louder than her father's. "Or at the least, to his priests, who have commissioned me for research at the hill temple. There are certain etched stones in the meditation rooms, as I take it?"

"Ah, are there not!" Reyman Bhar exclaimed. "You are in for a course of study, my friend. Be advised, buy a pair of nightsight lenses before you ascend. The meditation rooms are ancient, indeed, and lit by oil."

"Do you say so?" Scholar Hafeez exclaimed, over certain creaks and groanings from the visitor's chair as it accepted his weight.

Inas, forgotten, huddled, soundless and scarcely moving in the alcove, listening as the talk moved from the meditation rooms to the wider history of the hill temple, to the progress of the report on which her father and Scholar Hafeez had collaborated, not so long since.

At some point, Nasir came in, bearing refreshments. The talk wandered on. In the alcove, Inas sank silently to her knees, drinking in the esoterica of scholarship as a thirsty man guzzles tea.

Finally, there came a break in the talk. Scholar Hafeez cleared his throat.

"I wonder, old friend– that *curiat* you bought in Hamid's store?"

"Yes?" her father murmured. "A peculiar piece, was it not? One would almost believe it had come from the old days, when Hamid's grandfather was said to buy from slavers and caravan thieves."

"Just so. An antique from the days of exploration, precious for its oddity. I have no secrets from you, my friend, so I will confess that it comes often into my mind. I wonder if you would consider parting with it. I will, of course, meet what price you name."

"Ah." Her father paused. Inas pictured him leaning back in his chair, fingers steepled before his chin, brows pulled together as he considered the matter. In the alcove, she hardly dared breathe, even to send a futile woman's prayer to the little god for mercy.

"As much as it saddens me to refuse a friend," Reyman Bhar

said softly, "I must inform you that the *curiat* had been purchased as a gift for a promising young scholar of my acquaintance."

"A strange item to bestow upon a youth," murmured Baquar Hafeez, adding hastily, "But you will, of course, know your own student! It is only that–"

"I most sincerely regret," Scholar Bhar interrupted gently. "The gift has already been given."

There was a pause.

"Ah," said Scholar Hafeez. "Well, then, there is nothing more to be said."

"Just so," her father replied, and there was the sound of his chair being pushed back. "Come, my friend, you have not yet seen my garden. This is the hour of its glory. Walk with me and be refreshed."

Inas counted to fifty after the door closed, then she rose, reshelved the two remaining volumes, and ghosted out of the study, down the hall to the women's wing.

*

Humaria's wedding was blessed and beautiful, the banquet very grand to behold, and even the women's portions fresh and unbroken, which spoke well for her new husband's generosity.

At the last moment, it was arranged between Reyman Bhar and Gabir Majidi that Shereen would stay with her sister for the first month of her new marriage, as the merchant's wife was ill and there were no daughters in his house to bear Humaria company.

So it was that Scholar Bhar came home with only his youngest daughter to companion him. Nasir pulled the sedan before the house and the scholar emerged, his daughter after him. He ascended the ramp to the door, fingering his keycard from his pocket–and froze, staring at a door which was neither latched nor locked.

Carefully, he put forth his hand, pushing the door with the tips of his fingers. It swung open onto a hallway as neat and as orderly as always. Cautiously, the scholar moved on, his daughter forgotten at his back.

There was some small disorder in the public room–a vase

overturned and shattered, some display books tossed aside. The rugs and the news computer–items that would bring a goodly price at the thieves market–were in place, untouched. The scholar walked on, down the hall to–

His study.

Books had been ripped from their shelves and flung to the floor, where they lay, spine-broke and torn, ankle deep and desolate. His notepad lay in the center of the desk, shattered, as if it had been struck with a hammer. The loose pages of priceless manuscripts lay over all.

Behind him, Scholar Bhar heard a sound; a high keening, as if from the throat of a hunting hawk, or a lost soul.

He turned and beheld Inas, wilting against the door, her hand at her throat, falling silent in the instant he looked at her.

"Peace–" he began and stopped, for there was another sound, from the back of the house–but no. It would only be Nasir, coming in from putting the sedan away.

Yes, footsteps; he heard them clearly. And voices. The sudden, ghastly sound of a gun going off.

The scholar grabbed his daughter's shoulder, spinning her around.

"Quickly–to the front door!"

She ran, astonishingly fleet, despite the hindrance of her robes. Alas that she was not fleet enough.

Baquar Hafeez was waiting for them inside the front hallway, and there was a gun in his hand.

*

"Again," Scholar Hafeez said, and the large man he called Danyal lifted her father's right hand, bent the second finger back.

Reyman Bhar screamed. Inas, on her knees beside the chair in which Scholar Hafeez took his ease, stared, stone-faced, through her veil, memorizing the faces of these men, and the questions they asked.

It was the curiat they wanted. And it was the curiat which Reyman Bhar was peculiarly determined that they not have. And why was that? Inas wondered. Surely not because he had made it a gift to a daughter. He had only to order her to fetch it from its hiding place and hand it to Baquar Hafeez. What could a daughter do, but obey?

And yet–*hidden knowledge has power.*

"The *curiat*, old friend," Scholar Hafeez said again–patient, so patient. "Spare yourself any more pain. Only tell me who has the *curiat,* and I will leave you and your household in peace."

"Why?" her father asked–a scholar's question, despite his pain.

"There are those who believe it to be the work of infidels," Scholar Hafeez said smoothly, and yet again: "The *curiat*, Reyman. Where is it?"

"It is not for you to know," her father gasped, his voice hoarse from screaming, his left arm useless, dislocated by Danyal in the first round of questions.

Scholar Hafeez sighed, deeply, regretfully.

"I was afraid that you might prove obstinate. Perhaps something else might persuade you."

It happened so quickly, she had no time to understand–pain exploded in her face and she was flung sideways to the floor, brilliant color distorting her vision. Her wrist was seized and she was lifted. More pain. She tried to get her feet under her, but she was pulled inexorably upward, sandals dangling. Her vision spangled, stabilized–Danyal's face was bare inches from hers. He was smiling.

Somewhere, her father was shouting.

"Your pardon, old friend?" Scholar Hafeez was all solicitude. "I did not quite hear the location of the *curiat*?"

"Release my daughter!"

"Certainly. *After* you disclose the location of the *curiat.* Such a small thing, really, when weighed against a daughter's virtue."

"Inas–" her father began, and what followed was not in the common tongue, but in that of her mother, and they were uttered as a prayer.

"Opportunity comes, daughter, be stout and true. Honor

your mother, in all her names."

Scholar Hafeez made a small sound of disappointment, and moved a hand. "The *ubaie*, Danyal."

Inas saw his hand move. He crumbled the fragile fabrics in his fist and tore them away, unseating her headcloth. Her hair spilled across her shoulders, rippling black.

Danyal licked his lips, his eyes now openly upon her chest.

There was a scream of rage, and from the corner of her eye she saw her father, on his knees, a bloody blade in his least-damaged hand, reaching again toward Hafeez.

Danyal still held her, his attention on his master; Inas brought both of her knees up, aiming to crush his man-parts, as Thelma Delance had described.

The villain gasped, eyes rolling up. His grip loosened, she fell to the floor, rolling, in order to confound the aim of the gun, and there was a confusion of noises, and her father shouting "Run!"–and run she did, her hair streaming and her face uncovered, never looking back, despite the sounds of gunfire behind her.

*

The house was in the merchant district of the city of Harap, a walk of many days from the prefecture Coratu, whose principal cities, Iravati and Lahore-Gadani, had lately suffered a sudden rash of explosions and fires and unexplained deaths. There were those who said it was a judgment from the gods; that Lahore-Gadani had become too assertive; and Iravati too complacent in its tranquility. The priests had ordered a cleansing, and a month long fast for the entire prefecture. Perhaps it would be enough.

In Harap, though.

In Harap, at that certain house, a boy crossed the street from out of the night-time shadows and made a ragged salaam to the doorman.

"Peace," he said, in a soft, girlish voice. "I am here to speak with Jamie Moore."

The doorman gave him one bored look. "Why?"

The boy hefted the sack he held in his left hand. "I have

something for him."

"Huh." The doorman considered it, then swung sideways, rapping three times on the door. It opened and he said to the one who came forward, "Search him. I'll alert the boss."

*

The search had discovered weapons, of course, and they had been confiscated. The bag, they scanned, discovering thereby the mass and material of its contents. Indeed, the search was notable in that which it did not discover–but perhaps, to off-worlders, such things mattered not.

The door to the searching chamber opened and the doorman looked in.

"You're fortunate," he said. "The boss is willing to play."

So, then, there was the escort, up to the top of the house, to another door, and the room beyond, where a man sat behind a desk, his books piled, open, one upon the other, a notetaker in his hand.

Tears rose. She swallowed them, and bowed the bow of peace.

"I'm Jamie Moore," the man behind the desk said. "Who are you?"

"I am Inas Bhar, youngest daughter of Scholar Reyman Bhar, who died the death to preserve what I bring you tonight."

The man looked at her, blue eyes–outworlder eyes–bland and uninterested.

"I don't have a lot of time or patience," he said. "Forget the theatrics and show me what you've got."

She swallowed, her throat suddenly dry. This–this was the part of all her careful plans that might yet go awry. She opened the bag, reached inside and pulled out the *curiat.*

"For you," she said, holding it up for him to see, "from Thelma Delance."

There was a long silence, while he looked between her and the box. Finally, he held out his hands.

"Let me see."

Reluctantly, she placed the *curiat* in his hands, watching

as he flicked the ivory hooks, raised the lid, fished out a volume, and opened it at random.

He read a page, the next, riffled to the back of the book and read two pages more. He put the book back in the box and met her eyes.

"It's genuine," he said and gave her the honor of a seated bow. "The Juntavas owes you. What'll it be? Gold? A husband with position? I realize the options are limited on this world, but we'll do what we can to pay fair."

"I do not wish to marry. I want . . ." She stopped, took a breath, and met the bland, blue eyes. "My father was a scholar. He taught me to be a scholar–to read, to reason, *to think.* I want to continue–in my father's memory."

He shrugged. "Nice work, if you can get it."

Inas drew herself up. "I speak five dialects and three languages," she said. "I am adept with the higher maths and with astronomy. I read the mercantile, scholarly and holy scripts. I know how to mix the explosive *skihi* and–" The man behind the desk held up a hand.

"Hold up. You know how to mix skihi? Who taught you that?"

She pointed at the curiat. "Page thirty-seven, volume three."

He whistled. "You found the cipher, did you? Clever girl." He glanced thoughtfully down at the box.

"You wouldn't have used any of that formula, would you? Say, back home or in Lahore-Gadani?"

Inas bowed, scholar to scholar. "They killed my father. He had no sons to avenge him."

"Right."

More silence–enough that Inas began to worry about the reasoning going on behind those blue outworlder eyes. It would, after all, be a simple thing to shoot her–and far more merciful than the punishment the priests would inflict upon her, were she discovered dressed in a boy's tunic and trousers, her face uncovered, her hair cut and braided with green string.

"Your timing's good," Jamie Moore said abruptly. "We've

got a sector chief checking in tomorrow. What I can do, I can show you to the chief, and the two of you can talk. This is sector chief business, understand me?"

Inas bowed. "I understand, Jamie Moore. Thank you."

"Better hold that until you meet the chief," he said, and the door opened behind her, though she had not seen him give a signal.

"We'll stand you a bath, a meal and a bed," he said, and jerked his head at the doorman. "Get her downstairs. Guard on the door."

He looked at her once more. "What happens next is up to you."

*

She sat on the edge of the *chatrue*–well, no she didn't. Properly a chatrue, a female's bed, would be hidden by a curtain at a height so that even a tall man could not see over. This was hardly a bed meant for a woman . . . .

She sat on the edge of the bed then, with the daybreak meal in dishes spread around her, amazed and appreciative at the amount of food she was given to break her fast.

But, after all–she had come to the house in the clothes of a boy, admitted to taking a son's duty of retribution to herself; and agreed to meet with the *sector chief.* These were all deeds worthy of male necessities; hence they fed her as a male would be fed, with two kinds of meat, with porridge of proper sweetness and with extra honey on the side, with fresh juice of the gormel-berry–and brought her clean boy's clothes in the local style, that she might appear before the sector chief in proper order.

She had slept well, waking only once, at the sound of quiet feet in the stairway. Left behind when she woke then was a half-formed dream: In it she had lost her veils to Danyal, but rather than leer, he had screamed and run, terrified of what he had seen revealed in her face.

Too late now to run, she thought as she slipped back into sleep, both Danyal and her father's false friend had fallen to her vengence. And the *curiat* was in the hands of the infidel.

Inas ate all the breakfast, leaving but some honey. There had been too many days since her father's death when food had been scarce; too many nights when her stomach was empty, for her to stint now on sustenance.

"Hello, child!" A voice called from outside the door. There followed a brisk knock, with the sound of laughter running behind it. "Your appointment begins now!"

*

The name of Jamie Moore's boss was Sarah Chang. She was small and round, with crisp black hair bristling all over her head, and slanting black eyes. Her clothing was simple– a long-sleeved shirt, open at the throat, a vest, trousers and boots. A wide belt held a pouch and a holster. Her face was naked, which Inas had expected. What she had not expected was the jolt of shock she felt.

Sarah Chang laughed.

"You're the one pretending to be a boy," she commented, and Inas bowed, wryly.

"I am an exception," she said. "I do not expect to meet myself."

"Here, you're an exception," the woman corrected, and pointed at one of the room's two chairs, taking the other for herself. "Sit. Tell me what happened. Don't leave anything out. But don't dawdle."

So, she had told it. The gift of the *curiat*; the visit of Scholar Hafeez to her father; Humaria's wedding; the violation of her father's study, and his brutal questioning; her escape into the night, and return to a house of the unjustly murdered–father, books and servant. Her revenge.

"You mixed a batch of *skihi*, blew up a couple buildings, disguised yourself as a boy and walked away from it," Sarah Chang said, by way of summing up. She shook her head. "Pretty cool. How'd you think of all that?"

Inas moved her hands. "I learned from Thelma Delance. The recipe for *skihi* was in her *curiat*. She disguised herself as a man in order to pursue her scholarship."

"So she did." The woman closed her eyes. "Any idea what I should do with you?"

Inas licked her lips. "I wish to be a scholar."

"Not the line of work women usually get into, hereabouts." Sarah Chang's eyes were open now, and watching carefully.

"Thelma Delance–"

"Thelma was an outworlder," the boss interrupted. "Like I am. Like Jamie is."

This woman possessed a man's hard purpose, Inas thought; she would do nothing for pity. She raised her chin.

"Surely, then, there is some place where I, too, would be an outworlder, and free to pursue my life as I wish?"

Sarah Chang laughed.

"How old are you?" She asked then.

"Fourteen winters."

The boss tipped her head. "Thirteen Standards, near enough. Regular old maid. And you've got a nice touch with an explosive."

"Skihi, for your information, is an extremely volatile mixture. Many explosive experts have the missing fingers to prove it." She bounced out of her chair and shook her head.

"All right, Inas, let's go."

She stayed in her chair, looking up into the slanting black eyes. "Go where?"

"Outworld," the boss said, and moved an impatient hand, pointing upward, toward the sky–and beyond.

This House

IT WAS SPRING AGAIN.

Mil Ton Intassi caught the first hint of it as he strolled through his early-morning garden –a bare flutter of warmth along the chill edge of mountain air, no more than that. Nonetheless, he sighed as he walked, and tucked his hands into the sleeves of his jacket.

At the end of the garden he paused, looking out across the toothy horizon, dyed orange by the rising sun. Mist boiled up from the valley below him, making the trees into wraiths, obscuring the road and the airport entirely.

Spring, he thought again.

He had come here in the spring, retreating to the house he had built, to the constancy of the mountains.

Turning his back on the roiling fog, he strolled down the pale stone path, passing between banked rows of flowers.

At the center of the garden, the path forked–the left fork became a pleasant meander through the lower gardens, into the perimeter wood. It was cunning, with many delightful vistas, grassy knolls, and shady groves perfect for tête-à-têtes.

The right-hand path led straight to the house, and it was to the house that Mil Ton returned, slipping in through the terrace window, sliding it closed behind him.

He left his jacket on its peg and crossed to the stove, where he poured tea into a lopsided pottery mug before he moved on, his footsteps firm on the scrubbed wooden floor.

At the doorway to the great room, he paused. To his right, the fireplace, the full wall of native stone, which they had gathered and placed themselves. The grate wanted sweeping and new logs needed to be laid. He would see to it later.

Opposite the doorway was a wall of windows through which he could see the orange light unfurling like ribbons through the busy mist, and, nearer, a pleasant lawn, guarded on the far side by a band of cedar trees, their rough bark showing pink against the glossy green needles. Cedar was plentiful on this side of the mountain. So plentiful that he had used native cedar wood for beam, post, and floor.

Mil Ton turned his head, looking down the room to the letterbox. The panel light glowed cheerfully green, which meant there were messages in the bin. It was rare, now, that he received any messages beyond the commonplace–notices of quartershare payments, the occasional query from the clan's man of business. His sister–his delm–had at last given over scolding him, and would not command him; her letters were laconic, non-committal, and increasingly rare. The others–he moved his shoulders and walked forward to stand at the window, sipping tea from the lopsided mug and staring down into the thinning orange mist.

The green light tickled the edge of his vision. What could it be? he wondered–and sighed sharply, irritated with himself. The letterbox existed because his sister–or perhaps it had been his delm–asked that he not make himself entirely unavailable to the clan. Had she not, he would have had neither letterbox, nor telephone, nor newsnet access. Two of those he had managed, and missed neither. Nor would he mourn the letterbox, did it suddenly malfunction and die.

Oh, blast it all–*what* could it be?

He put the cup on the sill and went down the room, jerking open the drawer and snatching out two flimsies.

The first was, after all, an inquiry from his man of business on the subject of re-investing an unexpected payout of dividend. He set it aside.

The second message was from Master Tereza of Solcintra Healer Hall, and it was rather lengthy, outlining an exceptionally interesting and difficult case currently in the care of the Hall, and wondering if he might bring himself down to the city for a few days to lend his expertise.

Mil Ton made a sound halfway between a growl and a laugh; his fingers tightened, crumpling the sheet into an unreadable mess.

Go to Solcintra Hall, take up his role as a Healer once more. Yes, certainly. Tereza, of all of them, should know that he had no intention of ever–he had told her, quite plainly– and his had never been a true Healing talent, in any case. It was a farce. A bitter joke made at his expense.

He closed his eyes, deliberately initiating a basic relaxation exercise. Slowly, he brought his anger–his panic–under control. Slowly, cool sense returned.

Tereza had been his friend. Caustic, she could certainly be, but to taunt a wounded man for his pain? No. That was not Tereza.

The flimsy was a ruin of mangled fiber and smeared ink. No matter. He crossed the room and dropped it into the fire grate, and stood staring down into the cold ashes.

Return to Solcintra? Not likely.

He moved his shoulders, turned back to the window and picked up the lopsided cup; sipped tepid tea.

He should answer his man of business. He should, for the friendship that had been between them, answer Tereza. He should.

And he would–later. After he had finished his tea and sat for his dry, dutiful hours, trying to recapture that talent which had been his, and which seemed to have deserted him now. One of many desertions, and not the least hurtful.

*

Spring crept onward, kissing the flowers in the door garden into dewy wakefulness. Oppressed by cedar walls, Mil Ton escaped down the left-hand path, pacing restlessly past knolls and groves, until at last he came to a certain tree, and beneath the tree, a bench, where he sat down, and sighed, and raised his face to receive the benediction of the breeze.

In the warm sunlight, eventually he dozed. Certainly, the day bid well for dozing, sweet dreams and all manner of pleasant things. That he dozed, that was pleasant. That he did not dream, that was well. That he was awakened by a voice murmuring his name, that was–unexpected.

He straightened from his comfortable slouch against the tree, eyes snapping wide.

Before him, settled casually cross-legged on the new grass,

heedless of stains on his town-tailored clothes, was a man somewhat younger than himself, dark of hair, gray of eye. Mil Ton stared, voice gone to dust in his throat.

"The house remembered me," the man in the grass said apologetically. "I hope you don't mind."

Mil Ton turned his face away. "When did it matter, what I minded?"

"Always," the other replied, softly. "Mil Ton. I told you how it was."

He took a deep breath, imposing calm with an exercise he had learned in Healer Hall, and faced about.

"Fen Ris," he said, low, but not soft. Then, "Yes. You told me how it was."

The gray eyes shadowed. "And in telling you, killed you twice." He raised a ringless and elegant hand, palm turned up. "Would that it were otherwise." The hand reversed, palm toward the grass. "Would that it were not."

Would that he had died of the pain of betrayal, Mil Ton thought, rather than live to endure this. He straightened further on the bench, frowning down at the other.

"Why do you break my peace?"

Fen Ris tipped his head slightly to one side in the old, familiar gesture. "Break?" he murmured, consideringly. "Yes, I suppose I deserve that. Indeed, I know that I deserve it. Did I not first appeal to Master Tereza and the Healers in the Hall at Solcintra, hoping that they might cure what our house Healer could not?" He paused, head bent, then looked up sharply, gray gaze like a blow.

"Master Tereza said she had sent for you," he stated, absolutely neutral. "She said you would not come."

Mil Ton felt a chill, his fingers twitched, as if crumpling a flimsy into ruin.

"She did not say it was you."

"Ah. Would you have come, if she had said it was me?"

Yes, Mil Ton thought, looking aside so the other would not read it in his eyes.

"No," he said.

There was a small silence, followed by a sigh.

"Just as well, then," Fen Ris murmured. "For it was not I." He paused, and Mil Ton looked back to him, drawn despite his will.

"Who, then?" he asked, shortly.

The gray eyes were infinitely sorrowful, eternally determined.

"My lifemate."

Fury, pure as flame, seared him. "You dare!"

Fen Ris lifted his chin, defiant. "You, who taught me what it is to truly love–you ask if I *dare*?"

To truly love. Yes, he had taught that lesson–learned that lesson. And then he had learned the next lesson–that even love can betray.

He closed his eyes, groping for the rags of his dignity . . .

"Her name is Endele," Fen Ris said softly. "By profession, she is a gardener." A pause, a light laugh. "A rare blossom in our house of risk-takers and daredevils."

Eyes closed, Mil Ton said nothing.

"Well." Fen Ris said after a moment. "You live so secluded here that you may not have heard of the accident at the skimmer fields last relumma. Three drivers were killed upon the instant. One walked away unscathed. Two were sealed into crisis units. Of those, one died."

Mil Ton had once followed the skimmer races–how not?–he had seen how easily a miscalculated corner approach could become tragedy.

"You were ever Luck's darling," he whispered, his inner ear filled with the shrieks of torn metal and dying drivers; his inner eye watching carefully as Fen Ris climbed from his battered machine and–

"Aye," Fen Ris said. "That I was allowed to emerge whole and hale from the catastrophe unit–that was luck, indeed."

Abruptly it was cold, his mind's eye providing a different scene, as the emergency crew worked feverishly to cut through the twisted remains of a racing skimmer and extricate the shattered driver, the still face sheathed in blood–two alive, of six. Gods, he had almost lost Fen Ris–

No.

He had already lost Fen Ris.

"I might say," Fen Ris murmured, "that I was the most blessed of men, save for this one thing–that when I emerged from the unit, Endele–my lady, my heart . . ." His voice faded.

"She does not remember you."

Silence. Mil Ton opened his eyes and met the bleak gray stare.

"So," said Fen Ris, "you did read the file."

"I read the summary Tereza sent, to entice me back to the Hall," he corrected. "The case intrigued her–no physical impediment to the patient's memory, nor even a complete loss of memory. Only one person has been excised entirely from her past."

"Excised," Fen Ris repeated. "We have not so long a shared past, after all. A year– only that."

Mil Ton moved his shoulders. "Court her anew, then," he said, bitterly.

"When I did not court her before?" the other retorted. He sighed. "I have tried. She withdraws. She does not know me; she does not trust me." He paused, then said, so low Mil Ton could scarcely hear–

"She does not want me."

It should have given him pleasure, Mil Ton thought distantly, to see the one who had dealt him such anguish, in agony. And, yet, it was not pleasure he felt, beholding Fen Ris thus, but rather a sort of bleak inevitability.

"Why me?" he asked, which is not what he had meant to say.

Fen Ris lifted his face, allowing Mil Ton to plumb the depths of his eyes, sample the veracity of his face.

"Because you will know how to value my greatest treasure," he murmured. "Who would know better?"

Mil Ton closed his eyes, listening to his own heartbeat, to the breeze playing in the leaves over his head, and, eventually, to his own voice, low and uninflected.

"Bring her here, if she will come. If she will not, there's an end to it, for I will not go into the city."

"Mil Ton–"

"Hear me. If she refuses Healing, she is free to go when and where she will. If she accepts Healing, the same terms apply." He opened his eyes, and looked hard into the other's face.

"Bring your treasure here and you may lose it of its own will and desire."

This was warning, proper duty of a Healer, after all, and perhaps it was foretelling as well.

Seated, Fen Ris bowed, acknowledging that he'd heard, then came effortlessly to his feet. "The terms are acceptable. I will bring her tomorrow, if she will come."

Mil Ton stood. "Our business is concluded," he said flatly. "Pray, leave me."

Fen Ris stood, frozen–a heartbeat, no more than that; surely, not long enough to be certain–and thawed abruptly, sweeping a low bow, accepting a debt too deep to repay.

"I have not–" Mil Ton began, but the other turned as if he had not spoken, and went lightly across the grass, up the path, and away.

*

Mil Ton had stayed up late into the night, pacing and calling himself every sort of fool, retiring at last to toss and turn until he fell into uneasy sleep at dawn. Some hours later, a blade of sunlight sliced through the guardian cedars, through the casement and into his face.

The intrusion of light was enough to wake him. A glance at the clock brought a curse to his lips. Fen Ris would be arriving soon. If, indeed, he arrived at all.

Quickly, Mil Ton showered, dressed, and went on slippered feet down the hall toward the kitchen. As he passed the great room, he glanced within–and froze in his steps.

A woman sat on the edge of the hearth, a blue duffel bag at her feet, her hands neatly folded on her lap. She sat without any of the cushions or pillows she might have used to ease her rest, and her purpose seemed not to be repose, but alert waiting.

Her attention at this moment was directed outward, toward the window, beyond which the busy birds flickered among the cedar branches.

He took one step into the room.

The woman on the hearth turned her head, showing him a round, high-browed face, and a pair of wary brown eyes.

Mil Ton bowed in welcome of the guest. "Good day to you. I am Mil Ton Intassi, builder of this house."

"And Healer," she said, her voice deeper than he had expected.

"And Healer," he allowed, though with less confidence that he once might have. He glanced around the room. "You came alone?"

She glanced down at the blue duffel. "He drove me here, and opened the door to the house. There was no need for him to wait. He knew I did not want him. You did not want him either, he said."

Not *entirely* true, Mil Ton thought, face heating as he recalled the hours spent pacing. He inclined his head.

"May I know your name?"

"Bah! I have no manners," she cried and sprang to her feet. She bowed–a completely unadorned bow of introduction–and straightened.

"I am Endele per'Timbral, Clan–" her voice faded, a cloud of confusion passed briefly across her smooth face.

"I am Endele per'Timbral," she repeated, round chin thrust out defiantly.

Mil Ton inclined his head. "Be welcome in my house, Endele per'Timbral," he said, seriously. "I am in need of a cup of tea. May I offer you the same?"

"Thank you," she said promptly. "A cup of tea would be welcome."

She followed him down the hall to the kitchen and waited with quiet patience while he rummaged in the closet for a cup worthy of a guest. In the back, he located a confection of pearly porcelain. He poured tea and handed it off, recalling as she received it that the cup had belonged to Fen Ris, the sole survivor of a long-broken set.

Healers were taught to flow with their instincts. Mil Ton turned away to pour for himself, choosing the lopsided cup, as always, and damned both Healer training and himself, for agreeing to . . .

"He said that you can Heal me." Endele spoke from behind him, her speech as unadorned as her bow had been. "He means, you will make me remember him."

Mil Ton turned to look at her. She held the pearly cup daintily on the tips of her fingers, sipping tea as neatly as a cat. Certainly, she was not a beauty–her smooth forehead was too high, her face too round, her hair merely brown, caught back with a plain silver hair ring. Her person was compact and sturdy, and she had the gift of stillness.

"Do you, yourself, desire this Healing?" he asked, the words coming effortlessly to his lips, as if the year away were the merest blink of an eye. "I will not attempt a Healing, against your will."

She frowned slightly. "Did you tell him that?"

"Of course," said Mil Ton. "I also told him that, if you wish to leave here for your own destination, now or later, I will not impede you. He accepted the terms."

"Did he?" The frown did not disappear. "Why?"

Mil Ton sipped tea, deliberately savoring the citrus bite while he considered. It was taught that a Healer owed truth to those he would Heal. How much truth was left to the Healer's discretion.

"I believe," he said slowly, to Endele per'Timbral's wary brown eyes, "it is because he values you above all other things and wishes for you only that which will increase your joy."

Tears filled her eyes, glittering. She turned aside, embarrassed to weep before a stranger, as anyone would be, and walked over to the terrace door, her footsteps soft on the wooden floor.

Mil Ton sipped tea and watched her. She stood quite still, her shoulders stiff with tension, tea cup forgotten in one hand, staring out into the garden as if it were the most fascinating thoroughfare in Solcintra City.

Sipping tea, Mil Ton let his mind drift. He was not skilled at hearing another's emotions. But the Masters of the Hall in Solcintra had taught him somewhat of their craft, and sometimes, if he disengaged his mind, allowing himself to fall, as it were into a waking doze–well, sometimes, then, he could see . . .

Images.

Now he saw images and more than images. He saw intentions made visible.

Walls of stone, a window set flush and firm, tightly latched against the storm raging without. Hanging to the right of the window was a wreath woven of some blue-leaved plant, which gave off a sweet, springlike scent. Mil Ton breathed in. Breathed out.

He felt, without seeing, that the stone barrier was all around the woman, as if she walked in some great walled city, able to stay safe from some lurking, perhaps inimical presence . . .

A rustle of something and the stones and their meaning faded.

"Please," a breathless voice said nearby. He opened his eyes to his own wood-floored kitchen, and looked down into the round face of Endele per'Timbral.

"Please," she said again. "May I walk in your garden?"

"Certainly," he said, suddenly remembering her profession. "I am afraid you will find it inadequate in the extreme, however."

"I was charmed to see your house sitting so comfortably in the woods. I am certain I will be charmed by your garden," she said in turn, and turned to place her cup on the counter.

He unlocked the door and she slipped through, walking down the path without a look behind her. Mil Ton watched her out of sight, then left the door on the latch and poured himself a second cup of tea.

*

By trade, he was a storyteller. A storyteller whose stories sometimes went . . . odd. Odd enough to pique the interest of the Masters, who had insisted that he was Healer, and taught him what they could of the craft.

He was, at best, a mediocre Healer, for he never had gained the necessary control over his rather peculiar talent to make it more than an uncertain tool. Sometimes, without warning, he would tell what Tereza was pleased to call a True Story, and that story would have–an effect. Neither story nor effect were predictable, and so he was most likely to be called upon as a last resort, after every other Healing art had failed.

As now.

Mil Ton thought about the woman–the woman Fen Ris had taken as lifemate. He remembered the impassioned speech on the subject of this same woman, on the night Fen Ris had come to tell him how it was.

He sighed then, filled for a moment with all the grief of that night, and recalled Fen Ris demanding, *demanding* that Mil Ton take no Balance against this woman, for she had not stolen Fen Ris but discovered him. Among tears and joy, Fen Ris insisted that they both had been snatched, unanticipated and unplanned, out of their ordinary lives.

And now, of course, there was no ordinary life for any of them.

He wondered–he very much wondered–if Endele per'Timbral would choose Healing.

Her blue bag still lay by the hearth, but it had been many hours since she had gone out into the garden. More than enough time for a sturdy woman in good health to have hiked down to the airport, engaged a pilot and a plane and been on her way to–anywhere at all.

Mil Ton sighed and looked back to his screen. When he found that he could no longer practice his profession, he had taught himself a new skill. Written stories never turned odd, and before his betrayal, he had achieved a modest success in his work.

The work was more difficult now; the stories that came so grudgingly off the tips of his fingers bleak and gray and hopeless. He had hoped for something better from this one, before Fen Ris had intruded into his life again. Now, he was distracted, his emotions in turmoil. He wondered again if Endele per'Timbral had departed for a destination of her own choosing. Fen Ris would suffer, if she had done so. He told himself he didn't care.

Unquiet, he put the keyboard aside and pulled a book from the table next to his chair. If he could not write, perhaps he could lose himself inside the story of another.

*

She returned to the house with sunset, her hair wind-combed, her shirt and leggings rumpled, dirt under her fingernails.

"Your garden *is* charming," she told him. "I took the liberty of weeding a few beds so that the younger flowers will have room to grow."

"Ah." said Mil Ton, turning from the freezer with a readimeal in one hand. "My thanks."

"No thanks needed," she assured him, eyeing the box. "I would welcome a similar meal, if the house is able," she said, voice almost shy.

"Certainly, the house is able," he said, snappish from a day of grudging, grayish work.

She inclined her head seriously. "I am in the house's debt." She held up her hands. "Is there a place where I may wash off your garden's good dirt?"

He told her where to find the 'fresher and she left him.

*

Dinner was enlivened by a discussion of the garden. She was knowledgeable–more so than Mil Ton, who had planted piecemeal, with those things that appealed to him. He kept up his side only indifferently, his vision from time to time overlain with stone, and a storm raging, raging, raging, outside windows tight and sealed.

When the meal was done, she helped him clear the table, and, when the last dish was stacked in the cleaner, stood awkwardly, her strong, capable hands twisted into a knot before her.

Mil Ton considered her through a shimmer of stone walls.

"Have you decided," he said, careful to keep his voice neutral–for this was *her* choice, and hers alone, so the Master

Healers taught–"whether you are in need of Healing?"

She looked aside, and it seemed that, for a moment, the phantom stones took on weight and substance. Then, the vision faded and it was only clean air between him and a woman undecided.

"They say–they say he is my lifemate," she said, low and stammering. "They say the life-price was negotiated with my clan, that he paid it out of his winnings on the field. They say, we were inseparable, greater together than apart. His kin–they say all this. And I say– if these things are so, why do I not remember him?"

Mil Ton drew a deep, careful breath. "Why should they tell you these things, if they were not so?"

She moved her shoulders, face averted. "Clearly, it *is* so," she whispered. "They– he–the facts are as they state them. I saw the announcement in the back issue of the Gazette. I spoke to my sister. I remember the rooms which are mine in his clan house. I remember the gardens, and the shopkeeper at the end of the street. I remember his sister, his brothers–all his kin! Saving him. Only him. My . . . lifemate."

Her pain was evident. One needn't be an empath to feel it. Mil Ton drew a calming breath . . .

"I am not a monster," she continued. "He–of course, he is bewildered. He seems– kind, and, and concerned for my happiness. He looks at me . . . I do *not* know him!" she burst out passionately. "I owe him nothing!" She caught herself, teeth indenting lower lip. Mil Ton saw the slow slide of a tear down one round cheek.

She was sincere; he remembered Tereza's report all too well:

This is not merely some childish game of willfulness, but a true forgetting. And, yet, how has she forgotten? Her intellect is intact; she has suffered no trauma, taken no drugs, appealed to no Healer to rid her of the burden of her memories . . .

"And do you," Mil Ton asked once more, "wish to embrace Healing?"

She turned her head and looked at him, her cheeks wet and her eyes tragic.

"What will happen, if I am Healed?"

Ah, the question. The very question. And he owed her only truth.

"It is the wish of your lifemate that you would then recall him and the life you have embarked upon together. If you do not also wish for that outcome, deny me."

Her lips tightened, and again she turned away, walked a few steps down the room and turned back to face him.

"You built this house, he said–you alone." She looked around her, at the bare wooden floor, the cedar beam, the cabinets and counter in-between. "It must have taken a very long time."

So, there would be no Healing. Mil Ton sighed–Fen Ris. It was possible to feel pity for Fen Ris. He bought a moment to compose himself by repeating her inventory of the kitchen, then brought his eyes to her face and inclined his head.

"Indeed, it took much longer than needful, to build this house. I worked on it infrequently, with long stretches between."

"But, why build it at all?"

"Well." He hesitated, then moved his hand, indicating that she should walk with him.

"I began when I was still an apprentice. My mother had died and left the mountain to myself alone, as her father had once left it to her. There had been a house here, in the past; I discovered the foundation when I began to clear the land." He paused and gave her a sideline look.

"I had planned to have a garden here, you see–and what I did first was to clear the land and cut the pathways . . ."

"But you had uncovered the foundation," she said, preceding him into the great room. She sat on the edge of the hearth, where she had been before. Fen Ris had himself perched precisely there on any number of evenings or mornings. And here was this woman–

Mil Ton walked over to his chair and sat on the arm.

"I had uncovered the foundation," he repeated, "before I went away–back to the city and my craft. I was away–for many years, traveling in stories. I made a success of myself; my tales were sought after; halls were filled with those who hungered for my words.

"When I returned, I was ill with self-loathing. My stories had become . . . weapons– horribly potent, uncontrollable. I drove a man mad in Chonselta City. In Teramis, a woman ran from the hall, screaming . . ."

On the hearth, Endele per'Timbral sat still as a stone, only her eyes alive.

"That I came here–I scarcely knew why. Except that I had discovered a foundation and it came to me that I could build a house, and keep the world safely away."

Oh, gods, he thought, feeling the shape of the words in his mouth, listening to his voice, spinning the tale he meant, and yet did not mean, to tell . . .

"I built the house of cedar, and laid the beams by hand; the windows I set tight against the walls. At the core, a fireplace–" He used his chin to point over her shoulder. "Before I finished that, the Healers came to me. News of my stories and the effects of my stories had reached the Masters of the Guild and they begged that I come to be trained, before I harmed anyone else." He looked down at his hand, fisted against his knee, and heard his voice continue the tale.

"So, I went and I trained, and then I worked as a Healer in the hall. I learned to write stories down and they did not cause madness, and so took up another craft for myself. I was content and solitary until I met a young man at the skimmer track." He paused; she sat like a woman hewn of ice.

"He was bold, and he was beautiful; intelligent and full of joy. We were friends, first, then lovers. I brought him here and he transformed my house with his presence; with his help, the fireplace went from pit to hearth."

He closed his eyes, heard the words fall from his lips. "One evening, he came to me– we had been days apart, but that was no unknown thing–he followed the races, of course. He came to me and he was weeping, he held me and he told me of the woman he had met, how their hearts beat together, how they must be united, or die."

Behind his closed eyes he saw image over image–Fen Ris before him, beseeching and explaining, and this woman's wall of stone, matching texture for texture the very hearth she sat on.

"Perhaps a true Healer might have understood. I did not. I cast him out at once, told him to go to his woman and leave me–leave me in peace. I fled—here, to the place which was built for safety . . ."

"How did you abide it?" Her voice was shrill, he opened his eyes to find her on her feet, her body bowed with tension, her eyes frantic. "How did you abide loving him? Knowing what he does? Knowing that they might one day bring his body to you? Couldn't you see that you needed to lock yourself away?"

His vision wavered, he saw stones, falling, felt wind tear his hair, lash rain into his face. In the midst of chaos, he reached out, and put his arms around her, and held her while she sobbed against his shoulder.

Eventually, the wind died, the woman in his arms quieted.

"I loved him for himself," he said softly, into her hair. "And he loved the races. He would not choose to stop racing, though he might have done, had I asked him. But he would have been unhappy, desperately so–and I loved him too well to ask it." He sighed.

"In the end, it came to *my* choice: Did I bide and share in our love, for as long as we both remained? Or turn my face aside, from the fear that, someday, he might be gone?"

In his arms Endele per'Timbral shuddered–and relaxed.

"As simple as that?" she whispered.

"As simple, and as complex." Words failed him for a moment–in his head now were images of Fen Ris laughing, and of the ocean waves crashing on stone beneath the pair of them, of arms reaching eagerly–

He sighed again. "I have perhaps done you no favor, child, in unmaking the choice you had made, if safety is what you need above all."

"Perhaps," she said, and straightened out of his embrace, showing him a wet face, and eyes as calm as dawn. "Perhaps not." She inclined her head. "All honor, Healer. With your permission, I will retire, and tend my garden of choices while I dream."

He showed her to the tiny guest room, with its thin bed and single window, giving out to the moonlit garden, then returned to the great room.

For a few heartbeats, he stood, staring down into the cold hearth. It came to him, as from a distance, that it wanted sweeping, and he knelt down on the stones and reached for the brush.

*

"Mil Ton." A woman's voice, near at hand. He stirred, irritable, muscles aching, as if he had slept on cold stone.

"Mil Ton," she said again, and he opened his eyes to Endele per'Timbral's pale and composed face. She extended a hand, and helped him to rise, and they walked in companionable silence to the kitchen for tea.

"Have you decided," he asked her, as they stood by the open door, inhaling the promise of the garden, "what you shall do?"

"Yes," she said softly. "Have you?"

"Yes," he answered–and it was so, though he had not until that moment understood that a decision had been necessary. He smiled, feeling his heart absurdly light in his breast.

"I will return to Solcintra. Tereza writes that there is work for me, at the Hall."

"I am glad," she said. "Perhaps you will come to us, when you are settled. He would like it, I think–and I would."

He looked over to her and met her smile.

"Thank you," he said softly. "I would like it, too."

Changeling

THE FIRST THING THEY told him when he emerged from the catastrophic healing unit was that his wife had died in the accident.

The second thing they told him was that her Clan was pursuing retribution to the fullest extent of the Code.

They left him alone, then, the med techs, with instructions to eat and rest. The door slid closed behind them with the snap of a lock engaging.

Out of a habit of obedience, he walked over to the table and lifted the cover from the tray. The aroma of glys-blossom tea rose to greet him and he dropped the cover, tears rising.

He had not known his wife well, but she had been pretty and bold and full of fun—one found it inconceivable, newly healed from one's own injuries and with the scent of her preferred blend in the air, that she was—that she was—

Dead.

The tears spilled over, blinding him. He raised his hands to cover his face and wept where he stood.

His name was Ren Zel dea'Judan, Clan Obrelt. He was twenty-one Standard years old and the hope of all his kin.

*

They were shopkeepers, Clan Obrelt. It scarcely mattered what sort of shop, as long as it wanted keeping. In the hundreds of years since the first dea'Judan took up the trade, Obrelt had kept flower shops, sweet shops, hardware shops, book shops, wine shops, green groceries and shops too odd to mention. The shops they kept were never their own, but belonged to other, wealthier, Clans who lacked Obrelt's genius for management.

Having found a trade that suited them, Obrelt was not minded to change. They settled down to the work with a will and achieved a certain reputation. Eventually, it came to be Obrelt managers that the High Clans sought to manage the stores the High Clans owned. In the way of commerce, the price that Obrelt might ask of Clans desirous of employing their shopkeepers rose.

The House became—not wealthy, not in any Liaden terms—but comfortably well-off. Perhaps not nearly so well-off by the standard of the far homeworld, Liad itself; but comfortable enough by the easy measure of outworld Casia.

A Clan of shopkeepers, they married and begat more shopkeepers, though the occasional accountant, or librarian, or Healer was born. These changelings puzzled the Clan elders when they appeared, but honor and kin-duty were served and each was trained to that which he suited, to the increase and best advantage of the Clan.

Into Clan Obrelt, then, in the last relumma of the year called Mitra, a boychild was born. He was called Ren Zel, after the grandfather who had first taken employ in a shop and thus found the Clan its destiny, and he was a normal enough child of the House, at first, second and third counting.

He was quick with his numbers, which pleased Aunt Chane, and had a tidy, quiet way about him, which Uncle Arn Eld noted and approved. No relative was fond enough to proclaim him a beauty, though all allowed him to be neatly made and of good countenance. His hair and eyes were brown; his skin a rich, unblemished gold.

As befit a House in comfortable circumstance, Obrelt was wealthy in children. Ren Zel, quiet and tidy, was invisible amid the gaggle of his cousins. His three elder sisters remembered, sometimes, to pet him, or to scold him, or to tease him. When they noticed him at all, the adults found him respectful, current in his studies, and demure—everything that one might expect and value in the child of a shopkeeper who was destined, himself, one day to keep shop.

It was Aunt Chane who first suspected, in the relumma he turned twelve, that Ren Zel was perhaps destined to be something other than a shopkeeper. It was she who gained the Delm's permission to take him down to Pilot's Hall in Casiaport. There, he sat with his hands demurely folded while a lady not of his Clan tossed calculations at him, desiring him merely to give the answer that came into his head.

That was a little frightening at first, for Aunt Chane had

taught him to always check his numbers on the computer, no matter how certain he was, and he didn't like to be wrong in front of a stranger and perhaps bring shame to his House. The lady's first calculations were easy, though, and he answered nearly without thinking. The quicker he answered, the quicker the lady threw the next question, until Ren Zel was tipped forward in his chair, face animated, brown eyes blazing in a way that had nothing tidy or quiet about it. He was disappointed when the lady held up her hand to show she had no more questions to ask.

Also that day, he played catch with a very odd ball that never quite would travel where one threw it—at least, it didn't the first few times Ren Zel tried. On his fourth try, he suddenly understood that this was only another iteration of the calculations the lady had tossed at him, and after that the ball went where he meant it to go.

After the ball, he was asked to answer timed questions at the computer, then he was taken back to his aunt.

She looked down at him and there was something . . . odd about her eyes, which made him think that perhaps he should have asked the lady's grace to check his numbers, after all.

"Did I do well, Aunt?" he blurted, and Aunt Chane sighed.

"Well?" she repeated, reaching to take his hand and turning toward the door. "It's the Delm who will decide that for us, youngling."

Obrelt Himself, informed in private of the outcome of the tests, was frankly appalled.

"Pilot? Are they certain?"

"Not only certain, but—enthusiastic," Chane replied. "The Master Pilot allows me to know that our Ren Zel is more than a step out of the common way, in her experience of pilot-candidates."

"Pilot," the Delm moaned and went over to the table to pour himself a second glass of wine. "Obrelt has never bred a pilot."

Chane pointed out, dryly, that it appeared they had, in this instance, bred what might be trained into a very fine pilot, indeed. To the eventual increase of the Clan.

That caught Obrelt's ear, as she had known it would, and he brightened briefly, then moved a hand in negation. "All very well to say the *eventual* increase! In the near while, have you any notion how much it costs to train a pilot?"

As it happened, Chane did, having taken care to possess herself of information she knew would lie near to Obrelt's concern.

"Twenty-four cantra, over the course of four years, apprentice fees for two years more, plus licensing fees."

Obrelt glared at her. "You say that so calmly. Tell me, sister, shall I beggar the Clan to educate one child? I allow him to be extraordinary, as he has managed to become your favorite, though we have prettier, livelier children among us."

"None of whom is Ren Zel," Chane returned tartly. She sighed then and grudgingly showed her lead card. "A first class pilot may easily earn eight cantra the Standard, on contract."

Obrelt choked on his wine.

"They say the boy will achieve first class?" he managed a few moments later, his voice breathless and thin.

"They say it is *not impossible* for the boy to achieve first class," she replied. "However, even a second class pilot may earn five cantra the Standard."

'May'," repeated Obrelt.

"If he brings the Clan four cantra the Standard, he will pay back his education right speedily," Chane said. Observing that her brother wavered, she played her trump.

"The Pilot's Guild will loan us his first two year's tuition and fees, interest-free, until he begins to earn wages. If he achieves first class, they will write paid to the loan."

Obrelt blinked. "As desirous of the child as that?"

"He is," Chane repeated patiently, "more than a step out of the common way. Master Pilot von'Eyr holds herself at your pleasure, should you have questions for her."

"Hah. So I may." He walked over to the window and stood looking down into the modest garden, hands folded behind his back. Chane went to the table, poured herself a glass of wine and sipped it, recruiting herself to patience.

Eventually, Obrelt turned away from the window and came forward to face her.

"It is a strange path we would set the child upon, sister, to a place where none of his age-mates may follow. He will sail between stars while his cousins inventory stock in back storerooms. I ask you, for you have given him his own room in your heart: Do we serve him ill or well by making him a stranger to his kin?"

And that was the question that needed to be asked, when all considerations of cantra-costs were ended. What was best done for Ren Zel himself, for the good of all the Clan?

Chane set her glass aside and met her Delm's eyes straightly.

"He is already a stranger among us," she said, speaking as truly as she knew how. "Among his age-mates he is a cipher—he is liked, perhaps, but largely ignored. He goes his own way, quiet, tidy, courteous—and invisible. Today—today, when the pilots returned him to me, it was as if I beheld an entirely different child. His cheeks glowed, his eyes sparkled, he walked at the side of the Master Pilot visible and proud." She took a breath, sighed it out.

"Brother, this boy is not a shopkeeper. Best for us all that we give him the stars."

And so it was decided.

*

Ren Zel achieved his first class piloting license on the nineteenth anniversary of his Name Day. He was young for the rank, especially for one who had not sprung from a piloting House, but not precocious.

Having thus canceled out half of his tuition and fees, he set himself to paying off the balance as quickly as possible. It had been plain to him for several years that the Clan had gone to extraordinary expense on his behalf and he did not wish his cousins to be burdened by a debt that rightly belonged only to himself. That being so, he had the Guild accountant write a contract transferring the amount owed from Clan Obrelt to Ren Zel dea'Judan Clan Obrelt, as a personal debt.

He was young, but he had a reputation among the elder

pilots with whom he'd flown for being both steady and level-headed, a reputation they were glad to broadcast on the Port.

That being so, contracts came his way—good contracts, with pay-outs in the top percentage of the Guild's rates. Often enough, there was a bonus, for Ren Zel had a wizard's touch with a coord string—or so his elders praised him. Those same elders urged him to go for Master, and he thought he would, someday.

After he cleared his debt.

*

It was night port at Casia by the time he finished shutdown and gave the ship into the keeping of the client's agent. Ren Zel slung his kit over a shoulder and descended the ramp, filling his lungs with free air. World air tasted different than ship air, though he would have been hard put to say which flavor he preferred, beyond observing that, of world air, he found Casia's the sweetest.

At the bottom of the ramp, he turned right and walked leisurely through the night-yard, then out into the thoroughfare of Main Port.

The job he had just completed had been profitable—an exhilarating run, in fact, with the entire fee paid up front and a generous bonus at the far end. A half-dozen more like it would retire his debt. Not that such runs were common.

Night-port was tolerably busy. He saw a pilot he knew and raised a hand in greeting. The other waved and cut across the crowded walkway.

"Ren Zel! I haven't seen you in an age! There's a lot of us down at Findoir's—come and share a glass or two!"

He smiled, but moved his hand in a gesture of regret. "I'm just in. Haven't been to Guild Hall yet."

"Well, there's a must," the other allowed cheerfully. "Come after you've checked in, do, for I tell you we mean to make a rare night of it. Otaria's gotten her first."

"No, has she? Give her my compliments."

"Come down after you've checked in and give them to her yourself," his friend said, laying a hand briefly on his sleeve. "Until soon, Ren Zel."

"Until soon, Lai Tor."

Warmed, he continued on his way and not many minutes later walked up the stairs into Casiaport Guild Hall.

The night clerk took his license, scanned it and slid it back across the counter. "Welcome home, Pilot." She tapped keys, frowning down at her readout. Ren Zel put his card away and waited while she accessed his file.

"Two deposits have been made to your account," she said, scrolling down. "One has cleared, and twelve percent Clan share has been paid. Eleven-twelfths of the balance remaining has gone against the Pilots Guild Tuition Account, per standing orders. No contracts pending . . ." She paused, then glanced up. "I have a letter for you, Pilot. One moment." She left the console and walked to the back.

Ren Zel frowned. A letter? A *paper* letter? Who would—

The clerk was back, holding a buff colored envelope. She used her chin to point at the palm reader set into the surface of the counter.

"Verification please, Pilot."

Obediently, he put his palm over the reader, felt the slight tingle, heard the beep. He lifted his hand and the clerk handed him the envelope. His fingers found the seal embossed on the sealed flap—Obrelt's sign.

Ren Zel inclined his head to the clerk.

"My thanks."

"Well enough," she replied and looked once more to her screen. "Status?"

He paused on the edge of telling her "on-call," feeling the envelope absurdly heavy in his hand.

"Unavailable," he said, fingers moving over the seal.

She struck a last key and inclined her head.

"So recorded."

"My thanks," he said again and, shouldering his kit, walked across the hall to the common room.

As luck would have it, the parlor was empty. He closed the door behind him, dropped his kit and slid his finger under the seal.

A letter from Obrelt? His hands were not quite steady as he unfolded the single sheet of paper. Paper letters had weight, and were not dispatched for pleasantries.

Has someone died? he wondered, and hoped that it might not be Chanc, or Arn Eld or—

The note was brief, written in Obrelt's Own Hand.

Ren Zel dea'Judan was required at his Clan house, immediately upon receipt of this letter.

His Delm judged it time for him to wed.*

It was morning when the taxi pulled up before Obrelt's house. Ren Zel paid the fare, then stood on the walkway until the cab drove away.

He had not come quite "immediately," there being no reason to rouse the House at midnight when so many were required to rise early and open the various shops under Obrelt's care. And he was himself the better for a shower, a nap and a change of clothes, though it was still not easy to consider the reason he had been summoned home.

Home.

Ren Zel turned and looked up the walk, to the fence and the gate and the tall town house beyond them. He had grown up in this House, among the noisy gaggle of his sibs and cousins; it was to this House that he had returned on his brief holidays from school. Granted, he had come back less often after he had finished with his lessons, but there had been flight time to acquire, techniques to master and the first class to win.

Once he held first class, of course, there had been contracts to fulfill, the debt to reduce. Between contracts, he had routinely kept his status on "on-call," which required him to lodge at the Guildhall. The debt shrunk, but so, too, did his contact with his family.

He looked at the gate, and took a deep breath, steeling himself as if for some dreaded ordeal. Which was nonsense. Beyond the gate were only his kin—his Clan, which existed to shelter him and to care for him and to shield him from harm.

He took a step up the walkway.

The gate in the wall surrounding Obrelt's house sprang

open and a woman emerged from the fastness beyond, walking briskly in her neat, shopkeeper's uniform and her sensible boots, a manager's clipboard cuddled against her breast.

She saw him and checked, eyes widening for the leather-jacketed stranger on Obrelt's very walk. Ren Zel held out his hands, palms showing empty.

"Eba," he said softly to his next eldest sister, "it is I."

"Ren Zel?" Her gaze moved over his face, finding enough of Obrelt there to soothe her into a smile and a step forward, hand extended. "Brother, I scarcely knew you!"

He smiled in his turn and went to take her hand.

"The jacket disarmed you, doubtless."

She laughed, kin-warm. "Doubtless. Jump-pilot, eh? It suits you extremely."

Eba had been his favorite sister—young enough not to entirely despise the childish projects of a younger brother, yet old enough to stand as sometimes ally against the more boisterous of the cousins. Ren Zel pressed her fingers.

"I find you well?"

"Well," she conceded, and then, playfully, "And well you find me at all, rogue! How many relumma have passed since you last came to us? I suppose it's nothing to you that I am tomorrow sent to Morjan for a twelve-day? I was to have left today, but necessity calls me to the shop. Say at least you will be at Prime!"

"I believe I shall," he said. "The Delm calls me home, on business."

"Ah!" She looked wise. "One had heard something of that. You will be pleased, I think." She dropped his hand and patted the leather sleeve of his jacket. "Go on inside. I must to the shop."

"Yes, of course." She read his hesitation, though, and laughed softly, shaking her glossy dark hair back.

"You cannot stand out on the walk all day, you know! Until Prime, Ren Zel!"

"Until Prime, Eba," he replied, and watched her down the walk. She turned at the corner without looking back. Ren Zel squared his shoulders, walked up to the gate and lay his palm against the plate.

A heartbeat later, he was within Obrelt's walls. Directly thereafter, the front door accepted his palmprint and he stepped into the house.

His nose led him to the dining room, and he stood on the threshold several minutes before one of the cousins caught sight of him, touched the arm of the cousin next to him, who turned, then spoke quickly—quietly—to the cousin next to *her* until in no time the whole busy, bustling room was still, all eyes on the man under the archway.

"Well." One stirred, stood up from her place at the table.

"Don't dawdle in the doorway, child," said Aunt Chane, for all the stars as if he were ten again. "Come in and break your fast."

"Yes, Aunt," he said meekly and walked forward. The cousins shook themselves, took up the threads of their conversations, poured tea and chose slices of sweet toast. Ren Zel came to the table and made his bow.

"Ma'am."

"Ren Zel." She held out a hand, beckoning, and he stepped to her side. Chane smiled, then, and kissed his cheek. "Welcome home."

*

Aunt Chane sat on the short side of the table across which Ren Zel and Obrelt Himself faced each other, in the Advocate's Chair. The wine was poured and the ritual sip taken; then the glasses were set aside and Obrelt laid the thing out.

"The name of the lady we propose for your wife is Elsu Meriandra, Clan Jabun," he said, in his usual bluff way.

Ren Zel blinked, for Jabun was a Clan old in piloting. Certainly, it was not Korval, but for outworld Casia it was very well indeed—and entirely above Obrelt's touch.

The Delm held up a hand. "Yes, they are beyond us absolutely—pilots to shopkeepers. But Obrelt has a pilot of its own to bring to the contract suite and Jabun was not uninterested."

But surely, Ren Zel thought, surely, the only way in which

Obrelt might afford such a contract was to cede the child to Jabun—and that made no sense at all. Jabun was a Clan of pilots, allied with other of the piloting Houses. What use had they for the seed of a child of Obrelt, bred of shopkeepers, the sole pilot produced by the House in all its history? He was a fluke, a changeling; no true-breeding piloting stock such as they might wish to align with themselves.

"The child of the contract," his Delm continued, "will come to Obrelt."

Well, yes, and *that* made sense, if Obrelt found pilot wages to its taste and wished to diversify its children. But, gods, the expense! And no guarantee that his child would be any more pilot than Eba!

"No," Aunt Chane said dryly, "we have not run mad. Recruit yourself, child."

Ren Zel took a deep breath. "One wishes not to put the Clan into shadow," he said softly.

"We have been made to understand this," Obrelt said, of equal dryness with his sister. "Imagine my astonishment when I learned that a debt contracted by the House for the good of the House had been reassigned to one Ren Zel dea'Judan Clan Obrelt. At his request, of course."

"My contracts are profitable," Ren Zel murmured. "There was no need for the House to bear the burden."

"The Clan receives a tithe of your wages," Aunt Chane pointed out.

He inclined his head. "Of course."

He looked up in time to see his Aunt and his Delm exchange a look undecipherable to him. The Delm cleared his throat.

"Very well. For the matter at hand—Jabun and I have reached an equitable understanding. Jabun desires his daughter to meet you before the lines are signed. That meeting is arranged for tomorrow evening, at the house of Jabun. The lines will be signed on the day after, here in our own house. The contract suite stands ready to receive you."

The day after tomorrow? Ren Zel thought, feeling his

stomach clench as it did when he faced an especially tricksy bit of piloting. Precisely as if he were sitting board, he took a breath and forced himself to relax. Of course, he would do as his Delm instructed him—obedience to the Delm, subservience to the greater good of the Clan, was bred deep in his bones. To defy the Delm was to endanger the Clan, and without the Clan there was no life. It was only—the matter came about so quickly . . .

"There was a need for haste," Aunt Chane said, for the second time apparently reading his mind. "Pilot Meriandra's ship is come into dock for rebuilding and she is at liberty to marry. It amuses Jabun to expand his alliances—and it profits Obrelt to gain for itself the child of two pilots." She paused. "Put yourself at ease: the price is not beyond us."

"Yes, Aunt," he said, for there was nothing else to say. Two days hence, he would be wed; his child to come into Clan, to be sheltered and shaped by those who held his interests next to their hearts. The Code taught that this was well, and fitting, and just. He had no complaint and ought, indeed, feel honored, that the Clan lavished so much care on him.

But his stomach was still uncertain when they released him at last to settle his business at the Port and to register his upcoming marriage with the Guild.

*

The lines were signed, the contract sealed. Elsu Meriandra received her Delm's kiss and obediently allowed her hand to be placed into the hand of Delm Obrelt.

"Behold, the treasure of our Clan," Jabun intoned, while all of Clan Obrelt stood witness. "Keep her safe and return her well to us, at contract's end."

"Willingly we receive Elsu, the treasure of Jabun," Obrelt responded. "Our House stands vigilant for her, as if for one of our own."

"It is well," Jabun replied, and bowed to his daughter. "Rest easy, my child, in the House of our ally."

The cousins came forward then to make their bows. Ren Zel stood at the side of his contract-bride and made her known to each, from Obrelt Himself down to the youngest child in the nursery—his sister Eba's newest.

After that, there was the meal of welcoming. Ren Zel, who held lesser rank in Obrelt than his wife held in Jabun, was seated considerably down-table. This was according to Code, which taught that Obrelt could not impose Ren Zel's status on Elsu, who was accustomed to sitting high; nor could her status elevate him, since she was a guest in his House.

He had eaten but lightly of the meal, listening to the cousins on either side talk shop. From time to time he glimpsed his wife, high up-table between his sister Farin and his cousin Wil Bar, fulfilling her conversational duty to her meal partners. She did not look down-table.

The meal at last over, Ren Zel and Aunt Chane escorted Jabun's treasure throughout Obrelt's house, showing her the music room, the formal parlor and the tea room, the game room and the door to the back garden. In the library, Aunt Chane had her place a palm against the recording plate. This registered her with the House computer and insured that the doors allowed to contract-spouses would open at her touch.

Departing the library, they turned left down the hall, not right toward the main stair, and Aunt Chane led the way up the private stairway to the closed wing. In the upper hallway, she paused by the first door and bowed to Elsu Meriandra.

"Your room, contract-daughter. If you find aught awry, only pick up the house phone and call me. It will be my honor to repair any error."

Elsu bowed in turn.

"The House shows me great kindness," she said, most properly, her high, sweet voice solemn. She straightened and put her hand against the plate. The door slid open and she was gone, though Ren Zel thought she looked at him, a flickering glance through modestly lowered lashes, in the instant before the door closed behind her.

Though it was not necessary, Aunt Chane guided him to the third and last door on the hallway. She turned and smiled.

"Temporary quarters."

This sort of levity was not like his Aunt and Ren Zel was startled into a smile of his own. "Thank you, ma'am."

"Thank us, is it?" She tipped her head, considering him in the hall's dim light. "Let the flowers aid you," she said softly. "It will be well, child."

He had his doubts, in no way alleviated by the few words he had actually exchanged with his wife, but it would serve no useful purpose to share them with Aunt Chane. The Clan desired a child born of the union of pilots: His part was plainly writ.

So, he smiled again and raised her hand, laying his cheek against the backs of her fingers in a gesture of kin-love. "It will be well," he repeated, for her comfort.

"Ah." She seemed on the edge of saying something further, but in the end simply inclined her head before walking, alone, back the way they had come.

After a moment, Ren Zel put his hand against the door and entered his temporary quarters.

He had been here yesterday, moving in his clothes and such of his books as he thought would be prudent. He had even opened the inner door and gone into the middle room—into the contract room itself—walking lightly on the lush carpet.

The bed was ornate, old, and piled high with pillows. The flowers twined up two bedposts and climbed across the connecting bars, spilling down in luxuriant curtains of green and blue. Sunlight poured down from the overhead window, heating the blossoms and releasing the aphrodisiac scent. Standing by the wine-table, Ren Zel had felt his blood stir and taken a step away, deliberately turning his back on the bed.

The rest of the room was furnished but sparsely: there was the wine-table, of course, and a small table with two chairs, at which two might take a private meal; and a wide, yellow brocade sofa facing a fireplace where sweet logs were laid, awaiting the touch of a flamestick. The solitary window was that above the bed; the walls were covered in nubbled silk the color of the brocaded sofa.

Across the room—directly across the room from the door by which he had entered—was another door. Beyond, he knew, was another room, like the room he had just quit, where his sisters were laying out those things Elsu Meriandra had sent ahead.

Some trick of the rising heat had filled his nostrils with flower-scent again and Ren Zel had retreated to his own quarters, locking the door to the contract-room behind him.

Now, showered and dressed in the robe his sisters had given him in celebration of his marriage, he paused to consider what little he knew of his wife.

She was his elder by nearly three Standards, fair-haired, wide-eyed and comely. He thought that she was, perhaps, a little spoilt, and he supposed that came of being the true-daughter of a High Clan Delm. Her manners were not entirely up in the boughs, however, and she spoke to Aunt Chane precisely as she ought. If she had little to say to him beyond those things that the Code demanded, it was scarcely surprising. He was in all things her inferior: rank, flight-time, age, and beauty. And, truth be told, they had not been brought together to converse.

That which had brought them together—well. He had taken himself to the sleep learner, to review the relevant section of Code, for the contract-bed was a far different thing than a breakshift tumble with a comrade—and there his wife had the advantage of him again. She had been married once already, to a pilot near her equal her rank, and Jabun had her child in its keeping.

Sighing, he straightened his garment about him, catching a glimpse of himself in the mirror: Ordinary, practical Ren Zel, got up in a magnificent indigo-and-silver marriage robe that quite overwhelmed his commonplace features. Sighing again, he glanced at the clock on the dresser.

The hour was upon him.

Squaring his shoulders under their burden of embroidery, Ren Zel went to the inner door, and lay his palm against the plate. The door opened.

Elsu Meriandra was at the wine table, back to him. Her hair was loose on her shoulders, her robe an expensive simplicity of flowing golden shadowsilk, through which he could plainly see her body. She heard the door open and turned, her eyes wide, lustrous with the spell of the bed-flowers.

"Good evening," she said, her high voice sounding

somewhat breathless. "Will you drink a glass with me . . . Ren Zel?"

His name. A good sign, that. Ren Zel took a breath, tasting the flowers, and deliberately drew the scent deep into his lungs. He smiled at the woman before him.

"I will be happy to share a glass with you, Elsu," he said softly, and stepped into the contract-room.

*

Ren Zel woke in the room he had been allotted, and stretched, luxuriating in his solitude even as he cataloged his various aches. The lady was not a gentle lover. He thought he could have borne this circumstance with more equanimity, had he any indication that her exuberance sprang from an enthusiasm for himself. To the contrary, she had brushed his attentions aside, as one might dismiss the annoying graspings of a child.

Well, he thought ruefully, he had heard that the flower did sometimes produce . . . unwarranted . . . effects.

So thinking, he rolled neatly out of bed, showered, and dressed in his usual plain shirt and pants. He stamped into his boots and picked up his latest book—a slender volume of Terran poetry. The habit of taking a book with him to breakfast had formed when he was a child and it had come to his notice that the cousins let him be, if he were diligently reading.

He was passing the game room on his way to the dining hall when the sound of child's laughter gave him pause.

It was not entirely . . . comfortable . . . laughter, he thought. Rather, it sounded breathless, and just a little shrill. Ren Zel put his hand against the door and, quietly, looked inside.

Elsu Meriandra was playing catch with young Son Dor, who had, Ren Zel remembered, all of eight Standards. She was pitching the ball sharply and in unexpected directions, exactly as one might do when playing with a pilot—or one destined to be a pilot.

Son Dor was giving a good accounting of himself, considering that he was neither a pilot nor the child of a pilot. But he was clearly at the limit of both his speed and his skill, chest heaving and face wet with exertion. As Ren Zel watched, he dove for the ball, reacting to its motion, rather than anticipating its probable course, actually got a hand on it and cradled it against his chest. He threw it, none too steadily, back to Elsu Meriandra, who fielded the toss smoothly.

"That was a good effort," she said, as Ren Zel drifted into the room, meaning to speak to her, to offer her a tour of the garden and thus allow Son Dor to escape with his melant'i intact.

"Try this one," Elsu said and Ren Zel saw her hands move in the familiar sequence, giving the ball both velocity and spin. Dropping his book, he leapt, extended an arm and snagged the thing at the height of its arc. He danced in a circle, the sphere spinning in a blur from hand to hand, force declining, momentum slowing, until it was only a ball again—a toy, and nothing likely to break a child's fragile fingers, extended in a misguided attempt to catch it.

"Cousin Ren Zel!" Son Dor cried. "I could have caught it! I could have!"

Ren Zel laughed and danced a few more steps, the ball spinning lazily now on the tips of his fingers.

"Of course you could have, sweeting," he said, easily. "But you were having so much fun, it was more than I could do not to join in." He smiled, the ball spinning slowly. "Catch now," he said to Son Dor, and allowed the toy to leave his fingers.

The child rushed forward and caught it with both hands.

"Well done!" Ren Zel applauded. Son Dor flushed with pleasure and tossed the ball back. Ren Zel caught it one-handed, and allowed his gaze to fall upon the wall clock.

"Cousin," he said, looking back to the child, "is it not time for history lessons?"

Son Dor spun, stared at the clock, gasped, and spun back, remembering almost at once to make his bow.

"Ma'am, forgive me. I am wanted at my studies."

"Certainly," Elsu said. "Perhaps we might play ball again, when your studies free you."

Son Dor looked just a bit uneasy about that, but replied courteously. "It would be my pleasure, ma'am." He glanced aside.

"Cousin . . ."

Ren Zel waved a hand. "Yes, all you like, but do not, I implore you, be late to Uncle Arn Eld. You know how he grumbles when one is late!"

Apparently Son Dor knew just that, and the knowledge gave his feet wings. The door thumped closed behind him and Ren Zel let out his breath in a long sigh before turning to face Elsu Meriandra.

She was standing with her head tipped, an expression of amused curiosity upon her face.

"He is not," Ren Zel said, stringently even, "a pilot. He will never be a pilot."

She frowned slightly at that and motioned for the ball. He threw it to her underhanded and she brought it, spinning hard, up onto her fingers.

"Are you certain of that, I wonder? Sometimes, when they are young, they are a little lazy. When that is the case, the spinball may be depended upon to produce the correct response."

Ren Zel moved his shoulders, letting the tension flow out of him. She did not understand—how could she? Pilot from a House of pilots. He sighed.

"The children of this House are shopkeepers. They have the reactions and the instincts of shopkeepers." He paused, thinking of Son Dor, laboring after a toss that a pilot's child would find laughably easy.

"He was striving not to disappoint," he told Elsu Meriandra. "What you see as 'a little lazy' is Son Dor's best reaction time. The spinball—forgive me—damage might well have been done."

Her face blanked. She caught the ball with a snap and bowed, unexpectedly low. "It was not my intention to endanger a child of the House."

She straightened and looked at him out of the sides of her eyes. "One was told, of course, but it is difficult to recall that this is not a House of pilots. Especially when there is yourself! Why, one can hardly hold a conversation in Guild Hall without hearing of your accomplishments!" She bowed again, more lightly this time.

"You do our Guild great honor."

She did not wait for his reply, but turned and crossed the room to put the ball away. After a moment, Ren Zel went to pick up his fallen book.

"What have you?" she asked from just behind him. He turned and showed her the cover.

She frowned at the outlandish lettering. "That is Terran, is it not?"

"Indeed. *Duet for the Star Routes* is the title. Poetry."

"You read Terran?" She seemed somewhat nonplused by this information.

"I read Terran—a little. I am reading poetry to sharpen my comprehension, since I find it a language strong in metaphor."

Elsu moved her gaze from the book to his face. "You speak Terran."

That was not a question, but he answered it anyway. "Not very well, I fear. I meet so few to practice against that my skill is very basic."

"Why," she asked, the frown back between her eyes, "would you wish to learn these things?"

Ren Zel blinked. "Well, I am a pilot. My craft takes me to many ports, some of them Terran. I was . . . dismayed . . . not to be able to converse with my fellows on those ports and so I began to study." He paused. "Do you not speak Terran?"

"I do not," she returned sharply. "I speak Trade, which is sufficient, if I am impelled into conversation with—with someone who is not able to speak the High Tongue."

"I see," Ren Zel murmured, wondering how to extricate himself from a conversation that was growing rapidly unpleasant for them both. Before he arrived at a solution, however, the lady changed the subject herself.

"Come, we are both pilots—one of us at least legendary in skill!" she said gaily. "What do you say we shake the House dust from our feet and fly?"

It sounded a good plan, he owned; for he was weary of being House-bound already. There was, however, one difficulty.

"I regret," he said, his voice sounding stiff in his own ears.

"Obrelt does not keep a ship. One is a pilot-for-hire."

"As I am," she said brightly. "But do not repine, if you haven't your own ship. I own one and will gladly have you sit second board."

Well, and that was generous enough, Ren Zel thought. Indeed, the more he thought about it, the better the scheme appeared. They were, as she said, both pilots. Perhaps they might win through to friendship, if they sat board together. Only look at what had lain between himself and Lai Tor—and see what comrades they had become, after shared flight had made their minds known to each other.

So—"You are generous," he told Elsu Meriandra. "It would be pleasant to stretch one's wings."

"Good. Let me get my jacket. I will meet you in the front hall."

"Well enough," he said. "I will inform the House."

*

Elsu's ship was a small middle-aged packetspacer, built for intra-system work, not for hyperspace. It would also, Ren Zel thought, eyeing its lines as he followed his contract-wife toward the ramp, do well in atmospheric flight. The back-swept wings and needle-nose gave it an eerie resemblance to the raptors that lived in the eaves of the Port Tower, preying on lesser birds and mice.

"There," Elsu used her key and the ship's door slid open. She stepped inside and turned to make him an exaggerated bow, her blue eyes shining.

"Pilot, be welcome on my ship."

He bowed honor to the owner and stepped into the ship. The hatch slid shut behind him.

Elsu led the way down the companionway to the piloting chamber. She fair flung herself into the chair, her hands flying across the board, rousing systems, initiating checks. From the edge of the chamber, Ren Zel watched as she woke her ship, her motions nearer frenzy than the smooth control his teachers had bade him strive to achieve.

She turned in the pilot's chair, her face flushed, eyes

brilliantly blue, and raised a hand to beckon him forward.

"Come, come! Second board awaits you, as we agreed! Sit and make yourself known to the ship!" Her high voice carried a note that seemed to echo the frenzy of her board-run and Ren Zel hesitated a moment longer, not quite trusting—

"So an intra-system is not to your liking?" she inquired, her voice sharp with ridicule. "Perhaps the legendary Ren Zel dea'Judan flies only Jumpships."

That stung, and he very nearly answered in kind. Then he recalled her as she had been the night before, inflicting her hurts, tempting him, or so it seemed, to hurt her in return—and he made his answer mild.

"Indeed, I took my second class on just such a ship as this," he said and walked forward at last to sit in the co-pilot's chair.

She glanced at him out of the edge of her eyes. "Forgive me, Pilot. I am not usually so sharp. The lift will improve my temper."

He could think of nothing to say to that and covered this lapse by sliding his license into the slot. There was a moment's considering pause from the ship's computer, then his board came live with a beep. Ren Zel initiated systems check.

Elsu Meriandra was already on line to the Tower, requesting clearance. "On business of Clan Jabun," Ren Zel heard and spun in his chair to stare at her. To characterize a mere pleasure-lift as—

His wife cut the connection to the Tower, looked over to him and laughed. "Oh, wonderful! And say you have never told Tower that a certain lift was just a little more urgent than the facts supported!"

"And yet we are not on the business of Clan Jabun," Ren Zel pointed out, remembering to speak mildly.

"Pah!" she returned, her fingers dancing across the board, waking the gyros and the navcomp. "It is certainly in the best interest of Jabun that one of its children not deteriorate into a jittercase, for cause of being worldbound." She leaned back in the pilot's chair and sighed. "Ah, but it will be fine to lift, will it not, Pilot?"

"Yes," Ren Zel said truthfully. "Whither bound, Pilot?"

"Just into orbit, I think, and a long skim down. Do you fancy a late-night dinner at Head o'Port when we are through?"

Ren Zel's entire quartershare was insufficient to purchase a dinner at Head o'Port, which he rather thought she knew.

"Why not a glass and a dinner at Findoir's? There are bound to be some few of our comrades there."

She moved her shoulders. The comm beeped and she flipped the toggle.

"*Dancer*."

While she listened to Tower's instruction, Ren Zel finished his board checks and, seeing that she was feeding coords into her side, reached 'round to engage the shock webbing.

"Pilot?" he inquired, when she made no move to do the same.

"Eh?" She blinked at him, then smiled. "Oh, I often fly unwebbed! It enhances the pleasure immeasurably."

Perhaps it did, but it was also against every regulation he could think of. He opened his mouth to say so, but she waved a slim hand at him.

"No, do not say it! Regulation is all very well when one is flying contract, but this is pleasure, and I intend to be pleased!" She turned back to her board. The seconds to lift were counting down on the center board. Ren Zel ran another quick, unobtrusive check, then Elsu hit the engage and they were rising.

It was a fine, blood-warming thing, that lift. Elsu flew at the very edge of her craft's limits and Ren Zel found plenty to do as second board. He found her rhythm at last and matched it, the two of them putting the packet through its paces. They circled Casia twice, hand-flying, rather than let the automatics have it. Ren Zel was utterly absorbed by the task, caught up entirely in the other pilot's necessity, enwrapped in that state of vivid concentration that comes when one is flying well, in tune with one's flight-partner, and—

His board went dead.

Automatically, his hand flashed out, slapping the toggle for the back-up board.

Nothing happened.

"Be at ease, Pilot!" Elsu Meriandra murmured, next to him. "I have your board safe. And now we shall have us a marvelous skim!"

She'd overridden him. Ren Zel felt panic boil in his belly, forced himself to breathe deeply, to impose calm. He was second board on a ship owned by the pilot sitting first. As first, she had overridden his board. It was her right to do so, for any reason, or for none—regulations and custom backed her on this.

So, he breathed deeply, as he had been taught, and leaned back in his chair, the shock web snug around him, watching the descent on the screens.

Elsu's path of re-entry was steep—Ren Zel had once seen a tape of a Scout descent that was remarkably like the course she had chosen. She sat close over the board, unwebbed, her face intent, a fever-glitter in her eyes, her hands hurtling across her board, fingers flickering, frenzy just barely contained.

Ren Zel recruited his patience, watching the screens, the descent entirely out of his hands. Gods, how long since he had sat passenger, wholly dependent on another pilot's skill?

The ship hit atmosphere and turbulence in the same instant. There was a bump, and a twitch. Ren Zel flicked forward, hands on his useless board—and sat back as Elsu made the recover and threw him an unreadable look from over-brilliant blue eyes.

"Enjoy the skim, Pilot," she said. "Unless you doubt my skill?"

Well, no. She flew like a madwoman, true enough, but she had caught that boggle just a moment ago very smoothly, indeed.

The skim continued, and steeper still, until Ren Zel was certain that it was the old Scout tape she had fashioned her course upon.

He looked to the board, read hull-heat and external pressure, and did not say to the woman beside him that an old packet was never the equal of a Scout ship. She would have to level out soon, and take the rest of the skim at a shallow glide, until they had bled sufficient momentum to safely land.

She had not yet leveled out when they hit a second bit of

turbulence, this more demanding than the first. The ship bucked, twisted—again Ren Zel snapped to his dead board, and again the pilot on first corrected the boggle and flew on.

Moments passed, and still Elsu did not level their course.

Ren Zel leaned forward, checking gauges and tell-tales, feeling his stomach tighten.

"Pilot," he said moderately, "we must adjust course."

She threw him a glance. "Must we?" she asked, dulcet. "But I am flying this ship, Ren Zel dea'Judan."

"Indeed you are. However, if we do not level soon, even a pilot as skilled as yourself will find it—difficult—to pull out. This ship was not built for such entries."

"This ship," she stated, "will do what I wish it to do." Incredibly, she kept her course.

Ren Zel looked to the screens. They were passing over the ocean, near enough that he could see the v-wakes of the sea-ships, and, then, creeping into the edge of screen four, towering thunderheads where the water met the land.

"Pilot," he said, but Elsu had seen them.

"Aha! Now you shall see flying!"

They pierced the storm in a suicide rush; winds cycled, slapping them into a spin, Elsu corrected, and lightning flared, leaving screen three dead.

"Give me my board!" Ren Zel cried. "Pilot, as you love your life—"

She threw him a look in which he had no trouble reading hatred, and the wind struck again, slamming them near into a somersault in the instant her hand slapped the toggle. The cabin lights flickered as Ren Zel's board came live, and there was a short, snapped-off scream.

Poised over the board, he fought—fought the ship, fought the wind, fought his own velocity. The wind tossed the ship like so many flower petals, and they tumbled again. Ren Zel fought, steadied his craft and passed out of the storm, into a dazzle of sunlight and the realization that the ground was much too close.

He slapped toggles, got the nose up, rose, rose—

His board snapped and fizzed—desperately, he slapped the toggle for the secondary back-up.

There was none.

The ship screamed like a live thing when it slammed into the ground.

*

On the morning of his third day out of the healing unit and his second day at home, his sister Eba brought him fresh clothes, all neatly folded and smelling of sunshine. Her face was strained, her eyes red with weeping.

"You are called to the meeting between Obrelt and Jabun next hour, brother," she said, her voice husky and low. "Aunt Chane will come for you."

Ren Zel went forward a step, hand outstretched to the first of his kin he had seen or spoken to since the accident. "Eba?"

But she would not take his hand, she turned her face from him and all but ran from the room. The door closed behind her with the wearisome, too-familiar sound of the lock snapping to.

Next hour. In a very short time, he would know the outcome of Jabun's pursuit of Balance, though what Balance they might reasonably take remained, after three full days of thought on the matter, a mystery to him. The Guild would surely have recovered the flight box. They would have run the tape, built a sim, proven that it had been an accident, with no malice attached. A tragedy, surely, for Jabun to lose a daughter. A double tragedy, that she should die while in Obrelt's keeping. There would be the life-price to pay, but—Balance?

He considered the computer in its alcove near the window. Perhaps today he would be allowed to access the nets, to find what the world knew of this?

But no, he was a pilot and a pilot's understanding was quicker than that. He knew well enough the conditions of his tenure here. All praise to Terran poetry, he even knew the proper name for it.

House arrest

Escorted by med techs, he'd arrived home from the Medical

Center, and brought not to his own rooms, but to the Quiet Suite, where those who mourned, who were desperately ill—or dying—were housed. There was a med tech on-call. It was he who showed Ren Zel the computer, the call button, the bed; he who locked the door behind him when he left.

There was entertainment available if one wished to sit and watch, but the communit reached only the med tech and the computer accessed only neutral information—no news, no pilot-net; the standard piloting drills did not open to his code, nor had anyone brought his books, or asked if he wished to have them. This was not how kin cared for kin.

Slowly, Ren Zel went over to the pile of clean clothes. He slipped off the silver-and-indigo robe, and slowly, carefully, put on the modest white shirt and dark trousers. He sat down to pull his boots on and sat a little longer, listening to the blood singing in his ears. He was yet low of energy. It would take some time, so the med tech told him—perhaps as long as a relumma—to fully regain his strength. He had been advised to take frequent naps, and not to overtire himself.

Yes, very good.

He pushed himself to his feet and went back to the table. His jacket was there. Wonderingly, he shook it out, fingering the places where the leather had been mended, pieced together by the hand of a master. As he had been.

The touch and smell of the leather was a reassuring and personal commonplace among the bland and antiseptic ambiance of the quiet suite. He swung the jacket up and on, settling it on his shoulders, and looked at the remaining items on the table.

His piloting license went into its secret pocket. For a moment, he simply stared at the two cantra pieces, unable to understand why there should be so much money to his hand. In the end, still wondering, he slipped them into the pocket of his jacket.

Behind him, he heard the lock snap, and turned, with a bare fraction of his accustomed speed, staggering a little on the leg that had been crushed.

Chane dea'Judan stepped into the room, the door sliding

silently closed behind her. He stood where he was, uncertain, after Eba and two days of silence, what he might expect from his own kin.

If Aunt Chane will not speak to me, he thought, I will not be able to bear it.

She paused at the edge of the table and opened her arms. "Ren Zel."

He almost fell into the embrace. His cheek against her shoulder, he felt her stroke his hair as if he were small again and needing comfort after receiving some chance cruelty from one of his cousins.

"It's gone ill, child," she murmured at last and he stirred, straightened, and stood away, searching her solemn face.

"Ill," he repeated. "But the life-price of a pilot is set by the Guild. I will take the—" He stopped, struck dumb by the impossible.

Aunt Chane was weeping.

"Tell me," he said then. "Aunt?"

She took a moment to master herself, and met his eyes squarely.

"A life for a life," she said. "Jabun invokes the full penalty. Council and Guild uphold them."

He stared at her. "The flight box. Surely, the Guild has dumped the data from the flight box?"

"Dumped it and read it and sent it by direct pinbeam to a Master Pilot, who studied it and passed judgement," Aunt Chane said, her voice edged with bitterness. "Jabun turned his face from the Master Pilot's findings—and the request to hold open review at Casiaport Hall! He called on three first class pilots from Casiaport Guild to judge again. I am told that this is his right, under Guild law." She took a deep breath and looked him squarely in the eye.

"The honored pilots of Casiaport Guild find you guilty of negligence in flight, my child, the result of your error being that Pilot Elsu Meriandra untimely met her death."

But this was madness. They had the box, the actual recording of the entire flight, from engage to crash.

"Aunt—"

She held up her hand, silencing him.

"I have seen the tape." She paused, something like pride—or possibly awe—showing in her eyes. "You will understand that it meant very little to me. I was merely astonished that you could move so quickly, recover so well, only to have the ship itself fail you at the last instant. . . " Another pause.

"I have also read the report sent by the Master Pilot, who makes points regarding Pilot Meriandra's performance that were perhaps too hard for a father to bear. The Master Pilot was clear that the accident was engineered by Pilot Meriandra, that she had several times ignored your warnings, and that she had endangered both ship and pilots by denying you access to your board during most of the descent. That she was not webbed in . . ." Chane let that drift off. Ren Zel closed his eyes.

"I heard her scream, but I could not—the ship . . ."

"The Master Pilot commends you. The others . . ."

"The others," Ren Zel finished wearily, "are allied to Jabun and dare not risk his anger."

"Just so. And Obrelt—forgive us, child. Obrelt cannot shield you. Jabun has demonstrated that we will starve if we reject this Balancing."

"Demonstrated?"

She sighed. "Eba has been released from her position, her keys stripped from her by the owner before the entire staff of the shop. Wil Bar was served the same, though the owner there was kind enough to receive the keys in the privacy of the back office. Both owners are closely allied with Clan Jabun."

Gods. No wonder Eba wept and would not see him.

"We will mourn you," Aunt Chane said softly. "They cannot deny us that." She glanced at the clock, stepped up and offered her arm.

"It is time."

He looked into his Aunt's face, saw sorrow and necessity. Carefully, tender of the chancy leg, put his hand on the offered arm and allowed himself to be led downstairs to die.

*

The House's Modest ballroom was jammed to overflowing. All of Clan Obrelt, from the eldest to the youngest, were present to witness Ren Zel's death. Fewer of Clan Jabun were likewise present, scarcely a dozen, all adult, saving one child—a toddler with white-blonde hair and wide blue eyes that Ren Zel knew must be Elsu's daughter.

On the dais usually occupied by musicians during Obrelt's rare entertainments was a three-sided table. On the shortest side stood Ren Zel; Aunt Chane and Obrelt Himself were together at one of the longer sides; Jabun and his second, a grey-haired man with steel-blue eyes, stood facing them.

In the front row of witnesses sat a figure of neither House, an old and withered man who one might see a time or two a year, at weddings and funerals, always wearing the same expression of polite sadness: Tor Cam tel'Vana, the Eyes of Casia's Council of Clans.

"We are here," Jabun lifted his voice so that it washed against the far walls of the room, "to put the death upon the man who murdered Elsu Meriandra, pilot first class, daughter of Jabun."

"We are here," Obrelt's voice was milder, but no more difficult for those in the back to hear, "to mourn Obrelt's son Ren Zel, who dies as the result of a piloting accident."

Jabun glared, started—and was restrained by the hand of his second on his sleeve. Thus moderated, he turned his hot eyes to Ren Zel.

"What have you in your pockets, dead man? It is my Balance that you go forth from here nameless, rootless and without possessions."

Slowly, Ren Zel reached into his jacket pocket and withdrew the two cantra pieces.

"Put them on the table," Jabun hissed.

"He will return them to his pocket," Obrelt corrected and met the other's glare with a wide calmness. "Ren Zel belongs to Obrelt until he dies. It is the tradition of our Clan that the dead shall have two coins, one to an eye." He gestured toward the short side of the table, still holding Jabun's gaze. "Ren Zel, your pocket."

Obediently, he slipped the coins away.

Once again, Jabun sputtered; once again, he was held back by his second, who leaned forward and stared hard into Ren Zel's face.

"There is something else, dead man. We will see your license destroyed ere you are cast away."

Ren Zel froze. His license? Were they mad? How would he work? How would he live?

"My nephew gave his life for that license, Honored Sir," Aunt Chane said serenely. "He dies because he was worthy of it. What more fitting than it be interred with him?"

"That was not our agreement," the second stated.

"Our agreement," said Obrelt with unbreached calm, "was that Ren Zel dea'Judan be cast out of his Clan, and made a stranger to his kin, his loss to Obrelt to precisely Balance the loss of Elsu Meriandra to Clan Jabun. Elsu Meriandra was not made to relinquish her license in death. We desire, as Jabun desires, an exact Balancing of accounts."

Jabun Himself answered, and in such terms that Ren Zel would have trembled, had there been room for fear beside the agony in his heart.

"You think to buy him a life? Think again! What ship will employ a dead man? None that Jabun knows by name." He shifted, shaking off his second's hand.

In the first row of witnesses, the aged man rose. "These displays delay and impair the death," murmured the Eyes of Council. "Only his Delm may lay conditions upon a dying man, and there is no death until the Delm declares it." He paused, sending a thoughtful glance to Jabun. "The longest Balance-death recorded stretched across three sundowns."

Jabun glared briefly at the Eyes, then turned back to the table.

"He may retain the license," he said, waving his hand dismissively. "May it do him well in the Low Port."

There was silence; the Eyes bowed toward the Balancing table and reseated himself, hands folded on his knee.

Obrelt cleared his throat and raised his voice, chanting in

the High Tongue.

"Ren Zel dea'Judan, you are cast out, dead to Clan and kin. You are nameless, without claim or call upon this House. Begone. Begone." His voice broke, steadied.

"Begone."

Ren Zel stood at the small side of the table, staring out over the roomful of his kin. All the faces he saw were solemn; not a few were tear-tracked.

"Begone!" snarled Jabun. "Die, child-killer!"

In the back of the ballroom, one of the smallest cousins began to wail. Steeling himself, not daring to look at Chane, nor anywhere, save his own feet, Ren Zel walked forward, down the three steps to the floor; forward, down the thin path that opened as the cousins moved aside to let him gain the door; forward, down the hallway, to the foyer. The door stood open. He walked on, down the steps to the path, down the path to the gate.

"Go on!" Jabun shouted from behind. Ren Zel did not turn. He pushed the gate open and walked out.

The gate crashed shut behind him and he spun, his heart slamming into overaction. Shaking, he flattened his palm against the plate, felt the tingle of the reader and—

Nothing else. The gate remained locked. His print had been removed from the House computer. He was no longer of Obrelt.

He was dead.

*

It was full night when he staggered into the Pilots Guildhall in Casiaport. He'd dared not break a cantra for a taxi-ride and his clan-credit had proven dead when he tried to purchase a news flimsy with the headline over his photograph proclaiming "Pilot Dead in Flight Negligence Aftermath." His sight was weaving and he was limping heavily off the leg that had been crushed. He had seen Lai Tor in the street a block or an eternity over, raised his hand—and his friend turned his face aside and hurried off in the opposite direction.

Dead, Ren Zel thought, and smiled without humor. Very well, then.

A ghost, he walked into the Guildhall. The duty clerk looked up, took him in with a glance and turned her face away.

"You are not required to speak to me," Ren Zel said, and his voice sounded not quite . . . comfortable . . . in his own ears. "You are not required to acknowledge my presence in any way. However." He pulled his license from its secret pocket and lay it face down on the reader. "This license—this valid license—has a debt on it. This license will not be dishonored. List the license number as 'on-call,' duty clerk. The debt will be paid."

Silence from the clerk. No move, toward either the license or the computer.

Ren Zel took a ragged breath, gathering his failing resources. "Is Casiaport Guildhall in the practice of refusing repayment of contracted loans?"

The clerk sighed. Keeping her eyes averted, she turned, picked up the license and disappeared to the back.

Ren Zel gasped, questioning the wisdom of this play, now that it was too late, his license possibly forfeit, his life and his livelihood with—

The clerk reappeared. Eyes stringently downturned, she placed a sheet of printout and his license on the countertop. Then she turned her back on him.

Ren Zel's heart rose. It had worked! Surely, this was an assignment. Surely—

He snatched up his license and slipped it away, then grabbed the paper, forcing his wavering sight to focus, to find the name of the client, lift time, location.

It took him all of three heartbeats to realize that he was not looking at flight orders, but an invoice. It took another three heartbeats to understand that the invoice recorded the balance left to be paid on his loan, neatly zeroed out to three decimal places, "forgiven" stamped across the whole in tall blue letters, and then smaller blue letters, where the Guildmaster had dated the thing, and signed her name.

Tears rose. He blinked them away, concentrating on folding the paper with clumsy, shaking fingers. Well and truly, he was a dead man. Kinless, with neither comrades nor Guildmates to support him. Worldbound, without hope of work or flight, without even a debt to lend weight to his existence.

The paper was folded, more or less. He shoved it into his jacket pocket, squared his aching shoulders and went out into the Night Port.

On the walk, he turned right, toward Findoir's, taking all of two steps before recollecting himself. Not Findoir's. Every pilot on Port had news of his death by now.

His comrades would turn their faces away from him, as Lai Tor had. He might speak to them, but they would not answer. He was beyond them—outcast. Nameless. Guildless. Clanless.

Dead.

The tears rose again. He blinked them away, aghast. To weep openly in the street, where strangers might see him? Surely, even a ghost kept better Code than that.

He limped a few steps to the left and set his shoulders against the cool stone wall of Casiaport Guildhall. His chest hurt; the bad leg was afire, and the street scene before him seemed somewhat darker than even night might account for.

Ren Zel took a breath, imposing board-calm. Dispassionately, he cataloged his resources:

A first-class piloting license. A jump-pilot's spaceleather jacket, scarred and multiple patched. Two cantra.

He leaned his head against the stone, not daring to close his eyes, even here, in the relative safety of Main Port.

They expected that he would go to Low Port, Clan Jabun did. They expected him to finish his death there. Obrelt had cast against that, winning him the right to hold his license; winning him, so he must have thought, a chance to fly. To live.

And how had Jabun countered? Briefly, Ren Zel closed his eyes, seeing again the three-sided table, the crowd of cousins, weeping and pale; heard Jabun snarl: "What ship will employ a dead man? None that Jabun knows by name."

And that was his doom. There was no ship on Casiaport that Jabun could not name.

Or was there?

Ren Zel opened his eyes.

Jabun's daughter—had not spoken Terran.

Perhaps then her father did not know the names of all the ships on port.

He pushed away from the wall and limped down the walk, heading for Mid Port.

*

The man behind the desk took his license and slid it into the computer. His face was bored as he scrolled down the list of Ren Zel's completed assignments.

"Current," he said indifferently. "Everything in order, except . . ." The scrolling stopped. Ren Zel's mouth went dry and he braced himself against the high plastic counter. Now. Now was when the last hope died.

The duty cler—no. The roster boss looked down at him, interest replacing boredom in his face.

"This note here about being banned from the big hall. That temporary or permanent?"

"Permanent," Ren Zel answered, and was ashamed to hear his voice shake.

"OK," the boss said. He pulled the license out of the slot and tossed it across the counter. Exhausted though he was, still Ren Zel's hand moved, snatching the precious thing out of the air, and sliding it safely away.

"OK," the boss said again. "Your card's good. Fact is, it's too good. Jump-pilot. Not much need for jump-pilots outta this hall. We get some intersystem jobs, now and then. But mostly the jumps go through Casiaport Guild. Little bit of a labor tax we cheerfully pay, for the honor of being allowed on-world."

It was an astonishment to find irony here. Ren Zel lifted his eyes and met the suddenly knowing gaze of the roster boss, who nodded, a half-smile on his lips.

"You got that, did you? Good boy."

"I do not," Ren Zel said, careful, so careful, of the slippery, mode-less Terran syllables, "require a jump-ship, sir. I am . . . qualified . . . to fly intra-system."

"Man's gotta eat, I guess." The boss shook his head, stared

down at the computer screen and Ren Zel stood rooted, muscles tense as if expecting a blow.

The boss let his breath out, noisily.

"All right, here's what. You wanna fly outta here, you gotta qualify." He held up a hand, though Ren Zel had said nothing. "I know you got a first class card. What I don't know is, can you run a Terran board. Gotta find that out before I turn you loose with a client's boat." He tipped his head. "You followin' this, kid?"

"Yes, sir." Ren Zel took a hard breath, his head aching with the effort of deciphering the man's fluid, idiomatic Terran. "I am . . . required . . . to, to demonstrate my worth to the hall."

"Close enough," the boss allowed, crossing his arms atop his computer. "The other thing you gotta do, after you pass muster, is post a bond."

Ren Zel frowned. "Forgive me, I do not—'bond'?"

"Right." The boss looked out into nothing for a moment, feeling over concepts, or so Ren Zel thought. "A bond is—a contract. You and me sign a paper that basically says you'll follow the company rules and keep your face clean for a Standard, and to prove you're serious about it, you give me a cantra to keep. At the end of the year, if you kept your side of the contract, I give you your money back." Again, he held up his hand, as if he expected Ren Zel's protest.

"I know your word binds you, you being all honorable and Liaden and like that, but it's Gromit Company policy, OK? You don't post bond, you don't fly."

"O. . . K," Ren Zel said slowly, buying himself a thimbleful of time while he worked the explanation out. He gathered, painfully, that the hall required him to post earnest money, against any misfortune that might befall a client's goods while they were under his care. In light of what had happened to the last item entrusted to him in flight, it seemed that the hall was merely prudent in this. However . . .

"If the . . . Gromit Company? . . . does not fulfill its side of the contract?"

The boss gave a short laugh. "Liadens! If the company don't fulfill its side of the contract, kid, we'll all be lookin' for work."

That didn't quite scan, but he was tired, and his head ached, and his leg did, and if he did not fly out of the Terran hall, who else on all of Casiaport would hire him? He inclined his head.

"I accept the terms," he said, as formally as one could, in Terran.

"Do you?" The boss seemed inclined to find that humorous as well. "OK, then. Report back here tomorrow Port-noon and we'll have you take the tests. Oh—one more thing."

"Yes."

The man's voice was stern. "No politics. I mean that. I don't want any Liaden Balances or vendettas or whateverthehell you do for fun coming into my hall. You bring any of that here and you're out, no matter how good a pilot you are. Scan that?"

Very nearly, Ren Zel laughed. Balance. Who would seek Balance with a dead man?

He took a shaky breath. "I understand. There is no one who . . . owes . . . me. Anything."

The boss held his eyes for a long moment, then nodded. "Right. Keep it that way." He paused, then sighed.

"You got a place to sleep?"

Ren Zel pushed away from the counter. "I . . . not. . ." He sighed in his turn, sharply, frustrated with his ineptitude. "Forgive me. I mean to say—not this evening. Sir."

"Huh." The boss extended a long arm and hooked a key off the board by his computer. "This ain't a guild hall. All we got here is a cot for the willfly. Happens the willfly is already in the air, so you can use the cot." He threw the key and Ren Zel caught it between both palms. "You pass the entry tests, you find your own place, got it?"

Not entirely, no. But comprehension could wait upon the morrow.

"Yes, sir," Ren Zel said respectfully, then spent two long seconds groping for the proper Terran phrase. "Thank you, sir."

The man's eyebrows rose in apparent surprise. "You're welcome," he said, then jerked his head to the left. "Second door down that hall. Get some sleep, kid. You're out on your feet."

"Yes," Ren Zel whispered, and managed a ragged

approximation of a bow of gratitude before turning and limping down the hall. He slid the key into the slot and the second door whisked open.

The room beyond was no larger than it needed to be to hold a Terran-sized cot. Ren Zel half-fell across it, his head hitting the pillow more by accident than design. He managed to struggle to a sitting position and pulled off his boots, setting them by long habit where he would find them instantly, should he be called to fly. After sober thought, he removed his jacket and folded it under the pillow, then lay down for a second time.

He was asleep before the timer turned the room lights off.

*

On its face, the case had been simple enough: A catastrophe had overtaken two first class pilots. First board was dead; second nearly so, and Guild law required that such matters be reviewed and judged by a Master Pilot. So the Guild had called upon Master Pilot Shan yos'Galan Clan Korval, Master Trader and Captain of the tradeship *Dutiful Passage*.

Shan had, he admitted to himself, ridden the luck long enough, having several times during the last three Standards been in precisely the wrong place to be called upon to serve as Master of Judgement, though his name had been next on the roster.

This time he was the only Master Pilot near, and in fact had already filed a flight plan calling for him to be on, the planet on which the fatal incident had occurred. Thus the Guild snared him at last, and offered a budget should he need to study what was left of the ship, or convene a board to do so.

A budget was all very good, but it did nothing to lessen Shan's dislike of this particular duty. Still, he had read the file, reviewed the raw data from the flight box and, finally, in a state of strong disbelief, flew the sim.

Even in simulation, flying fatals is—unpleasant. It was not unknown that Master Pilots emerged weeping from such flights.

Shan emerged from flying the Casia fatal in an all-but-incandescent fury.

First board was dead because she was a fool—and so he stated in his report. More—she had allowed her stupidity to endanger not only the fine and able pilot who had for some reason found it necessary to sit second to her, but unnamed and innocent civilians. That the ship had finally crashed in an empty plain was due entirely to the skill of the pilot sitting second board, who might have avoided the ground entirely, had only the secondary back-up board required by Guild regulations been in place.

Shaking with rage, Shan pulled the ship's maintenance records.

The pilot-owner had not even seen fit to keep to a regular schedule of routine maintenance. Several systems were marked weak in the last recorded mechanic's review—three Standard years past!—at which time it was also noted that the co-pilot's back-up board was non-operational.

Typing at white heat, Shan finished his report with praise for the co-pilot, demanded an open hearing to be held at Casiaport Guildhall within a day of his arrival on-Port, and shunted the scalding entirety to the Tower to be pinbeamed to Guild Headquarters, copy to Casiaport Guildmaster.

He had then done his best to put Casia out of his mind, though he'd noted the name of the surviving pilot. Ren Zel dea'Judan Clan Obrelt. *There* was a pilot Korval might do well to employ.

*

"Ren Zel, get your ass over here." Christopher's voice was stern.

Ren Zel checked, saw the flicker of anger on his co-pilot's face and waved her on toward the gate. "Run system checks. I will be with you quickly."

"Yah," she said, grumpily. "Don't let Chris push you around, Pilot."

"The schedule is tight," Ren Zel returned, which effectively clinched the argument and sent her striding toward the gate. Ren Zel altered course for the counter and looked up at the roster boss.

"Christopher?"

The big man crossed his arms on top of his computer and frowned down at him. "What'd I tell you when you first signed on? Eh? About what I didn't want none of in this hall?"

"You wished no vendettas, Balance or whateverthehell I might do for fun to disturb the peace of the hall," Ren Zel recited promptly, face betraying nothing of the puzzlement he felt.

An unwilling grin tugged at the edge of Christopher's mouth. "Remember that, do you? Then you remember that I said I'd throw you out if you brought anything like that here."

"Yes . . ." What was this? Ren Zel wondered. Half-a-relumma he had been flying out of the Terran hall. And now—

"Guy come in here last night, looking for you," the boss said now. "Fancy leather jacket, earrings, uptown clothes. Blonde hair going gray; one of them enameled rings, like the House bosses wear. Talked Trade, and I wouldn't call him polite. Seemed proud of his accent. Reeled off your license number like it tasted bad and wanted to know if it was registered here." Christopher shrugged. "Might've told him no—ain't any business of his who flies outta this hall—but your number was right up there on the board, with today's flight schedule. He didn't talk Terran, but he could read numbers quick enough."

Jabun? was Ren Zel's first thought—a thought he shook away, forcefully. There was no reason for Jabun to seek him; he was dead and it was witnessed by the Eyes. Surely Jabun, of all the Clans on Casia, knew that.

In the meantime, Christopher was awaiting an explanation, and his co-pilot was awaiting him at the ship they were contracted to lift in a very short while.

"I—do not know," he told the roster boss, with what he hoped was plain truth. "There is no one—*no one*—who has cause to seek me here. Or to seek me anywhere. I am . . . outside of Balance." He hesitated, recalled his co-pilot's phrase and offered it up as something that might be sensible to another Terran: "*I am no longer a player.*"

"Huh." The boss considered that for a moment, then shook his head. "OK, but it better not happen again." He glanced to one side. "Look at the clock, willya? You gonna lift that ship on time,

Pilot?"

"Yes," said Ren Zel, taking that for dismissal. He turned and strode quickly toward the gate. The leg that had been crushed had not—entirely—healed, and was prone to betray him at awkward moments, so he did not quite dare run, though he did move into a trot as he passed the gate onto the field.

The client's ship—a packet somewhat older than the one that had belonged to Elsu Meriandra—was mercifully near the gate, the ramp down and the hatch open. Ren Zel clattered up-ramp, slapped the hatch closed as he sped through and hit the pilot's chair a heartbeat later, automatically reaching over his shoulder for the shock strap.

"Tower's online," Suzan said, her fingers busy and capable on the second's board. "We got a go in two minutes, Pilot."

"Yes." He called up his board, flickering through the checks; reviewing the flight plan and locking it; pulling in traffic, weather and status reports. "Cargo?"

"Port proctor's seal on it."

"Good. Please tell the Tower we are ready."

He and Suzan had flown together before—indeed, they were already seen as a team among certain of the clients, who had made a point to ask Christopher to "send the pilots we had last time." This was good; they made a name for themselves—and a few extra dex.

Suzan was a solid second classer with more flight time on her license than the first class for whom she sat co-pilot. She flew a clean, no-nonsense board, utterly dependable; and Ren Zel, cautiously, liked her. From time to time, she displayed a tendency to come the elder kin with him, which he supposed was natural enough, considering that she overtopped him, outmassed him, and could easily have given him twelve Standards.

"Got the go," she said now.

"Then we go," Ren Zel replied, and engaged the gyros.

*

Night port was in its last hours when Ren Zel and Suzan walked through the gate and into the company's office. Christopher's second, a dour person called Atwood, waved them over to the counter.

"Guy in here looking for you, Ren Zel."

His blood chilled. Gods, no. Let it not be that Christopher was forced to send him away.

Some of his distress must have shown on his face, more shame to him, for Suzan frowned and put her big hand on his sleeve. "Pilot?"

He shook her off, staring at Atwood, trying to calm his pounding heart. "A—guy. The same who asked before?"

Atwood shook her head. "New. Chris says," she glanced down, reading the message off the computer screen: "Tell Ren Zel there's another guy looking for him. This one's a gentleman. Asked for him by name. Might be a job in it." She looked up. "It says he—the guy—will be back here second hour, Day Port, and wants to talk to you."

He took a breath, imposing calmness. *By name?* And who on Casia would speak his name, saving these, his comrades, Terrans, all. Ah. Christopher perhaps would . . . understand . . . *Terran* gentleman. How such a one might have the name of Ren Zel dea'Judan was a mystery, but a mystery easily solved.

He glanced at the clock over the schedule board: last hour, Night Port, was half gone. Too little time to return to his room, on the ragged edge of Mid Port. Too long to simply wait on a bench in the hall . . .

" 'Bout enough time to have a bite to eat." Suzan grinned and jerked her head toward the door.

"There's a place couple streets down that actually brews real coffee," she said. "C'mon, Pilot. My treat."

*

Coffee, Ren Zel thought, some little while later, was clearly an acquired taste.

The rest of the meal was unexceptional—even enjoyable—in its oddness. The one blight was the lack of what Suzan styled 'poorbellows'. An inquiry after this unknown and absent foodstuff gained Ren Zel the information that poorbellows were a kind of edible fungus, after which the coffee tasted not quite as bitter as he had at first thought it.

The meal done, Suzan drained her third cup and went to the front to settle the bill, stubbornly refusing his offer to pay for his share with a, "Told you it was my treat, didn't I?"

Ren Zel shrugged into his jacket and followed her slowly. "Treat" was a Terran concept, roughly translating into "a gift freely given," with no Balance attending. Still, it went against his sense of propriety, that his co-pilot should give him a gift. Perhaps he might search out some of these poorbellows elsewhere on port and make her a gift in return? He considered it, then found his thoughts drifting elsewhere, to the mysterious "gentleman" whom he was, very soon now, to meet.

That the "gentleman" was Terran seemed certain. That he would, indeed, offer Ren Zel dea'Judan a jump-pilot's contract, as Christopher seemed to think, was—not so certain.

But if the offer was made? Ren Zel wondered, stepping out onto the walkway and slipping his hands in the pockets of his jacket. If the unknown gentleman offered a standard jump contract, with its guarantee of setting the pilot on the world of his choice after the terms were fulfilled, then Ren Zel might yet prosper, though in a solitary, Terran sort of way. If he chose his port wisely, he—

"There!" The unfamiliar voice disrupted his thoughts, the single word in Liaden. He looked toward the sound, and saw a gaggle of five standing half-way to the corner. All were dressed in Low Port motley; four also wore the leather jackets of jump-pilots.

And not one of them, to Ren Zel's eye, was anything like a pilot.

The foremost, perhaps the one who had spoken, bowed, slightly and with very real malice.

"Dead man," he said with mock courtesy, "I am delighted to find you so quickly. We are commissioned to deliver you a gift."

Yes—and all too likely the gift was a knife set between his ribs, after which his jacket would become a prize for the fifth in the pack.

"All right, Pilot, let's get us back to hall and see this mystery man of—" Suzan froze, the door to the restaurant still balanced on the ends of her fingers, looking from Ren Zel to the wolf pack.

"Friends of yours?"

He dared not take his eyes from the face of the leader, who seemed dismayed by the advent of a second, much larger, player in the game.

"No," he told Suzan.

"Right," she said, and pushed the door wider, rocking back on her heel. "There's a back door. After you."

Keeping his back to the wall, he slithered past her, then followed as she sped through the main dining room, down a short hallway and into the kitchen. She raised a hand to a woman in a tall, white hat, and opened the door in the far wall. In keeping with a co-pilot's duty, she stepped through first, then waved him after.

"OK. Down this alley about two blocks, there's a beer joint. Tom and Gina hang out there on their downshifts. We'll pick 'em up and all go back to the hall together."

It was prudent plan, Tom and his partner being no strangers to street brawls, if even half of their stories were to be believed. Ren Zel inclined his head. "Very well."

"Great. This way."

They had gone perhaps a block in the direction of the tavern, when Ren Zel heard a noise behind them. A glance over his shoulder showed him the wolf pack just entering the alley by the rear door to the restaurant.

Suzan swore. Ren Zel saw the gleam of metal among the pack as they moved into a ragged run nothing like the smooth flow of pilot motion. Though it would serve. And when they were caught, the wolf pack would not care whether they killed one or two.

He already had one death on his hands.

"Go on," he said to Suzan. "I will speak with them."

She snorted, "Pilot, I thought you knew I wasn't as big a fool as I look. Those boys don't want talk—they want blood." She reached down and grabbed his arm.

"Run!"

Perforce, he ran, stretching to match her pace, willing the bad leg not to betray him. Behind, he heard their pursuers, chanting—"Dead man! Pilot slayer! Dead man!"—and found time to be grateful, that Suzan did not speak Liaden.

"Here," she gasped and pulled him with her to the right. One massive shoulder hit the plastic door, which sprang open, and they were eight running paces into a dark and not overcrowded room before Suzan let him go, shouting, "Vandals right behind us! Call the Watch!"

Several of the patrons of the room simply dropped the long sticks they had been holding and bolted for the front door, for which Ren Zel blamed them not in the least. Left on his own, he spun, fire lancing the bad leg, which held, thank the gods, and looked about him for a weapon.

There were several small balls on the green covered table just beside him. Before he had properly thought, he had snatched the nearest up. The ball was dense for something so small, but that was no matter. His hands moved in the familiar pattern, the thing was spinning and then airborne as the first of the wolf pack charged into the room.

The ball caught the fellow solidly in the nose. He went down with a grunt, not quite tripping the man immediately behind him. That one, quick enough, if not pilot-fast, leapt his comrade and landed on the balls of his feet, a chain dangling from his hand.

He saw Ren Zel and smiled. "Dead man. But still alive to pain, eh?" The chain flashed as the man jumped forward. Ren Zel ducked, heard metal scream over his head, grabbed one of the fallen long sticks and came up fast, whirling, stick held horizontal between his two hands.

The chain whipped again. Ren Zel threw the stick into the attack. The chain wrapped 'round the gleaming wood twice, and Ren Zel spun, trying to pull the weapon from his adversary's grip.

With a laugh, the wolf jumped forward, grabbed the stick and twisted. Ren Zel hung on, then lost his grip, danced back a step, and then another as the man raised the weapon in both hands and swung it, whistling, down.

Once again, action preceded thought. Ren Zel dove, rolling under the green covered table, heard chain and stick hit the floor behind him, and came up on the far side of the table just in time to see Suzan place a well-considered bar stool into the back of his opponent's head.

Elsewhere in the room, the remaining three of the pack were engaged with those of the patrons who had not run. Suzan waded back into the melee, swinging her bar stool with abandon. Thinking that he might yet have use for a weapon, Ren Zel, went 'round the table to retrieve the long stick. The thing was shattered, the pieces still wrapped in chain. That he let lie, judging he was more likely to harm himself than any adversary, should he try to wield such an unfamiliar weapon. He straightened, ears pricked. Yes—from the open front door came the sound of a siren, growing rapidly louder. The Port Proctors would soon arrive, Ren Zel thought, with a sinking sense of relief. All would be—

Across the room, the pack leader dropped his man with a flickering knife thrust. He spun, seeking new blood, saw Suzan's unprotected back—

" 'Ware!" Ren Zel screamed, but the word was in Liaden; she would not know . . .

Ren Zel jumped.

The knife flashed and he was between it and his co-pilot, one shoulder, covered in tough space-leather, taking the edge and turning it. Ren Zel spun with the force of the blow, deliberately using it as he came back around—

And the bad leg failed him.

Down he went, the wolf leader atop, and it was a muddle of shouts and blows and kicks before the quick shine of the knife, snaking past the leather this time, slicing cloth and flesh. Ren Zel lashed out, trying to escape the pain. The knife bit deeper, twisting. He screamed—and was gone.

*

"Master Pilot, I regret," Casiaport Guildmaster was all but stuttering in distress. "Notification should have been sent. I swear to you that I will learn why it was not. However, the fact remains that no hearing has been scheduled. The case was adjudicated by three first class pilots, fault has been fixed and the matter is closed."

Shan lifted his eyebrows, feeling the woman's guilt like sandpaper against his skin, and she rushed on, babbling.

"Guild rule is plain, as the Master Pilot surely knows. Three first class pilots may judge, in the absence of a Master—and may overturn, in the case of a disputed judgement."

"Guild rule is plain," Shan agreed, in the mode of Master to Junior, which was higher than he usually spoke with another pilot. "Though it is considered good form to allow the Master Pilot in question to know that his judgement has been disputed."

"Since I am here in any wise," he continued, "I will see the file."

The Guildmaster gasped; covered the lapse with a bow.

"At once, Master Pilot. If you will step down to the private parlor, the file will be brought."

Shan inclined his head. "Bring also Pilot dea'Judan, if he is on-Port."

"Pilot dea'Judan?" the Guildmaster repeated, blankly.

"Pilot Ren Zel dea'Judan Clan Obrelt," Shan explained, wondering how such a one had risen to the rank of Guildmaster of even so backward a port as Casia. "Surely you recall the name?"

"I—Indeed I do." She drew a deep breath and seemed to recruit her resources, bowing with solemn precision. "I regret. Ren Zel dea'Judan Clan Obrelt is dead."

Shan stared. "And yet I ran the license number through the port's own database just before departing my ship and found it listed as valid and active."

The Guildmaster said nothing.

"I see," Shan said, after several silent moments had elapsed. "I will review the case file now, Guildmaster." He turned and walked down the hall to the private parlor.

The file, brought moments later by a pale-faced duty clerk, was thin enough, and Shan was speedily master of its contents. True enough, his judgement had been set aside in favor of the cooler findings of three first class pilots, all of whom flew out of Casiaport

Guildhall. Shan sighed, shaking his head as his Terran mother had sometimes shaken hers, expressing not negation so much as ironic disbelief.

There was a computer on the desk. He used his Master Pilot's card to sign onto the newsnet and spent a few minutes tracking down the proper archives, then shook his head again.

The legal notices told the story plainly: Obrelt had been cruelly Balanced into banishing their only pilot and naming him dead. None that kept strict Code would deal with a man who had no Clan to stand behind his debt and honor . . .

It was the description of the circumstances surrounding death, fully witnessed by the Eyes of Council, that sent him once again into the public ways of Casiaport and finally to the Gromit Company's shabby Mid Port office.

There, the luck was slightly out, for Pilot dea'Judan was flying. The man behind the counter, one Christopher Iritaki, had suggested he return early next morning and had promised to let the pilot know that an appointment had been set in his name.

Shan presented himself at Gromit Company slightly in advance of the appointed hour, to find Mr. Iritaki's second on duty.

"I'm sure they'll be back any minute, sir," Ms. Atwood said, sending a faintly worried look at the clock. "They just went a couple streets over for a bite and a cup of coffee. Ren Zel's solid. He wouldn't miss an appointment for anything short of catastrophe."

"I'm sure you're right," Shan said soothingly. He smiled at the roster boss and had the satisfaction of seeing the worry fade from her face.

"I could fancy some coffee myself," he confided. "Do you happen to know which shop the pilots favor? Perhaps I won't be too late to share a cup with them."

It happened that Atwood did know which shop, which was a favorite among the company's pilots. "Only place on Casia you can get real coffee," she said, and Shan would have sworn there were tears in her eyes.

A few moments later, possessed of directions to this mecca,

and having extracted Ms. Atwood's promise to hold Pilot dea'Judan, should he arrive back at the Hall in the meantime, Shan sauntered out into the sharp air and rumble of early morning Casiaport.

Though there was nothing in his face or his gait to betray it, Shan was in a fever to shake the dust of Casia from his feet. His evening had been spent delving deeper than was perhaps good for his peace of mind into the affairs of Casiaport Guildhall and a certain Clan Jabun. The information he uncovered was disturbing enough that he found he had no choice, as a Master Pilot who owed duty to the Guild, but to call Jabun before a full board of inquiry.

However, he thought, stretching his long legs and turning into the street where he would find the "best damn coffee on Casia," that job of form-filing would certainly wait until he had Ren Zel dea'Judan safely in hand.

The coffee shop hove into view on his left, precisely as promised. Shan checked his long stride, but did not approach the door, which was crowded around with people, all staring up-street, where a commotion was in progress.

Shan felt the hairs shiver on the nape of his neck. What was it that Ms. Atwood had said? That nothing would keep Ren Zel from an appointment except calamity?

The scene up-street had every trapping of calamity, including the white trucks and flashing blue lights of Casiaport Rescue, clustered in such abundance that the Port Proctor's sun-yellow scooters were scarcely noticeable.

Shan stretched his legs again, moving quickly toward the hubbub.

He had no trouble walking through the cordon thrown up by the Proctors—he was never stopped by guards if he did not wish to be—and into what the sign by the door dignified as "Wilt's Poolroom and Tavern."

Inside—well.

All about were knots of med techs, attending the wounded. Elsewhere, Proctors questioned several unmistakable grounders who were for some reason wearing pilots' leathers. Toward the back of the room, a figure was shrouded in a white plastic sheet. Not far distant lay another figure, blood a black pool on the floor. Shan touched a stud on his belt, alerting every Dutiful Passage crewmember on Port that there was a comrade down and in danger. Help was on the way. Now . . .

Directly before him, a Terran woman was shouting at a med tech.

"Hey!" she yelled in Trade, grabbing the tech's arm. "There's somebody over there who needs you."

The tech turned, glanced along the line of the Terran's finger, then slid his arm free, sighing slightly.

"I am not allowed to tend that one."

"What?" the Terran gaped. "You just patched up four of the worst desperadoes I've seen on this Port in a long time and you ain't allowed to tend a pilot who was wounded while protecting his co-pilot?"

"He is Clanless," the tech said, with a note of finality in his soft, Liaden voice.

"He'll be *lifeless* if you people don't do something for him soon!"

The tech turned his back.

The Terran pilot raised her hand, and Shan swung forward, catching her lightly 'round the wrist.

"Precisely how will being arrested for assault help your pilot?" he inquired in Terran.

The woman spun, pulling her wrist free. She stared at him; took a deep breath.

"He's gonna *die*."

Shan glanced at the still figure in its pool of black blood, noting the ragged breath, and the sweat on the pale, unconscious face. He looked back to the Terran pilot.

"Perhaps not. Just a moment." He stepped forward, claiming the med tech's attention with a genteel cough and bowed when the man turned.

"Good-day. I am Shan yos'Galan Clan Korval, Captain of *Dutiful Passage*."

Recognition moved in the tech's eyes. "Captain yos'Galan, I am honored." He bowed, deeply.

Shan inclined of the head, then pointed across the room to the downed pilot.

"That person is one of my crewmen, med tech. His contract started today. I understand that you may not tend him, but my melant'i is clear. I require the use of your kit."

Relief flickered across the tech's face; he held the kit out with alacrity. "Certainly, sir. Please return it when you are through."

"I will," Shan inclined his head once again and turned, gathering the Terran pilot with a glance and lifted eyebrow.

"What'd you say?" she asked, following him to where her pilot lay, alone in the midst of all the official bustle.

"That I required the use of his kit in order to perform first aid on my crewman." Shan knelt down, heedless of the blood, and began to remove the towels she had used to try to staunch the blood.

"He ain't your crew," she protested.

"Ah, but he is a pilot, and I am partial to pilots. Besides, he might well have *been* mine, if he'd managed to stay out of trouble long enough to . . ." His breath caught. The wound was bad—deep and ragged. Immediately, reflexively, he ran a quick mental sequence to relax and focus himself.

"Knife," the Terran said, succinctly. "He took it for me. At least," she amended, as Shan opened the med kit and poked among the various tools of the tech's trade, "the first strike was meant for me. Got between me and the blade—I coulda handled it, but he's so *damned* fast. He'd've been OK, except the bum leg went out on him and the hood was on him like a terrier on a rat . . ."

Shan had found what he was looking for—a suture gun. "Unpleasant, but effective," he commented, fingering the settings. "At least he's unconscious. We'll just do a quick patch, I think—something to hold him together until we can get him up to the *Passage*."

The Terran blinked. "You're the guy the pilot was supposed to meet at the hall this morning."

He met her eyes. "In fact, I am—and I am remiss. My name is Shan yos'Galan Clan Korval."

She sucked air, eyes going wide. "Tree and Dragon," she said, possibly to herself, then inclined her head, roughly, but with good intent. "I'm Suzan Fillips."

Shan nodded. "Suzan Fillips, your pilot needs you. Please hold him while I do the patch."

She did and Shan bent to the unpleasant task, sending up indiscriminate petitions to all the gods of mercy, that the boy beneath his hand remain unconscious.

At last the thing was done. He set the suture gun aside and sat back on his heels. Suzan Fillips took her hands slowly from the downed pilot's shoulders and looked up.

"Tell me about this 'bad leg,' " Shan said. "Had he been injured before today?"

"He was in a crash not too long ago and the leg never healed right," Suzan said, meeting the eyes straitly. "You know about the crash—you're the Master Pilot. I remember your name from the report."

"Do you?" He look at her with renewed interest. "Where did you get the report, I wonder?"

She snorted. "I'm a registered pilot on this port. I used my card and pulled the file. Even Terrans hear rumors—and we'd heard one about a crackerjack pilot who'd been drummed outta the local Guild for not having the good taste to die in a crash. I read the reports—yours and the one they liked better. Tried to get the sim, too, but the Guild won't lend it."

The slanted white brows pulled together. "Won't lend it? Yet you are, as you point out, a pilot on this port."

"Jabun." The voice was faint and none too steady. Both Shan and Suzan jumped before staring down at the wounded pilot. His eyes were open, a dilated and glittering black, the brown hair stuck to his forehead in wet, straggling locks.

"Jabun," he repeated, the Liaden words running rapidly and not altogether in mode. "Not enough that they had me cast out. I must die the true death, if he must hire a wolf pack to the task. Dishonor. Danger! They must not find—" He struggled, trying to get his good arm around.

Shan put his hands firmly on the boy's shoulders. "Pilot.

Be at ease."

The unseeing black eyes met his. "When will they have done?" he demanded. "When will they—"

Shan pushed, exerting force as well as force of will. "Lie *down,*" he said firmly, in a mode perilously close to that hc would use with a feverish child. "You are wounded and will do yourself further injury."

"Wound—" Sense flickered. "Gods." He twisted, weakly; Shan held him flat with no trouble.

"Suzan!"

She snapped forward, touching his unwounded shoulder. "Here, Pilot. I'm OK, see?"

Apparently, he did. The tension left him and he lay back, understanding in his eyes now. Shan frowned.

"You accuse Clan Jabun seriously," he said, in the Liaden mode of Comrade, and thinking of his own discoveries of the evening before. "Have you proof?"

"The pack leader . . ."

He glanced at Suzan, who jerked her head to the left, where two Port Proctors were talking to sullen man in a scarred leather jacket.

"All right," he said, in Terran, for Suzan Fillips' benefit. "I will speak to the pack leader. Pilot dea'Judan, you will remain here quietly with your co-pilot."

The glittering eyes stabbed his. "Yes."

One of the Proctors looked up as he approached and came forward to intercept him. "Master Trader?" he inquired courteously.

Shan considered him. "One hears," he said, delicately, "that yon brigand was hired by a House to deal death to a dead man."

The Proctor sighed. "It produces the name of Jabun—but this is not unusual you know, sir. They grasp at anything they hope will win them free of the present difficulty."

"Just so," Shan murmured, and drifted back toward Suzan Fillips and Ren Zel dea'Judan.

"I believe you," he said to the wounded pilot's hot eyes, and looked thoughtfully at the Terran.

From the entrance came the sounds of some slight agitation among the guards, who parted to admit a pilot of middle years, his pale hair going to gray, his leather gleaming as if new-made.

"It's him!" shouted the man who had been the wolf pack leader, and was silenced by his guards.

A Proctor moved forward, holding his hands up to halt the newcomer.

"Sir, this is the scene of a death by misadventure; I must ask you to leave unless you—"

"Ah, is it a death?" The man's face displayed such joy that Shan swallowed, revolted. "I must see for myself!"

The Proctor moved his hand as if to deny, but another signed assent and the three of them strode across the room to the covered form.

"Your Lordship is to understand that this is . . . unpleasant," the first Proctor said. "The nose has been forcibly crushed into the brain by a blow . . ."

"That is of no matter," the newcomer snapped, "show me!"

The Proctors exchanged glances, then bent and lifted the covering back. Shan rose to his feet, eyes on His Lordship's proud, eager face, glowing with an anticipation so—

"What nonsense is this?" the man shouted. "This is not he!"

"I am here . . . Suzan, help me stand. Jabun, I am here!"

The voice was barely a croak, nearly inaudible. The bloodied figure gained his feet, more than half-supported by his grim-faced co-pilot.

"The dead man you want . . . the dead man you want is here!" Ren Zel gritted out, and Shan stepped back, giving Jabun clear sight of his victim.

"You!" Jabun flung forward one step, hatred plain in his comely face, then froze, as if he had abruptly understood what he had done.

"Speaking to a dead man?" Ren Zel rasped. "Out of Code, Jabun." He drew a sobbing breath. "Look on me—dead by your malice. One death was not enough, one Balance insufficient . . ."

He swayed and Shan moved to offer his support as well. Ren Zel gasped.

"You, who deal in life and death—you will be the death of all you are pledged to hold!"

A gasp ran through the room, and Shan felt a tingle in the close air of the poolroom, as if a thunderstorm were charging.

Jabun stood as if struck; and Shan heard a med tech mutter, "Dramliza, you fool! Will you play Balance games against a wizard?"

Ren Zel straightened, informed by an energy that had nothing to do with physical strength.

"Jabun, you are the last delm of your House. The best of your line shall lifemate a Terran to escape your doom. The rest of your kin will flee; they will deny their name and their blood, and ally themselves with warehousemen and fisherfolk for the safety such alliances buy!

"Hear me, Jabun! In my blood is told your tale—witness all, all of you see him! See him as he is!"

"Pilot—" began Suzan, but Shan doubted Ren Zel heard her worried murmur, lost as he was in the dubious ecstasy of a full Foretelling.

"It is Jabun the pod-pirate," he cried, and Shan felt the hairs raise on his arms, recalling his own researches. "Jabun the thief! Jabun the murderer! Beware of his House and his money!"

The poolroom was so completely quiet that Shan heard his own heartbeat, pounding in his ears.

Jabun was the first to recover, to look around at the faces that would not—quite—return his regard.

"Come, what shall you? This—this is a judged and Balanced murderer, dead to Code, clan and kin. It is raving, the shame of its station has no doubt broken its wits. We have no duty here. It is beneath our melant'i to notice such a one."

"Then why," came the voice of man Suzan had identified as the wolf pack leader, "did you give us a cantra piece to beat him to death?"

Jabun turned and stared at his questioner, moved his shoulders under the bright leather. "Proctors, silence that person."

"Perhaps," murmured one of the two who had shown him the dead brigand. "I fear I must ask you to remain here with us, Your Lordship. We have some questions that you might illuminate for us."

"I?" Jabun licked his lips. "I think not."

"We have authority here, sir," the second Proctor said, and stepped forward, beckoning. "This way, if you will, Your Lordship."

"Of your kindness, pilots," Ren Zel dea'Judan said, his Liaden slurring and out of mode, "I would sit . . ."

Shan and Suzan got him into a chair, where he sagged for a moment before reaching out none-too-steadily to touch his co-pilot's sleeve

"Tell Christopher," he managed, and his Terran was blurred almost out of sense. "I—apologize. The hall—his pilots—I did not know. It is not done . . ."

Suzan patted his knee. "It's OK, pilot. You leave Chris to me."

Shan nodded, reached into his sleeve and pulled out a card. He held it out to Suzan Fillips, who blinked and shook her head.

Patiently, he held the card extended, and looked seriously into her eyes.

"Should you find yourself at risk over this incident," he said, "use the beam code on the card."

She licked her lips. "I—"

"Take. It." The wounded pilot's voice was barely audible, but the note of command was strong. The woman's hand rose. She slipped the card out of Shan's fingers and slid it immediately into her license pocket.

"Good," said Ren Zel, and Shan saw now only a wounded pilot, with no trace of the power of Foretelling, nor voice of command . . .

There was a clatter at the door. Shan looked around and spied Vilt and Rusty of his own crew, raised a hand, and then glanced down at Ren Zel dea'Judan.

"Pilot, I offer you contract: A Standard year's service on

the *Dutiful Passage*, after which we will renegotiate or, if you wish, you will be set down on the world of your choice."

Ren Zel swallowed, and looked up to meet his gaze firmly. "You are Liaden," he managed. "I am dead."

"No," Shan said, in earnest Terran. "You really must allow my skill to be better than that."

Almost, it seemed that the wounded boy smiled. The lids drooped over the fevered eyes.

"I accept," he murmured. "One Standard year."

Heirloom

HE WOKE, PANTING, out of a snare of dreams in which he over and over ran to succor a child, hideously suspended over a precipice, the slender branch clutched in terrified small fingers bending toward break beneath the slight weight–

While he ran–ran at the top of his speed. And arrived, over and over, full seconds after the branch gave way and the tiny body plummeted down . . . .

He opened his eyes–not too far–and swallowed as the dim light assaulted him. Lashes drooping, he took careful stock.

The dream–it had somehow become *the dream* of late it seemed–was both frequent and bothersome enough that he'd considered once or twice taking it to the Healers.

On other mornings, those not quite so fraught with physical complaints, his considerations had always led him to reject the notion that the dream was prophetic, for hadn't he been tested by the dramliz, several times over, at the order of the Delm-in-Keeping as well as at the order of his mother? And the dream never gave face to child, nor location to tree or cliff . . . .

The dramliz tests were remarkably similar to the piloting tests–somehow he always managed to fail without knowing exactly what it was expected of him. Of course the wizards claimed they *weren't* expecting anything of him, but neither his mother nor anyone else seemed pleased by the results–not fast enough for pilot, nor possessed of whatever *something* the dramliz probed for–

Well, and he had long ago understood that neither the Clan's ships nor the Clan's allies among the Healers or the dramliz would provide his sustenance, and he had begun casting about for what he could do to support himself, for he was a young man, holding in full measure all the stubborn pride of his House. He would take not a dex from the Clan that could not use him. His quartershares could accumulate in his account until the cantra overran the bank and flowed down the streets of Solcintra.

So he had cast about. He could shoot, of course, but one could scarcely make a living as a tournament shooter. Uncle Daav's happy experiment of giving him a gun and target practice at Tey Dor's had brought him close to the gaming set, who had no qualms about dealing with someone not a pilot, or not able tell the future through true prophecy...

Early last evening, however, he had a moment of prophecy. It came when he overheard his mother speaking with Guayar Himself. It seemed that Guayar knew a certain house which had need of one well-placed, and well-taught, and well-versed in the Code, and able to travel with a group of children, teaching as well as protecting. She'd suggested that she knew of *just* such a person.

Travel with *children*?

He had been on his way out, intending to stop at the parlor only long enough to take graceful leave of his parent and exchange pleasantries with her guest. Rag-mannered though it was, he allowed himself to forgo these duties and instead left immediately by a discreet exit that did not require him to pass the occupied room.

Once outside, he had gone, not to Tey Dor's, which had been his first, and perhaps best, inclination, but to a minor establishment which catered to the aspiring gamester. There he had accepted most of the proffered beverages, which was not his habit.

Now, his head hurt abominably, of course, and his stomach was uneasy, though not quite in revolt. Mixed fortune, there. He supposed he should rise, shower and prepare himself to meet the dubious pleasures of the day. After all, it wasn't as if he had never been drunk before.

In truth, he was rarely drunk, being a young man of fastidious nature. Certainly, he was *never* drunk while gaming, and last night's losses at the piket table were ample illustration of his reasons, thank you.

Sighing, he raised his hands and scrubbed them, none-too-gently, over his face, relishing the friction.

Gods, what a performance! He was entirely disgusted with himself, and not the most for his losses at cards. At least he had retained sense enough not to enter the shooting contest proposed by pin'Weltir!

At least–he thought he had. His memory of the later evening was, he discovered to his chagrin, rather . . . spotty.

His stomach clenched, and he took a deeper breath than he wanted–and another– forcing himself to lie calmly, to wait for the memories to rise . . . There.

He *had* turned pin'Weltir down, and when the man insisted, he had refused even more forcefully–by claiming his cloak and calling for a cab. He remembered that, yes. Too, he remembered entering the cab, and the driver asking for his direction. He remembered saying, "Home," an idiotic reply emblematic of his state, and the driver asking again, doggedly patient, as if she dealt with drunken lordlings every night–which, he thought now, in the discomfort of his bed, she might very well.

After that, he remembered nothing, though he supposed he must have managed to give her the direction of his mother's house–and if his mother had been late at her studies and had observed his return–

He wondered if people died of hangovers, and, if so, how he might manage it.

A spike of red pain shot through his head and he twisted in the bed, gagging, eyes snapping open to behold–

Not the formal bedchamber he occupied in his mother's house, but the badly shaped, sloped ceiling chamber where he had spent many peaceful childhood nights.

Despite the headache, Pat Rin smiled. Drunk into idiocy he may have been, but his heart had known the direction of home.

*

Some while later, showered and having taken an analgesic against the headache, he glanced at last night's bedraggled finery, flung helter-skelter on the simple, hand-tied rug. He bit his lip, ashamed of this further untidy evidence of his debauch, then gathered it all up and took it into the 'fresher, where he bundled the lot into the valet to be cleaned and pressed.

Returning to his bedroom, he paused at the old wooden wardrobe, coaxed open the sticky door and was very shortly thereafter dressed in a pair of sturdy work pants and a soft, shapeless shirt.

Closing the wardrobe, he considered himself in the thin mirror: A slender young man, dark of hair and eye, cheekbones high, brows straight, chin pointed, mouth stern. In his old clothes, he thought he looked a laborer, or a dock worker, or a pilot at leave–then he glanced down at his long, well-kept hands and sighed.

Looking back to the mirror, he frowned at the mass of wet hair snarled across his shoulders. The *torentia* was all the kick this season, and Pat Rin yos'Phelium Clan Korval, apprentice at play, naturally wore his hair so, spending as much as an hour a day combing and curling the thick, unruly stuff into the long, artful chaos fashion demanded.

But not today. Today, he turned 'round, snatched a comb up from the low bureau and dragged it ruthlessly through the tangled mass until it hung, sodden and straight. Putting the comb aside, he raised both hands, pulled his hair sharply back, holding the tail in one hand while he rummaged atop the bureau, finally bringing up a simple wooden hair ring, which he snapped into place.

The lad in the mirror presented a more austere face, now, without the fall of hair to soften it. Indeed, he might have been said to be quite fox-faced, were it not the general policy in the circles in which he lately moved that Pat Rin yos'Phelium was comely.

Poppycock, of course, and tiring, too. Almost as tiring as Cousin Er Thom insisting upon endless repetitions of tests taken and proved–

No.

He would not think of Cousin Er Thom–of Korval-pernard'i. And he assuredly would not think of tests. In fact, he would go downstairs to tell Luken that he was to house.

*

"Good morning, boy-dear!" Luken said, looking up with a smile. The manifest he had been studying lay on the tabletop amidst the genteel ruins of a frugal breakfast, the tree-and-dragon–Korval's seal–stamped in the top left corner of the page.

Despite everything, Pat Rin smiled, and bowed, gently,

hand over his heart.

"Good morning, father," he replied, soft in the mode between kin. "I trust I find you well?"

"Well enough, well enough!" His foster father waved a ringless hand toward the sideboard. "There's tea, child, and the usual. Have what you will and then sit and tell me your news."

His news? Pat Rin thought bitterly. He turned to the sideboard, taking a deep breath. Luken, alone of all his relatives could be trusted to honestly care for Pat Rin's news, and to take no joy in his failures.

He poured himself a glass of tea, that being what he thought he might coax his stomach to accommodate, and returned to the table, taking his usual seat across from Luken, there in the windowed alcove. Outside, the sky shone brilliant, the sun fully risen. Odd to find Luken so late over breakfast, dawn-rising creature that he was.

"Are you *quite* well?" Pat Rin asked, around a prick of panic. "I had looked to find you in the warehouse . . . ."

Luken chuckled. "Had you arisen an hour earlier, you would have found me precisely in the warehouse," he said. "What you see here is a second cup of tea, to aid me in puzzling out just what it is that Er Thom means me to do with these." He picked up the manifest and rattled it gently before dropping it again to the table.

In addition to his melant'i as Korval-in-trust, Er Thom yos'Galan wore a master trader's ring. Interesting goods, therefore, had a way of coming into his hand, and it had long been his habit to send the more interesting and exotic textiles to Luken's attention.

Pat Rin assayed a tiny sip of tea, eyeing the manifest half-heartedly. "Sell them?" he murmured, that being the most common outcome of rugs sent by Er Thom, though two, to Pat Rin's knowledge, were on display in museums, and one covered the white stone floor of the Temple of Valiatra, at the edge of the Festival grounds.

"Not these, I think," Luken said picking up his tea glass. "It seems that the clan is divesting itself of the Southern House and the place is being emptied–including the back attics, which I daresay is where these were found."

Korval was selling the Southern House? Not a heartbeat too soon, in Pat Rin's opinion. He had been to the place once, and had found it dismal. Nor was he alone in his assessment. While most of Korval's houses enjoyed more-or-less steady tenancy, the Southern House most often sat empty, undisturbed by even the housekeeper, who had his own quarters in another building on the property.

"Perhaps Cousin Er Thom wants a catalog made?" Pat Rin offered, taking another cautious sip of tea. Though rugs Luken dismissed as back attic fare hardly seemed likely candidates for cataloging and preservation.

"He doesn't write. Only that the house is being cleared, and that these might interest me." Luken sipped his tea, and moved a dismissive hand. "But, enough of that. *Your news*, boy-dear–all of it! I haven't seen you this age. Catch me up, do."

It hadn't quite been an age, the two of them having dined together only a twelveday ago, though there was, after all, the news which was no news at all . . . .

Pat Rin looked down into his glass, then forced himself to raise his head and meet Luken's gentle gray eyes.

"Korval-pernard'i bade me take the test again, yesterday." He felt his face tighten and fought an impulse to look away from Luken's face. "I failed, of course."

"Of course," his foster father murmured, entirely without irony, his expression one of grave interest.

"I don't know why," Pat Rin said, after a moment, "I can't be left in peace. How many times must I fail before they will understand that I am *not* a pilot, nor ever will be?" He took a breath, and did glance down, his eye snagging on the manifest, the upside down tree-and-dragon, sigil of the clan in which he was second of two freaks, his mother being the first. "If I am asked to take the test again, I will not," he stated, and raised his glass decisively.

"Well," Luken said after a moment. "Certainly it must be tedious to be asked to take the same test repeatedly, especially when it is so distressful for you, boy-dear. But to speak of turning your face aside from the word of Korval-pernard'i–that won't do all. Husbanding the clan's pilots falls squarely within his duty–and determining who might be a pilot, as well. He doesn't send you to the testing chamber only to plague you, child. If you were feeling more the thing, you'd see that."

It was gently said, but Pat Rin felt the rebuke keenly. Yet Luken, as nearly all the rest of his kin, was a pilot. Granted, a mere third-class, and there had lately been a time when he would have given all of his most valued possessions, had he only been given in exchange a license admitting that Pat Rin yos'Phelium was a pilot, third class.

He told himself he didn't care; that five failures would teach *him* the lesson Cousin Er Thom refused to learn.

He told himself that.

"Child?" murmured Luken.

Pat Rin looked up and smiled, as best as he was able around the headache.

"I hope I didn't disturb your rest when I came in last night," he said softly.

Luken moved his shoulders. "In fact, I had been late in the showroom, and was just coming up myself when you were dispatched from your cab."

Blast. He didn't remember that. Not at all.

"I'm afraid that I was a trifle disguised, last night," he said, around a jolt of self-revulsion.

"A trifle," Luken allowed. "I guided you to your room, we said our sleepwells and I retired."

None of it. Pat Rin bit his lip.

"I made rather a fool of myself last night," he said. "Not only did I fall into my cups, but then I was idiot enough to play cards–and lost most wonderfully, as you might expect."

"Ah." Luken finished off his tea and put the glass aside. "You also told me last night, as we were negotiating the stairway, that you had come away early because a certain– pin'Weltir, I believe?–had become boorish in his insistence that you shoot against him, then and there. Which is not, perhaps, entirely idiot."

He had already determined that for himself, but a part of

him was eased, that Luken thought so, too.

"Some things," he admitted, "I did correctly." He tipped his head, then, and shot a quick glance into Luken's face, where he found the gray eyes attentive

"Do you care, father? The trade I have set myself to learn, that is."

Luken spread his hands. "Why should I care? From all I understand, it's a difficult study you undertake in order to ascend the heights of a profession which is exhilarating and not without its moments of risk." He smiled. "I would expect, of course, that you will rise to become a master, if masters of the game there be."

"Not–by that name," Pat Rin said, thinking of those who had undertaken his education. "But, yes. There are masters."

"And you aspire to stand among them?"

Well of course he did. Who of Korval, present or past, had not sought to stand among the masters of whatever profession or avocation they embraced? Certainly not Luken.

"Yes," he said. "I do."

"It is well, then," his foster father judged. "That you will mind your melant'i and keep the honor of your House pure, I have no need to ask."

He paused for a moment, reaching absently to his empty glass, and letting his hand fall with a slight sigh. Pat Rin got up, bore the glass to the sideboard, refilled it and brought it back.

"Gently done," Luken murmured, his thoughts clearly somewhere else. "My thanks."

"It is my pleasure to serve you, father."

"Sweet lad." He had a sip from the refilled glass and looked up.

"I wonder if you've given thought to setting up your own establishment," he said. "It occurs to me that bin'Flora has a townhouse for lease in a location near the High Port."

Most of Solcintra's gambling houses were located at the High Port. There were several residential streets just beyond the gate, none of them unsavory, though one or two not as . . . fashionable . . . as they might be.

bin'Flora traded in textile–bolt goods more usually than

rugs–and the present master of the house, one Sisilli, and Luken had enjoyed a friendly rivalry for possibly more years than Pat Rin had been alive. Therefore, it was likely that the house in question was on–

"Nasingtale Alley," Luken murmured. "Third house on the right, as you walk out from the High Port."

Pat Rin sipped tea. "Rents on Nasingtale Alley are certainly above my touch," he said to Luken. "I am yet a student."

"Yet an able student, for that," Luken said. "And the rent may not be . . . quite ruinous."

"Ah." He considered the face across from him thoughtfully. "*Shall* I set up my own establishment, father?"

Luken sighed. "It's a prying old man, to be sure," he said. "But I will tell you what is in my heart, boy-dear.

"Firstly, and true enough, I worry about you, walking about the port with large amounts of coin on you." He raised a hand. "I know your reputation with the small arms, but it would be best not to employ them."

"I agree," Pat Rin murmured, and Luken inclined his head.

"Too, it makes sense to hold a base near your daily business, and this house bin'Flora offers is certainly that.

"And lastly . . ." His voice faded and he glanced aside.

Pat Rin felt his stomach clench.

"You know your mother and I have no love lost between us," Luken said slowly, "despite that which the Code tells us is due to kin. And you know that, as a youngling, you were moved from your mother's care into mine, by the word of the Delm."

The Delm. That would have been Daav yos'Phelium, his mother's brother, gone from the clan these years, on a mission of Balance. There had been no love lost between his mother and her brother, either, Pat Rin knew, though as a child he had adored his tall, easy uncle.

"I confess that I was a bit puzzled when you went to live with your mother, after your schooling was done." He raised a hand. "I don't ask your reasons, boy-dear, though I know you had them. Nor will I speak ill of your mother to you. I will say that, drawing on my knowledge of you–and of her–perhaps you might consider if you would be more . . . relaxed in your own small establishment."

That he certainly would be, Pat Rin thought, for his mother was a high stickler and kept stringent Code. He supposed that was inevitable, given her reputation as Liad's foremost scholar of and expert on the Code. She also held rank among Solcintra's leading hosts, and it was for that reason that Pat Rin, returning home from university and fixed upon the trade that he would follow, had taken up residence with his parent, rather than moving back into his comfortable place with Luken.

Kareen yos'Phelium could–and did, for who knew better what was due the heir of a woman of her impeccable lineage and melant'i?–launch him into society. Luken cared little for society, though his clientele came largely from the High Houses. And Pat Rin had needed the final polish and the ties to the High which only his mother could give him.

He wondered, here and now, sitting in Luken's sunny alcove, if he would have chosen differently, had he known the cost beforehand. For life with his mother was not easy, or comfortable, though he was surrounded by every luxury. He was required to live to his mother's standard, and to study the Code until he was very nearly an expert himself. He studied other things, as well, so that he would have a store of graceful conversation available; he attended all the fashionable plays, patronized his mother's excellent tailor, wore gems of the first water, and was never seen at a stand.

The one . . . relaxation he allowed himself was target practice every other morning, on the lifetime membership to Tey Dor's Club which Uncle Daav had given to him.

Of course, he saw now–had seen last evening with sudden clarity–that his mother had never believed his assertions that he intended to make his way without recourse to the funds of the Clan. She had heard him, for she was a courteous listener, precisely as the Code instructed–heard him, but did not believe. And he had never quite seen that there would need be an *after* to his plan.

"Pat Rin?" Luken murmured.

He blinked back into now, and inclined his head.

"You understand," he said slowly. "That I attempt to . . . produce a certain, and very specific, effect. Produce, and sustain it."

Luken smiled. "I am not quite an idiot, boy-dear."

"Of course not," he murmured, more than half caught in his calculations. "So, the question before me now is whether the effect will remain fixed, should I retire to my own establishment."

"I should think," Luken said, "that the key would be not to retire, but to continue as you have been, only from the comfort of a bachelor's dig."

A townhouse on Nasingtale Alley could scarcely be called a 'dig'–and Luken, as he so often was, despite one's mother's contention that the rug merchant was no more nor less than a block–Luken was right. Pat Rin had only to carry on as he was. The invitations would continue to arrive–and he might even host a small entertainment or two, himself. The gods knew, he had assisted with enough of his mother's entertainments to know how the thing was done.

"Please consider," Luken said carefully. "You are now well known among the Houses. Your melant'i is your own, no matter that it in some measure reflects your mother's, and your Clan's, as it must. But–it would hardly do for you to regularly best your mother's houseguests while you yourself sleep under her roof. Nor would it be best for you, seen among the elders of many a House as a biddable young man always at your mother's call, to have to rigorously make a point . . ."

Pat Rin grimaced at this description of himself, while allowing that, from the outside, it might appear thus.

". . . as I say, if you need to press an honest advantage across a table, it might be best if you do it first among the lesser members of the Houses until Lord Pat Rin is more fully known as himself. If being Lady Kareen's son is not your occupation, my boy, then having your own place will afford you both more flexibility in your evenings and more company in the mornings. I say this as one who was, alas, once young myself."

Seated, Pat Rin bowed the bow of apprentice to master.

"It might do," he said, and glanced to Luken's face. "If

bin'Flora's rate is possible."

Luken smiled. "Please, know that there are two partners in every trade. The place would have been rented anytime the last two relumma were the matter simply one of cash flow. Not all would-be renters are High House, my boy. Nor," he said with sudden emphasis– "are all High House equally acceptable. Whatever the Code may teach."

"I will mention your interest to Sisilli," Luken concluded, and drank off the rest of his tea.

"As much as I enjoy your company, child, I am afraid that I must leave you for an appointment."

Pat Rin inclined his head, his gaze snagging on the manifest, lying forgotten on the table. He extended a slender hand and plucked the page up, running an eye trained by Master Merchant Luken bel'Tarda down the list of items.

"Shall I inventory these, while you are gone?" he asked Luken. "That will have to be done, whatever else Cousin Er Thom intends."

"So it will," Luken said, coming to his feet. "If you have the leisure, boy-dear, the work would be appreciated. You'll find the lot of them in the old private showing room. And also, since you will wish to have clear sight if not a clear head, I suggest you make use of some of the tea you will find there. It will have Terran wording on it–*McWhortle's Special Wake-Up Blend*–and it should be taken just as the directions instruct. Shall we plan on dining at Ongit's this evening?"

"I would enjoy that," he said truthfully. "Very much."

"Then that is what we shall do," Luken declared. "Until soon, my son."

"Until soon, father," Pat Rin responded and rose to bow Luken to the door.

*

It appeared that Luken had been correct in his assessment of the lot of rugs from the Southern House, as well as in his understanding of the utility of McWhortle's Special Wake-Up Blend.

The tea was surprisingly tasty for something avowedly of Terran extraction, and equally efficacious.

The rugs . . . He sighed. Not all of the pilots of Korval–put together!–knew what Luken did of rugs, and some had, alas, displayed an amazing lack of both color sense and fashion awareness.

The first rug, indifferently rolled and protected by nothing more than a thin sheet of plastic, was synthetic. He threw it across the flat onto the show-zone, where the mass and size were automatically recorded–the overhead camera recorded detail, but really–there wasn't much to say for it. Machine stamped in a small, boring floral pattern, backed with nothing more than its own fibers, with a density on the low side, it might as well be sent as a donation to the Pilot's Fund used-goods outlet in Low Port.

Pat Rin dutifully entered these deficiencies into his clipboard, slotted the stylus, and touched a key. The clipboard hummed for a moment, printing, and a yellow inventory tag slid out of the side slot. Pat Rin picked up the stitch gun and stapled the tag to the corner of the rug, before rolling it, bagging it in a bel'Tarda-logo light-proof wrapper, and dragging the sorry specimen over to the storage bin which he had marked with Cousin Er Thom's number and the additional legend, "Southern House."

Straightening, feeling somewhat better for the tea and in fact much more clear eyed– he looked suddenly to the shelf above the bin, where a long-haired white cat with excessively pink ears lounged, very much at her leisure. Likely she'd been there the while; that he hadn't noticed her was a further testament to his excesses of the evening before.

"Niki," Pat Rin murmured, extending a finger, but not quite touching the drowsing animal.

Her eyes slitted, then opened to full emerald glory. Yawning, she extended a pink-toed and frivolously befurred foot to wrap around his fingertip, her claws just pricking the surface of his skin.

Pat Rin smiled and used his free hand to rub the lady softly beneath her delicate chin. Niki's eyes went to slits again and her breathy purr filled the air between them. The claws withdrew from his captive finger and he let the freed member fall to his side, while moving his other hand to her ears. His exertions there were shortly rewarded with an increase in her audible pleasure, and he smiled again.

One's mother did not keep cats, or any other domestic creature, aside the occasional servant. It made for an oddly empty feel about the house, even when it was full with guests.

"Thank you," he whispered, giving her chin a last rub and stepping back. Niki squinted her eyes in a cat-smile, purring unabated.

Pat Rin turned back to his work.

The next rug was intriguingly and thickly wrapped in what must have been a local newspaper. He fussed the sheets off and found the rug rolled backing out, tied at intervals with what might have once been elegant hair-ribbons. He sat on his heels and smiled. This, he would examine last. It had good weight and somehow the smell of a proper rug–and would be his reward for doing a careful inventory of the rest of the obviously unsuitable specimens tumbled about them.

He used a utility blade to slit the plastic sealing the next rug, noting the ragged jute backing, and unrolled it onto the scale with a casual kick before bending to retrieve the clipboard.

The work was–comforting. Despite that Kareen yos'Phelium had declared that she would not have her heir made into a rug salesman–had in fact complained of him coming up with callused hands–Luken had trained him well, and he knew himself to be the master of the task he had set for himself. It could not be said that he completely shared his foster father's ecstatic enthusiasm for carpet, or his encyclopedic knowledge of their histories, but he owned to a fondness for the breed, and knew a certain pleasure in being once more among them.

The unrolled carpet was a geometric, hand-loomed in bronzes, browns and dark greens, with pale green fringe along the two short sides. It glistened in the light, inviting him to believe that it was silk. But he had seen the backing and was not taken in.

As counterfeits went, it was rather a good one. The

traditional Arkuba pattern had been faithfully reproduced, the measurements precisely those to which all Arkuba carpets adhered, to the very length of the pale fringe, and the vegetable-dyed thread. Alas, the luster which would, in the genuine article, be testimony to the silken threads that had gone into its manufacture, was in this case misleading. Rather than silk, the carpet before him had been woven with specially treated cotton thread.

A perfectly serviceable and attractive rug, really, setting aside for the moment those issues surrounding a counterfeit hall mark. Pat Rin merely hoped that the nameless ancestor who had purchased the thing had known it for what it was and had paid accordingly.

He entered his observations, tapped the stylus against the print button, and slid it into its slot while the clipboard hummed its tuneless tune and in the fullness of time extruded an inventory ticket which he stapled to the corner of the rug before bagging and dragging it over to the bin.

Niki was still on the shelf overhead, profoundly asleep. He smiled, but did not disturb her.

The protective plastic over the next carpet had been torn at some time–possibly as recently as the move from the Southern House to Luken's warehouses. Pat Rin slit what was left of the sheet, approving, as he did so, the plentitude of painstakingly tied knots along the carpet's underside, and the foundation of wool.

Once more, a kick sent the rug rolling out–and he sighed aloud. Insects had gotten in through the breached plastic. The wool in spots was eaten down to the backing, leaving the skeleton of a handsome rectilinear design he did not immediately recognize. No, this damage had not occurred in the warehouse, being both too extensive and too old.

Sighing yet again, he reached for the clipboard to record the loss–

"Cousin Luken?" The voice was clear and carrying–and unfortunately familiar.

Pat Rin closed his eyes, there where he rested on one knee beside the ruined rug, and wished fervently that she would overlook this room. There was little chance that she would, of course. His cousin Nova was nothing if not thorough. Unnaturally thorough, one might say.

"Cousin Luken!" she called again, her voice nearer this time.

Pat Rin opened his eyes, picked up the clipboard, fingered the stylus free and entered a description of the damage. The mechanism hummed and in due time a red tag emerged. He reached for the stitch gun–

"Oh, there you are, cousin!" Nova said from the doorway at his back.

Amidst the sound of approaching light footsteps, Pat Rin stapled the red tag to a corner of the ruined rug.

"Father sent me to help you catalog the rugs from the–" She stopped, aware, so Pat Rin thought, that she had made an error.

Gently, he placed the stitch gun on the floor next to the clipboard, and turned his head slightly so that she could see the side of his face.

"Cousin Pat Rin!" she exclaimed, with a measure of astonishment that he found not particularly flattering.

He inclined his head. "Cousin Nova," he stated, with deliberate coolness. "What a surprise to find you here."

The instant the words left his lips, he wished them back. He had spent the last year and more deliberately honing his wit and his tongue until they were weapons as formidable as the palm pistol he carried in his sleeve. Surely, it was ill-done of him to loose those weapons on a child.

"Is Cousin Luken to house?" she asked stiffly.

He rose carefully to his feet and turned to face her.

Nova's twelfth name day had been celebrated only a relumma past, and already she showed warning of the beauty she would become. Her hair was gilt, her eyes amethyst, her carriage erect and unstrained. She had, so he heard, passed the preliminary testing for pilot-candidate, an unsurprising fact which had nonetheless woken a twist of bitterness in him.

Today found her dressed in sturdy shirt and trousers, well-scuffed boots on her feet, passkey clenched in one hand, and a glare on her face for the ill-tempered elder cousin–for which he blamed her not at all.

"Alas, one's foster father is away on an appointment," he said, moderating his tone with an effort. "May I be of service, cousin?"

Her glare eased somewhat as she glanced about her.

"Father sends me to help Cousin Luken sort the carpets from the Southern House," she said tentatively. "However, I find you at that task."

It was not meant to be accusatory, he reminded himself forcefully. She was a child, with a child's grasp of nuance.

Though she had grasped the nuance of his greeting swiftly enough. He had the acquaintance of adults who would have not have taken his point so quickly–if at all.

So–"Cousin Er Thom had not written us to expect your arrival and assistance," he answered Nova, deliberately gentle. "I happened to be at liberty and took the work for my own."

She blinked at him, jewel-colored eyes frankly doubtful.

"You are aware, are you not," Pat Rin said, allowing himself an edge of irony, "that I am Luken's fosterling?"

"Ye-e-s-s," Nova agreed. "But Cousin Kareen–I heard her speaking with my father and she . . ." Here she hesitated, perhaps nonplused to discover herself admitting to listening at doors.

Pat Rin inclined his head. "One's mother was adamant that I not be trained as a rug merchant," he said smoothly. "Alas, by the time she recognized the danger, the damage had long been done."

Nova's straight, pale mouth twitched a little, as if she had suppressed a smile.

"Will you come into Cousin Luken's business?" she asked, which was not an unreasonable question, from a daughter of the trade Line. Still, Pat Rin felt his temper tighten, spoiling the easier air that had been flowing between them.

"I've gone into another trade, thank you," he said shortly, and swept his hand out, showing her the pile of rolled rugs waiting to be inventoried. "For all that, I am competent enough in this one."

He sighed, recalling his mother's plans for him, and shook

the memory away.

"If you like, you may assist me," he murmured, and that was no more than the Code taught was due from kin to kin: Elders taught those junior to them, freely sharing what knowledge and skill they had, so that the Clan continued, generation to generation, memory and talent intact.

Nova bowed, hastily. "I thank you, cousin. Indeed, I would be pleased to assist you."

"That is well, then. The sooner we address the task, the sooner it will be done. Attend me, now."

He moved over to the pile and kicked a smallish roll out into the work area. Dropping to knee, he slit the plastic, revealing a plain gauze backing. A push unrolled it onto the scale, and Pat Rin looked up at Nova, standing hesitant where he had left her.

"Please," he said, "honor me with your opinion of this."

Slowly, she came forward, and knelt across from him, frowning down at the riot of woolen flowers that comprised the rug's design. She rubbed her palm across the surface, gingerly.

"Wool," she said, which was no grand deduction, and flipped up the edge near her knee. The gauze backing disconcerted her for a moment, then she returned to the face, using her fingers to press into and about the design.

"Hand-hooked," she said then, and was very likely correct, Pat Rin thought, but as it stood it was no more than a guess. He held up a hand.

"Hooked, certainly," he murmured. "Where do you find the proof for 'handmade?' "

Eagerly, she flipped back the edge, and pointed to the row of tiny, uneven stitches set into the gauze.

"Ah." He inclined his head. "I see that your conclusion is not unreasonable. However, it is wise to bear in mind that carpets are sometimes adjusted–fringe is added, or removed, backings are sewn on–or removed–holes are rewoven. Therefore, despite the fact that someone has clearly sewn the backing on by hand, the rug itself might yet have been made by machine. The preferred proofs are . . ."

He extended a hand and smoothed the wool petal of a

particularly extravagant yellow flower, displaying a stitching of darker thread beneath.

"Maker's mark."

Nova bit her lip.

"Or," Pat Rin continued, flipping the little rug entirely over with a practiced twist of his wrists. He put his palm flat on the backing and moved it slowly, as if he were stroking Niki. He motioned Nova to do the same–which she did, gingerly, and then somewhat firmer.

"What do you feel?" he asked.

"Knots," she replied. "So it *is* handmade–I was correct."

"It is handmade," he conceded, "and you were correct." He lifted a finger. "For the wrong reason."

She sighed, but – "I understand," was what she said.

"Good. If you will, of your goodness, hand me the clipboard, I will make that notation and then we may proceed with the rest of the inspection."

She picked up the clipboard in one hand and held it out to him over the rug. He took it, his thumb accidentally nudging the stylus out of its slot, sending it floorward in a glitter of silver–

Nova swept forward, her hand fairly blurring as she scooped the stylus out of the air, reversed it and held it out to him.

He blinked. A *child*, he thought, all of his bitterness rising . . . .

Some part of it must have shown on his face. Nova hesitated, hand drooping.

"I was too fast, wasn't I?" she said, sounding curiously humble. "I do beg your pardon, cousin. Father is trying to teach me better, but I fear I am sometimes forgetful."

"Teach you better?" Pat Rin repeated, and his voice was harsh in his own ears. "I thought speed was all, to those who would be pilots."

"Yes, but one mustn't be too fast," Nova said solemnly. "It won't do to frighten those who are not pilots–or to rush the instruments, when one is at the board."

He closed his eyes. Five times, since his eleventh name-day. Five times, he had tested for pilot and failed. Always, the tests found him too slow. Too slow–and this child, his cousin, must learn not to be *too fast.* He tried to decide if he most wished to laugh or to weep and in the end only opened his eyes again and took the stylus from her hand.

"My thanks," he murmured, and bent his head over the clipboard while he took his time making the initial entry.

"Now," he said when he could trust his voice for more than a few words. He looked over to Nova. "We must assess general condition, wear patterns, repairs, stains–that sort of thing. What say you?"

Seriously, she scrutinized the gauze backing, then turned the rug over, clumsily, to study the face, her hands chastely cupping her knees.

"Hands," Pat Rin murmured. "Use your hands."

He demonstrated, elegant fingers–ringless for this work–petting, gripping, pushing– his palms flowing about the top and bindings.

"Feel the nap. Is there a stiff spot which may be a stain invisible to the eye? Pull on the loops–do they hold or come loose? Smell the carpet–is it musty? Sour? All of these details are important."

She sent him one startled glance out of vivid purple eyes before bending forward, her right hand stroking and seeking. She bent her face closer–and sneezed.

"Dusty," she said.

He inclined his head.

She continued her inspection with that solemness which was characteristic of her, and at last sat back on her heels and looked at him across the rug.

"The threads are good, the stitches are firm. There is no staining visible to eye or to hand. The carpet is dusty, but fresh."

"Very good," he said, and plied the stylus once more.

When the yellow tag appeared, he handed it across to her.

"Use the stitch gun to staple the tag to the near corner."

He helped her wrestle the wrapper on it, and used his chin to point at the waiting carpets.

"Please choose our next subject and unroll it while I put this in its proper place."

She rose, a thing of pure, careless grace, and moved lithely to the pile. Pat Rin gritted his teeth and carried the little rug across to the bin.

Niki was sitting tall on the shelf. She blinked lazy green eyes at him as he stroked her breast.

Somewhat soothed, Pat Rin turned back to the work area, expecting to find the next specimen unrolled and awaiting inspection.

Indeed, a rug had been liberated from the pile, and he felt a momentary pang–she had chosen the one he had wanted to study himself. It displayed a promising underside, thick with knots. He sighed, then wondered about the delay.

Knife at her knee, Nova crouched over the roll, head bent above the single corner she had curled into the light. Her shoulders were rounded in an attitude of misery–or defiance.

"Unroll it!" he said, perhaps a little sharply, but Nova only knelt there.

Gods, what ailed the child? Pat Rin thought, irritably, and moved forward.

"Don't . . ." Nova moaned, "I *know* this rug!"

But that was nothing more than nonsense. Likely the thing had been away rolled in a dusty attic for a dozen dozen Standards . . . .

He moved down the cylinder, pulling the ribbon ties rapidly.

"Nova, help me roll this out."

She crouched lower, fingers gripping her corner . . .

Pat Rin delivered a smart kick and the thing unrolled with alacrity, as if the carpet had been yearning for its freedom.

Beside him, cowering now, head even closer to the floor and the corner of carpet she clung to, Nova gasped.

He looked down at the top of her bright head, frowning. Nothing he knew of Nova encouraged him to believe that she was a malingerer. Nor was it possible to imagine Cousin Er Thom or his lady wife, Cousin Anne, tolerating this sort of missish behavior for anything longer than a heartbeat.

"Are you ill?" he asked. "Cousin?"

She shuddered, and raised her head as if it were a very great weight.

"No," she said on a rising note, as though she questioned her answer even as she gave it. "I . . . beg your pardon, cousin. A passing–a passing stupidity." She rose, slowly and with a quarter of her previous grace. "Pray . . . do not regard it."

He considered her. Carpets woven of certain esoteric materials did sometimes collect ill humors in storage. It was doubtful that this rug, which he had already tentatively classified as a Tantara of some considerable age, woven with vegetable dyed zeesa-wool thread that wore like ship-steel, had collected anything more than a little must, if that.

He glanced from her pale face to the rug. Yes–certainly it was an older Tantara, a geometric in the ivory-and-deep-green combination which had been retired for a dozen-dozen Standards, and in an absolutely enviable state of preservation, saving a stain on a wide section of the ivory-colored fringe.

Bending, he ran his hand over the nap near the stain–stiff fibers grazed his palm. Whatever the substance was, it had gotten into the rug, too, which meant that there would be more to repairing the damage than simply replacing the fringe. It was odd that the carpet had been rolled away without being cleaned–and unfortunate, too. Most stains could be eradicated, if treated when fresh. A stain which had set for dozens of years, perhaps–it might be impossible to entirely remove the mar.

"We will need the kit for this," he said briskly, straightening. "I'll fetch it while you do a preliminary inspection."

"Yes," she whispered, and he sent another frown into her pale face.

"Nova," he said, touching her hand. "Are you well?"

"Yes," she whispered again, and turned away to find the clipboard.

Irritated, he strode off to the supplies closet.

The diagnostic kit was hanging in its place on the peg-board wall. Despite this, Pat Rin did not immediately have it down and hurry back to the work area. The stained rug had languished for years without care. A few heartbeats more would do it no harm.

Leaning against the wall, he closed his eyes and took stock. The headache was the merest feeling of tightness behind his eyes, his stomach was empty, but unconcerned. In all, he had managed to come out of last evening's adventures in fairly good order. His present irritability was not, he knew, the result of overindulgence, but rather the presence of one of his pilot kin, innocent herself of any wrong-doing–and a poignant reminder of all that he was not. Nor ever would be.

"Be gentle with the child," he said to himself. "Did Luken show temper with you, thrust upon him unwarned and very likely unwanted?"

But, there. Luken was a gentle soul, and never showed temper, nor ever raised his voice, no matter how far he was provoked. He had other means of exacting Balance.

Pat Rin took another deep breath–and another. Opening his eyes, he could not say that he felt perfectly calm–but it would suffice. He hoped.

One more inhalation, for the luck. He had the kit off the peg and headed back to the workroom, and his assistant, and was brought up short on the threshold.

Nova stood in the center of the rug, shoulders and chin thrust forward in a distinctly truculent attitude, surveying the pattern.

"It is a beautiful rug, indeed," she said nastily, as if speaking to someone who stood next to her rather than one on the other side of the room.

"Indeed, show off the pattern. Tell us that it is an antique Quidian Tantara, unblemished, heirloom of a clan fallen on hard times, a clan of rug dealers who have kept this treasure until the last, until your wonderful trading skills brought its true glory to us! And how *like* you to bring it here as subterfuge, hiding the truth of it, magnifying yourself to the detriment of others, and to the Clan. Almost, you got away with it . . . ."

What was this? Was she speaking to him, after all? Had she discovered a pedigree card tucked into the end of the rug? In fact, from his view now, it might well be a Quidian, the rarest of the rare. . .

She turned and stared directly at him.

"How many times more will you fail?" she shouted.

Pat Rin froze, caught between astonishment and outrage. How *dare*–

"One failure should certainly have been enough," he said, struggling to keep his tone merely courteous and his face smooth. "That there are more can be laid to your father's account."

"Kin will suffer for your lapses!" Nova snarled, moving forward one slow, threatening step.

"Yes, very likely!" he snapped, all out of patience. "But never fear, *cousin.* The clan will not suffer because of me. I will make my own way."

"You fail and fail again, always blaming others," ranted the girl on the rug, as if he hadn't spoken. "You will die dishonored and your kin will curse your name!"

Now *that,* Pat Rin thought, his anger abruptly gone, was coming rather too strong. It wasn't as if Korval had never produced a rogue. Rather too many, if truth were told–and most especially Line yos'Phelium. Taking up trade as a gamester was the merest bagatelle, set beside the accomplishments of some of the honored ancestors.

He came to the edge of the rug. Nova continued to stand at menace in the center, her attitude too–old, somehow. Too tense. And now that he brought his attention to it, he saw that her face was tight with an adult's deep and hopeless grief–and that her eyes were black, amethyst all but drowned in distended pupils.

Too, she stood in something very close to a fighter's stance . . . and was not *quite* looking at him.

Pat Rin frowned. Something decidedly odd was going on. Perhaps she was acting out some part from a melant'i play? Though why she should do so, here and now, was beyond his understanding.

He held the diagnostic kit up before those pupil-drowned eyes.

"Come now!" He said, with brisk matter-of-factness.

"We'll be at work into the next relumma if we stop every hour to playact!"

The blind, grief-ridden face turned away from him.

"How many times will you fail?" she whispered–and the voice she spoke in was not *her* voice.

Pat Rin felt a frisson of horror. He cleared his throat.

"Nova?"

"Die dishonored," she mourned and sagged to her knees, palms flat against the carpet. "Cursed and forgotten."

He caught his breath. This was no playacting. He couldn't, offhand, think of any swift-striking disease that caused hallucination. There were recreational pharmaceuticals which produced vivid visions, but–

"Cursed," Nova moaned, in the voice of–The Other. And there was no drug that Pat Rin knew of which would produce *that* effect.

Come to that, it was not unknown for Korval to produce Healers, though such talents usually did not manifest until one came halfling. Not that this . . . fit . . . bore any resemblance to his limited experience of Healer talent.

Dramliza?

But those talents, like Healing, usually came with puberty. And, surely, if one were dramliza . . . .

Crouched on the rug, Nova looked distinctly unwell. Her grief-locked face was pale, the black eyes screwed shut, now; and she was shivering, palms pressed hard against the carpet.

Clearly, whatever the problem was, she needed to be removed from the carpet, and brought away to a place where she might lie down while he called a medic to her–and her father.

Pat Rin put the diagnostic kit on the floor and went forward. When he reached the grieving girl, he knelt and put his hands, gently, on her shoulders.

"Nova."

No reply. Her shoulders were rigid under his fingers. He could see the pulse beating, much too fast, at the base of her slender throat.

Fear spiked Pat Rin–the child was *ill!* He made his decision, braced himself, slipped his arms around her waist and rose, lifting her with–

The quiescent, grieving child exploded into a fury of fists and feet and screams. He was pummeled, kicked, and punched–one fist landing with authority on his cheek.

Pat Rin staggered and went down on a knee. Nova broke free, rolled, and snapped to her feet, the carpet knife held in a blade-fighter's expert grip.

Blindingly fast, she thrust. Pat Rin threw himself flat, saw her boots dance past him and rolled, coming to his feet and spinning, body falling into the crouch his defense teacher had drilled him on, ready to take the charge that did not come.

Nova looked at him–perhaps she did look at him–and tossed the blade away, as if it were a stylus or some other harmless trifle, ignoring it as it bounced away, safely away, across the rug and onto the workroom floor. Niki, brought down from her comfort-spot by the noise, stalked it there, tail rigid, and smacked it smartly with a clawed paw.

Slowly, Pat Rin straightened, forcing himself to stand at his ease.

Something terrible was happening, and he was entirely out of his depth. He should, he thought, call the Healers now. And then he thought that he should–he *must*–get her off of the rug.

Perhaps persuasion would succeed where force had failed. He took a breath and shook the hair that had come loose from the tail out of his face. His cheek hurt and he would make odds that he would have a stunning bruise by evening. No matter.

He cleared his throat.

"Nova?"

No answer. Pat Rin sighed.

"Cousin?"

She raised her head, her eyes were pointed in his direction.

Ah, he thought. Now, how to parley this small advantage into a win?

He shifted, and looked down at the carpet. An old carpet, a treasure–a Quidian Tantara, the pattern as old as weaving itself.

How Luken would love this rug.

Alas, he sorely missed Luken and his endless commonsense just now. What would *he* do in this eldritch moment? Cast a spell? Trap the offending spirit in a tea box?

Pat Rin looked up.

"Cousin," he said again, to Nova's black and sightless eyes. "I . . . scarcely know you. If you must treat with me this way, at least show respect to our common Clan and tell me clearly which melant'i you use. "

He bowed flawlessly, the bow requesting instruction from kin.

Something changed in her face; he'd at least been seen, if not recognized.

"Melant'i games? You wish to play *melant'i games* with me? I see."

Chillingly, she swept a perfect bow: Head of line to child of another line.

"Lisha yos'Galan Clan Korval," she said in that strange voice, and bowed again, leading with her hand to display the ring it did not bear. "Master Trader. It is in this guise, Del Ben, that I became aware of your perfidy in dealing with bel'Tarda."

Del Ben? The name struck an uneasy memory. There had been a Del Ben yos'Phelium, many years back in the Line. Indeed, Pat Rin recalled, there had been three Del Ben yos'Pheliums–and then no more, which was . . . peculiar . . . of itself. He remembered noticing that, during his studies of the Diaries and of lineage. And he remembered thinking it was odd that a yos'Phelium had died without issue, odder still that the death was not recorded, merely that Del Ban vanished from the log books between one page and the rest . . .

Nova's black eyes flashed. She laughed, not kindly. "Look at you! Hardly sense enough to see to your wounds! Well, bleed your precious yos'Phelium blood out on the damned rug if you will, and live with the mark of it. This–I am old. I am *slow*. I could never have touched the man you wish to be. But you–always, you do just enough to get by, just enough to cause trouble for others, just enough–"

"Bah," she said, interrupting herself with another bow: Cousin instructing cousin.

"This one? Well, cuz, I had thought myself well beyond the time of my life where I must marry at contract. But not only will I wed a bel'Tarda because of you, I will bring them into the Clan because of you."

Pat Rin froze–what was *this*?

She swept on, a child chillingly, absolutely convincing in the role of Clan elder.

"Ah, yes, smirk. I have seen the contracts. Tomorrow, I will sign them. Do you know that the dea'Gauss and bel'Tarda's man of business met this week? No–you might have, had you checked your weekly agendas, but when have you ever done so? Did you know that, between them, they decided that your life was insufficient to Balance the wrong done bel'Tarda?"

There was a laugh then, edgy and perhaps not quite sane. "Do you know that we are forbidden by Korval to kill you? But no matter, cuz, I am to both carry the bel'Tarda's heir, who will replace the man who suicided as a result of your extortion, and to oversee the rebuilding of their business–likely here on Liad!–since the heir and his heir died in the fire. The only proper Balance is to offer our protection, bring them into Korval, and insure that their Line lives on. For you–you nearly destroyed the whole of it! And you?"

Another frightening bow, this one so complex it took even Pat Rin's well-trained eye a moment to decode it: The bow of one who brings news of a death in the House.

Pat Rin, mesmerized, saw the play move on–

"You may see the Delm, if you dare, or you may choose a new name–one that lacks Korval, and one that lacks yos'Phelium. You may eat while you are in this house, you may sleep in this house, you may dress from the clothes you already own–but you will bring me your Clan rings, your insignia, your pass-keys. Bring them to me now. If you will speak to the Delm I will take you, else . . . .

"Hah, and so I thought, " she said, spitting on the rug. "Remove this rug and bring me the items I named . . .

Know that if you leave–if you go beyond the outside door–it will not readmit you."

With that the girl-woman kicked at the rug and stormed off of it, turning her back and crumpling into the pose Pat Rin had seen before . . . .

"I shall take the rug!" Pat Rin announced with sudden fervor, not certain that she'd heard.

He rolled it quickly, slung it manfully across his back in the carry he had learned so long ago from Luken, and hustled it out into the hall, where he dumped it hurriedly on the back stairs to his loft room, and clicked the mechanical lock forcefully.

He snatched the portable comm from its shelf and rushed back to the door of the display room, where he could see the girl huddled in sobs amid the ribbons that had once bound the cursed rug.

His fingers moved on the comm's keypad and he wondered who they had called. A faint chime came out of the speaker . . . another–and a woman's voice, speaking crisply.

"Solcintra Healer Hall. Service?"

*

The Healers–a plump, merry-faced man and a thin, stern woman–arrived. The woman went immediately to Nova where she crouched and wept against the floor. The man tarried by Pat Rin's side.

"Did you move anything?"

"I took the carpet away, as she commanded," he said. "I locked the carpet knife in a drawer."

The Healer inclined his head. "We will wish to see both, later." He glanced about him and used his chin to point at the ceiling camera. "Is that live?"

"Yes," Pat Rin murmured. "Shall I–?"

"We will want a copy of the recording, yes, sir," the Healer said. "If you could have that done while we are examining your kinswoman, it would be most helpful."

"Certainly," Pat Rin said, and the Healer patted his arm, as if they were kin, or old and comfortable comrades, and strolled away across the floor.

Glad of being given a specific task, Pat Rin moved to the control desk, keeping an eye on the huddled group. The Healers blocked his sight of Nova, but, still, he was her nearest kin present and the Code was explicit as to his duties–until her father arrived to take them over.

Behind the control desk, he touched keys, taking the current camera off-line and activating the back-up. He accessed the first's memory, and started the preliminary scan.

Murmurs came from across the room as he worked, but the thin, hopeless sobbing had at last ceased, and Pat Rin drew a deep breath of relief. The Healers were here; surely they would put all to rights–

The sound of rapid footsteps sounded in the hallway, a shadow flickered in the doorway, and Er Thom yos'Galan was in the room, face set and breathing as easily as if he had not all but run down the long hall–and quite possibly all the way from Port. He paused, scanning, discovered the Healers, kneeling together on the show room floor, took a step– and checked, turning slightly until he spied Pat Rin behind the desk.

His mouth tightened and he came forward. Pat Rin touched the 'pause' key and drew himself straight.

"Where is your cousin?" Er Thom asked, without greeting, in a voice so stringently calm that Pat Rin felt a small shiver of pity for stern and commonsense Cousin Er Thom.

He inclined his head. "The Healers have come. Already, I believe the situation improves."

Er Thom glanced over his shoulder. "Could you not have moved her from the floor?"

"She . . . did not know me," Pat Rin said carefully, and put light fingertips against the cheek Nova had punched. "I had tried to move her, earlier, and she fought like a lyr-cat protecting her litter." He took a breath. "It seemed best not to make a second attempt, with the Healers on the way."

"So." Er Thom drew a careful breath of his own. "What do you?"

"The Healers requested a copy of the tape."

"Tape?"

Pat Rin swept a hand out, encompassing the showroom. "We were making an inventory of the rugs you had sent from the Southern House," he murmured. "The camera was on, of course."

"Of course," Korval-pernard'i said politely, and cast one more look at the Healers. Pat Rin could all but see his longing to go to his child's side–and then saw discipline snap into place. A wise man–a man who wished the very best outcome for his wounded child–that man did not interrupt Healers at their work.

Er Thom took a hard breath and stepped 'round the corner of the desk.

"Show me the film," he ordered.

*

The female Healer had gone, taking Nova, Er Thom and the copy of the work session recording with her, leaving her partner to examine the carpet knife–which he proclaimed harmless–and the carpet.

"Ah, I see," he murmured, as for the second time that afternoon Pat Rin unrolled the thing on the showroom floor. The Healer stepped onto the carpet, and Pat Rin tensed, half-expecting to see his face twist into that expression of angry pain.

But whatever haunted the rug appeared to have no hold on the Healer. He knelt, carefully, at a corner and put his hands flat on the ivory-and-green pattern. Closing his eyes, he moved his hands over the rug, walking forward on his knees as he did so, as if he wished to stroke every fiber.

Pat Rin, relieved that there would apparently be no second playing of the tragedy, removed himself to the control desk once more, and began to shut down for the day. He would inventory the remaining carpets tomorrow, he told himself. Alone.

There was a small burble of sound and a flash of flyaway fur. Niki landed on silent pink toes by the control board. Pat Rin smiled and held out his hand; the cat rubbed her cheek against his fingers, then sat down, wrapped her tail neatly 'round her toes and squinted her eyes in a cat-smile, as if to assure him that all was well.

Yes, precisely.

He returned to his task, comforted by the routine and her silent presence–

"What were your plans for that rug?"

"Eh?" Pat Rin blinked, and looked up at the sudden Healer. "Truly, sir, it is not my place to have plans for it. I do not hide from you that it is an extremely valuable carpet, even if the stain cannot be removed, and that it belongs to Line yos'Galan."

"Stain?" murmured the Healer, tipping his head to one side. "There is no stain, young sir."

Pat Rin felt the hairs rise along the back of his neck.

"Most assuredly," he said, moving round the desk and marching toward the rug in question, "there *is* a stain."

"Here," he said, arriving. He swept a hand downward, his eyes on the Healer's face. "Only look here and you will see where the fringe has– "

The Healer was watching his face, calmly. Pat Rin looked down.

There was no brown stain marring the wave of ivory fringe. He bent, stroked the supple woolen nap which had scant hours before been stiff with–blood. Del Ben yos'Phelium's blood.

"I believe that the most excellent yos'Galan will not favor this rug, young sir," the Healer murmured. "Perhaps you might take charge of it." He raised his hand as if he had heard Pat Rin's unspoken protest. And perhaps, thought Pat Rin, he had.

"I will speak with your cousin on the matter, for it comes to me that such a rug, gotten at such cost, ought not to be destroyed, no matter the pain it has unwittingly brought to a daughter of the House." The Healer cocked his head. "Keep it by, do."

Pat Rin bowed.

"Very well," the other said, with a sigh. "I leave you now, sir. A pleasure to make your acquaintance."

"Wait– " Pat Rin put out a hand as if he would physically restrain the man.

The Healer paused. "Yes?"

"My cousin Nova–what ailed her? Will she mend? How

shall–?"

"Peace, peace," the Healer laughed. "The Masters must have their chance at diagnosis, but it seems to me that your cousin has a very rare talent in the dramliz spectrum."

Dramliza. Pat Rin closed his eyes. "What talent?" he asked, 'round the pain in his heart.

"Why, she remembers," the Healer said, as Pat Rin opened his eyes. "That's all." He gave the carpet one more long glance.

"I really must–ah, a moment, of your kindness!" He leaned forward, and before Pat Rin knew what he intended, had cupped the injured cheek in a warm and slightly moist palm.

There was a small tingle–and the pain flowed away, leaving only warmth.

The Healer stepped back, placed his hand over his heart and bowed.

"Peace unto you, Pat Rin yos'Phelium. Long life and fair profit."

"Healer–" Pat Rin began.

But the Healer was gone.

*

pin'Weltir had gone some hours ahead of the rest, pleading another appointment, which seemed odd at that hour of the morning–but who was Pat Rin yos'Phelium to comment upon the arrangements of a mere acquaintance? He did note, privately, that pin'Weltir had not recalled this second appointment until Luken had roundly trounced him at piket, lightening his brash lordship's purse by a considerable number of coins.

Still, and excusing the early departure of a guest not much missed in his absence, Pat Rin counted this first party in his own establishment a success. He was quite sincerely exhausted by his hostly duties, yet exhilarated.

The last, late-staying guest bowed out, and the door locked, Pat Rin moved down the hall to the room he had made his study. There, as he expected, he found his foster father, seated in Pat Rin's reading chair, thoughtfully gazing at the ivory-and-green carpet.

Pat Rin hesitated in the doorway. Luken looked up, face

roguish in the soft yellow light.

"Well, boy-dear! Well, indeed. A most glorious crush, hosted with grace and style! I daresay you will sleep the day through, now."

"Not quite now," Pat Rin murmured.

Luken smiled. "A bit in the upper key, is it? Never mind it–very shortly Lord Pat Rin will find hosting a party three times this to be a mere nothing!"

Pat Rin laughed. "Verily, Lord Pat Rin shall be nothing more nor less than a fidget-about-town. I wonder how you might bear with so slight a fellow."

"Now, there," Luken said, with sudden seriousness, "you touch near to a topic I wished to bring before you. I wonder–have you thought of entering the lists at Tey Dor's?"

Pat Rin blinked, and drifted into the room, across the Tantara, to prop a hip against the desk and looked down into his foster father's face.

"I had never thought of competing at Tey Dor's," he said then. "Should I have?"

"You might find that you will wish to do so," Luken said, "as you consider the . . . *effect* you wish to sustain. For I do not think, boy-dear, that you would do very well in a long-term role either as fidget or as mushroom."

"Ah." Pat Rin smiled. "Lord Pat Rin shall be flamboyant, shall he?"

Luken raised a finger. "Lord Pat Rin, if you will permit me, boy-dear, shall be *accomplished*."

"I'll grant that's a happier thought," his son said after a moment. He inclined his head. "Allow me to consider the matter, when my head is done spinning."

"Surely, surely." Luken paused before murmuring. "I wonder if you have heard that young Nova takes lessons at the dramliz school now–and has passed the preliminary for third-class pilot."

Pat Rin inclined his head. "She was by a three-day gone, with a gift for the house. We drank tea and she caught me up with her news."

"Ah?" Luken said. "And how do you find yourselves aligned, if an old man might ask it."

"We are–comfortable," Pat Rin said after a moment. "She–I do not know how such a thing might be, but–she remembers both sides of the . . . incident, and we have, thereby, an understanding."

There was a small silence. "Good," Luken said, simply, and pushed himself out of the chair. Pat Rin leapt forward to offer him an arm.

"Must you leave?" he asked, and Luken laughed.

"I daresay the two of us might now repair to the Port for a game or six, were I thirty years younger!" He said, patting Pat Rin's hand. "But you must have pity on an old man and allow me to seek my bed."

"Certainly," Pat Rin replied, walking with him toward the hallway. "I will summon a cab."

"Assuredly you will, sir!" Luken turned suddenly, face serious. "Lord Pat Rin will have servants to attend to these small matters for him."

"I daresay he might," Pat Rin retorted, with spirit, "for those who are merely guests. But if Lord Pat Rin should ever fail of attending the father of his heart personally, I shall know him for a worthless dog, no matter his *accomplishments.*"

Luken paused, then extended a hand to cup Pat Rin's cheek. "Sweet lad." He let the hand fall away and smiled, softly. "Call for the cab, then, and be welcome."

Quickly, Pat Rin stepped back into his study and made the call. Turning back, he saw Luken framed in the doorway, his eyes dreaming once more upon the Tantara.

"Father?" he said, abruptly.

Luken looked up, face mild. "Child?"

Pat Rin cleared his throat. "I–do you mind?" he blurted. "The carpet–it is yours; the treasure of your Line. It should–"

Luken held up a hand. "Peace." He glanced down at the ivory-and-green design, smiling slightly as he once again met Pat Rin's eyes.

"I allow it to be a gem, and everything that is graceful. Even,

I allow it to be a family heirloom. Who best to have the keeping of such a treasure, than my son?"

Pat Rin's eyes filled. "Father– "

"Nay, I'll brook no argument, willful creature! Hark! Is that the cab?"

It was. Luken fastened his cloak and together they went down the steps to the walk. Pat Rin opened the door and saw his father comfortably disposed. That done, he handed the driver a coin.

"Good-night, boy-dear," Luken said from the back. "Sweet dreams to you."

"Good-night, father," he returned, stepping back from the curb. "Sweet dreaming."

The cab pulled away, accelerating smoothly down the long, dark street.

Quiet Knives

THE TURTLES HAD CANCELED, the tidy kill-fee deposited to ship's funds before the message had hit her in box.

Just as well, thought Midj Rolanni, wearily. She sagged back into the pilot's chair and reached for the cup nestled in the armrest holder. She'd hadn't really wanted to reconfigure the flight deck for two turtles, anyway.

The 'toot wasn't exactly prime grade and being cold didn't improve it. She drank it anyway, her eyes on the screen, but seeing through it, into the past, and not much liking what she saw.

She finished the cold 'toot in a swallow, shuddered and threw the cup at the recycler. It hit the unit's rim, shimmied for a heartbeat, undecided, and fell in, for a wonder. Midj sighed and leaned to the board, saving the turtles' cancellation with a finger-tap, and accessing the stored message queue.

There wasn't much there besides the turtles' message–the transmittal, listing the cargo she'd paid Teyope to carry for her; the credit letter from the bank, guaranteeing the funds, half on cargo transmittal, half on delivery.

And the letter from Kore. Pretty thin letter, really, just a couple lines. Not what you'd call reason for off-shipping a perfectly profitable cargo onto a trader just a little gray–". . . just a little gray," she repeated the thought under her breath–and Teyope *did* owe her, which even he acknowledged, damn his black heart, so the cargo was in a fine way to arriving as ordered, where ordered, and not a line of the guarantees found in violation.

She hoped.

Her hand moved on its own, fingers tapping the access, though she could have told the whole of Kore's note out from heart. Still, her eyes tracked the sentences, few as they were, as if she'd never read them before.

Or as if she hoped they'd say something different this time.

Her bad luck, the words formed the same sentences they had since the first, the sentences making up one spare paragraph, the message of which was–trouble.

Midj. You said, if I ever changed my mind, you'd come. Cessilee Port, Shaltren, on Saint Belamie's Day. I'll meet you. Kore.

"And for this," she said out loud, hearing her voice vibrate against the metal skin of her ship. "For this, you shed cargo and take your ship–your home and your livelihood–onto Juntavas headquarters?"

It wasn't the first time she'd asked the question since the letter's receipt. Sometimes, she'd whispered it, sometimes shouted. *Skeedaddle*, now. Her ship didn't tell her nothing, but that she needed to go. She'd promised, hadn't she?

And so she had–promised. Half her lifetime ago, and the hardest thing she'd done before or since was closing the hatch on him, knowing where he was going. She'd replayed their last conversation until her head ached and her eyes blurred, wondering what she could have said instead, that would have made him understand . . .

But he *had* understood. He'd chosen, eyes open, knowing her, knowing how she felt. He'd said as much, and say what you would about Korelan Zar, he was no liar, nor ever had been.

"You go, then," the memory of her voice, shaking, filled her ears. "If this job is so important you gotta take up the Juntavas, too–then go. I ain't gonna stop you. And I ain't gonna know you, either. Walk down that ramp, Korelan, and you're as good as dead to me, you hear?"

She remembered his face: troubled, but not anything like rethinking the plan. He'd thought it through–he'd told her so, and she believed him. Kore'd always been the thinker of the two of them.

"Midj," he said, and she remembered that his voice hadn't been precisely steady, either. "I've got to. I told you–"

"You told me," she'd interrupted, harsher maybe in memory than in truth. She remembered she'd been crying by then, with her hand against the open hatch, and the ramp run down to blastcrete, a car waiting, its windows opaqued and patient, just a few yards beyond.

"You told me," she'd said again, and she remembered that

it had been hard to breathe. "And I told you. I ain't comin' with you. I ain't putting *Skeedaddle* into Juntavas service. You want to sell yourself, I guess you got the right. But this ship belongs to me."

His face had closed then, and he nodded, just once, slung his kit over his shoulder and headed down the ramp. Chest on fire, she'd watched him go, heard her own voice, barely above a whisper.

"Kore . . ."

He turned and looked up to where she stood, fists braced against her ship.

"You change your mind," she said, "you send. I'll come for you."

He smiled then, so slight she might've missed it, if she hadn't known him so well.

"Thanks, Midj. I'll remember that."

In the present, Midj Rolanni, captain-owner of the independent tradeship *Skeedaddle*, one of a dozen free traders elected as liaison to TerraTrade–respectable and respected– Midj Rolanni drew a hard breath.

Twenty Standards. And Kore had remembered.

*

She set down as prearranged in Vashon's Yard and walked over to the office, jump-bag on her shoulder.

Vashon himself was on the counter, fiddling with the computer, fingers poking at the keys. He looked up and nodded, then put his attention back on the problem at hand. Midj leaned her elbows on the counter and frowned up at the ship board.

Rebella was in port–no good news, there–and *BonniSu*, which was better. In fact, she'd actively enjoy seeing Su Bonner, maybe buy her a beer and catch up on the news. Been a couple Standards since they'd been in port together, and Su had bought last time . . . .

"Sorry, Cap," Vashon said, breaking into this pleasant line of thought. "Emergency order, all good now. What'll it be?"

All spacers were "Cap" to Vashon, who despite it was one of the best all-around spaceship mechanics in the quadrant–and maybe the next.

"Ship's *Skeedaddle*, out of Dundalk," she said, turning from the board. "Got an appointment for a general systems check. Replace what's worn, lube the coils, and bring her up to spec–that's a Sanderson rebuild in there, now, so the spec's 're–"

"Right, right . . ." He was poking at the keys again, bringing up the records. "Got it all right here, Cap. How're them pod-clamps we fitted working out for you?"

"Better'n the originals," she said honestly, which was no stretch, the originals having seen a decade of hard use before *Skeedaddle* ever came to her, never mind what she'd put on 'em.

"Good," he said absently, frowning down at his screen. "Now, that Sanderson–we have it on-file to tune at ninety percent spec, that being efficient enough for trade work, like we talked about. You're still wantin'–"

"Bring her up to true spec," Midj interrupted, which she'd decided already and, dammit, she wasn't going to second-guess herself at this hour. If she was a fool, then she was, and it wouldn't be the first time she'd made the wrong call.

Not even close.

Vashon was nodding, making quick notes on his keypad. "Bring her to true-spec, aye, Cap, will do." He looked up.

"You'll be wanting the upgraded vents, then, Cap? If you're going to be running at spec, I advise it."

She nodded. "Take a look at the mid-ship stabilizer, too, would you? Moving her just now, I thought I noticed a slide."

" 'Cause you come in without cans," he said, making another note. "But, sure, we'll check it–ought to ride stable, cans or no cans." He looked up again.

"Anything else?"

"That's all I know about. If you find anything major that needs fixing, I'll be at the Haven."

"Haven it is," he said, entering that into the file, too. "Cash, card, or ship's credit?"

"Ship's credit."

"Right, then." He gave her a crabbed smile. "She ought to be good to go by the end of the week, barring we find anything unexpected. You can check progress on our stats channel, updated every two hours, local. Ship's name is your passcode."

"Thanks," she said, and shifted the bag into a more comfortable position on her shoulder. "I'll see you at the end of the week, barring the unexpected."

She nodded and he did and she let herself out the door that gave onto the open Port.

*

"Going *where*?" Su Bonner paused with her beer halfway to her mouth.

"Shaltren," Midj repeated, trying to sound matter of fact, and not at all reassured by the other woman's decisive headshake.

"Shaltren's not the place you want to be at this particular point in time, Captain Rolanni, me heart." Su put her beer down on the table with an audible thud. "Trust me on this one, like you never have before."

"I trust you plenty," Midj said, spinning her own beer 'round the various scars on the plastic tabletop, that being a handy way to not meet her friend's eyes. "You know I do."

"Then you've given over the idea of going to Shaltren." Su picked up her beer and had a hefty swallow. "Good."

Midj sighed, still navigating the bottle through the tabletop galaxy. "So, what's wrong with Shaltren? Besides the usual."

"The usual being that it's Juntavas Headquarters? That'd be bad enough, by your lights and by mine. Lately, though, there's more. Chairman Trogar, they say, is not well-loved."

Frowning, Midj glanced up. "Must break his heart."

"Not exactly, no." Su had another swallow of beer and shook two fingers at the bartender. "What I heard is, he means to keep it that way. Anybody who talks across him or who doesn't rise fast enough when he yells 'lift!'–they're dead right off. He's got himself an aggressive expansion plan in motion and he doesn't mind spending lives–that's anybody's but his own–to get what he wants."

Midj shrugged. "The Juntavas always grabbed what they could."

The new beers came, the 'keeper collected Su's empty, looked a question at Midj and was waved away.

"Not always." Su was taking her last comment as a debating point. "I'm not saying every decent spacer should sign up onto the Juntavas workforce, but I will say they've been getting carefuller in later years. They're still trading in all the stuff nobody ought, but they haven't been as gun-happy as they were back in the day . . ." She raised a hand, showing palm.

"Cold comfort to you and yours, I grant. The fact remains, there was a trend toward less of that and more . . . circumspection–and now what rises to the top of the deck but Grom Trogar, who wants a return to the bad old days–and looks like getting them."

"Well." Midj finished her beer, set the bottle aside, and cracked the seal on the second.

"*So*," Su said into the lengthening silence. "You changed your mind about going to Shaltren, right? At least until somebody resets Mr. Trogar's clock?"

Midj sighed and met her friend's eyes. "Don't see my business waiting that long, frankly."

"What business is worth losing your ship, getting killed, or both?"

Trust Su to ask the good questions. Midj kept her eyes steady.

"You remember Korelan Zar," she not-asked, and Su frowned.

"Tall, thin fella; amber eyes and coffee-color skin," she said slowly. "I remember thinking that skin was so pretty-looking." She fingered her beer. "Your partner, right? He was the one that told you one day he take you to Panore for a vacation, right?"

Midj nodded, said nothing.

Su's sip was nearly a chug, then she continued into the silence.

"Right. Always wondered what happened to him. Never got around to asking. Must be–what? Fifteen, eighteen Standards?"

"Twenty." Her voice sounded tight in her own ears. "What happened to him was he figured he had to sign on with another crew–he had reasons, they seemed good to him, and that's all twenty

Standards in the past. Thing is, I told him, if he ever needed to ship out– call, and I'd come get him."

Su was quiet. Midj had a swig of beer, and another.

"And where he is, is Shaltren," Su said eventually, after she enjoyed a couple of swigs, herself. "Midj–you don't owe him."

"I owe him–I promised." She closed her eyes, opened them. "He asked me to come."

"Shit." More quiet, then–"How soon?"

St. Belamie's Day had begun as a joke; at need, it had become a code–he'd remembered that, too, and trusted her to do the same. It was a moving target, calculated by finding the square root of the diameter of *Skeedaddle*, multiplying by the Standard day on which the message was sent and dividing by twelve. Accordingly, she had about twenty Standard Days on Kago before she lifted for Shaltren.

She'd wanted to time it closer, but there was the ship to be brought up to spec, and she daren't gamble that Vashon would find nothing wrong. Likely he wouldn't, but it wasn't the way to bet, not with Kore waiting for her, with who knew what on his dance card.

"Couple weeks, local," she said to Su, and the other woman nodded.

"Let's do this again, before I ship out," she said, and finished off her beer in one long swallow. She thumped the bottle to the table. "For now, gotta lift. Business."

"I hear that," Midj said, dredging up a grin. "I'm at the Haven for the next while, then back on-ship. Gimme a holler when you know you got time for dinner. I'll stand the cost."

"Like hell you will," Su said amiably. She got her feet under her and was gone, leaving Midj alone with the rest of her beer and the tab.

*

He walked down the ramp easy, not hurrying, a pilot on his way to his ship, that was all. He turned the corner and froze, there on the edge of the hallway, still out of range of the camera's wide eye–and the woman leaning against the wall, gun holstered, waiting.

Waiting for him, he had no doubt. He knew her–Sambra Reallen–who hadn't been anybody particular, and now ran in Grom Trogar's pack; high up in the pack, though not so high that calling attention to herself might get fatal. If she was here, calmly waiting for him go through the one door he had to go through–then he was too late.

He nodded, once, turned, and went back up the hall, walking no faster than he had going down, and with as little noise.

Too late, he thought, as he reached street-level. Damn.

There were two ways to play it from here, given that he'd sworn not to be a damn' fool. The strike for the ship, that might've been foolish, though he'd had reason to hope that the fiction of the Judge's continued residence would cover him. The Judge's absence would still serve as cover, since he *was* the Judge's courier. But the fact that one of Chairman Trogar's own had been waiting for him–that was bad. He wondered how bad, as he ran his keycard through the coder.

If they'd been waiting for him at the ship, then they likely knew some things. They probably knew that the Judge and most of the household was gone, scattered, along with all the rest of the Judges and staff who had managed to go missing before Grom Trogar thought to look for them. It was unlikely that they knew everything–and they'd figure that, too. Which meant he had a bad time ahead of him.

Nothing to help it now–if he ran anywhere on Shaltren, they'd catch him, and the inconvenience would only make his examination worse. If he waited for them, and went peaceably–it was going to be bad. Chairman Trogar would see to that.

If they'd been at the ship, they'd be *here* soon, if they weren't already.

The door to the house slid open.

He stepped inside, playing the part of a man with nothing to fear. His persona had long been established–a bit stolid, a bit slow, a steady pilot, been with the Judge since his itinerant days.

He flicked on the lights–public room empty. So far, so

good. They'd take their time coming in–Judges and their crews, after all, had a reputation for being a bit chancy to mess with.

There was a some urgency on him, now. He'd planned for back-up; it was second nature anymore to plan for back-up. At the time it had seemed prudent and, anyway, he'd meant to be gone before it came to that.

Meant to, he thought now, walking quick through the darkened rooms, heading for the comm room and the pinbeam. *Meant to isn't 'will.'*

He'd put a life in danger. Might have put a life in danger. If the first message had gotten through. If she hadn't just read it and laughed.

I'll come for you, she whispered from memory, the tears running her face and her eyes steady on his. He moved faster now, surefooted in the dark. She'd come. She'd promised. Unless something radical had happened in her life, altering her entirely from the woman he had known–Midj Rolanni kept her promises.

He'd had no right to pull her in on this. *Especially this.* Even as a contingency back-up that was never going to be called into play. No right at all.

He slapped the wall as he strode into the comm center. The lights came up, showing the room empty–but he was hearing things now. Noises on his back path. The sound, maybe, of a door being forced.

Fingers quick and steady, he called up the 'beam, fed in the ID of the receiver. The noises were closer now–heavy feet, somebody swearing. Somewhere in one of the outer rooms, glass shattered shrilly.

He typed, heard feet in the room beyond, hit *send,* cleared the log, and spun, hands up and palms showing empty.

"If you're looking for the High Judge," he said to man holding the gun in the doorway. "He's not home."

*

Vashon not finding anything about to blow down in *Skeedaddle's* innards, and the vent upgrade going more smoothly than the man himself had expected, Midj was back on-board in good order inside of eight local days.

She stowed her kit and initiated a systems check, easing into the pilot's chair with a sigh of relief. The ship was quiet, the only noises those she knew so well that they didn't register with her anymore, except as a general sense of everything operating as it should. Of all being right in her world, enclosed and constrained as it was.

When she ran with a 'hand–never with a partner, not after Kore–the noises necessarily generated by another person sharing the space would distract and disorient her at first, but pretty soon became just another voice in the overall song of the ship.

And whenever circumstances had her on-port for any length of time, she came back to the ship with relief her overriding emotion, only too eager to lower the hatch and shut out the din of voices, machinery and weather.

Hers. Safe. Comfortable. Familiar. Down to the ancient *Vacation on Incomparable Panore* holocard Kore'd given her as a promise after one particularly hard trade run.

She'd thought before now that maybe it was time to start charting the course of her retirement. Not that she was old, though some days she felt every Standard she'd lived had been two. But she did have a certain responsibility to her ship, which could be expected to outlive a mere human's span–hell, it had already outlived two captains, and there wasn't any reason it wouldn't outlast her.

She ought to take up a second–a couple of the cousins were hopeful, so she'd heard. The time to train her replacement was while she was still in her prime, so control could be eased over gradual, with her giving more of her attention to TerraTrade, while the captain-to-be took over ship duty, until one day the change was done, as painless as could be for everyone. That's how Berl took *Skeedaddle* over from Mam, who had gone back to the planet she'd been born to for her retired years, and near as Midj had ever seen on her infrequent visits, missed neither space nor ship.

Berl, now. Midj shook her head, her eyes watching the progress of the systems check across the board. In a universe without violence–in a universe without the Juntavas–Berl would've been standing captain yet, and his baby sister maybe trading off some other ship. Maybe she'd been running back-up on Skeedaddle, though that wasn't the likeliest scenario, her and her brother having gotten along about as well as opinionated and high-tempered sibs ever did.

Still and all, he hadn't deserved what had come to him; and she hadn't wanted the ship that bad, having found a post that suited her on the Zar family ship. Suited her for a number of reasons, truth told, only one of them being the younger son, who came on as her partner once she'd understood Berl was really dead, and *Skeedaddle* was hers.

Full circle.

The board beeped; systems checked out clean, which was nothing more than she'd expected. She had a cold pad spoke for at the public yard; some meetings set up across the next couple days–couple of independents on-port she still needed to get to regarding their views on TerraTrade's proposed "small trade" policies. She'd write that report before she lifted, send it on to Lezly, in case . . .

In case.

Well.

She reached to the board, opened eyes and ears, began to tap in the code for the office at the public yard–and stopped, fingers frozen over the keypad.

In the top left corner of the board, away from everything else on the board, a yellow light glowed. Pinbeam message waiting, that was.

Most likely it was TerraTrade business, though she couldn't immediately call to mind anything urgent enough to require a 'beam. Still, it happened. That's why emergencies were called emergencies.

She tapped the button, the message screen lit, sender ID scrolled–not a code she recognized, offhand–and then the message.

Situation's changed. Don't come. K

*

The room was softly lit, his chair comfortable. For the moment, there were no restraints, other than those imposed by the presence of the woman across the table from him.

"Where is the High Judge, Mr. Zar?"

Her voice was courteous, even gentle, despite having asked this selfsame question at least six times in the last few hours.

"Evaluation tour, is what he told me," he answered, letting some frustration show.

"An evaluation tour," his interlocutor repeated, a note of polite disbelief entering her cool voice. "What sort of evaluation?"

"Of the other judges," he said, and sighed hard, showing her his empty hands turned palm up on his knee. "He was going to visit them on the job, see how they were doing, talk to them. It's a regular thing he does, every couple Standards." That last at least was true.

"I see." She nodded. He didn't know her name–she hadn't told him one, and she wasn't somebody he knew. She had a high, smooth forehead, a short brush of pale hair and eyes hidden by dark glasses. One of Grom Trogar's own–his sister, for all Kore knew or cared.

What mattered was that she could make his life very unhappy, not to say short, unless he could convince her he was short on brains *and* info.

"It seems very odd to me," she said now, conversationally, "that the High Judge would embark on such a tour without his pilot."

They'd been over this ground, too.

"I'm a courier pilot," he said, keeping a visible lid on most of his frustration; "not a big ship pilot. I fly courier work, small traders, that kind of thing. I stay here, in case I'm needed."

She hesitated; he could almost taste her weighing the question of the rest of the household's whereabouts against his own actions. Questions regarding his actions won out.

"You went to the courier shed this afternoon, is that correct?"

"Yes," he said, a little snappish.

"Why?" Getting a little snappish, herself.

"I had a 'beam from the Judge, with instructions."

"Instructions to lift?"

"Yes."

"And yet you didn't lift, Mr. Zar. I wonder why not."

He shrugged, taking it careful here. "There was a guard on the door. It smelled wrong, so I went back to the house and sent a 'beam to the Judge."

"I see. Which guard?"

He had no reason to protect the woman who'd been waiting for him. On the other hand, he had no reason to tell this woman the truth.

"Nobody I'd seen before."

She shook her head, but let that line go, too. Time enough to ask the question again, later.

"Once more, Mr. Zar–where is the High Judge?"

"I told you–on evaluation tour."

"Where is Natesa the Assassin?"

She was trying to throw him off. He gave an irritable shrug. "How the hell do I know? You think a courier assigns Judges?"

"Hm. What was the destination of the lift you did not make?"

He shook his head. "High Judge's business, ma'am. I'm not to disclose that without his say. If you want to 'beam him and get his OK . . . ."

She laughed, very softly, and leaned back in her chair, sliding her dark glasses off and holding them lightly between the first and middle fingers of her right hand. Her eyes were large and pale gray, pupils shrinking to pinpoints in the dim light.

"You are *good*, Mr. Zar–my compliments. Unfortunately, I think you are not quite the dull fellow you play so well. We both know what happens next, I think? Unless there is something you wish to tell me?"

He waited, a beat, two . . . .

She shook her head–regretfully, he thought, and extended a long hand to touch a button on her side of the table. The door behind her slid open, admitting two men, one carrying a case, the other a gun.

The woman rose, languidly, and motioned them forward. Kore felt his stomach tighten.

"Mr. Zar has decided that a dose of the drug is required to aid his memory, gentlemen. I'll be back in ten minutes."

*

Don't come . . . .

Midj stared at the message, then laughed–the first real laugh she had in–gods, a Standard.

"Don't come," she snorted, leaning back in the chair in the aftermath of her laugh. "Tell me another one, Kore."

Shaking her head, she got up, went down the short hall to the galley and drew herself a cup of 'toot, black and sweet.

Sipping, she walked back to the pilot's chamber and stood behind the chair, looking down at the message on the screen.

"Now, of all the things he might've expected me to remember, wouldn't that have been one of 'em?" She asked her ship. There was no answer except for the smooth hum of the air filtering system. But, then, what other answer was needed? *Skeedaddle* knew Kore as well as she did.

As well as she *had.*

Twenty-six years ago, Midj Rolanni had been taken up as trader by Amin Zar, and set working beside the least of Amin's sons, one Korelan, who also had a head for trade. Their eighth or ninth stop, they were set to meet with one of the Zar cousins, who was a merchant on the port. Taking orbit, they collected their messages, including one from the cousin: "Don't come."

Amin Zar, he took a look at that message, nodded, broke open the weapons locker and issued arms. They went down on schedule, whereupon Amin and the elder sibs disembarked, leaving Kore, Midj, and young Berta in care of the ship.

Several hours later, they were back, Amin carrying the cousin, and a few of the sibs bloodied–and Midj still had bad dreams about the lift outta there.

After it all calmed down, she'd asked Kore why they'd gone in, when they'd clearly been warned away.

And he'd laughed and told her that "Don't come," was Zar family code for "help."

She sipped some more 'toot, took the half-empty cup over to the chute and dumped it in.

The time, she thought, going back and sitting in her chair, had come to face down some truths.

Truth Number One: She was a damn fool.

Truth Number Two: So was the Korelan Zar she had known, twenty Standards ago. Who but a damn fool left the woman, the ship and the life that he loved for a long shot at changing the galaxy?

And who but a damn fool let him go alone?

What came into play now was those same twenty Standards and what they might have done to the man at his core.

She noted that he never had said he'd changed his mind, in that first, brief call for her to come get him. The Kore she knew had never been a liar, preferring misdirection to outright falsehoods. It looked like he'd kept that tendency, and its familiarity had been the one thing that had convinced her the letter was genuine; St. Belamie giving her a second.

And this–this was the third validation, and the most compelling reason to continue on the course she had charted, in case she was having any last minute doubts.

"You gonna die for twenty Standards ago?" She asked herself, and heard her voice echo off the metal walls of her ship.

You gonna turn your back on a friend when he needs your help? Her ship whispered in the silence that followed.

No, she thought. No; she'd done that once, and it had stuck in her craw ever since.

One good thing–she could go on her own time, now, since the way she saw it, "don't come" trumped St. Belamie.

Smiling, she reached to the board and opened a line.

"Tower, this is *Skeedaddle*, over at Vashon's Yard. How soon can I lift outta here?"

*

There were restraints this time, uncomfortably tight, and

a violent headache.

So, he thought, laboriously. *You wanted to make the guy with the gun use it, and he did. Quitcherbitchin.*

"He's back," a man's voice said breathlessly from somewhere to the left.

He'd managed to land some blows of his own, which didn't comfort him much, since he was still alive.

A man hove into view, his right cheek smeared with blood and a rising shiner on his left eye.

Good, he thought, and then saw the injector. *Not good.*

He tried to jerk away, but the cords only tightened, constricting his breathing–some kind of tangle-wire, then. He might be able to–

"No, you don't, fly-boy," the man with the injector snarled, and grabbed his chin in an iron grip, holding him immobile while the cold nozzle came against his neck.

There was a hiss, a sharp sting, and the injection was made. The man with the black eye released him and stepped back, grinning.

He closed his eyes. *Fool,* he thought.

The drug worked fast. The irritation of the wire was the first to fade from his perception, then the raging headache. He lost track of his feet, his fingers, his legs, his heartbeat, and, finally, his thoughts. He hung, limbless, without breath or heartbeat, a nameless clot of fog, without thought or volition.

"What is your name?" A voice pierced the fog.

"Korelan Zar," another voice answered, slowly. Inside the fog, something stirred, knew the voice and the name. Recognized, dimly, peril.

"Good," said the first voice. "Where is the High Judge?"

"I don't know," he heard himself say.

"I see. Why were you going to your ship?"

"Orders."

"What orders?"

He was listening in earnest now, interested in the answer; expecting to hear another, "I don't know . . . ."

"Orders to get out, if it looked like it was going to hell."

Well, he thought, inside the thinning fog, *that certainly makes sense.*

"And things in your opinion were going to hell?"

He'd said so, hadn't he? "Yes."

"Ah," said the voice. That not being a question, he found himself speechless. Time passed; he felt the fog growing dense about him again.

"What," the voice said, sharp enough to shred the fog and cut him where he hung, defenseless. "What was the text of the last message you sent to the High Judge?"

"Situation stable," he heard himself answer.

"When was that?"

"Four weeks ago, local."

More silence; this time, he found he was able to concentrate and thin the fog further. He could feel the shadows of the tangle-wire binding him to the chair; a breath of headache . . . .

"You were at the comm when we located you earlier this evening. Who did you send to?"

A question had been asked; the drug compelled him to answer with the truth, but the truth had facets . . . .

"An old girlfriend."

"Indeed. What is your old girlfriend's name?"

The answer formed; he felt the words on his tongue, swelling, filling his mouth, his throat . . .

"Impressive," the voice didn't-ask, releasing him. Exhausted, he fell back into the fog, felt it close softly around him, hiding the restraints, the pain, the sense of his own self.

"What," the voice asked, soft now, almost as if it were part of the fog, "is the code of the last receiver to which you sent a pin-beam?"

Calmly, his voice told out the code, while he sank deeper into the fog and at last stopped listening.

*

She set *Skeedaddle* down in the general port, calling some minor attention to herself by requesting a hot pad. Tower was so bland and courteous she might have been back on Kago, which didn't comfort her as much as it maybe should have.

Sighing, she levered out of the pilot's chair and stretched, careful of her back and shoulders, before moving down the hall.

She pulled a pellet pistol from the weapons locker, and a needle gun–nothing more than a trigger, a spring and the needle itself. Completely illegal on most worlds, of course, though she'd come by it legal enough: It had been with Berl's body, when it came back, with his ship, to his sister.

She slipped the needle gun into a hideaway pocket, and clipped the pistol to her belt. That done, she straightened her jacket, sealed the locker and went back to the galley for a cup of 'toot and a snack while the hull cooled.

*

The fact that they hadn't killed him was–worrisome. That they kept him here, imprisoned, but not particularly misused, indicated that they thought there was more he could tell them.

He'd had time to consider that; time to weigh whether he ought to file his last flight now and preserve what–and who–he could.

The end of that line of consideration was simply that he wanted to live. His one urge toward suicide had failed and he couldn't say, even considering present conditions, that he was sorry on that score. If it came down that he died in the line of doing something useful, then that was how it was. But to die uselessly, while there were still cards in play – no.

That decision left open the question of what he could do of use, confined and maybe being used as bait. Not that the Judge would fall for bait, but Grom Trogar might not know that. In fact, Chairman Trogar might well see the Judge's concern for his household and his courier as a weakness to be exploited. Big believer in exploiting other people's weaknesses, was Mr. Trogar.

Having the time, he thought about his life past, and what he might've done different, if he hadn't been your basic idealistic idiot. Put that way, he could see himself staying with Midj, leading a trader's prosperous life, raising up a couple of kids, maybe getting into politics. There were more ways to change the galaxy than the route he had chosen. And who was to say that change was the best thing?

He'd been so sure.

*

She had a plan, if you could call it that. Whoever had done the alias for the pinbeam Kore'd sent his last message from had been good, and if she'd started with no information, she'd right now be on a planet known as Soltier, somewhere over in the next quadrant. Knowing that Kore was on Shaltren made the exercise of tracking the 'beam something easier, and she thought she had a reasonable lock on his last location.

Nothing guaranteed that he'd still be at that location, of course, but it was really the only card she had, unless she wanted to go calling on the chairman, which she was holding in reserve as her Last Stupid Idea.

For her first trick, she needed a cab.

There was a cab stand at the end of the street, green-and-white glow-letters spelling out *Robo Cab! Cheap! Quick! Reliable!*

Right.

She leaned in, hit the call button, and walked out to the curb to wait.

Traffic wasn't in short supply this planet-noon, and the port looked prosperous enough. If you didn't know you were on galactic crime headquarters, in fact, it looked amazingly normal.

Up the street, a cab cut across three lanes of traffic, angling in toward her position, the green-and-white Robo Cab logo bright in the daylight. It pulled up in front of her, the door opened and she stepped in.

Mistake.

"Good afternoon, Captain Rolanni," said the woman pointing the gun at her. "Let's have lunch."

The door snapped shut and the cab accelerated into traffic.

*

It was going to take a bit to disable the camera, but he

thought he had a workable notion, there. The hard part was going to be getting out the door. After that, he'd have to deal with the details: scoping out where, exactly, he was, and how, exactly, to get out.

He'd read somewhere that it was the duty of prisoners taken in war to attempt to escape; in order, so he guessed, to make the other side commit more resources to keeping their prisoners where they belonged. It had occurred to him at the time that the efficient answer to that might be to shoot all the troublemakers at hand, and institute a policy of taking no prisoners. On the other hand, Mr. Trogar having erred on the side of prisoner-taking, he supposed there was a certain usefulness to confounding the home guard.

Or, as the Judge was a little too fond of saying, "Let's throw a rock in the pond and see who we piss off."

*

Surprisingly enough, it *was* lunch, and if there was a guard mounted outside the door of the private parlor, and her host was armed, nobody had gotten around to taking the gun that rode openly on her belt, much less searching her for any hidden surprises she might be carrying.

Lunch was simple–pre-made sandwiches, hand pastries, coffee, and some local fruit.

To hear her tell it, the host's name was Sambra Reallen, which was as good as any other name. She professed herself a not-friend of the current chairman, on which point Midj reserved judgment, considering the manner of their meeting. Since she also seemed to hold some interesting information, Midj was willing to listen to her for the space it took to eat a sandwich and savor a couple cups of the real bean.

"You're here for Korelan Zar," Sambra Reallen said, and it was disturbing to hear that fact stated so baldly, no "am -I-right?" about it.

There being no use playing games, Midj nodded slowly and sipped her coffee. "Man asked me to give him a ride off-world. That against the law?"

The other woman grinned, quick and feral. "At the moment, the law here is the chairman's whim. Given that–yes, I'm afraid it is."

"That's too bad," Midj said, hoping she sounded at least neutral.

"You could say that," Sambra Reallen agreed. She wasn't drinking coffee, and she hadn't even bothered to look at the sandwich in front of her. "Captain Rolanni, do you have any idea who Korelan Zar *is?*"

Well, that was a question, now, wasn't it? Midj shrugged. "Old friend. Called in a favor. I came. That's how we do things, out where the chairman's whim counts for spit."

Another quick grin. "I'll take that as a long 'no,' " she said. "Korelan Zar is the High Judge's courier."

Midj sipped coffee, considering. She decided that she didn't really care what the Juntavas had to do with judges or judging, and looked up to meet Sambra Reallen's sober gaze.

"Kore was a hell of a pilot," she said, which was nothing but the truth.

The Juntava snorted. "So he was and so he is. He's also been with the High Judge for twenty Standards–maybe more. The two of them came out of nowhere–the High Judge, he wasn't a Judge then; the closest we had to Judges were the Enforcers–and that wasn't close at all. He sold the Justice Department idea to the then-chairman–the chairman that the present whimsical guy we've got replaced, you understand. The two of them–Zar and the Judge–they set up the whole system, recruited Judges, trained 'em and set 'em loose. I don't know how many Judges there are now–the last number I heard was thirty, but I think that's low–very low. The High Judge isn't a man who shows you all the cards he's got in his hand–and Korelan Zar's just like him."

It was a fair description of Kore, all things weighed. And the project itself jibed with the one he'd tried to sell her on, sitting across from her in *Skeedaddle's* tiny galley, holding her hands so hard she felt the bones grinding together. Bunch of crazy talk, she'd thought then. Now... Well, say the years had given her a different understanding of what was necessarily crazy.

"Not that I'm disinterested in your problems," she said now to Sambra Reallen, "but I'm not quite grasping what this has to do with me."

The other woman nodded vigorously. "Thank you, yes. You do need to know what this has to do with you." She leaned forward, face intent, eyes hard.

"The High Judge, his household, all the Judges I know about and all those I don't–are gone. Say that they are not blessed with the chairman's favor. I don't doubt–*I know*–that the High Judge had a plan. He must have foreseen–if not the current situation, at least the *possibility* of the current situation. He would have planned for this. His very disappearance forces me to conclude that he does have a plan, and has only withdrawn for a time to marshal his forces and his allies."

Midj shrugged. "So?"

"So." Sambra Reallen leaned deliberately back in her chair. "About a month ago, local, the chairman realized the High Judge had not been seen in some while. That, indeed, the entire network of Judges, as far as they are known, had slipped through the hands of his seekers. He realized, indeed, that the sole member of the High Judge's household remaining upon Shaltren was–"

"The courier." Midj put her cup down, all her attention focused on the other woman.

Sambra Reallen nodded. "Precisely. The word went out that Korelan Zar should be brought to the chairman. How Zar heard of the order, I don't know, but I'm not surprised that he did. He made a strike for his ship, as I was sure he would, and I waited for him there, hoping to divert him to a safe place. Something must have spooked him; he returned to the High Judge's house–and was taken into custody shortly thereafter."

"Hm. How 'bout if it was you spooked him?" Midj asked. "I'm thinking that altruism isn't exactly your style. What'd you want from Kore in exchange for the safe berth?"

The other woman's face tightened. "Information! The High Judge must be planning something–I must know what it is! The chairman can't be allowed to continue–he's already lost us ground on three significant worlds and will loose Stelubia entirely, if he's not stopped. All of that would be reason enough, if there weren't Turtles in the mix, too!"

Midj blinked. "Turtles? Clutch Turtles?"

"There's another kind?"

"Not that I know of. These would be two, and asking after the health of a couple of humans they adopted, am I right?"

Sambra Reallen nodded, sighed.

"Indeed," she said finally, finding her pastry's icing a fascinating diversion from the discussion as she weighed some inner necessity.

"These things are too big to be secret," she continued, "no matter how hard any of us wish to hide them. Here you are, fresh in, and already the word is out."

The pilot relaxed slightly, realizing that the Juntava was apparently too focused on her own set of woes to pursue Midj's familiarity with the doings of the Clutch.

"I've been reading history, Captain Rolanni. The vengeance that these two beings may visit upon the entire organization if their petition is mishandled–and there is no possibility that the chairman will *not* mishandle it–doesn't bear thinking about. I–Action needs to be taken. But I must know what the High Judge is planning."

"And you think Kore knows."

"Yes."

"But Kore's been taken by the chairman," Midj pointed out, trying to keep the thought– and its implications–from reaching real nerve endings. "If he's as ruthless as he say, he's already cracked Kore's head open and emptied out everything inside." *Including my name, my ship's name, and the fact that I was coming for him.* That did touch a nerve, and she picked up her cup, swigging down the last of the cold coffee.

"The chairman tried to do exactly that," Sambra Reallen said. "Mr. Zar's defenses are formidable–also, as I discover from my study of the session transcript, he wasn't asked the right question."

"You got my name from the transcript, then."

"No." The Juntava shook her head. "I got your pinbeam receiver ID from the transcript. Mr. Zar could not be persuaded to part with your name, though he was obviously experiencing some . . . discomfort for withholding the information."

The receiver ID was enough to sink her–present company being evidence–but she'd made it extra easier for them by coming on-world–and the joke was on her, if she'd taken an honest warn-away for code.

"So, what do you want from me?" Might as well ask it straight out, though she thought she had a good idea what it would be.

"I want you to pull him out of custody. I can provide you with his location, weapons if you need them, and a safe place to bring him to."

Yup, that was it. Midj shook her head.

"And what do I get?"

The Juntava pushed the untouched sandwich away and leaned her elbows on the table.

"What do you want?"

Just like that: Name a price and the Juntavas would meet it. No problem. She felt a hot flash of fury, felt the words, *I want my brother back* rising and kept them behind her teeth with an effort. Sat for a couple of heartbeats, breathing. Just that.

When she was sure she could trust her voice, she met the other woman's bland eyes.

"What I want is Kore, free and in shape to leave, if that's what he still wants. And I want us both to have safe passage out of here, and a guarantee that we won't either of us be pursued by the Juntavas after."

There was a pause.

"I could promise you these things," Sambra Reallen said eventually, "but until I hear what Korelan Zar has to tell me–if he will tell me anything–I can't know if my promise will hold air." She raised a hand, palm out. "I understand that you have no reason to love the Juntavas, Captain. The best I can promise at this point is that, if Chairman Trogar leaves the game, I will do my best to ensure that your conditions are met."

About what she'd figured; as good as she was going to get, and no time to negotiate anyway, with Kore's life on the line.

"Why hasn't the chairman killed him?" she asked.

The Juntava shrugged. "It could be that the chairman thinks Korelan Zar still retains some potential for amusement."

Right. Midj sighed.

"I'll need a diversion. If Kore's high-level, then there are high-level people interested in him who'll have to be drawn off."

Sambra Reallen nodded. "I'll call a department chair meeting."

Midj blinked. "You can do that?"

The Juntava smiled, letting a glimmer of genuine amusement show. "Oh, yes," she said. "I can do that."

*

Getting out the door hadn't been so hard after all, though there was going to be hell to pay if–well, there was going to be hell to pay; it wasn't any use thinking there could be a different outcome to this.

He was sorry he wouldn't be on hand to see the finish of it, since he'd been in on the beginning. It had been a grand, beautiful scheme, so logical. So–simple. Introduce a justice system into Juntavas structure. Feed and nurture and protect it and its practitioners for twenty, thirty, fifty Standards–they hadn't been sure of the timing, but hoped to see results within their lifetimes–easily that. Lately, he thought they'd been optimistic–and not only of the timing.

Still, he had a gun, courtesy of a guard even stupider than he was, and he knew where he was, and where he was going, more or less right down to his final breath. It was . . . freeing in a way. He felt at peace with himself, and with his purpose. If he could kill Grom Trogar, then he could depart as happy as a man filled full of pellets could be, and the plan– his plan, that he'd given up his life of small happinesses to see through–would have a second chance at continuing.

It was convenient that his holding room was in the chairman's building. Convenient that he had committed the layout of that building, along with several others, to memory years ago. He knew where the secret stair was and the code that opened the hatch. He eased the panel shut behind him and began to climb.

He paused to catch his breath just below the fourteenth landing. Only one more landing, if his memory could be relied upon–and since he'd already decided that it could why worry about it now? The hatch opened in what used to be a supply closet in the chairman's suite. He steeled himself for the unpleasant truth that he might need to kill blameless people before he got to his target. He wasn't an assassin; even killing Mr. Trogar himself, much as it was needed, wasn't going to be a home joy. The important thing was not to freeze, not to hesitate. To acquire his target and shoot. He might only get one shot, and it was important to make it count.

Leaning against the wall, he once again went over his stolen gun. It was a good gun, loaded, well-oiled with an extra clip of pellets riding in the handle. The guard had taken good care of his weapon. Points for the–

Above him and to the left, where the ongoing flight angled off the landing, there was a noise. A very slight noise, not immediately repeated, as if someone had scuffed a boot against the edge of a step.

He went to one knee on the step, raised the gun in two hands, and waited, breathing slow. *Easy . . .*

Another scuff, and a dim shadow on the dim wall of the landing. His finger tightened on the trigger. Silence–

And a sudden appalling rush of sound, as a dark figure hurtled hit the landing, flat-footed, gun out and pointing at his head. He had a moment to feel anger, then–

"Kore!"

He blinked. Stared up into a pale face and dark brown eyes, short dark hair showing a blaze of gray going back from the temple.

"Midj?" Slowly, he lowered the gun. "What the hell are you doing here?"

"Back atcha." She lowered her own weapon and stood, a little stiffly, he thought. "But it's gonna hafta to wait. I'm supposed to be getting you out of here, to a safe place."

He frowned. "Safe by whose standards?"

"Woman by the name of Sambra Reallen."

He thought about it, shook his head. "Can't trust her."

"Can't not trust her," she countered. "She picked me up in port. Could've just as easy been the chairman, the way I hear it. She wants him gone and she don't want to jinx the High Judge's play, if he has a play. Which you're supposed to tell her."

He snorted. "She wouldn't believe me." He thought again. "How were you supposed to get me out of here?"

"Same way I came," she said, jerking her head up the stairs. "We walk up to the roof. There's a monowing waiting to lift us out."

"OK," he said, and came to his feet. He smiled, then, and it felt like his soul was stretched so wide it might burst a seam.

"Midj. Thank you."

"No problem."

*

They were two steps below the fifteenth landing when the alarm went out. Kore threw himself onto the landing, fingers moving rapidly on the code bar. The panel slid open as Midj came up beside him.

"What's going on?"

"Damned if I know. But the doors will seal in ten seconds–go!" He pushed her through and followed, into the dimness of the supply room.

"Where are we?"

Trust Midj to ask the question. "Chairman Trogar's office."

"Great."

"Could be worse. Let's see . . ."

Carefully, he eased open the closet door. The receptionist's desk was empty, he could hear voices, out in the hall, and slipped forward, barely hearing Midj's curse as she followed him.

He crept to the hall door and peered around–and abruptly gave up stealth.

In the center of the hall, surrounded by gaping humans, stood two large green– persons. On the floor beyond them, he could see a form, a shock of white hair, a widening pool of blood, a–weapon, though what sort of weapon he scarcely knew.

The largest of the two green persons–sang. There was a flash! of pinpoint light, a snap! of sound and the weapon was molten metal, mixing with liquid red.

There was a stifled scream from the crowd; a shifting of bodies, and then from the crowd, one stepped forward and bowed.

"I am called Sambra Reallen, Chairman Pro Tem," she said softly. "How may I serve you, Aged Ones?"

*

Skeedaddle was well away, on course for Clarine, and a chat with Teyope, should he have actually happened to deliver the cargo as commissioned. At least, that's what Sambra Reallen knew. It was the least of what Sambra Reallen knew, and Midj hoped she had joy of her new status. Talk about being in a position to honor promises.

"She'll have to be certified by the department heads." Kore sat down on the edge of the co-pilot's chair and held out a steaming cup. " 'toot?"

"Thanks." She took it, spinning her chair to face him. She drew a breath, thinking she might be about to say something, found her mouth dry, and drank some 'toot instead.

"I wanted to say." Kore was holding his cup between both palms, staring down as if the hot liquid were a navigation screen.

"I wanted to say–I'm sorry. I had no right to pull you into that, Midj, knowing you –and knowing what it could become. My arrogance. I thought I was ahead of the trouble."

"Well," she said, softly. And then again, "Well."

He looked up, amber eyes wary. The black hair showed some shine of silver, his face marked with the lines of responsibility and worry.

"Your plan. I mean your old plan. Is that playing out the way you'd hoped?"

He tipped his head, considering. Had a sip of 'toot.

"Not exactly. There were compromises needed. Somehow, I hadn't thought of there needing to be compromises. Some good people died, and I never meant that. Justice . . . ." The ghost of a laugh. "Justice isn't always easy to cipher. I didn't expect that at all." He sighed.

"That said–we've made progress. In some direction. We've introduced another player into the game, and another set of rules. Is that a good thing, a bad thing, or a null-value?" He shrugged. "Don't know."

Right.

Midj sipped her 'toot; used her chin to point at the board.

"Course is set for Clarine; it's easy to change, if you're expected somewhere. Or I can set you down where you say. Or you can stay on."

There, it was out in the open.

Kore was looking at her like he thought hard.

"Stay on?"

"If you want to." The cup of 'toot trembled a bit in her hand, belying her attempt at a casual tone.

She cleared her throat and met his eyes square. "Thinking over it all–I had the idea we'd been a damn good team, Kore. Had the idea we might be again, if you're wantin' it."

She felt a moment of panic then–a moment brought on in part by twenty years of the voice in her head nagging at her in odd moments telling her *He joined up with his eyes open, Midj–they'll never let him go–* "That is, "she said with a challenge, "if you want it and if they'll *let* you . . ."

A pause, getting long while he–and she–sipped at their cups. Then . . . .

"There isn't anything I want more," Kore said slowly. "But I–Midj, maybe we need to do this in stages. First, I gotta get back to the Judge. I've got to let him know where I am, how it is with me. And–I'd like you to meet him. Talk with him."

Meet the Juntava who had stolen away Kore and twenty years of their life? She felt the anger rise–shook it off as he kept talking.

"Then, well, I got a couple standard years of vacation time coming. We could go somewhere . . . like maybe Panore."

He favored her suddenly with a grin that made her sway as she laughed.

"A couple years vacation? On Panore, is it? What did you do? Loot the strongbox?"

His grin faded; and Midj felt a chill. Suppose he had looted the joint?

"Nah," he admitted wryly, "I didn't. It's just that I never really took much time off. I mean the Judge project, it kept me pretty busy. And . . ."

"But Panore? I'd have thought you'd forgot that . . ."

He shook his head then, and snorted a quiet laugh, and kind of talked into his cup for a minute like he was afraid, or too shy, to look at her.

"Nah. I always did mean to get out to Panore, you know. And I always kept hoping there'd be some way I could maybe get you to go with me. So when I got a chance, I put some of my money into a condo-building out there . . . one unit's mine."

He looked up, caught the look of amaze that had left her mouth half open. She felt the words spill out unbidden.

"What? Panore's for fatcats! Do you have any idea of what it costs to live on a place like that? I, I . . . "

He signed a quick yes in pilot's hand-talk as he finished his 'toot.

"So yeah, I do know. But now that you brought it up, why don't we find us a cargo or two that'll take us out that way, make sure we can still work together. Then, we can make sure we can still play together."

He put the cup down, unexpectedly reached his hand to hers. "Tell me it's a deal, and I'll sign the book as co-pilot right now, if you like. "

"Deal," she said, and squeezed his hand before pulling the logbook out on it's trip tray.

Lord of the Dance

IT WAS SNOWING, of course.

The gentleman looked out the window as the groundcar moved quietly through the dark streets. His streets.

And really, he said to himself irritably, *you ought to be able to hit upon some affordable way of lighting them.*

"What are you thinking, Pat Rin?" His lady's voice was soft as the snow, her hand light on his knee. And he was a boor, to ignore her most welcome presence in worries over street lamps.

He leaned back in the seat, placed his hand over hers, and looked into her dark eyes.

"I was thinking how pretty the snow is," he murmured.

She laughed and he smiled as the car turned the corner—and abruptly there was light, spilling rich and yellow from all of the doors and windows of Audrey's whorehouse, warming the dark sidewalks and spinning the snowflakes into gold.

*

"Boss. Ms. Natesa." Villy bowed with grace, if without nuance, and pulled the door wide. "You honor our house."

Great gods. Pat Rin carefully did not look at his lady as he inclined his head.

"We are of course pleased to accept Ms. Audrey's invitation," he murmured. "It has been an age since I have danced."

The boy smiled brilliantly. "We hoped you'd be pleased, sir." He pointed to the left, blessedly returning to a more Terran mode. "You can leave your coats in the room, there, then join everybody in the big parlor."

"Thank you," Pat Rin said, and moved off as the bell chimed again, Natesa on his arm.

"Who," he murmured, for her ear alone, "do you suppose has been tutoring Villy in the Liaden mode?"

"Why shouldn't he be teaching himself?" she countered, slanting a quick, subtle look into his face. "He admires you greatly, master."

"Most assuredly he does," Pat Rin replied, with irony, and paused before the small room which served as a public closet for the clients of Ms. Audrey's house. Natesa removed her hand from his arm and turned, allowing him to slip the long fleece coat from her shoulders. The remains of snowflakes glittered on the dark green fabric like a spangle of tiny jewels. He shook it out and stepped into the closet.

The hooks and hangers were crowded with a variety of garments: oiled sweaters, thick woolen shirts, scarred spaceleather jackets, and two or three evening cloaks in the Liaden style.

Pat Rin removed his own cloak and hung it carefully over Natesa's coat. Shaking out his lace, he stepped back into the hallway, where his lady waited in her sun-yellow gown.

He paused, his heart suddenly constricted in his chest. Natesa's black eyebrows rose, just slightly, and he moved a hand in response to the question she did not voice.

"You overwhelm me with your beauty," he said.

She laughed softly and stepped forward to take his arm again.

"And you overwhelm me with yours," she answered in her lightly accented High Liaden. "Come, let us see if together we may not overwhelm the world."

*

The doors between the public parlor and the visitors' lounge had been opened and tied back; the furniture moved out of the public parlor and the serviceable beige rug rolled up, revealing a surprisingly wide expanse of plastic tile in a deep, mostly unscarred brown. A refreshment table was placed along the back wall, directly beneath–

Pat Rin blinked.

When not pressed into duty as a dance hall, the public parlor of Ms. Audrey's bordello displayed certain . . . works of art . . . as might perhaps serve to beguile the mind away from the cares of the day and toward the mutual enjoyment of pleasure.

This evening, the walls had been–transformed.

The artwork was gone, or mayhap only hidden behind

objects, which, had anyone dared challenge Pat Rin to describe twelve items belonging to Korval that he least expected to find on public display, he would certainly have placed within the top six.

Nursery rugs, they were–the design based upon a star map. Three rugs together formed the whole of the map, the original of which he had himself seen, preserved in Korval's log books.

One rug had lain on the floor of the nursery at Jelaza Kazone. The second, in the schoolroom at Trealla Fantrol. The third–the third had covered the floor in the small private parlor the boy Pat Rin had shared with his foster-father, Luken bel'Tarda.

And yet on the wall directly across from him–the rug, the very rug, from Trealla Fantrol. And on the wall to his right, the rug from Jelaza Kazone.

Carefully, Pat Rin turned his head, and–yes, there on the wall behind them was the rug from his childhood, looking just as it always had, close-looped and unworn, its colors as bright as–

"Pat Rin?" Natesa murmured. "Is something amiss?"

He shook himself, and turned his head to smile at her.

"Merely–unexpected, let us say." He waved a languorous hand. "What a crush, to be sure!"

This was not strictly the case. Still, the big parlor was comfortably crowded, the conversation level somewhat louder than one might perhaps have expected at a similar gathering in Solcintra. Bosses of several of the nearer territories were present, including Penn Calhoon, as well as the Portmaster, and a good mix of local merchants.

Across the room, white hair gleaming in the abundant light, his cousin Shan stood in deep conversation with Narly Jempkins, chairman of the nascent Surebleak Mercantile Union.

"We arrive among the last, as suits our station," Natesa said softly, which bait he ignored in favor of inclining his head to their hostess, who was approaching in a rustle of synthsilk, her pale hair intricately dressed, and an easy smile on her face.

"Boss. Natesa. I'm real glad you could come."

"Audrey." Natesa smiled and extended a hand, which the older woman clasped between both of hers.

"Winter has been too long," Natesa said. "How clever of

you to think of a dance!"

Audrey laughed. "Wish I could say it was all my idea! Miri was the one put the seed in my head, if you want the truth. Said she had too much energy and no place to spend it, which I'll say between the three of us ain't the usual complaint of new-birthed mothers."

"Miri is an example to us all," Pat Rin murmured, which pleasantry Audrey greeted with another laugh.

"Ain't she just–and your brother's another one! When I invite a man to a dance, I don't expect him to bring his keyboard and set up with the band. That's just what he's done, though–take a look!" She pointed down the room, where was collected a fiddle, a guitar, a drum set, a portable omnichora – and several musicians wearing what passed for stage finery on Surebleak, clustered about a slender man in a ruffled white shirt and formal slacks that would have been unexceptional at any evening gather in Solcintra.

It had been . . . disconcerting . . . to find that Audrey, with the rest of Pat Rin's acquaintance on Surebleak, assumed that Val Con, his cousin and his Delm, was in fact his younger brother, brought in to care for the transplanted family business while the Boss undertook the important task of putting the streets in order.

As the misapprehension only amused Miri, and Val Con's sole comment on the matter was a slightly elevated eyebrow, Pat Rin gave over attempting to explain their actual relationship and resigned himself to having at his advanced age acquired a sibling.

"For a time, he and Miri sang for their suppers," he said now to Audrey. "Perhaps he misses the work."

"Could be," she answered, as the sound of footsteps and voices grew louder in the hall behind them. She sent a look over his shoulder, extended a hand and patted his sleeve lightly.

"The two of you go on in and circulate. Dancing ought to be starting up soon."

Thus dismissed, Pat Rin followed Natesa deeper into the parlor.

*

Ms. Audrey's big parlor, already crowded, grew more so. Deep in a discussion with Etienne Borden and Andy Mack, which involved free-standing solar batteries, and the benefits of light level meters over mechanical timers, Pat Rin still registered an abrupt lowering of the ambient noise and looked around, thinking that the promised music was at last about to begin. But no.

It was his mother entering the room, on the arm of no one less than Scout Commander ter'Meulen, dressed for the occasion in High House best, his face oh-so-politely bland, and his mustache positively noncommittal.

Pat Rin, who had all his life known Scout ter'Meulen, could only wonder at the reasons behind such a display–not to mention the why and wherefore of Lady Kareen accepting his arm for anything at all. They were neither one a friend of the other, though it had always seemed to Pat Rin that the greater amusement was on Clonak's side and the greater dislike on his mother's.

Surely –

Audrey bustled forward to welcome these newest arrivals, her high, sweet voice easily rising above the other conversations in the room.

"I *knew* you'd turn the trick, Mister Clonak!" she said gaily, patting him kindly on the shoulder. This was apparently a dismissal, as Clonak adroitly disengaged himself from the lady's arm, took two steps into the parlor and was lost in the general crush.

Audrey turned to face Kareen squarely, and Pat Rin's stomach tightened, as he contemplated disaster. Even had he not counted Audrey a friend, he thought, it was surely no more than his duty to stand between her and Lady Kareen yos'Phelium, in the same way that it was his duty as Boss to stand between the residents of his streets and mayhem.

He murmured something quick and doubtless unintelligible to the Colonel and the assistant portmaster, and slipped through the press of bodies, moving as quickly as he was able.

"Lady Kareen," Audrey said clearly. "Be welcome in my house."

It was the proper sentiment, properly expressed, thought Pat Rin, working his way forward. Though what–and from whom–his mother might exact as Balance for being made welcome at a whorehouse–

"Well met, cousin!" Val Con murmured, astonishingly slipping his arm through Pat Rin's. "Where to in such a rush?"

"If you would not see a murder done–or worse–" Pat Rin hissed into the frigid silence that followed Audrey's greeting–"let me tend to this!"

"Nay, I think you wrong both our host and your lady mother," Val Con said tranquilly, his grip on Pat Rin's arm tightening. "Besides, the hand is dealt."

"You know what my mother is capable–"

"Peace," his cousin interrupted. "My aunt is about to play her first card."

"Who speaks?" Lady Kareen's Terran was heavily accented, but perfectly intelligible; her tone as frigid as the wind in high winter.

It was of course quite mad to even consider that he might extricate himself from the brotherly embrace of one who was both a pilot and a Scout. Nonetheless, Pat Rin took a careful breath to camouflage his shift of weight–and felt warm fingers around his unencumbered hand. He looked down, equally dismayed and unsurprised to see Miri grinning up at him, grey eyes glinting.

"Take it easy, Boss," she whispered. "Audrey's good for this."

He began to answer, then closed his mouth tightly. The fact that this had been planned–that Audrey had been coached on form and manner . . .

"That's right," their host was saying equitably to his mother. "You won't know that. I'm Audrey Breckstone, boss of this house. I'm happy to see you."

Not for nothing did Lady Kareen stand foremost among the scholars of the Liaden Code of Proper Conduct. She not only knew her Code, but she practiced it, meticulously. Rather too meticulously, as some might think. But there was perhaps, Pat Rin thought now, an advantage–to Audrey, to the house, and to Kareen herself–in an extremely nice reading of Code in regard to this particular circumstance.

It was not for a mere son to say what weights and measures were called into consideration as his mother stood there, head tipped politely to one side, face smooth and emotionless, but surely the unworthy scholar who had studied Code at her feet might make certain shrewd and informed guesses.

Whether Audrey possessed the native genius to have added that guileless, "I'm happy to see you," to her introduction, or whether she had been coached in what she was to say mattered not at all. That she had uttered the phrase in apparent sincerity placed her *melant'i* somewhat in regard to the *melant'i* of Kareen yos'Phelium. Here was, in fact, a delm–at most–or a head of Line–at least–so secure in her own worth and the worth of her house that she not only welcomed, but was *happy to receive*, the burden of a visit from a high stickler who might ruin her and hers with a word.

Or, to phrase the matter in the parlance of Surebleak, Audrey had in essence said to Kareen: *I see that you're armed, and I'm your equal.*

"I am pleased to accept the greeting of the house," Lady Kareen stated, and bowed– Expert to Expert–which allowed a certain limited equality between herself and her host, and placed a finer measuring into the future, after more data had been gathered and weighed.

To her credit–or that of her tutor–Audrey did not attempt to answer the bow. Instead, she smiled, and offered her arm.

"There's going to be music and dancing for the youngers in just a bit, now," she said. "But I'm betting that a woman of good sense would like to have a glass of wine in her hand."

There was a slight hesitation as Kareen performed the mental gymnastics necessary to untangle this, then she stepped forward and placed her hand lightly on Audrey's sleeve.

"Thank you," she said austerely. "A glass of wine would be most welcome."

The two ladies moved off toward the refreshment table as the rest of the guests shook themselves and returned to interrupted conversations.

Pat Rin remembered to breathe.

"See?" Miri gave his hand a companionable squeeze before

releasing him, and sending another grin up into his face . "Piece o'cake."

"As an author of the joke you might well say so," he replied, with feeling. "But consider how it might seem to those who had no–"

"Indeed, it was ill-done of us," Val Con murmured, slipping his arm away. "We had not taken into account that your duty would place you between the two ladies."

Pat Rin turned to stare, and Val Con inclined his head, for all the worlds like a proper Liaden, and murmured the phrase in High Liaden–"Forgive us, cousin. We do not intend to distress you, but to attain clarity."

Sighing, Pat Rin also inclined his head, "It is forgotten," rising reflexively to his lips.

"Next time, we'll send you a clue ahead of time," Miri said.

He eyed her. "Must there be a next time?"

"Bound to be," she answered, not without a certain amount of sympathy. Her eyes moved, tracking something beyond his shoulder.

"Band's settin' up," she said to Val Con.

"Ah," he returned, and lifted an eyebrow. "Cousin, I am wanted at my 'chora."

"By all means, go," Pat Rin told him. "Perhaps Ms. Audrey will induce my mother to stand up with Andy Mack."

The band played surprisingly well, and in a rather wider range than Pat Rin had expected, fiddle and guitar at the fore, Val Con's omnichora weaving a light, almost insubstantial, background.

At Ms. Audrey's insistence, he and Natesa had stood up for the first dance–a lively circle dance not dissimilar to the *nescolantz*, which had been a staple at young people's balls when he had been considerably younger. He spied Ms. Audrey, with Lady Kareen and Luken bel'Tarda at her side, observing the pattern of the dance from the edge of the rug. Further on, Clonak ter'Meulen was in animated conversation with Uncle Daav and Cheever McFarland.

At the end of the first dance, he relinquished Natesa to

Priscilla with a bow, and started for the refreshment table. He'd scarcely gone three steps before his hand was caught.

"Come," said his cousin Nova. "I claim you for the next dance!"

"Ah, do you?" He laughed, and allowed himself to be led back onto the floor. "Then let us hope the band pities me and produces a less spirited number!"

Alas, his wish had not reached the ears of the band leader, for the next dance was something akin to a jig, requiring intricate footwork which he learned from step to step by the simple expedient of observing Nova and reproducing her movement.

He'd done the same thing many times in the past, of course–a person of *melant'i* would naturally take care to acquire the movements of a variety of dances, so that he might do his proper duty as a guest; however, no one but a scholar of the form could hope to know the intricacies of all possible dances. A quick eye and a flair for mimicry were therefore skills that a young person who wished to move without offense through Solcintra's party season would do well to acquire.

Having survived the jig unbloodied, Pat Rin bowed to his fair partner, handed her off to his Uncle Daav, and turned, setting his sights on a glass of wine and perhaps more discussion of solar arrays with Andy Mack, who he could see speaking with Clonak to the left of the refreshment table.

This time, he was claimed by a smiling Villy, who led him back out onto the floor with something very like a skip in his step. At least, Pat Rin thought, the gods were at last kind: it was a square dance, with he and Villy facing off as sides one and two, Shan and Priscilla taking up the third side and the fourth.

The slower pace was more than balanced by a complex, cumulative pattern of exchanges with one's partner, thus: step forward, touch right hands, step back/step forward, touch right hands, then left, step back–and so on, until the tune turned on itself and one began to subtract a gesture at the exchange, and each dancer was at last back in their place, having regained all that had been given.

The music stopped the instant the second partner pair fell

back into place. There was a moment of tension, as if the dancers awaited another phrase from the musicians–then laughter, and light applause. Their little square evaporated, Pat Rin moving with determination toward the refreshment table, Shan and Priscilla amiably keeping pace. He was sincerely thirsty now, and thinking in terms of a cool glass of juice.

"Do you find the party agreeable?" he asked Priscilla.

"Perfectly agreeable," she said, with a seriousness that was belied by the glimmer of a smile in her eyes. "Ms. Audrey said that she meant to host the dance of the winter."

"Which we thought would be no great challenge," Shan continued. "There being so few dances held in the winter. Or the summer. Or the spring, come to belabor it."

Pat Rin considered him. "If you find a lack, cousin, you might host a ball or two yourself."

"Well, I might," Shan allowed. "If it weren't for the fact that the Delm has some foolish notion in his head about bringing Surebleak up to a mid-tier spaceport, with a timetable of roughly *right now*. Perhaps he's spoken to you on the subject?"

"He has," Pat Rin said, "and I must say that the Delm and I are as one on the matter."

"Well, then, what choice have I–a mere master trader!–commanded as I am by both the Delm of Korval and the Boss of Surebleak? Duty, as always, must bow before pleasure, and so it is that tomorrow I regretfully shake the snow of Surebleak from my boots and betake myself to Terran Trade Commission headquarters, there to enlist their aid in the Delm's necessity. There will be no dances held at yos'Galan's house–had we a house, which of course, we don't–until my task is done. Unless, Priscilla, you would care to host a ball or six while I'm gone?"

"I thought I'd go with you, instead," his lifemate replied in her calm deep voice. "To keep you and Padi out of trouble."

This was news. Pat Rin looked up. "Your heir accompanies you on this mission?"

Shan grinned, silver eyes glinting. "Now pity me, truly. Bearding the Terran Guild is as nothing when measured against the prospect of introducing one's daughter to the intricacies–not to say the politics–of trade."

They had reached the refreshment table. Pat Rin poured wine for the two of them, and a glass of cider for himself. He then inclined his head as Shan moved off to answer a hail from Portmaster Liu – and again a moment later as Priscilla was called over to join Thera Calhoon, Penn's lady wife.

Momentarily alone, Pat Rin sighed, had another sip of cider, and closed his eyes. Now that he had extricated himself from dancing, the band was–of course!–playing smooth and undemanding strolling music, the voice of the omnichora somewhat stronger than it had been previously.

Opening his eyes, Pat Rin looked out over the crowded dance floor. Uncle Daav was dancing with Natesa, Nova with Clonak ter'Meulen, and Villy with Etienne Borden. He sipped more cider and reminded himself that it was a boon to be warm in the depths of Surebleak's winter.

"Hey, there, Boss." Miri's cheerful voice interrupted his reverie. "Feeling OK?"

He considered her gravely, one eyebrow up, which only widened her grin.

"You look like Daav when you do that," she said, reaching around him for the cider bottle.

"There's punch, if you'd rather," Pat Rin murmured, and Miri laughed as she poured cider into a cup.

"Think I don't know better'n Audrey's punch?" she asked.

"The wine, then," Pat Rin countered. "It's quite pleasant."

She sent a sparkling glance up into his face. "Oughta be, considering it came out of our cellar." She sipped. "That's good," she sighed, and gestured vaguely with the cup. "Only way we could get Shan to come was to promise there'd be something drinkable on the table."

"Doubtless," Pat Rin said dryly, and she laughed again.

"Cut a fine figure out on the floor," she commented, her eyes on the languid dancers. "Bet you could dance all night, if there was need."

It was his turn to laugh, softly. "I hope that I do not shame my host or my lady," he murmured. "But I have long since given over dancing until dawn."

"Not quite 'til dawn, I'm guessing," Miri said, as the music swept into a crescendo, the 'chora's voice suddenly and achingly clear. She knocked back the last of her cider and put the cup on the table.

Pat Rin glanced at his cup, finished the last swallow and thought about pouring another before he went in search of Andy Mack, and–

"Over here!" Miri called, and put her hand on his arm.

Pat Rin went still. "What?" he snapped.

"Easy. It ain't nothin' more than this special dance Audrey has it in her head we all gotta do together. Family thing."

"I have already danced–"

"One more!" Villy cried, arriving in a swirl of exuberance. "You have to, sir! You're the Boss!"

"Ah." He considered the boy's flushed face. "How if I appoint Boss Calhoon to stand up in my place?"

"Won't work," Miri said. "Penn gets the least bit warm and his glasses fog up on him."

"Besides not being family?" he asked, but she only grinned, and nodded toward the floor, where stood surely all the members of Clan Korval present at the party, saving herself, Val Con, and Lady Kareen, who was at the edge of the rug, between Clonak ter'Meulen and Andy Mack, her face so perfectly bland that Pat Rin shivered.

"Miri . . ." He began, but she was gone, walking toward the group assembled in a loose circle at the center of the floor.

"Come on, sir!" Villy tugged his hand. "They're waiting for you!"

It was on the edge of his tongue to snap that they might wait for him until the snow melted. However, good manners overcame bad grace, and he allowed himself to be led out onto the floor. Hoots and whistles came from some of the spectators on the rug, and Lady Kareen's face grew blander still.

At the edge of the circle, Villy relinquished his hand,

bowed his liquid, meaningless bow, and skipped back toward the refreshment table.

Pat Rin gave a sigh–and another as Natesa came forward to put her hand on his arm.

"A round dance, my love," she murmured, as she eased him into the circle. "Audrey has asked us most especially to honor her."

If one's host desired it, there was nothing more to be said. And certainly he was able for one more dance. Still . . . He looked into Natesa's eyes.

"Do I know this dance, I wonder?" he murmured.

She smiled. "I believe you will find that you do," she answered, and guided him to a gap in the circle between Nova and Priscilla. Having seen him situated, she moved away, slipping into place between Luken and Daav, and smiling at him across the circle.

The drummer beat out a rapid tattoo, sticks flashing, and struck the cymbal a ringing blow, the sound quickly muffled by a cunning hand on the rim.

The room stilled admirably as Ms. Audrey walked out onto the floor, head high, back straight, as proud and as easy as any delm might be within the jewel of her own entertainment.

She raised her hands and spun slowly, showing herself to all gathered.

"You might be wondering," she said conversationally to the room at large, "why it is that I decided to throw a party in the middle of the winter. One reason is that Miri Robertson over here was getting the silly-stirs, her being a woman who had to go off-world to find enough going on to keep her busy–" She paused to let the general laughter die back, then tipped her head and smiled.

"There's two other reasons for this gathering, though. And I'm thinking they're both important enough to want some explaining.

"So, the next reason for the party is that we're in the middle of a special kinda winter. The first winter in my memory and in all of yours where there ain't a turf war going on, when the road to the spaceport stands open for its whole length, and where there are not less than five Bosses in this room right now."

Much shouting, stamping, and whistling erupted. At the edge of the rug, Andy Mack reached out, grabbed Penn Calhoon's arm and yanked it high into the air. Here and there around the room, the other Bosses were being given similar treatment. The applause ebbed, then swelled again, going on until the drummer rapped out a short, sharp rebuke.

Ms. Audrey waited while the room quieted, then held up her hands.

Silence fell, more or less immediately, and she grinned broadly.

"That's right. Now, you'll remember I said *three* reasons and here's the third–" She turned, bringing the room's attention to the circle of Korval, standing ready at the center of the dance floor.

"Boss Conrad and his organization are the reason we can have this party, now, in the middle of winter, without worrying we'll attract the attention of a rival fatcat." She looked around the room, spinning slowly on her heel.

"Remember this. Remember this night, this party. And remember who made it all happen."

The room was utterly quiet for the beat of three, then Andy Mack called out from Lady Kareen's side, "First of many nights just like it!"

"First of many!" The room took up the cry, hurled it against the ceiling, sustained it–

Once again, the drummer intervened. The shouting subsided slowly, and by the time quiet was more or less achieved, Ms. Audrey was making one of the little group about Lady Kareen, her arm tucked companionably through Clonak's, and Cheever McFarland had waded out of the rug-bound observers and onto the dance floor.

It was rare, Pat Rin thought, that one saw Cheever McFarland dressed in other than utilitarian clothing–tough sensible trousers and shirt in neutral colors, sturdy boots, and the inevitable jump pilot's jacket. Tonight, however–tonight, the big Terran positively turned heads as he moved toward their small circle.

The theme was black–a silk shirt so deep that it shone like

onyx, with no ruffles or ballooning sleeves which might entangle a pilot, while the trousers were not so tight as to bind, should a pilot need to move quickly, nor the shiny black boots too snug, should a pilot need to run. Over the shirt was not the usual battered spaceleather jacket but a vest in opal-blue brocade, embroidered with silver rosebuds.

Someone from the group on the rug whistled; Pat Rin suspected Andy Mack. Cheever only grinned his easy grin and raised a big, unringed hand.

"Now, what we're going to be doing here is something like what's called a round dance in Boss Conrad's hometown, and what they called a cue dance back when I learned how, at pilot school. Either name makes sense–a round dance on account it moves 'round in a circle and a cue dance on account there's somebody stands outside the circle, who's got what you might call the big picture, and they're the one responsible for shouting out signals about what steps to dance." He put his hand on his chest, and the drummer executed a long, showy roll, which got a laugh from those watching, and a grin from Cheever himself.

"Boss Conrad and his kin, they learned round dancin' because where they come from it's what polite people learn to dance. Me, I learned in a piloting seminar because we was bored and needed some legal way to work it off. That being the case, the cues are a little different.

"So, what we're gonna do is show you a round dance like Boss Conrad learned it, and then a cue dance like I did."

"Where'd Miri learn how?" somebody–Pat Rin didn't recognize the voice–called from the back.

"From the Boss' brother," Miri sang back. "You?"

The drummer hit the block twice and struck the cymbal hard, to general laughter.

"Any more questions?" Cheever called, and continued without taking a breath. "Fine. We're ready whenever the band gets around to it."

Immediately, the omnichora launched six bright notes, like skyrockets, toward the hidden winter sky, the fiddle player spun clear around and enthusiastically put her bow across the strings, the guitarist plucked out a quick pattern of sound and the drummer beat the rim, counting out three, six, twelve.

The music shifted, twisted, slowed . . .

"Bow to your partner," Cheever directed, against the mannerly rising of "Tiordia's Stroll."

Pat Rin received Nova's bow, bowing to her in turn. At Cheever's instruction, they joined hands, crossed, turned, and slid two steps forward, two steps right, three steps backward, three left, crossed, turned, and changed partners. Pat Rin's left hand slipped out of Nova's as his right hand met Priscilla's. He and his new partner stepped together, then apart, changed sides and danced four steps left and five steps back, six steps forward, turn about four steps right . . .

Relaxed and smiling, Pat Rin performed his part in the dance with ease, warmed and oddly comforted by the familiar movements. He did, in that portion of his mind neither attentive to nor lulled by the dance, own himself astonished to find Cheever McFarland so able a dance master.

Truly, he thought, as he and Priscilla crossed and turned; *there is no end to the good pilot's talents . . . .*

The dance continued its pleasant course, until each dancer had partnered with every other dancer in the set. Perfectly on-cue, he left Luken's side, his hand finding Nova's precisely on the beat. They turned, crossed, and dropped hands to the caller's commands; bowed, holding it for twelve beats, and straightening just as the last note from the 'chora trembled into silence.

The room was entirely quiet as they straightened, and in that moment, Pat Rin saw his mother, attended now by no one less than Portmaster Liu. Her face was calm, perhaps even relaxed, as if the dance had soothed her as well. She inclined her head slightly in his direction, then turned to address the Portmaster.

A wholly unexceptional procedure, Pat Rin thought, and not at all too much effort to expend for the pleasure of one's host. He was slightly warm, but nothing that another glass of cider couldn't put–

"All right," Cheever McFarland was saying, his big voice shattering the quiet. "That's what a round dance looks in Boss

Conrad's old turf. Now we're gonna show you how I learned it. First thing you'll notice is different, is the cues. Pilots, they can't leave anything alone if there's a way to maybe tweak it. Next thing you'll notice is there's some extra bits added in, 'cause pilots tend toward boredom and makin' trouble if they don't have six things to do at the same time."

Pat Rin frowned and turned to cock an eyebrow at Nova, who replied with a bland glance that would have done justice to his mother.

"Last thing," Cheever was saying, "is that pilots? They're competitive. So this dance, it's a kind of a contest, too."

Contest? thought Pat Rin, feeling his stomach tighten. He looked across the circle for Natesa, but she was turned away, watching something in the room beyond.

"Just as soon as the band's ready," Cheever said.

The drummer snapped out a twelve-count, then the guitar came in, followed by the fiddle, the omnichora singing softly in support. The tune was somewhat brisker than "Tiordia's Stroll"–and completely unfamiliar.

"Acknowledge your co-pilot," Cheever instructed, and Pat Rin turned to exchange bows with Nova, who smiled at him.

"Comp–" he began, but–

"Check your board," Cheever called, which Pat Rin's feet somehow knew to be a glide and change sides.

"Bring up the screens!"

Warned by the set of Nova's hip, Pat Rin managed to spin as instructed, though raggedly.

"Strap in," Cheever instructed. Nova's hand moved, Pat Rin caught it in his; they turned, separated–

"Lift!"–each danced six steps to their right–"Establish orbit!"–a half-turn, so Pat Rin was looking over Nova's shoulder at the starry rug that had covered the floor in Luken's small private parlor in their quarters above the warehouse–

"Outer ring adjust," Cheever said. Pat Rin kept his place while Nova slid three steps to left. His view of the rug was now unimpeded.

"Lay in coords!" Cheever called.

Lay in–

But Cheever was giving the coordinates. Rapidly. Pat Rin focused on the rug–on the *map*–found the first coord, slid forward two steps, located the second, slipped to the left three steps, the third–the third? There!–and forward again, four steps.

"Roll starboard!" came the instruction, and Pat Rin spun to the right with the rest, noting in a sort of mental gasp that the music was moving quicker now, that the 'chora's voice was louder, and the fiddle's entirely gone.

"Lay in coords!"

This time, it wasn't a complete shock; Pat Rin had time to face the map–the less familiar rug that had graced the schoolroom floor at Trealla Fantrol–and focus before Cheever intoned the first coord, then another, and another–a set of six full coordinates this time, and Pat Rin slipped, spun, circled, and lunged as directed, finishing the sequence damp and limp, but oddly triumphant. He hadn't missed a step!

Luken, however, had not had the same good fortune. Pat Rin spied him walking away from the circle, Andy Mack leaving the crowd at the edge of the rug to meet him–then Cheever called them to roll once more and he was facing the map from Jelaza Kazone.

The music was much too quick now, Pat Rin thought, tucking up his lace, and shaking his hair out of his eyes. More a jig than a round dance, which the 'chora gave shape in a continuing twisty flow of brilliantine notes.

Val Con must be ready to drop, he thought–and there was another thought, linked to that–but it was lost in the need to accept the coordinates, and he plotted his course with his feet and his hips, barely registering when Miri dropped out at the eighth coord–and Priscilla, at the twelfth.

The next round came and as he glimpsed the nearest celestial rug, he all but felt the controls beneath his hands; in truth he missed the cabin of *Fortune's Reward,* as he missed the thrust against his back, and the comfort of sitting First Board. The rug was before him, and another as he danced, and the calculations went thus and so and turn and step, and by rights now there should be

Jump glare and stars on the screens ahead, and stars behind, with stars underfoot, and a planet to find.

But the dance –

"Orient!" Cheever called, and the four remaining dancers came together in the center, joined hands, ran–*too fast!* Pat Rin thought, with a sudden spike of panic–'round, three times, six–

"Establish orbit!"

As one, they dropped hands, each spinning away, two-four-six revolutions, and came to rest, facing–the entranced spectators.

At the fore of them all stood his mother, considering him with a sort of distant interest, as one might inspect an insect.

"Check your board!" Cheever directed, and Pat Rin executed the required glide and change, aware of the weight of his limbs. It was hot, and his head ached, and really, he had every reason to be tire–

The omnichora shouted, notes streaming like lift beacons, and there was Miri next to his mother, and Priscilla approaching–

"Lay in coords!"

There was no map this time. Pat Rin closed his eyes.

Cheever chanted the coordinates–a short set of three. Forward, back, turn left–

"Sign your co-pilot!"

Pat Rin extended a hand–and his eyes snapped open in astonishment as it was caught in a warm grip.

"Well done!" Uncle Daav whispered, under cover of the music, and–

"Clear your board!"

The two of them crossed, separated, and came back together.

"Lock it down!"

Natesa's fingers wove comfortably with his. Shan, on her other side, extended his hand and caught Daav's free hand.

"Dim the lights," Cheever said softly, and the four of them walked sedately widdershins, three times, the 'chora slowing, slowing, almost down to a proper round . . .

"Open hatch."

Obediently, they dropped hands.

"Go to town," Cheever all-but-whispered, and the four of them turned to face the rug and those watching, as the 'chora finished with a flurry and a flare–and the shouts and whistles began.

*

Pat Rin shook his lace out and reached for his glass. With Natesa's connivance, he'd slipped through the crowd to the back room that had been set aside for the band's use. Finding a bottle of autumn wine before him, he poured and sipped, and sipped once again before making the attempt to make himself seemly.

The dance–the dance had been an odd thing, to be sure; in memory not nearly so harrowing as in actuality. Had it gone on much longer, he had no doubt but that he would have joined Luken, Miri, and Priscilla at his mother's side.

He paused, frowning, recalling the moment when he had met his mother's eyes . . .

"Ah, here he is, keeping the wine to himself!" Clonak ter'Meulen's voice overfilled the little room. Pat Rin sighed, and turned to face not only the portly Scout, but Luken and Daav, and Shan, Priscilla, Natesa, Andy Mack, Nova, Cheever, Miri–and Val Con, green eyes sparkling, the renegade lock of hair sticking damply to his forehead.

"Well met, cousin," he murmured, and Pat Rin held out his glass.

"I thought the 'chora was overextended," he said. "Drink."

"My thanks." Val Con took the glass and sipped; sighed. Pat Rin considered him, doing a different sort of calculation.

"More clarity?" he asked, but it was Miri who answered.

"No complaints, Boss. Sent you a clue, fair and square," she said.

He eyed her. "Hardly in advance."

"But in advance, nonetheless," Val Con said, with a note of finality in his quiet voice. "Come, let us not bicker. There is business to be done–and quickly, so that Clonak is not long kept from the wine."

"That's a touching regard for my well-being," Clonak said, and suddenly pulled himself up straight, looking not so pudgy, nor foolish at all.

"Pat Rin yos'Phelium Clan Korval," he intoned, the syllables of the High Tongue falling cool and sharp from his lips, "has stated in the hearing of pilots and of master pilots not once but several times that he holds a first class limited license under false pretenses. The pilot's solo rating flight was conducted in a Korval safe-ship, programmed to fly, should there be no pilot available. Pat Rin yos'Phelium has stated his belief that it was the ship which overcame the challenges of the pilot's solo, not the pilot." Clonak gave Pat Rin a level look.

"These are serious concerns and the pilot erred not in laying them before master pilots. Therefore, and after consultation, it was agreed that a retesting should be done. The testing is now completed, and I call upon the master pilots present to render their opinions: Is Pat Rin yos'Phelium Clan Korval a pilot or does he hold a license wrongly? Speak, masters!"

Daav stepped forward, black eyes serious.

"Though he is perhaps not as conversant with the basic coord book as might be desirable, it is my estimation as a master pilot that Pat Rin yos'Phelium is worthy of the license he carries." He fell back a step, cocking an eyebrow at Andy Mack, lounging against the wall. The lanky pilot shook his head, white hair moving softly across his shoulders, and took a sip of his beer.

"Been sayin' it, ain't I? Boy's a pilot. Tell by lookin' at him."

Shan stepped forward. "It is my estimation as a master pilot," he said seriously, "that Pat Rin yos'Phelium is worthy of the license he carries." He fell back a step, and Priscilla came forward, then Nova, Cheever and at last Natesa, who made her declaration with the cool, emotionless intonation of a Judge, then smiled at him and stepped forward to take his hand.

"You did well, Pat Rin," she murmured.

"In fact," said Clonak, "he did. I say this as one who doubted the damn' dance would work out at all, but young Shadow carried the day. So." He looked sharply at Pat Rin. "In my estimation as a master pilot, having observed the whole of the testing, Pat Rin yos'Phelium is worthy of the license he carries and I'll thank you to stop doubting yourself, you young whippersnapper! Between you and your lady mother, you're a devil's brew, make no mistake!"

Pat Rin blinked. "My mother?"

"It happens," Priscilla said surprisingly, "that Lady Kareen is, after all, of the dramliz. She appears to have only one talent, which is rare, but not unknown."

Pat Rin looked at her, foreknowing . . . "And that talent is?"

Priscilla smiled at him. "She may impose her will–to a very limited extent–upon the unwary." Her smiled deepened. "And now that you are warned, you are armed."

His mother a *dramliza*? It was only slightly mad, Pat Rin thought, considering the facts of Shan and Anthora in the present generation. But that one talent . . .

"I think you are saying that it was my mother's influence that kept me from qualifying as pilot?"

"At first, boy dear," Luken said, gently. "By the time you had failed two or three times, you were quite able to fail all on your own." He smiled, sadly. "It was my sorrow, my boy, that I could never allow you to see anything other than your own unworthiness."

Pat Rin blinked against tears; Natesa's finger's tightened around his. "You did so much else, Father . . ."

A small pause, and then was Val Con abruptly before him, raising his hand so that Korval's ring gleamed.

Pat Rin lifted an eyebrow. "Korval?"

"You will," Korval stated, "arrange time to study with Clonak ter'Meulen. You will learn the core coordinates, and such protocols as Scout ter'Meulen finds worthy. You will come to your delm inside of one local year and submit to such verification as may be demanded."

"Ah. And my streets? My duties as boss?"

Val Con smiled, and put his hand on his lifemate's shoulder.

"You'll think of something," he said.

Pat Rin drew a breath–to say what he hardly knew, or perhaps he meant only to laugh. The opportunity for either, however, was snatched from him by Cheever McFarland.

"Right then," the big man said. "Time to finish it up."

*

The fiddler provided a sprightly, skipping little melody as they filed into the parlor and took up position on a clear space on the rug, Val Con leaving them at the last to tend his 'chora once more.

Pat Rin stood in the first row of pilots, Natesa on his right, Luken on his left, Daav directly behind. The room was quiet, all eyes on them. Especially, Pat Rin saw, were Lady Kareen's eyes on them, from her position between Audrey and Penn Calhoon. His mother's face betrayed the faintest hint of boredom, as would perhaps be worthy of an adult who had been teased into attending a gathering of halflings.

The fiddler finished her tune as Cheever McFarland and Miri Robertson stepped up before the rest them, mercifully blocking Pat Rin's view of his mother's face. From behind, the 'chora began to whisper a faint line of a tantalizingly familiar song. Pat Rin strained his ears, trying to identify the music–then forgot about it as Cheever began to speak.

"I'm going to impose on your patience once more, here, if Ms. Audrey'll let me," he said.

In the first row, Audrey laughed, and called out, "It don't strain my eyes any looking at you, Mr. McFarland! Speak on!"

"Thank you, ma'am." The big man bent a little at the waist–*a bow*, Pat Rin thought, *Cheever McFarland style*–then raised his voice so that it carried to the far corners of the room–and likely the rooms abovestairs, as well.

"Now, I know you all heard me say that pilots is competitive, and you might've thought that just meant that them who missed their steps had to drop outta the dance. But there was a little more to it than that. We was also looking to judge who among the pilots dancing had danced best, according to their level, their flight time, and their training. Miri here–you all know Miri's partnered with the Boss' brother, right? And when there's a question comes before either of them, they got this arrangement where both are understood to answer? Makes the family business run smoother. Anyhow, Miri here's gonna announce the winner."

Whistles, hoots, and stamping filled the room. The drum tried to bring order, without success, until–

"PIPE DOWN!" Miri ordered, loud enough to make Pat Rin's ears ring–and silence fell like a knife.

"That's better," she said, in a more conversational tone. "I won't take long. Just want to say that it's the judgment of the master pilots we assembled here to watch that the winner of tonight's competition is–Boss Conrad!"

More noise erupted, shaking the rugs hung against the walls, and he walked forward to stand between Miri and Cheever. Smiling hugely, Villy danced forward with a bouquet of dried leaves tied with bright ribbons and presented it with a bow.

Pat Rin inclined his head, received the offering, and stood while the cheering went on, his eye inexorably drawn to the place where his mother stood, silent and bland-faced.

She met his eyes, her own as hard as stones–and turned her face away.

Pat Rin took a breath–sighed it out, and looked up with a smile as his lady came to his side.

"Shall we go home, love?" she asked, slipping her arm through his.

He looked into her face, and then around the room, heard the drummer begin his count –and looked back to her.

"I believe," he said, smiling. "That I would like to dance with my lifemate. There are still some hours until dawn."

Letters From Home, August 2007

Hi there, thrill seeker!

If you missed Liaden Universe® Companion, Volume One... this is not it. This is Volume Two. We expect to be writing another Letter from Home for Volume Three, eventually. Call it habit. We press on.

Habit, alas, has not been sufficient of late when it comes to having an orderly writing life.

First, Embiid Publishing went out of business last year. Embiid was a fine habit, and we miss them. Having weathered that we were blind-sided this spring when Meisha Merlin closed with little warning in April. Suddenly we were without another publisher. Enough to make it hard to concentrate on writing!

Meanwhile, the folks at Baen, having asked to publish our exisiting Liaden novels and chapbooks as ebooks at Baen Webscriptions, went a step beyond and offered us a contract for two fantasy novels, which are in progress as we prepare this book. Fans and writers rejoice!

In SF fandom, if it happens once, it's a tradition. Despite the setbacks inherent in losing a publisher, we knew there were people, fans of ours, friends of ours, who already regard the appearance of a Liaden Universe® Companion as a kind of summer tradition, every few years, and so we asked for and got your support to continue.

So this has been a hectic, roller-coasterish couple of years. We're glad you've decided to take part in the tradition, and that you've made reading our work habit. And as for us? Yeah, same for us. Rough year or not, Liaden stories are our habit and tradition. We press on.

Thanks!

—Sharon Lee and Steve Miller

Acknowledgments:

Any work of art is a community effort. Some, it turns out, more than others. This particular collective work of narrative art drew heavily on the skills, goodwill, good nature, and support of the community. In particular, we'd like to thank:

Anne McCaffrey for continuing encouragement and the occasional (needed) kick in the pants

Thomas Peters, for producing beautiful cover art at lightspeed

Elektra Hammond, for master-class proofreading

The Copycenter, including but not limited to Peter, Aron, Carla, and Ryan, for ongoing assistance, education, patience, and fortitude.

Mary Grow, who helps more than she knows

The many, many readers who generously took advance subscriptions, so that this book could become a reality

...and, as ever and always, the **Friends of Liad**

Sharon Lee and Steve Miller
Unity, Maine
August 2007

Recent Liaden Universe® Awards

Scout's Progress, Prism Award for Best Futuristic of 2002. Given by the Fantasy, Futuristic and Paranormal Chapter of the RomanceWriters of America.

Local Custom placed second for the above award, same year.

Scout's Progress, RomanticTimesBookClub Reviewers Choice for Best Science Fiction Novel, 2002.

Balance of Trade, Hal Clement Award for Best Young Adult Science Fiction Novel of 2004. Given by the Golden Duck Awards -- www.goldenduck.org

Lee & Miller Bibliography
through February 2007

Ace Books

Local Custom, February 2002
Scout's Progress, May 2002
Conflict of Honors, August 2002
Agent of Change, November 2002
Carpe Diem, February 2003
Plan B, May 2003
I Dare, August 2003
Balance of Trade, February 2006
Crystal Soldier, March 2007

AST, Russia

Partners in Necessity
Plan B
I Dare
The Tomorrow Log
Balance of Trade

Buzzy Multimedia

Local Custom, July 2005

Del Rey Books

Agent of Change, February 1988
Conflict of Honors, June 1988
Carpe Diem, October 1989

Embiid Publishing electronic editions

Conflict of Honors, May 2000
Agent of Change, June 2000
Carpe Diem, July 2000
Plan B, August 2000
Local Custom, February 2001
Scout's Progress, February 2001
The Tomorrow Log, July 2002

Balance of Trade, October 2003
Crystal Soldier, October 2004
Crystal Dragon, October 2005

Heyne Verlag, Germany

Agent of Change
Conflict of Honors
Carpe Diem

MAG, Poland

Agent of Change
Conflict of Honors
Carpe Diem

Meisha Merlin Publishing

Plan B, February 1999
Partners in Necessity, February 2000
Pilot's Choice, February 2001
I Dare, February 2002
The Tomorrow Log, February 2003
Low Port, (editors) September 2003
Balance of Trade, February 2004
Crystal Soldier, February 2005
Crystal Dragon, February 2006

Phobos Impact

Sword of Orion, October 2005

Science Fiction Book Club -- www.sfbc.com

Partners in Necessity, December 2000
Balance of Trade, November 2004

Reading Order for Liaden Universe® Novels As Suggested by the Friends of Liad

The *Agent of Change* Sequence (Clan Korval)

***Agent of Change* (in *Partners in Necessity*)**
***Conflict of Honors* (in *Partners in Necessity*)**
***Carpe Diem* (in *Partners in Necessity*)**
Plan B
***Local Custom* (in *Pilots Choice*)**
***Scout's Progress* (in *Pilots Choice*)**
I Dare

The *Great Migration Duology* (Cantra and Jela)

Crystal Soldier
Crystal Dragon

The *Master of Trade* novels (Jethri Gobelyn)

Balance of Trade

Not necessarily Liaden

The Tomorrow Log
Sword of Orion
***Low Port*, Sharon Lee & Steve Miller, editors**

A Partial Liaden Universe® Dictionary

A'jilata

Clutch word for dragon or dinosaur equivalent

a'nadelm

Heir to the nadelm

a'thodelm

Head-of-Line-to-Be

a'trezla

Lifemates

accazi

Mercenary patois for "Do you understand" or "Got that?"

al'bresh venat'i

Formal phrase of sorrow for another Clan's loss, as when someone dies.

Al'kin Chernard'i

The Day Without Delight

Astong

An area known for it's wines

Balance

Liaden custom of reaching a social equilibrium; often a much finer and more complex thing than mere revenge

Balent'i Kalandon

Our local galaxy

Balent'i tru'vad

The starweb of all creation

blood-test

A Circle ritual in some witch communities

bornduggle

Part of a nerligig

c'smerlaparek

A game played by young Clutch turtles

cantra

A Liaden unit of money, named after Cantra yos'Phelium, the smuggler pilot who was the first Korval.

cha'leket

Heartkin (heartbrother, heartsister)

cha'trez

Heartsong

chernubia

Confected delicacy, also of a person — sweet one

Chiat'a bei kruzon

Dream sweetly.

Ckrakec

(derived from the Yxtrang) Approximately "Master Hunter"

coab minshak'a

'Necessity exits'

conselem

An absurdity or exclamation, similar to "darn"

c'neschopita

Clutch turtle word meaning (very approximately) — pretty

Delm

Head of Clan (Delm Korval, Korval Himself/Herself)

Delmae

Lifemate to the Delm, sometimes the same as "co-delm"

denubia

Darling

dex

a fractional common coin, worth much less than a cantra

dramliza

A wizard. PLURAL: dramliz (The dramliz...)

dri'at

Left (direction)

eklykt'i

Unreturned

Eldema

First Speaker (usually the Delm)

Eldema-pernard'i

First-Speaker-In-Trust

entranzia volecta

Good greetings (High Liaden)

fa'vya

an aphrodisiac laced wine sold at Festival

Flaran Cha'menthi

'I(/We) Dare'

galandaria

Confederate, Countryperson, or native of one's own world

Ge'shada

Mazel tov; congratulations

Glavda Empri

yo'Lanna's house

I'ganin brath'a, vyan se'untor

Play with the body, rest the mind

i'lanta

Right (direction)

Ilania frrogudon palon dox

(approx) Young ladies should speak more gently

Illanga kilachi

(no translation available)

Indra

Uncle

Jelaza Kazone

The Tree, also Korval's Own House. 'Jela's Fulfill ment'

Lazenia spandok

compare to "son of a bitch" in Terran

Megelaar

The Dragon on Korval's shield

melant'i

Who one is in relation to current circumstances. ALSO who one is in sum, encompassing all possible persons one might be.

menfri'at

A Liaden martial art

Mirada

Father

misravot

Altanian wine; blue in color.

nadelm

Delm-to-Be

nubiath'a

Gift given to end an affair of pleasure

palesci modassa

Thank you (High Liaden)

prena'ma

Storyteller

prethliu

Rumorbroker

qe'andra

Man of business

qua'lechi

Exclamation of horror

relumma

Division of a Liaden year, equaling 96 Stan dard days. Four relumma equal one year.

Thawla

Mother (Low Liaden; approximately Mommy)

Thawlana

Grandmother

Thodelm

Head of Line

tra'sia volecta

Good morning (Low Liaden)

Trealla Fantrol

Offiical yos'Galan house.

Tree-and-Dragon

sigil of Clan Korval

V**alcon Berant'a**

Dragon's Price or Dragon Hoard, the name of Korval's valley.

Valcon Melad'a

Dragon's Way, the Delm's Own ship

van'chela

beloved friend

va'netra

charity case, lost puppy, clueless newbie

vya

the base herbal ingredient in fa'vya

wachmalog

part of a nerligig

zerkam'ka

kinslayer